S0-AQM-936

The Palace

Chelsea Quinn Yarbro

WARNER BOOKS

An AOL Time Warner Company

If you purchase this book without a cover you should be aware that this book may have been stolen property and reported as "unsold and destroyed" to the publisher. In such case neither the author nor the publisher has received any payment for this "stripped book."

WARNER BOOKS EDITION

Copyright © 2002 by Chelsea Quinn Yarbro

All rights reserved. No part of this book may be reproduced in any form or by any electronic or mechanical means, including information storage and retrieval systems, without permission in writing from the publisher, except by a reviewer who may quote brief passages in a review.

Published in arrangement with Stealth Press, a division of Stealth Media Corp.

Cover design by Diane Luger
Cover illustration by Phil Heffernan

Warner Books, Inc.
1271 Avenue of the Americas
New York, NY 10020

Visit our Web site at www.twbookmark.com

 An AOL Time Warner Company

Printed in the United States of America

First Paperback Printing: March 2003

10 9 8 7 6 5 4 3 2 1

ATTENTION: SCHOOLS AND CORPORATIONS
WARNER books are available at quantity discounts with bulk purchase for educational, business, or sales promotional use. For information, please write to: SPECIAL SALES DEPARTMENT, WARNER BOOKS, 1271 AVENUE OF THE AMERICAS, NEW YORK, NY 10020

RI'S PAPERBACKS
2 Price Used Books
92 Buttonwoods Ave
Warwick, RI 02886
(401) 738-6339

A STRANGER TO DEATH

"San Germano, I told them I was a heretic." Demetrice shook her head slowly in disbelief. "I had to tell them: They wouldn't have stopped if I hadn't."

"It's not important." Her confession was expected.

"But I'll burn," she said calmly. "In this world and the next."

"There is one chance." Ragoczy's eyes brightened. "Demetrice, I can give you a kind of...deliverance. If you share blood with me, your change is assured. Now. Tonight."

"There is still the stake," she said softly, not daring to hope that he might save her...

ACCLAIM FOR CHELSEA QUINN YARBRO AND THE SAINT-GERMAIN SERIES

"A remarkable combination of historical accuracy, exciting plot, and believable characters dominated by Ragoczy himself—a demon-lover anyone would welcome with open veins!"
—Michael Moorcock

"Readers hooked on Lestat would do well to investigate Saint-Germain. He's altogether different yet at least as complex and satisfying.
—Kirkus Reviews

"There's a lot of atmosphere here for Gothic fans who like their stories steeped in history. Highly recommended."
—Library Journal

"Saint-Germain is just as fresh as the day Chelsea Quinn Yarbro introduced him to the world. . . . Yarbro reminds us that there are things on this earth far more evil than vampires."
—Charlaine Harris, author of *Dead Until Dark*

ALSO BY CHELSEA QUINN YARBRO

Hôtel Transylvania

INTRODUCTION

Although the setting and many of the characters are based on real places and people, this is wholly the product of the writer's imagination. While every effort has been made to present Renaissance Florence as accurately as possible, the work is a fantasy and should be regarded as such.

With the exception of the poetry in Part I, chapter 8, all poetry credited to Lorenzo de' Medici was written by him. The variant spellings are of standard 15th century Italian usage. Lorenzo signed his letters to friends Laurenzo or Lauro and that style is used in this novel.

The Florentine calendar actually changed on Lady Day (March 23rd), not January first, but I have standardized the year to modern usage for the sake of clarity.

PART ONE

Laurenzo Di Piero De' Medici, Called Il Magnifico

Quant 'è bella giovinezza
Che si fugge tuttavia
Chi vuol esser lieto, sia;
Di doman non c'è certezza

How beautiful a thing is youth
Which so completely flees us
Whoever desires to be merry, let him;
For tomorrow is never certain.

—LAURENZO DE' MEDICI

TEXT OF A document confirming the sale of land filed with la Signoria in Fiorenza on November 5, 1490:

Know by this statement and testimony that I, Giovanni Baptiste Andreo di Massimo Corsarrio, merchant of the city of Fiorenza and citizen of the Repubblica, freely, on this day, have transferred all claim to land owned by me beyond the grounds of SS. Annunziata near the wall of the city to the alchemist Francesco Ragoczy da San Germano for the sum of six hundred fifty fiorini d'or.

It is further stipulated that neither I nor my heirs nor debtors may lay any title or claim to this land, and that it is the property of said Francesco Ragoczy da San Germano until such time as he, his heirs or debtors dispose of it under the rights and obligations of the laws of la Repubblica.

Francesco Ragoczy da San Germano declares that it is his intention to build a palazzo in the Genovese style on this land, and to that end has hired my own builders to do the work, in accordance with the regulations of the Arte, and to that end has deposited with me four cut diamonds valued by Tommaso Doatti Capella, the jewel merchant, at one thousand four hundred fiorini d'or, against payment of wages to the builders for construction of the palazzo, which shall begin immediately.

All conditions of transfer being satisfactorily met, this testament is to be regarded as complete and final.

Sworn to this day, the Feast of San Zachario, in Fiorenza, in 1490

Giovanni Baptiste Andreo di Massimo Corsarrio, cloth merchant, Fiorenzeno
his seal, a blue hand upraised on a field of red and white lozenges

Francesco Ragoczy da San Germano, alchemist, stragnero
his seal, the eclipse on a field of silver

witnesses:
Tommaso Doatti Capella, jewel merchant, Veronese
Laurenzo di Piero de' Medici, banker, Fiorenzeno

CHAPTER 1

IN SPITE OF the cold wind, Gasparo Tucchio was sweating. He swung the ninth sack of gravel onto his broad shoulder and began the careful, dangerous walk down into the large pit that would be the foundation of the foreigner's new palazzo. He shifted the weight experimentally and swore.

"Ei! Gaspar', not so fast!" Lodovico da Roncale said as he, too, shouldered a load. "Careful, careful, do not slip," he said somewhat breathlessly as they made their way into the excavation.

"Damned foreigner," Gasparo muttered as he took careful, mincing steps down the steep incline. " 'Dig it out to half again the height of a man,' he says. 'Fill it a hand's breadth with gravel,' he says. He will supply us with cement, he says. He will tell us how to mix it. Arrogant. Arrogant. He wants the gravel level, he wants the corner mountings dug down even farther. He must think he's some kind of old Roman."

Behind him Lodovico chuckled through his panting. "You're too stiff-rumped, Gaspar'. Even foreigners have good ideas once in a while."

Gasparo snorted. "I've been a builder all my life, and so was my father before me. He helped raise the Duomo of Santa Maria del Fiore. I've worked every day that I could since I grew a beard, and never, *never* have I worked on anything like this. Say what you want, Ragoczy is mad." To punctuate this opinion he swung the sack off his shoulder and onto the floor of the deep, broad pit.

"Good, good," said Enrico, their supervisor, as the sacks were spilled out. "Another five or more sacks and there will be enough."

"Five?" Gasparo demanded. "It's too cold. It's late. Sundown comes soon. We can finish tomorrow."

Enrico smiled blandly. "If you carry one more, and Lodovico carries one more, and if Giuseppe and Carlo bring down their sacks now, and carry one more each, then there will be six sacks. It is not too difficult, Gasparo."

Gasparo made no reply. He glared at the carefully dug hole and shook his head. "I don't understand it," he said to himself.

Giuseppe dropped his sack of gravel beside Gasparo's. "What do you not understand, you old fake?" His leather doublet was open to the waist, so that his rough-woven shirt hung loosely around him. "You hate work, that's all. It wouldn't matter if Laurenzo himself had ordered the work, you'd still complain."

The others laughed at this, nodding their agreement, which annoyed Gasparo. "Are you so eager to work for that foreigner, then? When have any of you been told how to make a building? It isn't right." He kicked tentatively at the gravel already spread over most of the bottom of the excavation. "If he were here, I'd tell him what I think, that's all."

An amused, beautifully modulated voice spoke from above. "And what would you say to me?"

The working men stopped, looked up. Gasparo shied a pebble across the gravel and said something under his breath.

At the rim of the pit stood Francesco Ragoczy da San Germano. His dark, fur-lined roundel over a black silk doublet and perfectly white camisa proclaimed him a stranger as much as his slight accent and the foreign Order around his neck on a silver chain that was studded with rubies. He wore heeled Russian boots on his small feet, embroidered black gloves, and a French chaperon on his unfashionably short dark hair. "Well? What is it?"

Gasparo glared. "I said," he lied, "that we might as well go home. It's going to rain."

"But not for some while yet. You need not fear to finish your work." He jumped lightly into the pit, landing easily on the unstable footing. The builders exchanged uneasy glances. None of them could have taken that drop without injury.

"You are doing well," Ragoczy was saying, walking across the gravel floor. "You should be ready to cement it."

Enrico bowed ingratiatingly. "I hope that you are satisfied, Patron. We have worked to your orders."

"All of you?" Ragoczy asked, looking at Gasparo. "Be

that as it may, I am satisfied. Yes. You have done well. I thank you."

"We are grateful, Patron." He waited, watching the foreigner stride around the graveled bed of the pit.

Ragoczy bent and picked up a handful of gravel. "Why? I thought my opinion meant little to you." He tossed one of the pebbles into the air and caught it, tossed it and caught it.

Three of the builders stopped their work, eyeing Ragoczy with suspicion, but Gasparo strode up to the black-clad stranger. "Your opinion is worth nothing," he said belligerently. "You know nothing of buildings. I have been a builder all my life, and my father before me. I tell you that all these precious instructions of yours are useless and a waste of time." He waited for the blow or the dismissal.

None came. "Bravo," Ragoczy said softly, smiling. "You may very well be right, amico mio. But nonetheless, you will do it my way."

Gasparo's jaw moved forward and he put his hands on his hips. "Yes? Why will we continue with this foolishness?"

"Because, carino, I am paying you. So long as I give you the money you earn, you will build whatever I tell you to, in whatever manner I tell you. Otherwise you may find your money elsewhere." He paused, still smiling. Although he was of slightly less than average height, something about him—it may have been the smile, or the dark clothes, or his disquieting air of command—dominated the builders in the pit. "If I were to tell you to build a Moorish citadel or a Chinese fortress, if you wanted to be paid, you would do it."

Even Enrico and Lodovico laughed at this, and Gasparo nodded his encouragement. "If you think, stranger, that you have any power here in Fiorenza . . ."

"I think," Ragoczy said wearily, "that money speaks a universal tongue. I think that even in Fiorenza you members of your Arte understand that." He threw the gravel in his hand away, listening as the stones spattered where they hit.

Again the builders exchanged looks and Lodovico nodded knowingly to himself.

"The way you build now in Fiorenza, this palazzo will stand . . . what?—perhaps three centuries." Ragoczy's face was desolate. "But what is that? Three centuries, four, five, are nothing. I want my palazzo to stand for a thousand years." He laughed ruefully. "Vain hope. But make the attempt, good builders. Humor me and build according to my outrageous instructions."

"A thousand years?" Gasparo was dumbfounded. He stared at the stranger, and thought that perhaps Ragoczy was mad. "What use will this be to you in a thousand years? Or in a hundred?"

"It is a home," Ragoczy answered simply.

Lodovico snickered and winked broadly at Giuseppe. "But the Patron has neither chick nor child. He has not even a wife. What heirs of his will live here in a thousand years? Or in a hundred?"

"Heirs?" It was as if a door had closed in Ragoczy. He stopped moving and his dark eyes narrowed, their penetrating gaze suddenly alarming. "Those of my blood will come after me, never fear. You have my Word on that."

There was silence in the foundation excavation and the cold wind whipped around them, but the chill the builders felt came more from the foreigner in black than from the air.

Gasparo beetled his brow as his indignation swelled. "We do not make funerary monuments, Eccellenza. If that is what you wish, talk to stonecutters, not to us."

There was a new light in Ragoczy's eyes as he looked at the thick-bodied builder. "Does it matter so much to you, amico?"

"I am a builder," Gasparo announced as he clapped one huge hand to his chest. "I make houses for the living, not the dead."

Behind Gasparo the other builders nodded nervously, and Carlo took courage, giving Gasparo an approving gesture.

"Admirable," Ragoczy said dryly.

"Mock me if you wish, Patron, it does not change the matter. You say you want us to build a house that will stand a thousand years. Va bene. You instruct us in our work. I do not like it, but you are the Patron. But even you cannot pay enough for me to put up a palazzo that is a shell only." He set his hands on his hips again and leaned forward. "You may mock me, but you will not mock my building!"

Ragoczy nodded. "What integrity!" There was neither bitterness nor condemnation in the words. "I promise you that I have no wish for any empty building. Why would I pay for so much special labor if I did not want to live here? Why else would I care how you lay the foundations? . . . Well?"

Gasparo shrugged. "As you say, we are being paid to build a palazzo for you. If you want it built with lacquered straw, what is it to me?" He folded his heavy arms over his chest.

Ragoczy nodded. "Precisely. And what can I be but flattered and grateful that you care so much for my home? You must let me thank you for your courtesy." He strode over to Gasparo, his arms open. "Come, will you not touch cheeks with me?"

Gasparo Tucchio was stunned. Never in his life had a gentleman offered him this familiarity. He flushed, rubbed his gritty hands on his workman's breeches. "Patron, I . . ."

Ragoczy embraced the builder heartily, and Gasparo realized what great strength was contained in that elegant, compact body. Very awkwardly he returned the hug, aware of the heavy stubble of his day-old beard on the smooth cheek of the foreigner.

The other builders watched, one or two of them acutely embarrassed. Though it was true Fiorenza was a Repubblica, this went far beyond the social equality they all took pride in. This was unheard of. Enrico soothed his wounded dignity—for as the supervisor, surely he was more entitled to this unbecoming display—by saying softly to Giuseppe, "Foreign manners. Outrageous. The Patron cannot know what he is doing."

Giuseppe nodded vigorously. "It is well enough for us of the Arte to touch cheeks, but not with one of his station."

But for Gasparo, at that moment if the foreigner in black with the unfathomable eyes had asked him to dig foundations from Fiorenza to Roma, he would have done it without question. There was no mockery in that handsome face, no insult to his conduct.

"Eccellenza . . ." he began, then faltered.

"Amico, I have been a prince, and I have been a beggar. I do not scorn you because you work with your hands. If you did not build, then all of Fiorenza would still live in tents, as it did when Romans first built their camp here next to the old Etruscan town."

Gasparo nodded eagerly. "As you say, Patron."

"Work well, then, my builders. You will all have proof of my gratitude." He managed to include them all in the sweep of his arm. Then he turned, ran two or three steps, and vaulted upward toward the edge of the pit, swung on his arms, landed cleanly but for a clod dislodged by the heel of one boot.

Lodovico made a low whistle, and Enrico blinked. Carlo and Giuseppe busied themselves with emptying their sacks. Only Gasparo smiled, and he smiled hugely.

From above them Ragoczy called down, "I am going to add to your woes, I am afraid." He gestured to someone or something out of sight. In a moment another man stood beside him. "This is Joacim Branco. He will be my lieutenant during the building. You are to follow his instructions to the very limit. I will be satisfied with nothing less than the best of what you are capable. I know your skill to be great. I know you will succeed."

The newcomer beside Ragoczy was amazingly tall, even by Fiorenzan standards. He had long, lean hands, a narrow body and a face like the spine of a book. He wore a rather old-fashioned houppelande in the Burgundian fashion and his unconfined hair drifted around his face like cobwebs. "Good afternoon, builders," he said in a voice so solemn that it tolled like the bell of San Marco.

"Another foreign alchemist," Lodovico said to Gasparo, just loud enough to be certain Joacim Branco could hear.

"That is correct," Ragoczy agreed, and smiled. "His skill is formidable. You will do well to obey him implicitly." Suddenly he laughed. "Come, you need not worry that he will disgrace you with ridiculous demands. Magister Branco is a reasonable man, much more reasonable than I am, I promise you."

Magister Joacim Branco achieved a sour smile. He bowed very slightly, very stiffly.

Enrico rolled his eyes heavenward and silently asked Santa Chiara what he had ever done to deserve this. "Welcome, Magister," he managed to say.

Ragoczy murmured something to the tall Portuguese at his side; then he addressed the men in the pit one last time. "There is special earth to be laid with the foundation. That you will do tomorrow. Today it is enough that you make the gravel even in preparation."

This time Gasparo's voice had real distress in it. "But, Patron, if it rains, we cannot lay a foundation. It will be ruined. It will not bear the weight of the building. It will crack . . ."

"I give you my word that there will be no rain tonight, or tomorrow, or tomorrow night. There will be enough time for you to set the foundation and to install the four corner pieces. After that, it will not matter if it rains; the foundation will be solid and you may make yourselves a shelter with the cornerpieces." With an expansive gesture Ragoczy turned away, leaving the Magister Joacim Branco alone at the edge of the excavation.

Giuseppe finished spreading the gravel from his sack and looked up. "Jesù, Maria," he whispered, and had to stop himself from making the Sign of the Cross.

Joacim Branco had come to the very edge of the pit, and in the cold wind the long sleeves of his houppelande flapped like tattered wings. He stood very still.

It was Enrico who broke the silence. "Magister? Would you care to come down?"

To the relief of the builders the alchemist did not jump into the pit, but made his way down the causeway. As he came nearer it was seen that he held several containers in his hands. He put these down on the gravel and turned to Enrico. "At the fence there are two carts. I will need them."

"How heavy are they?" Lodovico asked, not willing to move.

"They are well-laden. It will take a man apiece to pull them." He turned back to his containers, having no more interest in the builders.

Enrico shrugged fatalistically and pointed to Giuseppe. "You and Carlo bring down the carts. Gaspar' and Lodovico can carry down the last of the gravel."

With a sigh Gasparo trudged back up the slope and reluctantly shouldered another sack of gravel. He thought for a moment about the Patron, about his social solecism, and he grinned.

He was still grinning later as he sat with Lodovico drinking a last cup of hot spiced wine. The night had turned cold, providing an excuse for a larger measure of drink.

"But eggs, Gaspar', *hen's eggs*!" Lodovico was saying for the third time.

"If it is what the Patron wants, we'll put eggs in the mortar. Shells and all." He raised his wooden cup. "To Francesco Ragoczy da San Germano, generous madman that he is."

"Ah, since he touched cheeks with you, you approve every foolish scheme he and that alchemist of his bring forth. If he wanted to cement the palazzo with blood, you'd wield a butcher's ax for him." He stared into the fragrant steam that rose from his wine. "Where is all your jeering now, Gaspar'?"

Gasparo Tucchio smiled again, and wondered if he was getting drunk. "It is nothing to me if he wishes to be a laughingstock. And think of other tales we'll have to tell the Arte. Who has done anything to compare with it? Oh, I know. You're thinking of Ernan', and his stories about building the cage for Magnifico's giraffe. But that is nothing to the tales we'll have. And when the others come to finish the walls and lay the floors, we'll have stories to amaze even them." He tossed off the rest of the wine and considered signaling the tavernkeeper for more.

"But why does he do it? What is his gain? For if money speaks a universal language, as he said, then he must profit by our work." Lodovico considered this, and his face grew wary. After a moment he extended his cup to Gasparo. "Here. My head is growing heavy. Finish this up."

Gasparo's reluctance was for form's sake only. "If you are sure . . . And the night is cold. Why not?" He took the cup and filled his mouth with the fragrant wine. How grand it felt, as if he were floating. What if he was a little drunk? It did a man good to drink on such a cold night.

"I wonder what happened to the rain?" Lodovico mused.

"It held off awhile, like the Patron said," Gasparo replied after he had swallowed and wiped his mouth on his sleeve.

"How did he *know* it would?" This question was more to himself than to Gasparo, and so he paid little attention to the answer.

"Well, he's an alchemist. They know things."

Lodovico frowned and shifted in his chair. "Hen's eggs he gives us, and clay, and special earth and special sand, which must be mixed in a certain order. Why?" He stood up, almost upsetting the bench he shared with Gasparo.

"Here, now," the older builder objected as his seat teetered dangerously. "Lodovico, stop it. Sit down and drink another cup, like a Christian."

For a moment Lodovico stiffened; then he forced his mouth to smile as he sank back down onto the bench. "Va bene. Landlord! Another for both of us." He set his face in a mask of good fellowship and leaned back.

As soon as their cups had been refilled and Gasparo had decided which of the cups was his, Lodovico smiled guilelessly. "Ah, it is hard for a man alone, is it not?"

Gasparo nodded heavily. "It is, amico mio. Tonight I can hardly bear to go home. You'd think," he said drinking deeply, "that a man widowed as long as I've been would get used to it. But no. This night, every night, I think of Rosaria. She was an excellent woman—thrifty, pleasant, agreeable, devoted—a treasure among women." He pulled his hands over his eyes and then picked up his cup again. "You're young, you're young. You don't know what it is to be old and alone."

"You are not old, Gasparo."

But Gasparo shook his head and wagged a finger at Lodovico. "I'm thirty-eight. Thirty-eight. Another ten years and I'll be a toothless old hulk. A lonely, toothless old hulk." His sorrow at this thought overcame him and he finished off the rest of his wine.

This was going better than Lodovico dared hope. "It's a pity that age is not respected as it should be." He leaned closer to Gasparo and switched his full cup for Gasparo's nearly empty one. "It's not enough that you should lose your family and wife, but there's hardly enough money to keep you alive when you can no longer work." This turned out to be a miscalculation. Gasparo pulled himself up straight and said, almost without slurring, "My father was sixty-eight before he stopped working. We Tucchios are strong folk. We work till we drop." His face sagged a little. "My father was a good man. A good man. He helped raise the Duomo of Santa Maria del Fiore . . ."

But Lodovico did not allow his companion to wander. "But think of that palazzo. Think of the wealth of the Patron. With even a little of it a man could live well."

"Here, now." Gasparo slewed around on Lodovico, a belligerent light in his eye. "Are you suggesting that we rob our Patron? We're builders, man, not thieves. We do not steal from our Patron, from any Patron."

"But he's *rich*," Lodovico protested. "And he's foreign."

"All the more reason." With pompous care Gasparo dragged himself to his feet. "We're Fiorenzeni, Lodovico. Well, *I* am, at least. We don't rob foreigners. You put that out of your mind." He leaned forward. "I see what it is. You're drunk. You shouldn't have had that last cup of wine." He swayed and steadied himself, "I'll forget what you said, Lodovico. It was the wine talking."

Inwardly Lodovico cursed but he managed a fatuous smile. "You're right," he agreed. "Too much wine."

With the tenacity of drunkenness, Gasparo persisted. "The thing is not to be thought of. Now, you go home, you sleep this off. I'll forget you ever spoke to me of this." He finished the last of his wine and put the cup down with exaggerated care.

"Thank you, Gaspar'," Lodovico said, making no attempt to disguise his sneer.

"Well," Gasparo said with a sudden change to the affable, "it's been pleasant. Very pleasant. Good to talk. We don't talk enough, Lodovico. Too much work. We should talk more."

Lodovico removed Gasparo's hand from his shoulder. "Tomorrow, perhaps. But I've got to leave now." It had, he thought, been a most unprofitable evening. But in time he might turn it to good use. He rose to his feet and shammed confusion. "Which way . . . ?"

Gasparo clapped an affectionate arm around his shoulder. "Ah, Lodovico, you're a good man. A good man. Now, there's the door. You'll be grateful for the wine when we're out in the night." He reeled toward the door, dragging Lodovico with him.

With a great deal of ingenuity Lodovico disengaged himself from Gasparo's bearlike embrace. "My head . . . My head . . . ." He leaned against the wall for support. "Go on ahead," he said, waving Gasparo toward the door.

Gasparo laughed good-naturedly, waved vaguely to

Lodovico and the landlord, lunged through the door and was gone.

"Another?" the landlord asked Lodovico.

"No. No." He stood in the center of the tavern for some little time, his face closed in thought, his bright eyes calculating. Then, with an unattractive smile, he tossed a coin to the landlord and went out into the bright, cold night.

THE TEXT OF a note from Donna Estasia Catarina di Arrigo della Cittadella da Parma, housekeeper for her cousin, Alessandro di Mariano Filipepi, to Francesco Ragoczy da San Germano. Delivered by hand to the house of the alchemist Federigo Cossa on the night of March 21, 1491:

> *Diletto mio,*
>
> *I pray that this finds you with your host, for my message is urgent. Sandro and Simone will be gone for four days following this Sunday. For those days I will be alone, and anxious for your company. I trust you will be so obliging as to continue our most pleasant diversions of last week.*
>
> *Should this be satisfactory, send me word, and I will receive you as before, in my apartments. I have put your gift upon the bed and look forward in anticipation to showing you how well it becomes me. Oh, say you will come. I grow mad for lack of your kisses.*
>
> *Do not fail*
>
> *Estasia*

CHAPTER 2

Until she looked up with a start, Demetrice Volandrai did not realize how dark it had become in the Medici library. On the trestle table in front of her three books lay open, their texts indistinct now in the suffused light. She put a hand to her eyes and told herself she had a headache rather than admit that her mind had been wandering. She hesitated briefly before closing the books and setting them aside for tomorrow. Reluctantly she tested the quill that lay beside her notes and was not surprised to find it dried, ink caked on it so thickly that she despaired of being able to trim it properly.

She rose slowly and went to the window. In the last burnished light of sunset her woefully old-fashioned gonella of rust velvet seemed more beautiful than it had ever been in better light. Her pale rosy-blond hair framed her face in chaste braids and her simple linen chamise, where it showed above the neck of her gown and puffed around the terribly plain brooches that joined her simple sleeves to her dress, was without stains or grime. If anyone had suggested to her at that moment that she was the most attractive woman in il Palazzo de' Medici, she would have laughed. Her amber-colored eyes were wistful as she watched the light fade.

"Oh, don't move," said a voice behind her as she started at last to turn away from the window.

The familiar sound of Sandro Filipepi's voice brought a rueful smile to Demetrice's firm mouth and she turned to him, her arms extended. "Botticelli, admit it: if you could order the sun to stop in the heavens you would do it, so that you could make a color study."

He shrugged, but did not deny it. "It was color that

brought me here this afternoon. That alchemist, Ragoczy, the one who's building the big new palazzo? You know him?" He waited a moment.

"I have met him once or twice." She remembered liking his wit and his gentleness, and the enigmatic expression in his dark eyes. "Was he here, too?"

"Briefly. It seems he has some new formulae for colors. Of course Laurenzo is interested, and he asked me and a few of the others to use the colors and tell him what we think of them." He paused. "I wish I knew what to make of him."

It would not do for Sandro to see her interest, so she smiled and said, "You know alchemists. They are always mysterious. Confess it, amico, you would be disappointed if he were like everyone else."

Sandro nodded. "True. And he is foreign. But his affectations. Always dressed in black, never eating with us, forever curious about metals and earths! Ah, well, he is entertaining, and he does know something about pigments and tinctures. I will give him that."

Demetrice had come around the table and touched cheeks with him. "How generous. Will you try his colors?"

"Of course." He peered around the darkened room. "Cataloging?"

"Yes. Pico is home for a while and Agnolo is in Bologna, so the task falls to me. I am afraid that today I haven't done it very well. These old manuscripts, you know, are very difficult to read."

Sandro's face had clouded at the mention of Agnolo Poliziano. "I don't know why Laurenzo tolerates his impudence." He held up his hand to forestall the answer. "Loyalty is one thing, Donna mia, but this is foolishness. Poliziano trades on Laurenzo's tolerance shamelessly. You know he does."

Demetrice had gone back to the table and busied herself with gathering her papers. "I don't understand it, Sandro. But it is what Laurenzo wants, and I will respect his wishes."

Disbelief filled Sandro's next question. "Do you *like* Agnolo? How could you like him?"

"No, I don't like him. He's waspish, he's ugly-minded and for all his erudition, he's unpredictable. But he is talented, and truly a scholar." Very gently she said, "I need not tell you, Sandro, that every gift has a price."

"And sometimes more price than gift." He walked across the room and put his long painter's hands on her shoulders. "If there is any justice in this world, Donna mia, you will not have to bear your poverty forever. If your uncle had been a citizen of Fiorenza, Laurenzo would long since have restored your fortunes."

Demetrice felt absurd tears in her eyes and she wiped them away impatiently. "Well, even Laurenzo cannot restore what no longer exists, so perhaps it is as well that Lione lived in Rimini." She tried to smile, but could not. "Laurenzo has been more than generous. He has housed me and fed me and clothed me for almost ten years. That is much more than any of my nearer kinsmen were willing to do." She stopped abruptly and moved away from him. "Pardon me, Sandro. It is not pleasing for me to talk this way of my family."

By now the room was almost dark. Sandro was just an indistinct shape with a voice on the other side of the table. Demetrice thought that the dark must have something to do with it, for she had never spoken to him this way before. She took comfort in his friendship and was grateful for his interest, but she insisted on a reserve between them, and it was as real as the trestle table that stood in front of her.

Sandro tacitly accepted her rebuff, but added one parting shot. "I am twice your age, Donna mia. And I tell you, do not depend on anything or anyone in Fiorenza beyond Laurenzo. Fiorenza is a city of passions, of obsessions, and there is as much dark in it as light."

"This from you, Sandro?" she said, glad to turn this somber warning to banter.

"Especially from me." Then he, too, abandoned the subject. In a different voice he said, "I am going away for a few days. Simone and I have business to attend to."

"I wish you a pleasant and safe journey," Demetrice said automatically. "Do you go far?"

"Only to Pisa. A simple matter. But I would like to ask a favor of you."

"Of course." The words were out before she thought about them, and as soon as she had spoken, she doubted their wisdom. "If Laurenzo does not require my help here," she added prudently.

"It is nothing difficult, I promise you." He stopped as a servant came into the room carrying a taper to light the lanterns that stood at either end of the room and the three candles on the reading desk beside the fireplace.

The strange air of intimacy that had surrounded them disappeared in the light. Demetrice said to the servant, "Will you start the fire, too? The room is really quite chilly."

"Yes, Donna," the servant answered, and bent to her task.

"So it is," Sandro agreed. He rubbed his hands together and adjusted the long folds of his lucco, the standard social dress of most Fiorenzeni. His was of brown wool and lacked the intricate pleating at the neck that more prominent men wore.

"What is the favor, Sandro?" Demetrice had gone nearer

the fireplace and was nodding to the servant as the first spurt of flame took hold of the logs laid there.

"Ah, the favor. Yes. It is about my housekeeper, my cousin. You have met Estasia, haven't you?"

"Yes." Her tone was cautious as she thought of Estasia della Cittadella, of her soft, sensuous body and vixen's face. The primness of Estasia's widow's coif did not deceive Demetrice, for she had seen the eager hunger in Estasia's hazel eyes and heard the coaxing languor in her voice when she spoke to attractive men.

"She does not like to be alone," Sandro said with some difficulty. "Would you be willing to call on her one of the afternoons I am gone?"

Before she could stop herself, Demetrice asked, "Why?"

"For me? Demetrice?" He hesitated. "She *is* lonely, you know. It is never easy for a widow. And she often has trouble with other women. If she had a lover, it would be different. She would be happier and would have someone to enjoy. But in my house, there is little opportunity, and Simone is very severe with her."

Demetrice watched as the fire at last began its steady burn, making a friendly rush and crackle like conversation in an unknown tongue. She frowned, wishing that she did not. "I don't know."

Sandro had come near her again, and the light from the flames deepened the lines in his craggy face. "Prego, carina. I would not ask it if it were a trivial thing. You see, Estasia has been very much upset by the sermons Simone has been preaching to her. Simone . . ." He hesitated, not wanting to condemn his brother. "Simone worries for her soul, and for that reason he cannot accept the way Estasia wants to live. Her vivacity troubles him. He does not see that she has fear, too."

Rather dryly Demetrice said, "I have heard him. He was

here once last year. He does not approve of the way Laurenzo lives, either. He told him so."

"San Gregorio protect me." Sandro was acutely embarrassed. "I didn't know. He should never have . . . He does not think, Demetrice. His fervor inspires him and he speaks out. You can imagine, then, how he berates Estasia, which only makes her more determined to have her pleasures." Again he paused, and searched for words. "It would mean a great deal to Estasia to have someone call on her. Someone who is kind."

"Very well." Demetrice sighed and looked at her companion. She wished the room were dark again, so that they could recapture that closeness. With the room lit by candles, lanterns and fire, she saw too much and knew too little. "Since you ask it, I will. But I do not know what to say to her. Tell me: what interests her?"

"Housewifery. She's an excellent housekeeper. Not even Simone can make complaint on that issue. She knows, particularly, a great deal about cooking. She has a way with pastry."

Demetrice laughed in spite of herself. "I know almost nothing about cookery. It is the price of being raised in a scholar's home. Now, if the recipes were in Greek, or even Seneca's Latin, he might have been moved to care about food. About the only dish I can make is honey cakes. But I know a little of lacemaking," she offered helpfully.

"Estasia is expert with her needle. Her embroidery is superb. Take your lace with you."

"Yes, but Sandro," Demetrice objected reasonably, "we can't sit there and stitch at each other."

Sandro shook his head and leaned against the mantel of the fireplace. "Talk of clothing, then. Compare velvets. Or gossip. Surely there is fruit enough for that in Fiorenza." He waited until the servant was gone from the room, then said, "I fear for her when she is alone. She is terrified, sometimes, thinking that she is forever abandoned. I cannot let her suffer because of me. She makes light of it, but I have seen her eyes when she has been alone too long, and they are bright like a trapped animal's." He sighed, turned to her. "It is not your responsibility. She is my cousin. I know that. But if you would help me, I'd be truly grateful. Who knows," he added impishly. "I might even do your portrait."

"With those new pigments Laurenzo wants you to test?" She, too, moved away from the fire. "It grows late, Sandro, and I have not yet eaten. Will you join me at table? I fear we must take it in the pantry, for the household sat down some time ago."

"No. But it is gracious of you to ask me." Sandro shook off his somber mood and strode to the door. "I, too, have not eaten and it is time I was home."

Automatically Demetrice glanced toward the windows and saw the last glow of dusk in the cold March sky. "I didn't realize we had talked so long. Yes. Perhaps you'd better leave. Have one of the servants accompany you with a lamp."

But Sandro laughed this suggestion away. "There's no need. The thieves are not that desperate. I'll be safe, I promise you."

She did not object, but when the door was closed behind him, a frown settled on her face once more and there was a kind of distress in her bearing. She lingered in the library until the young Slavic slave who slept there arrived. Sure that the room was safe, Demetrice left it and hurried to the bottom floor in hope of having a light meal with the stewards.

The stairs of il Palazzo de Medici were narrow and

treacherously steep. Demetrice negotiated them with care, reminding herself as she went that she had fallen once, four years before, and the bruises and sprains had been many weeks in fading.

The understeward, Sergio, greeted her casually and offered to get her a dish of veal-and-pork pie that was left over from supper. "There are some tortolini and some broth, if you'd like that."

To her surprise, Demetrice discovered that she was hungry, and she accepted this offer, spooning pine nuts over the pie when it was brought to her.

Massimillio, the Medicis' enormous cook, swaggered into the pantry and favored Demetrice with a huge smile that spread over his moon face like butter. "Ah, it is la bella Demetrice, who is so kind and who loves my food."

Demetrice knew what was expected. "Massimillio, the food is superb, as always. The tortolini are savory and your pie is delicious."

"Let me pour you some Trebbiano," the cook offered, reaching for the wine flask. "And when you are finished, I have some confetti."

"A thousand thanks," Demetrice said, although she did not particularly like either white wine or sugared almonds.

"Chè piacer!" sighed the cook as he poured himself a generous portion of the Trebbiano and stared into its straw-colored depths. "Now, you, Donna mia, appreciate my art. But Laurenzo!" With his free hand he made a gesture of despair. "He would not care if I made nothing but sausages, so long as he got his chestnuts. I have boiled in wine and roasted barrels of chestnuts, I think." He shook his large head and his chins wobbled.

"You must make allowances, Massimillio. Since Laurenzo cannot smell, he misses much of your wonderful cooking." Demetrice sipped her wine and had another bite of pork-and-veal pie.

"Poor man!" He finished his wine and replenished his cup. "Trebbiano is very nice," he said judiciously. "For all the talk of it being workingman's wine, it is very nice."

By this time Demetrice had eaten most of the pie and her tortolini were nearly gone. She smiled warmly at the cook and said mendaciously, "How much I would like confetti, but I fear, Massimillio, that it is such a cold night, and your excellent food is so satisfying, that I had much better have some broth, to keep me warm."

Grudgingly Massimillio admitted this was wise and turned back to the cavernous kitchens to heat the broth. As he put the kettle on the coals of the hearth, he remarked, "That foreigner, the one Laurenzo likes so much. With the unchristian name."

"Ragoczy?" Demetrice suggested.

"That is the man. He has us all in an uproar. I have heard that his kitchen is going to be terribly odd. Now, you may say that is his foreign ways, and no doubt it would account for it, but," he added darkly, drawing down the corners of his mouth, "you may be sure that he will have to find cooks elsewhere if he intends to make us change our ways." As he spoke, he reached into one of the small drawers of the divided chest that flanked his cooking table, and pulled out a handful of seeds. "I am adding more coriander, to help keep you warm."

"You are kind, Massimillio." Demetrice had come to the door and stood watching the huge man as he added his finishing touches to the broth, which had begun to simmer.

"Ah, Donna Demetrice, it is a simple matter to be kind to you. You are good, you are pleasant, you like what I cook. I don't mind making special meals for you, because you enjoy them and it pleases me to watch you eat." He poured some of the steaming broth into a large wooden mug. "There. Now, when you have finished that, I fear you must leave, for I have much to do before tomorrow. Two Bolognese merchants and the officers of the Arte della Lana and the Arte di Calimala are to take their meal at midday tomorrow with Laurenzo. They will speak of nothing but cloth and money and will not taste so much as the ginger in my savor sanguino."

"Poor Massimillio." Demetrice felt genuine sympathy for the huge man. "Well, if you will, save me some leftovers and we can share a late meal together."

The cook turned to her, startled. "Will you not be eating with the others?"

"Not if they mean to talk only of cloth and money." There was a teasing light in her eyes as she stretched out her hand to him. "It will be much more pleasant to have my meal here, with you. Il comestio is nicer in good company."

"All meals are nicer in good company," Massimillio announced with awful hauteur. Then he relented somewhat, saying, "It will be a treat to share the meal with you. I am making a berlingozzo and a minestra of spring lamb, for we have just got the first new lambs."

Although these were not the greatest delicacies available to the Fiorenzan upper class, they were still special treats. Demetrice smiled delightedly. "If they do not enjoy your art, Massimillio, be certain that I will."

"Bella mia, I will perish of joy," he announced, and took back the empty cup she handed him. "Now, you must rush off to your bed, or the virtue of the broth will be for nothing."

Demetrice thanked him again, and left the kitchen for her small bedroom, three floors above. She tasted the ginger, garlic and coriander long after she had extinguished the candle and pulled the worn damask hangings around her bed.

TEXT OF A letter from Alessandro di Mariano Filipepi to Leonardo da Vinci:

> *To Leonardo in Milano, his friend Botticelli sends his affectionate greetings on our Beato Antoninus' Day:*
>
> *I am sending with this a wallet containing some new tinctures that may interest you. Laurenzo's new friend, the alchemist I have told you of before, developed them. I have used them myself and have found that the colors they produce are of rare luminosity. Try them, I urge you.*
>
> *I had your letter of March 27 in good time. If you are as much distressed by the Sforzas as you say, then why do you remain? You know that Laurenzo would welcome your return, and surely there is work for you to do in Fiorenza that will interest you as much as your work in Milano. Consider, then, caro amico, for you are much missed here. Even that sharp-tongued Poliziano speaks of you affectionately.*
>
> *You will perhaps be saddened to learn that Laurenzo has not been well. As has been his practice in the past, he has taken the waters and he insists that he is better. But I am worried. His hands often swell and he is sometimes weak without reason. Often of late, his kinswoman Donna Demetrice Volandrai reads to him, sometimes the works of Plato, sometimes new tales. It has become his habit to spend his evenings thus. Yet*

his mind is keen, and he is, as always, seeking out gifted artists. That young student of Ghirlandajo is part of the Medici household now, and for all your loathing of marble sculpture, you would admit that young Buonarroti has talent. Laurenzo is pleased with his progress, which, considering his youth, is remarkable. I think that Magnifico would prefer it if his own sons showed the promise of Michelangelo Buonarroti. Giovanni is for the Church, of course, and his mind is as tenacious as it is agile. But Piero is another matter: Piero has done little but indulge himself since he was old enough to ask his father for favors. He has not changed since you knew him—he is as capricious as a child, forever making demands.

Yet all is not bleak here. There was a great festival on Ascension Day, and all Fiorenza went into the fields to catch grasshoppers and to sport. There was a special Requiem Mass that day, at San Lorenzo, in memory of Giuliano. That deed will forever be a stain on the house of Pazzi, who would appear to be well-named, so insane was that act.

We have heard that you are still in the habit of buying birds in the market and setting them free. A friend of that alchemist I already mentioned has recently come from Venezia, and made a stop in Milano while the city was still talking about your most recent escapade. Leonardo, amico, you will not save the birds. They will only be caught again and someone else will eat them. How is it that you can invent such terrible weapons of war, and think nothing of examining the bodies of the dead most thoroughly, but balk at eating songbirds?

In reference to your love of machines, you would be delighted at the new palazzo that Ragoczy, the alchemist, is building. It is in the Genovese style, and he has added every innovation imaginable. The builders all gossip about it. He has modified his bath, and made a special chamber for storing and heating water, instead of making a holocaust. The chamber is about the size of two traveling chests and adjoins the bath closely. It is tarred and lacquered so that it cannot leak, and the water is fed to the bath through a pipe with a spigot. He has also invented a new sort of oven for his cooks, one made of metal, which he claims more efficient (though why he should want cooks when he never dines, I cannot conceive). Many of the cooks in the city have said they would have nothing to do with such an instrument. I understand that he has a very simple, hard bed, but that everything else is wholly magnificent. If you do not want Laurenzo for a patron, then consider Ragoczy. He has a great deal of wealth and loves beautiful things almost as much as the Medicis. When I told him of your silver lute, the one you fashioned in the shape of a horse's head, he was delighted. You need not fear his generosity—he is quite wealthy and completely honorable. I have myself seen some of his jewels, and their size and beauty would stagger even you. At Christmas he presented Laurenzo with an emerald as large as the pietra dura bowl of Laurenzo's silver cup. He, Ragoczy, knows many secret processes with metals. You would enjoy his conversation as well, Leonardo, for he is an erudite conversationalist and his range of interests is broad.

I pray you will consider coming once again to Fiorenza. We all here miss you. We miss your songs as much as your excellent work, for all you say you never finish anything. Whatever Milano offers you, Fiorenza can give you. Remember that you are loved here, and that the blessings of your friends follow you wherever you go, even home.

My cousin Estasia calls me to table, so I must end this. With the hope that our next greeting will be face to face, this brings you the affection of your friend

Sandro

In Fiorenza, on the 10th day of May, 1491

Chapter 3

NOT ALL THE morning mist had cleared yet, though there was the promise of heat in the air. Fiorenza shimmered in the spring light, so that the tall, stone-fronted buildings seemed touched with gold. On this splendid day the streets were full, the people already preparing for yet another festival. At la Piazza della Signoria banners of all the Artei were already being strung, each proclaiming the importance and function of one of the powerful guilds that were the heart and breath of the city.

"Well, mio caro stragnero," Laurenzo said to the alchemist who rode beside him and had shared his morning gallop, "what have you in your distant home to compare to this?"

Ragoczy smiled, but his dark eyes were remote. "We

have nothing like this, Magnifico." His gray horse scampered over the stone paving, still fresh, still playful, and the sound of his hooves echoed crisply off the street.

"And even if he did," drawled the third member of the riding party, "he is much too well-mannered to say so, at least to you, Medici."

Laurenzo's attractive, ugly face darkened, but he made no reply, occupying himself with the sportiveness of the big roan stallion he rode. When he had brought his mount even with Ragoczy's he turned to the other man. "Agnolo, he need hardly concern himself with courtesy when you are by."

Agnolo Poliziano barked out a laugh, then said more somberly, "I do not know why you allow *me* such liberty, then, Laurenzo. Or is it out of respect for Ragoczy's rank? He says nothing of his birth, but I will wager you half of the gold in your damned bank that he is better-born than any of us, though he is a foreigner."

At this Laurenzo smiled, and though the smile did not come as easily as it had a few years ago, it was still utterly charming and even Agnolo Poliziano could not resist answering it with one of his own. "Neither of us is nobly born, Agnolo. We cannot be. You, I, we are simply citizens of Fiorenza. But you"—he turned to Ragoczy—"you undoubtedly have a title recognized somewhere. I have often wondered what it is. Francesco Ragoczy da San Germano. Da San Germano." He tasted the words. "Where is San Germano, Francesco Ragoczy, and what is it to you?"

By now they had crossed the Ponte alle Grazie, and not far ahead la Palazzo della Signoria pointed its spire into the festive morning. Fiorenza was a city of towers and turrets, but the topheavy spire of il Palazzo della Signoria was the symbol of la Repubblica, and therefore was unique in the city.

Laurenzo motioned Ragoczy and Poliziano to rein in their horses. "It is very crowded. We will need another way." He thought for a moment, and took advantage of this hesitation to repeat his question to Ragoczy. "Where is San Germano?"

Ragoczy did not answer Laurenzo's inquiry at once. He had turned similar probings aside before. His eyes were fixed in the distance, on the gently rolling Tuscan hills with their villas keeping watch over Fiorenza, but his expression was far more remote than the hills he watched. "My homeland is . . . far away, in ancient mountains, where even now Turks and Christians are slaughtering each other. It is called Wallachia now, and Transylvania." He stopped rather abruptly, looking once again at Laurenzo. "It is a happier thing to be simply a citizen of Fiorenza, Magnifico, than to be a Prince of the Blood and a lifelong exile."

A band of youngsters surged out of la Via de' Benci and at the sight of Laurenzo set up the shout of "Palle! Palle!"

Laurenzo acknowledged this with a nod and a wave, calling out a few friendly words after them, then turned again to the haunted face of his foreign friend. "Exile," he said, and there was despair in his voice.

Ragoczy said nothing; his dark eyes were enigmatic.

"Better an exile in Fiorenza than King of the World," Agnolo Poliziano said nastily as he watched the children run down a side street. "Why else did you recall me after sending me away? Certainly you must value life in Fiorenza above all others. Or are you anxious to send me away again, to remind me about exile? What excuse will you find this time, now that your wife is dead, and cannot object to me?"

Once again Laurenzo de' Medici hesitated before speaking. "When I am most tempted to see you flung into the Arno, bellissimo Agnolo," he said at last, "I have only to touch myself here"—he fingered a long scar on his throat—"and I recall that if you had not been there on that bloody Easter, I would have died beside my brother, and the Pazzis would rule Fiorenza. You cannot provoke me, my friend. I am too much in your debt."

"Admirable. *Ad*mirable. What splendid sensibility. What sublime philosophy," Poliziano marveled. "And without me you cannot finish your library, not that that enters into it. But remember that I have not finished ransacking Bologna for you yet." He swayed dangerously in his studded saddle as his horse bucked at the sudden sound of trumpets. "The devil take Beato Antoninus! I wish him heavenly joy of that clamor!"

"The procession will begin soon," Laurenzo said to no one in particular. "We'd better hurry."

"As you wish." Ragoczy was grateful for this change in their conversation. "Perhaps if you do not want to take part in these festivities, you might enjoy inspecting my palazzo? It will be finished shortly, and I have not had the honor of showing you through it. Today would be an excellent time, Magnifico. The builders are all at the festival and we may browse through it at leisure."

"Bleeding wounds of God!" Poliziano burst out. "What is there to see but walls? You may paint them this shade or that, and have tapestries to cover them, or pictures. But in the end they are still walls, and only slightly different from any others you may see. Some are wider, some are more fancifully decorated, but they are nothing more than walls."

At this Ragoczy smiled. "Ah, you forget, Poliziano, there are also floors and ceilings, though to be sure, they are only to walk on and to hold up the roof."

His last few words were drowned in a new trumpet blare. The horses moved skittishly and the three men had to turn their attention to their mounts, tightening the reins, moving forward in the high saddles.

"What a noise they make!" Poliziano had jobbed the bit and his neat bay gelding now tossed its head and sidled restively.

"It is a celebration, Agnolo," Laurenzo explained patiently and unnecessarily. "Make up your mind, Agnolo. When the people of Fiorenza take to the street, they are a tide, and only the buildings have the strength to withstand them. We must leave quickly or be swept onto la Piazza della Signoria."

"But to waste another day seeing some new palazzo." Poliziano's small bright eyes narrowed and his mouth set. "Very well, very well. I have heard that this palazzo is in the Genovese manner. It might have all sorts of surprises."

"Yes," Ragoczy agreed ironically. "There's no telling how the walls are placed. They may lean at amazing angles." He turned to Laurenzo. "Do you truly not wish to see the festival, Magnifico?"

"I have seen it often. I have not seen your palazzo. And Piero is attending the festival." Laurenzo's attitude was thoughtful and his strong Medici jaw thrust even farther forward. "I will not live forever, and Piero must learn. It is time he discovered that this city is not merely his plaything. He must become accustomed to his civic duties." He twitched the end of his reins with crippled, lean fingers. "You see, mio caro stragnero, my son Piero is something of a fool. Perhaps it is not too late to change him."

Agnolo's angry laugh cut into this. "I would not depend on that, and I tutored him. Look at what he has. Think of the adulation. He is beautiful, and all Fiorenza loves him."

"By which you mean that Piero is beautiful and I am not?" Laurenzo did not wait for a response. He tapped his horse with his heels and began to move forward through the steady stream of people making their way toward la Piazza della Signoria. "I know well enough what I look like. Giuliano was the beautiful brother. Va ben'. Perhaps it is my face that makes me love beautiful things. Come, take this turn. We'll go through la Piazza della Santa Croce." Plainly he wanted to end the bickering.

Agnolo was not through with his barbs. "Such modesty, Laurenzo, Magnifico. But you have read Plato many times. You know that Socrates was sought after by every handsome young man in Athens. You must not despair. Your virtues will save you." With an impatient slap of his reins Poliziano sent his horse trotting ahead.

"Undoubtedly in Athens my face would be as ugly as it is now." There was neither rancor nor self-pity in this admission. At the next turn Laurenzo contrived to take the lead, shifting in his saddle so that the gold embossed LAUR. MED. that marked all his possessions would be visible.

Ragoczy followed, a faint smile curling his wry mouth. He shook his head as Poliziano once again maneuvered to get ahead of Laurenzo, and Medici let him keep that lead for a bit, and then skillfully reclaimed it. In a few more blocks the whole pattern was repeated, Laurenzo, as always, regaining the lead.

They were almost abreast of la Chiesa di San Marco when Poliziano tired of the game. He let his horse fall back and he shrugged. "What does it matter, after all? You ride better than I do, Laurenzo. You always have. I know it. But I want to be the better." His smile had an innocent delight. "Damn your infernal tolerance, Medici. If I were you, I would not have allowed me back in Fiorenza, no matter what the debt."

"Someone had to take Piero in hand. And he is hardly a reward for anyone." He shook his head and was about to address a remark to Ragoczy, still a few lengths behind them, when Poliziano began again.

"San Marco. How can anyone bear to live so near these sanctimonious Domenicani?" This attack was plainly directed at the man behind them. "Or do they like monks in your country, da San Germano?"

Ragoczy raised his fine brows. "That depends on whether you are a Turk or a Christian, I suppose. They do not bother me."

"They bother *me*," Poliziano said in a louder voice. "That boring preacher. The new one. He came here last year. What's his name, Laurenzo? The one who's always describing disaster. He was here for a while some years ago. You know which I mean."

"Girolamo Savonarola." Laurenzo sighed. "Give him credit, Agnolo. He may preach about the suffering of the damned and the worthlessness of the world, but he is sincere and he does not meddle in what does not concern him."

"You mean he stays out of politics?" Poliziano made an obscene gesture toward the church. "That's because he hasn't tasted power yet. You should not have allowed him to come back, Laurenzo. It was a mistake."

"Turn into the next street, Magnifico," Ragoczy called, even though Laurenzo undoubtedly knew the way.

"Of course." He nodded to Ragoczy, but continued his conversation with Poliziano. "You should not say such things, Agnolo. To me you may say what you like. But do not make remarks like that where they can cause trouble. You make the monk more important than he is. We have difficulties enough without making Savonarola angry. Let him preach his austerity and piety. There are some of our citizens who take comfort in mortification, and if they follow him, what is that to you or me? It harms no one. But the one sure way to bring him into politics is to malign him and make mock of his beliefs. If he is forced to defend himself, he will find allies, and that will be worse for Fiorenza than the Venezian pox and war with Milano." He pulled at the rein and let his stallion trot down the newly flagged street.

Poliziano shook his head, and he let the jeering note come back into his voice. "What? a Medici afraid of the truth? Very well. Keep your ridiculous policy if you insist. You have convinced yourself that you must be magnanimous with the Church for your damnable son-in-law. What does it matter if his father is Pope? You need not placate a preacher to keep peace with Innocento." Suddenly the sarcasm was gone and his little mouth narrowed in a deadly serious line. "I tell you that preacher is dangerous. I warn you: he will destroy you." Then he made as elaborate a bow as he could in the saddle. "Do not heed me, then. Who are you but a simple citizen of Fiorenza? What right have you to dictate to the Pope?"

Laurenzo was silent, but his jaw became more tense, so that the muscles stood out along the bone. His wide-brimmed hat shadowed his eyes, but Ragoczy could see anger and sorrow there.

Once again Poliziano's tone changed. "Don't think *me* more of a fool than *you* are, Laurenzo."

There was no answer. Laurenzo had already pulled up his horse in the unfinished gateway of an incomplete building. Scaffolding stood in the courtyard, and stonework and mortar showed that raw newness which was a substitute for character in the palazzo. As Laurenzo swung out of the saddle, he tugged his reins over the big roan's head and secured them to the nearest scaffold's supports. "I have never thought you a fool, Agnolo," he said, somewhat more acidly than before.

Ragoczy had also dismounted and was securing his reins to the new hinge mounts that would eventually hold the fantastic cast-iron grillwork of the gate. "Do you want to join me, Poliziano, and see the walls and floors and ceilings? Or would you rather stay here in the courtyard and let my servant bring you some wine to drink?"

This invitation delighted Poliziano. He kicked his feet free of the stirrups and slid off his horse. "I gladly accept the offer of wine, Ragoczy. And I thank you for sparing me the unending boredom of viewing your palazzo. The walls, I see, are upright, and certainly I can get the full effect of the building from here." His glance took in the unfinished courtyard.

For a moment Ragoczy's dark eyes rested enigmatically on Poliziano's face. "Can you?" Then the mood was gone. He shrugged lightly. "There are benches for you to sit on. I am sure the builders won't mind if you use them. The mosaics on that side of the court have just been laid. I pray you won't walk on them."

Poliziano had secured his horse's reins to the topmost of a stack of iron window grilles. He glanced around the courtyard in a perfunctory way, saying, "Pretty, very pretty. A handsome court. Those mosaics remind me of something I saw in Roma once. Where is that servant of yours who will bring me wine?"

Ragoczy still stood in the shadows, and because of the black clothes of Venezian silk he wore, he seemed one with them, almost unreal. "In a moment, Agnolo. I will summon him. Ruggiero!"

The sudden loudness of his call brought Laurenzo away from his inspection of the gate's fittings and decorations. "Ragoczy, what are the markings around your arms? I don't think I know the words. I thought it was Greek, but I cannot read it. Is it in the Russian tongue, perhaps?"

There was a certain aloofness in his manner as he turned to Laurenzo. "No, Magnifico, it is not Greek. Nor Russian." He contemplated the black disk with erect wings above it displayed against a silver field.

"But what does it say?" Laurenzo had stepped back and was slapping some dust away from his buff-colored belted riding mantle. "For some reason I find it . . . disquieting. The device is elegant, caro mio, much more than my red balls, but there is something almost frightening about it. What does the motto say?"

Ragoczy narrowed his eyes. "It is not easily said in your language, Magnifico. But I will try to tell you. Roughly, then, it is 'From the greatest darkness eternally reborn.' The device is the eclipse, of course. The arms are old." He looked away. "Very old."

"And very striking," Laurenzo said. He had pulled off his mazzocchio, though it was not customary to remove hats in- or out-of-doors. "It's warm for May."

There was a tap of hard-soled shoes in the far hall which connected the courtyard with the loggia at the front of the house. A figure could be seen moving toward them, and very shortly Ragoczy's servant stepped into the warm golden light. He was a slender man of slightly more than middle age. His weathered face was beardless and he wore a house-man's gown of belted linen. He paused and bowed with great dignity.

"Ruggiero, this man"—he indicated Agnolo Poliziano, who stood with one foot on a joiner's bench—"has done me the honor of being the first to accept my hospitality in this palazzo. Bring him wine, and some of the Persian sweets."

"As you wish, master."

"And, Ruggiero, bring a cup of almond milk to the upper gallery after you have served Signor Poliziano." He sketched a nod in Agnolo's direction, then turned to Laurenzo. "I am right, am I not, Magnifico? You do like almond milk?"

The stern set of Laurenzo's mouth relaxed and he grinned reluctantly. "Well done. You surprised me."

"I?" Ragoczy gave Ruggiero a sign of dismissal, then crossed the mosaic pavement to a shallow pit where a fountain would be in another month. "Surely you did not think that I would not offer you anything that might suit your fancy. Do you want more than almond milk? I have fruit, I think, and there must be some bread in the kitchen."

Laurenzo, too, crossed the mosaics. "No, food is all one to me. Almond milk will refresh me." He looked down at the mosaics. "What made you choose these intricate designs? They're classical enough to be old Roman."

Ragoczy was tempted to say that the mosaic designs were exactly the same as certain of those in imperial Roma, but he bit back the words. Instead, he smiled. "Thank you, Magnifico. I confess it was the effect I hoped for."

"Then you have succeeded." Laurenzo looked back toward Agnolo.

"Are you sure you will not change your mind, Poliziano, and come with us?"

"When wine and sweets are being brought?" His small eyes brightened. "Enjoy yourself, Laurenzo. For I will be quite happy on my own."

Laurenzo's response was resigned. "Then I will not concern myself." He lengthened his stride and joined Ragoczy in the shadow beneath the gallery. "I like these columns. Are they continued above?"

"Yes. And I am planning murals on the walls there to complement the mosaics. Will you recommend someone for this? I know that Sandro is too busy, but there might be others? Perhaps young Buonarroti?"

"Perhaps. Let me think on it." They had now entered the hall through which the servant Ruggiero had come. "I like your arrangement for lanterns," Laurenzo said.

Ragoczy went along with the turn in conversation. "Yes, they give excellent light."

"But if you had a mirror behind them, you would have even more light." Laurenzo stopped and pointed out the mountings. "It would be a simple matter to add mirrors. Then this hall would be wonderfully bright."

"I see." Ragoczy nodded, knowing that Laurenzo was used to having his advice followed. He studied the arrangement as if it were new to him, and then said, "Of course. You are right. I only hope that I can bring the glass from Venezia without mishap. If it were less fragile, I think I might install mirrors in the loggia, as well."

Laurenzo's civic pride was ruffled. "Venezia? Why not order your mirrors here?" He was as well aware as Ragoczy that the Venezian mirrors—indeed, all Venezian glass—were superior to anything produced in Fiorenza. He smiled reluctantly and relented. "Polished metal would do as well, or almost as well. Silver would be particularly appropriate. And Fiorenza produces much finer metalwork than Venezia."

Inwardly relieved, Ragoczy laughed. "Polished metal, then, and made in Fiorenza." He motioned them on with a gesture, and a few steps brought them to a wide loggia. "I think you will like this, Magnifico. The windows are particularly large, and set back from the street."

"You might find them too large in winter," Laurenzo warned, but without condemnation.

"Ah, but then I will have shutters over them, with louvers to let in some light. I have thought it out, you see." Ragoczy stood back and with a host's gesture left Laurenzo on his own.

Laurenzo did not speak as he paced out of the room, but there was an appreciative expression in his large brown eyes. "Even though it is Genovese, mio caro stragnero, it is beautiful. I particularly like this grand double staircase. It is quite unlike anything in Fiorenza. What will you use there, at the landing, to set it off?" He did not pause, but answered his own question. "A painting! Perhaps two of them, or possibly three smaller works. Or a statue, a small one in bronze or marble." He turned expectantly to the palazzo's owner.

"Well, no." Ragoczy mounted the stairs beside Laurenzo. "I have plans for elaborate wood paneling carved in very deep relief. It is more in the custom of my people to do so." He did not add that the paneling would better conceal the door to the three hidden rooms beyond the landing.

"Wood paneling carved in deep relief. Yes. A very pretty idea. It is too restrained for me, but I suppose you miss your homeland, and want it near you. It is good that your house reflects your country. I mean that this, too, is your home." He turned on the landing and continued up the left flight to the second floor. "The proportions are always pleasing to the eyes. From here, looking into the loggia, how pleasant the aspect is. You have quite . . ." He broke off on a sudden gasp as his normally sallow-tan complexion went chalky white.

Ragoczy caught Laurenzo around the waist and held him,

feeling the tension grow worse as Laurenzo fought against his weakness and increasing pain.

"No . . . No . . ." There was a sheen of sweat on Laurenzo's face now, and his long-fingered hands shook, locked like claws in the black silk damask of Ragoczy's Spanish pourpoint.

"Magnifico . . ." Ragoczy's beautiful foreign voice was low, with none of the alarm he felt allowed to color his words. "What should I do?"

"Christe and San Giovan'!" Laurenzo hissed through clenched teeth. His rather prominent eyes were squeezed shut and he would have sunk to his knees had not Ragoczy taken the weight of the taller man onto his shoulder. Carefully, gently, he lowered Laurenzo onto the shallow marble treads of the staircase. There was distress in his face as his small hands worked loose the collar of Laurenzo's riding mantle so that he could unbutton the giaguetta and untie the camisa underneath. When he tried to pull Laurenzo's fingers away they tightened convulsively.

"Francesco . . . No . . . Stay." With a visible effort Laurenzo opened his eyes and forced the worst of his anguish from his face. "There. I am . . . better. Stay, Francesco."

Ragoczy nodded. "Very well, if you wish it. But I would much rather get help. I have servants, and Poliziano . . ."

"*No!*" He drew several deep breaths, then went on. "As soon shout it through the city." Again he had to stop. When he could speak, he said with terrible intensity, "Tell no one. Swear by your life you will tell no one!"

"By my life?" Ragoczy smiled sardonically, then nodded and put his small hands over Laurenzo's big ones. "I swear it. By my life and by my native soil."

Laurenzo nodded, and some of the worry went out of his

eyes. "It is good. It is good." With a sigh he turned his head away.

When there had been silence for some little time, Ragoczy ventured to speak. "Magnifico?"

There was a strange lassitude in his voice when he answered. "In a moment, Francesco." At last he opened his hands and freed the fine cloth of Ragoczy's pourpoint. Mechanically he rubbed at his swollen knuckles. "Gout. How it plagues my family."

"Gout?" There was polite disbelief in Ragoczy's voice.

"It killed my father," Laurenzo stated simply, and left the rest unsaid.

"I was unaware that your father collapsed when the gout was on him." Ragoczy kept his tone neutral. He felt a cold fear for Laurenzo il Magnifico.

"He didn't." Now Laurenzo turned to him and raised himself on his elbow. "But he had the disease for many years. I have not been much troubled with it until recently. Before then it touched me rarely, and with much less severity." He pulled himself to his knees, his pugnacious jaw set with effort. He ignored Ragoczy's outstretched hand.

"My friend," Ragoczy said kindly as Laurenzo at last struggled to his feet, "if you won't disdain it, you may have my aid at any time, and for any reason."

Laurenzo swayed dangerously, then steadied himself. "I thank you, caro stragnero. Who knows? I may avail myself of your kindness."

There came the sound of booted feet and Ruggiero appeared at the foot of the staircase. He carried a tray with a single gold cup. "Master?" he ventured.

Ragoczy was back on his feet now. "Yes. Bring up the almond milk, Ruggiero."

Laurenzo put up an objecting hand, but Ragoczy overruled him. "You need nourishment, Magnifico. It is not yet time for il comestio. Drink this now. This has been a strenuous morning."

As Ruggiero came up the stairs, Laurenzo tried to be more lighthearted. "You should have known me twenty years ago, amico. I would have found this morning dull and insipid. But twenty years make a difference."

"I suppose they do," Ragoczy said uncertainly and took the cup from the tray to hand it to Laurenzo. "My cook, a rogue from Napoli, is Amadeo, and he is, in his own way, a genius."

"If you insist." Laurenzo took the cup. "I fear much of this is wasted on me. But it is sweet, I allow that." He finished the almond milk and was about to hand back the cup when Ragoczy bowed.

"Do me the honor of accepting the cup, as a token of my affection and hospitality."

Slowly Laurenzo was regaining his strength. He held up the cup. "This is a princely gift, Francesco."

"You distinguish it too much, Magnifico." Ragoczy started back down the stairs as he spoke. "But I doubt if Poliziano will want to wait much longer."

Glad for this excuse to leave, Laurenzo started down the stairs, saying, "Lend me your arm, Francesco. Let us have no formality."

Immediately Ragoczy was beside him, and the casual, courteous linking of arms successfully concealed the support Ragoczy gave Laurenzo as they came down the stairs.

Ruggiero followed after them, and when they once again stood in the loggia, he inquired, "Is there any other service you will want?"

"No, thank you, Ruggiero. You may leave us." Ragoczy made a sign of dismissal. When his servant was gone, he said, "Do you still need assistance, Magnifico?"

"I don't think so." Laurenzo began to walk down the hall toward the courtyard. His steps were somewhat shaky, but as he neared the courtyard and the familiar sarcasm of Agnolo Poliziano, he straightened his clothes and forced himself to stride as he usually did, and stretched a smile over his teeth.

"Seen enough walls?" Poliziano asked. "You were mighty quick about it." He finished the cup of wine he held and put it down beside a jug that was still half-full.

Laurenzo ignored this jibe. "If I am to meet with I Priori this afternoon, I must change, Agnolo. It is hardly fitting to walk in as if I had just come from the fields." He went to his horse and pulled the reins from the scaffold. Only Ragoczy saw how cramped his hands were and how badly his fingers trembled.

"Up to your old tricks, Magnifico?" Agnolo reached for his reins as well. "Very well. By all means, let us be off."

"Ragoczy." Laurenzo had already pulled himself into the saddle, and he looked down at the black-clad foreigner. "I would hate to see you leave Fiorenza in the near future. Let us hope that it is not necessary."

With a covert, compassionate smile Ragoczy acknowledged the significance of Laurenzo's remark. "I assure you, my friend, that it will not be."

But Laurenzo was not yet satisfied. "I would be most displeased to learn otherwise." He paused before making the threat. "Believe me, I would pursue the matter with all the resources at my command."

"Oh, San Michele! is Ragoczy involved in intrigue?" Poliziano held his horse ready, and his bored words broke the spell.

"No," Laurenzo said shortly to mask his concern. He clenched his free hand, and his swollen knuckles turned white. Though Ragoczy saw this, he said nothing, nor did he, by so much as the flicker of his eyebrow, draw attention to what he saw. In a gentler tone Laurenzo added, "And I do not think he is likely to be." His eyes met Ragoczy's for a moment and there was a plea and a beginning of trust in them. Then he pulled the big roan's head around and planted his heels so smartly that the stallion bounded through the unfinished gate of Palazzo San Germano.

Ragoczy walked through the gate and watched them go, Laurenzo setting a brisk pace and Poliziano behind him, a resentful angle to his shoulders. Even after they were out of sight he remained in the gate for some little time. At last he turned to lead his horse off to the temporary stables behind the courtyard. His striking, irregular face was troubled, and as he walked, the trouble deepened.

T EXT OF A letter from Gian-Carlo Casimir di Alerico Circando to Francesco Ragoczy da San Germano:

To his revered friend and excellent instructor, Francesco Ragoczy in Fiorenza, Gian-Carlo sends his profoundest respects:

This will come with Joacim Branco, and should arrive, as you stipulated in your letter of July 24, by the middle of September, barring misfortune, arrest, and brigands. Both Magister Branco and Baldassare Secco carry a complete and accurate list of the herbs, spices and medicinals for your verification upon their arrivals. The metals and ores you requested will be sent later, as Paolo Benedetto's ship has been delayed by foul weather and will not arrive in Venezia for some weeks yet. I have had word that he has laid over at Cyprus and will not be able to leave for some days. When the ores arrive in Venezia, I will send them on to you by the hand of Guido Frescomare and Fra Bonifacio.

Niklos Aulirios has sent word that the water wheel you made for him some time ago, the one that ran on the power of the tides, has been burned down. He indicated that he will flee into Egypt soon, and will contact you through Olivia when he is able.

Here your home is safe and all goes as it should. Il Doge is anxious for your return, as he wants more of your gold. But I have told him it will be some considerable time yet until you return. I have, in your absence, authorized the making of enough gold to fill one Venezian wine cask and will present it to il Doge on the Feast of Advent on your behalf. This undoubtedly will delight him, and add much to your credit here in Venezia.

Your own gondola has been completed to your specification. It is quite large, your arms are blazoned on it, and the ballast is of the earth you entrusted to me. You have only to send word, and it and your gondoliere will be waiting to bring you home.

The price of pepper has again risen outlandishly. Do you want me to hold your stores, or shall I sell off a few sacks? Your affairs stand in excellent order and there is more than enough money to run your household and see to your instructions, but there is a great deal of profit to be made just now. The English merchants, particularly, are willing to give top prices for pepper. Let me know by messenger if you want me to sell, and how much. As it stands now, prices will be high until Lent.

This to you by my own hand and through the good offices of Magister Joacim Branco, with sincerest regards I commend to you myself and my work.

> Gian-Carlo Casimir di Alerico Circando
> In Venezia, on the 19th day of August, 1491

CHAPTER 4

ONLY A FEW candles were burning at the house of Sandro Filipepi in la Via Nuova. The artist himself had retired two hours before and even his austerely fanatical brother Simone had at last finished his prayers and was vainly attempting to sleep on his hard bed.

Donna Estasia sat brushing her luxurious chestnut hair. She sang softly to herself as she plied the brush. The tune was a languid one, sensuous, like the expression in her eyes.

O veramente felice e beata
notte, che a tanto ben fusti presente;
o passi ciechi, scorti dolcemente
da quella man' suave a delicata.

Laurenzo's poetry made her smile. She, too, anticipated a happy and well-blessed night.

Voi, Amor e 'l mio core e la mia amata
donna . . .

She would have liked to be able to change the words so that the lover was a man, not a woman, but it would not fit the rhyme. She hummed the phrase over and went on.

> *. . . sapete sol, non altra gentre,*
> *quella dolezza che ogni umana mente*
> *vince, da uom giammai non più provata.*

Yes, it was true for her, too. Only her heart and her love knew the overwhelming source of her joy.

The night was warm and the air fragrant with summer. Estasia sighed and put her brush aside, looking for her jar of malmsey-ambergris-and-musk paste so that she could massage it into her hands and face to make them soft and sweet-smelling. At last she found it by the mirror Sandro had given her and which Simone despised so much. She pulled off the ivory stopper and began to anoint her skin. When that was done, she opened her nightshift impulsively and spread the salve over her breasts. Slowly, her eyes half-closed, she worked the fragrant paste into her flesh.

She was about to rise and seek her bed when she felt two small hands brush her shoulders and pluck her nightshift away. The startled cry that rose in her throat changed to a sigh of anticipation as she turned in the circle of Ragoczy's arms.

"Francesco," she murmured, pressing her gorgeous body against him. "You frightened me." The purr in her voice belied her.

"Did I." He cupped her pointed vixen's face in his hands and drew her nearer. "And are you frightened now?" he asked when he had kissed her.

She laughed almost nervously. "No. Never that." She kicked her discarded nightshirt away. "But I am anxious, Francesco. I have not been pleasured for eleven days." She touched his loose gown of Persian taffeta. "I have been too much with myself. Take me out of myself. Take me." She moved sensuously in his embrace, then stepped back and raised her breasts in her hands. "See? I have perfumed them for you. They are soft-feeling." She rose on tiptoe and stretched provocatively. "Tell me you like me. Tell me of your desire to possess me."

He laughed low in his throat. "What do you want me to say? Do you want me to tell you that your skin is softer and more fragrant than the finest spices of the East? Do you want me to tell you that I will roam over your body like a thirsty traveler searching for drink?"

Estasia's face was flushed and her opulent flesh was gilded in the candlelight. Her breath had quickened as he spoke to her and at last she reached out for him. "Francesco."

Clasping her outstretched hands, he gathered her close to him and lifted her easily into his arms, where she made a delicious, almost swooning burden. Her arms clung to his neck as he made his way to her bed. With an easy gesture he pulled back the sheet and stretched her beneath him.

"Do more. Say more." Her hazel eyes had darkened as her passion rose. Now she pulled urgently at his gown. "Hurry. Hurry."

But he held back. "Gently, Estasia. Slowly. Gently." As he spoke, his small hands stroked her, calming and arousing her at once. Lingeringly he sought out each sensation, now at her lips, now at her breasts, now in the petal softness of her thighs.

Estasia moaned, her head rolled back and a rapturous tension grew in her, so that her body thrummed like the plucked strings of a lute. She reached to push his hands away, but he would not be stopped. Unendurably, until it seemed that release would surely fragment her into a thousand shards of glowing light, he drew from her ever more dizzying delight until shuddering waves of fulfillment possessed her. From the penetration of his kiss to the magic in his hands, he and her appeased hunger stilled the tempest in her soul.

She turned on her pillow, a strange smile in her eyes. "Will you love me again before you leave?" She reached out and ran one finger along the strong, clean-shaven jaw.

"Is that what you want?" He did not frown, although he knew that her desire for him was becoming an obsession. She needed his hands, his lips to shield her from the fear that lay coiled inside her mind. And her demand increased in intensity each time he lay with her.

"Yes. Yes. I want you to do me again and again and again until I am dissolved." She turned her pillow so that her head was lifted. "Tell me you will."

He still tasted the frenzy of her need. "Perhaps. Sleep, now, Estasia."

"Swear that you will not leave me while I sleep!" She said this more desperately, reaching out to take his hand.

"Bella mia," he said gently as he pulled away from her. "I told you when we began that I will not be your servant. If you wish that, you must find someone else."

Estasia hesitated, a kind of panic in her eyes. "But you want me. You *want* me."

"Of course. That was our understanding. Your widowhood makes you freer than an unmarried girl, or a matron, for that matter. It was convenient for you to take me as your lover." He had moved away from her and he spoke too coolly.

"You sound as if you are performing an act of charity."

"Hardly charity," he said, some of the humor back in his dark eyes. "It's delightful to be with you, bellina. And as long as you have desires I can satisfy, and you're willing to satisfy mine, why should either of us deny ourselves? No one expects a widow of your age to lock herself away from the company of men."

"They did in Parma," she said darkly, remembering the many stormy scenes with her husband's family after his death.

"But you are in Fiorenza," he reminded her. "Here such matters are understood, are they not?"

There was a remoteness about him that was new, and it frightened her. "You said that you needed me," she insisted. "You told me that. Before we began."

"And you had no need?" Against his best intentions he turned toward her and touched her face. "There. Do not frown, Estasia. It does not please me to see you frown." He did not say that it was the ghost of age on her face that filled him with foreboding. In so little time she would be gone. And she sensed it, fought it with abiding hatred, devouring her youth in passions of the senses. If her voracious hunger increased, she would be terribly dangerous later.

Her face glowed, but she scolded him. "It was cruel of you to speak to me that way. I have half a mind to refuse myself to you next time you come. What will you do then, Francesco? Where will you go?"

Ragoczy hated this kind of taunting and his eyes grew coldly penetrating. "You may send me away if that's what you wish." He started to rise.

She reached out quickly, holding his arm through the fine Persian cloth. "No. You mustn't go!"

"Estasia . . ."

Her fingers tightened. "I didn't mean it. I didn't. Francesco, *I didn't mean it!*"

Ragoczy stopped, neither resisting nor relenting. Then slowly he reached out to touch her splendid flesh. "Tell me, bella Estasia: do I leave or stay?"

Eagerly she guided his hand over her body. "Stay. Yes, stay." Already her breath had quickened and she moved nearer to him. "Forgive me, Francesco. Show me you forgive me."

His appetite for her was already sated, but he felt her need rising again. He leaned across her and kissed her deeply.

"That's better," she said with a knowing smile as she looked up into the handsome, irregular face above her. She touched his dark hair and tweaked one of the loose short curls that clung to his head. "I like your hair, Francesco. You scent it with sandalwood, don't you?"

"Yes." His lips lingered over the delicious softness of her breasts. Estasia sighed, but there was an air of discontent in her response. "What is it?" he asked, interrupting his expert arousal.

Estasia closed her mouth petulantly. "Oh, you will be angry if I tell you." She pressed his head to her lovely body. "Do that some more."

But Ragoczy held off. "Are you regretting our delights? Do you wish now that I were like your other lovers, and would take you as they do?" There was no accusation in his words, only a gentle inquiry. "You needn't be ashamed to say that to me, Estasia. I know you have desires I cannot meet."

Suddenly she was all contrition. "No, no. You are more than any of the others. Truly, Francesco. No one has pleasured me as much as you do. But . . ."

"But?" he prompted kindly.

She gathered her courage and asked in a rush, "Francesco, are you a eunuch?"

Ragoczy's laughter surprised her as much as the amusement that glowed in his dark eyes. When he could speak he said, "No, Estasia, I am not a eunuch. As you should realize."

"But I *don't* realize it," she objected. "You've never . . . never . . ."

"Filled you?" he suggested lightly as his small hands sought out her intimate joys.

"Filled me, pierced me. I have never had your body *in* me." She moved her legs to accommodate his hand. "Oh. Oh, yes. There. There."

A knowing wry smile curved Ragoczy's mouth as he explored Estasia's passion to the limits. In the last moments she was transfigured as her spasms shook her, and her face was the face of a saint in holiest ecstasy.

When she was calmer he said, "Do you still think I'm a eunuch?"

She answered slowly. "I don't know. I'd hate it if you had another woman whom you loved as other men do."

He pulled back her heavy chestnut hair. "Rest assured, I have not touched a woman in that way since I was very young. And that was a long, long time ago."

"You are not so old."

"Am I not?" He reached to the foot of the bed and pulled her sheet up to cover her.

"No older than Laurenzo, certainly, and he is little more than forty." She pulled her pillow nearer.

"I am rather more than that," he said dryly.

Estasia was drowsy now, and her hazel eyes were fuzzy with sleep. "Truly?" she mused.

He smiled in the golden gloom. "Sleep, Estasia. It is late. Already there are birds singing in the fields and there is a faint glow in the sky the color of silver." He rose and blew out the candles. A soft gray light hung beyond the window and framed him, a darker shadow in the darkened room.

"You will come again, Francesco? Say you will come again." Even half-asleep there was urgency in her words.

"If that is what you want," he said.

"Yes. It's what I want." Her voice trailed off and in a moment the window was empty and Ragoczy was gone.

A LETTER FROM Laurenzo di Piero de' Medici to the Augustinian monk Fra Mariano:

To the reverend brother of San Agostino, Fra Mariano, Laurentius Medicis sends his grateful thanks on this, the feast day of the patron saints of his house, Cosmo and Damiano.

It is with a humble heart that I write, good Brother, for you have been of so great worth to our faith and our city that I search in vain for the adequate expression of my obligation to you.

Your superb example of mercy and tolerance on the occasion of the tenth of this month, when there was that lamentable confrontation in the Piazza di Santa Maria Novella, places all Fiorenza in your debt. How I wish that our other citizens had your goodness. And, though I am always a faithful and devoted son of Holy Church, I cannot help but grieve that those few overly zealous Domenicani would stray so far from their duties as to incite their congregations to battle in the streets. That you were willing to preach to the people in so dangerous a situation speaks most eloquently of your devotion both to the Words of Our Lord and to the people of Fiorenza.

*I beg you will not trouble yourself over the pro-
nouncement of the Domenicano Savonarola. It is God,
and not he, who will say what time I will die. He is
presumptuous to announce to the world that he knows
more than his superiors. Certainly I must die, as all
men, but that is the decree of Heaven, not Girolamo
Savonarola.*

*Your prayers on my behalf during my recent indis-
position are much valued by me, and I deeply appreciate your willingness to address the Mercy Seat on
my behalf. Certainly such piety as yours has helped
me very much in my recovery. Unfortunately, as this
letter must tell you, I still have a degree of weakness,
and so I have to ask you to forgive the poor quality of
my hand. It is sufficiently difficult for me to hold a pen
that I have yet to finish a sonetto this morning, which
is a hard thing for a poet.*

*Most humbly and reverently I commend myself to
you, good Brother, and with profoundest respect thank
you for your great service.*

Laurentius Medicis
*In Fiorenza, on the Feast of SS. Cosmo and Dami-
ano, September 27, 1491.*

CHAPTER 5

On his way up the grand staircase, Ruggiero stopped to
watch as a team of joiners eased the last section of the elaborately carved wood paneling into place at the landing.

Below, the loggia glowed with light, for the new fixtures were burning, their polished metal reflectors diffusing the golden glow throughout the large room and turning the recently carved oak the color of copper.

"Excellent. This is well done." Ruggiero had stepped forward, his houseman's gown just touching the floor where it brushed the last of the sawdust. "My master will be pleased." He ran his hand over the almost invisible joining and pushed on the middle section to be sure that the door it concealed would not open by force of the weight of the carving.

Teobaldo, the supervisor of the joiners, stood back as his Arte brothers began to screw the last section into place. "The Patron has been very generous," he remarked to Ruggiero. "He has promised each of us four fiorini d'or if we are finished by Advent." He laughed. "For that, we would fit each wall of the loggia."

"There are still the alcoves to do," Ruggiero reminded him, reserve in his smile. "But my master has faith in you."

"With good reason." Teobaldo squinted at the houseman, at the bronze-tan gown he wore, at his ring of keys tied to his belt. Though he disliked this foreigner, he added good-naturedly, "In other places, I daresay that it might be otherwise. But we in Fiorenza are the best artisans in the world."

Ruggiero, who had seen the temples of Burma and China and had watched Frankish monks illuminate parchment manuscripts, and who had, himself, once helped to raise a Roman bridge, nodded. "Indeed."

Something in Ruggiero's face made Teobaldo uneasy, so he went on, "It's not usual for a Patron to be so generous."

"It is not," Ruggiero agreed. "I have served him many years, and would serve no other."

That was too much for Teobaldo, who shook his head.

"He's a worthy Patron, that's certain. But I know of no one who could command such loyalty of me." He waited arrogantly for Ruggiero's reply.

"You mistake me," Ruggiero said slowly, staring at the joiner through old eyes. "He does not command anything of me but what I willingly give." He turned on his heel and strode on up the right side of the divided staircase, leaving the joiners to mutter among themselves about the unpredictability of foreigners.

At the top of the staircase he hesitated, studying the half-completed room on the other side of the gallery. Then, his mind made up, he moved toward the sound of sawing.

"Oh, it's you, Ruggiero," Gasparo Tucchio said with a friendly wave as he set down his mallets. "I'm glad of a break. The day is almost over."

Giuseppe followed Gasparo's example and set his saw aside. "It's nearly sunset. It's been getting cold at night."

"Where's the Patron?" Gasparo asked familiarly. "I saw him leave earlier. Dressed very fine, he was, all black brocade and a doublet of white velvet under his mantle."

Ruggiero was not offended by Gasparo's easy manner, or the disparaging comments of the other three. "My master has gone to the house of Federigo Cossa. He will do himself the honor of serving the prandium to the man who was his host for so long."

"Oh, the old alchemist." Gasparo dismissed Federigo Cossa with a laugh. "I built a new room for him once. He's almost as finicky as Ragoczy." He added, somewhat more respectfully, "So the Patron is serving the meal? That's just like a proper Fiorenzeno. I remember when Laurenzo used to serve his guests when they came to his table. He doesn't do it much anymore."

Lodovico managed to keep the contempt out of his voice.

"Ragoczy's becoming very Fiorenzan. I have heard that he has also distributed clothing to the poor."

"He has been told by Medici that this is expected of all rich men in Fiorenza." Ruggiero spoke evenly as he studied Lodovico closely.

Carlo put down his saw and slapped Lodovico on the back. "The trouble with you, amico, is that you're hungry." He turned his attention to Ruggiero. "You know how it is: a man gets hungry, he gets snappish."

Lodovico had already realized his mistake and gladly seized on Carlo's explanation for his surliness. "I have been famished this last hour," he admitted with an ingenuous smile for Ragoczy's manservant. "I'll be glad of prandium."

To this Gasparo added, "I get cross as a Turk when I miss a meal." He sighed and pushed his sawhorse toward the nearest wall. "We'll be through here in a month or so. There's the rest of this floor and the next to do. Then the joiners can finish everything. A pity. It's been good work."

Giuseppe sighed. "It has," he agreed, somewhat unexpectedly. "I'll never work on another building like this one, I know that."

Gasparo seemed to remember at last that Ruggiero had asked for this interview. "Well?" He stood up, much more businesslike. "Is that what you wanted to talk to us about? I have the men you requested here."

The air grew tenser as Ruggiero took a turn about the room. "You are all men without families," he said at last. "You are all masters of your trade. You have been remarkably loyal to your Patron."

The four builders preened uneasily under this praise, which was suddenly disturbing.

"My master has learned a great deal about you. He is

willing to pay you substantial money if you will perform two services for him."

"What services?" Lodovico asked, eyes narrowed.

"In a moment." Ruggiero hesitated, then explained.

"There is work to be done here that no one must know of. Those who work on it will be paid double your usual wages for the work"—this extraordinary announcement caused a number of exclamations—"and at the end of it, you must leave Fiorenza forever. You will be provided with work, wherever you go, and with a certain annual sum for your maintenance."

"Leave Fiorenza?" Gasparo demanded, torn between anger and utter amazement. "*Leave Fiorenza? What non-sense is this?*"

"No nonsense," Ruggiero said coldly. "It is my master's condition for the work you are to do."

Carlo had said nothing, but he ventured the question that Lodovico longed to ask. "What would the annual sum be? And how do we know we'll be paid?"

"Carlo!" Gasparo turned on him. "Would you do this?"

Carlo shrugged awkwardly. "As Ruggiero has said, I am without family. If there is work for me elsewhere, and money besides, I am willing to go. I have better skills than most of the workmen elsewhere." He refused to meet Gasparo's eyes. "I have never seen another city. My whole life has been lived in the shadow of il Palazzo della Signoria."

"And for that you should fall on your knees and thank Merciful Heaven!" Gasparo thundered. "Don't you real-ize—?"

But Ruggiero interrupted him. "Gaspar', let him make up his own mind."

"You!" Gasparo rounded on Ruggiero, seeking another target for his wrath. "Do you tell me that Ragoczy thought I would leave Fiorenza? Did he think that a bribe was enough to make me turn my back on my Arte and my city?"

"No," Ruggiero said kindly. "He did not."

This disarmed Gasparo completely. "But . . . you said . . ."

"It is necessary that one man remain in Fiorenza, to be certain that the others keep their word. Of course, my master wishes you to be that man. He trusts to your honor, Gasparo."

"And how should I trust to his? What security will he give me?" The builder had his big hands on his hips and his face thrust forward. "Do not mistake me, Ruggiero. I am willing to serve the Patron at any time. But I will not do so blindly. I must have assurances, for my men as well as myself."

Ruggiero smiled blandly but there was steel in his voice as he spoke. "My master has never broken his Word, not in all the years I have known him. Sometimes he has risked much to keep his Word. He is honorable in all things." He met Gasparo's challenging glance calmly and then touched the tips of his fingers together.

"Yet you make this offer; he does not. Why should he hold himself to your promises?" Lodovico asked almost flippantly. "Do you tell us that he'll take on this obligation because you say he will?"

The builders murmured a moment. Each of them shared some of the doubts in Lodovico's question, and Carlo added, "He may leave Fiorenza without warning and we would not see him again."

There was a certain boredom in Ruggiero's response. "My master is known in Venezia as well as Wien and Fiorenza. If you like, payment may be authorized from his holdings in either of those cities."

Gasparo had retreated from his aggressive stance and asked with new consideration, "Why are you so certain of him, Ruggiero? It's not often a man trusts his master overmuch."

For an answer Ruggiero walked to the unframed window and looked down into the courtyard. "I know of one instance when a runaway bondsman begged him for help. There was no reason for my master to trust this man, or to endanger himself on the bondsman's behalf. But he did. He sheltered the bondsman, restored him to health, and though the bondsman had been declared a criminal, my master saw that he was exonerated and that the man who had bonded and tortured his bondsman was punished." The distant expression cleared from his eyes and he turned away from the window. "If da San Germano would do so much for a man he found bleeding in rags, you may be sure that he will honor his Word to you."

"Did Ragoczy tell you this, or the bondsman?" Lodovico asked, and gave Giuseppe a surreptitious jab in the ribs.

Ruggiero did not answer immediately. "It was in Roma, and I had hidden for days. If he had not found me, I would have died there in the shadows of the Flavian Circus. He cared for my wounds and brought me back to life. The bondsman, good artisans, was myself."

Even Gasparo was silent: Roman excesses were legendary, and he nodded grimly at the picture of abuse Ruggiero had painted. "Well," he said in a bit, "if it is as you say, I'm willing to learn more of what the Patron offers us. And I will trust him for your sake, Ruggiero." He glared at the others, daring them to contradict him.

"I'm interested," Giuseppe said eagerly, and rubbed his ribs where Lodovico's elbow had poked him.

"So am I." Carlo stepped forward. "I have a cousin who

is a sailor. He told me of London, and the English. I'd like to go there, if it is permitted."

The foreign name was magic. Giuseppe grinned broadly. "I've heard that there is a city in Poland where the women are as fair as lilies of gold."

"Krakow will please you, I think," Ruggiero said with the ghost of a smile. "You may not find the women to your taste, but you will like the city."

"Wait!" Gasparo ordered. "This is not settled."

Lodovico shrugged and gestured to the others. "How is it not settled? Giuseppe will go into Poland, Carlo will go to London and I . . . I will go to Lisboa, if it please you." Portugal was far enough away to avoid suspicion, but close enough for him to make speedy return to Fiorenza, should that prove worth his while.

With a sigh, Gasparo raised his hands in resignation. "Very well, if you are all content, what is it to me?" He looked steadily at Ruggiero. "I will expect to hear regularly of these men. You will arrange that?"

"Certainly. And you will be furnished with proof that the sums have been paid, annually."

"Va ben'. There is nothing more to say. What must be done to earn this money and exile?" Gasparo gestured to the other builders. "We will not do anything contrary to the laws of la Repubblica, the Church and our Arte."

"I don't expect you to." Ruggiero nodded to the builders again. "You are all men of some intelligence. Perhaps you have noticed that this palazzo is built upon different lines than other buildings in Fiorenza?" He did not expect an answer and got none other than nods. "There are several reasons for this, most of which need not concern you. But there is one reason that is of paramount importance. Behind the landing on the grand staircase there are two concealed rooms. There is a third concealed room in the wall of the stable. These rooms must be finished, and to my master's specifications."

"What is the purpose of these rooms?" Gasparo demanded. "We will not be party to crimes."

"There is no crime," Ruggiero said in such a way that none of the builders doubted him. "My master is an alchemist. He does not want to work publicly, as much for the safety of those around him as for his privacy." He held open his hands. "It is not what he does is contrary to the laws, good artisans, it is that there is danger in the work."

Lodovico's eyes brightened. He knew now that he could turn this knowledge to good use, either as a way to force more money from Ragoczy or as a reward from a grateful city for revealing an unknown hazard to them. "What do we have to do?" he asked more eagerly than he had intended. "When do we begin?"

"Tomorrow," Ruggiero said shortly. "But there is something you must do first."

"What?" Gasparo was suspicious again.

"You must swear a Holy Oath never to reveal what you do here. On your souls you must swear, as you hope for Paradise." He clapped his hands sharply and in a few moments Joacim Branco appeared, his long robe flapping around his legs like broken wings.

"Do you have the document?" Ruggiero asked.

"I have it." The Portuguese alchemist held up an inscribed sheet of parchment. "It is ready."

Ruggiero looked at the builders. There was a steadiness in his manner that took away the doubts they might have felt. "Which of you can read?" he asked in the same tone he would have asked for a table to be moved, or a branch of candles lit.

There was an awkward moment in ... last Gasparo said, "I do, a little. But I hav...

"This is in your own tongue," Ruggiero sa... document from Joacim Branco. "I will read i... you, Gasparo, will read with me, so that there can b... ... ... ception. My master orders it be done this way."

The agreement was long, but its language was simple, and at the end, the builders were more than willing to consent to its conditions.

"It is well," Ruggiero said, and added, "You must make your marks in your own blood."

The builders stopped, and once again there was suspicion in their faces. Gasparo set his jaw. "Why?"

Joacim Branco was about to take issue with them when a quick gesture from Ruggiero quieted him. "There is a reason," he assured the builders. "My master makes this request of you."

"If there is a reason"—and from Lodovico's tone of voice it was obvious that he doubted it—"then you should be willing to tell me what it is. If there is not, your caprice is not reason enough for me to sign in blood."

Gasparo took up this attitude. "He will have our sworn words, given on the honor of our souls and salvation. Surely that's enough. Or is there something more precious than our souls?"

This was the question that Ruggiero had been waiting for. He made a solemn sign. "No, there is nothing more precious than your souls. And for that reason, you must guard it. Certainly now you put honor and trust in your salvation. But what if you are seduced by evil? Then there is no honor in your salvation. Then, good artisans, your blood will bind you."

Carlo guffawed. "There is nothing that would make me do that."

"Isn't there?" Ruggiero studied his hands. "Would you still be held by this oath if your mother were being racked, I wonder?"

The builders were silent, and even Lodovico admitted to himself that Ruggiero had made a powerful argument. At last he said, "After all, why not? If the foreigner knows us so little, we should oblige him."

The others hesitated, but when Ruggiero handed Lodovico a small knife and Lodovico confidently cut his finger and made his sign, the rest stepped forward.

"This is most satisfactory," Ruggiero said while the marks on the parchment dried. "In his appreciation for your kindness, my master asks that you go to the kitchen. You will find that Amadeo has made a repast for you. It is a full prandium, with two pies instead of one." This was flying in the face of the Fiorenzan sumptuary laws, but none of the builders objected.

Lodovico, remembering that he had claimed to be hungry, was the first to accept this invitation, hurrying out of the room into the lamplit dusk of the palazzo.

Only Gasparo waited. "I will want to talk to the Patron, Ruggiero, and discuss this document."

Ruggiero's expression was one of faint surprise. "Do you have objections now that you have signed it?" he wondered aloud.

"No. But I wish to know how the conditions will be met, and when we will be able to arrange a way to make payments."

"Well," Ruggiero said, "he should be back within the hour, and if you like, you may wait for him. Or, if you prefer, tomorrow morning he will spend an hour with you."

Gasparo remembered the meal waiting below. "The morning will be fine." He was about to leave, then added,

"If he comes before we are finished with the prandium, I'll talk to him then." He reached for a sack and put his tools into it, humming and occasionally breaking into song. He paid no attention to the alchemist and houseman until he interrupted himself. "That's been in my mind all day. Have you ever had that problem? You get a song into your thoughts, and do what you will, it won't leave?" He shook his head, stowed the tied sack near the sawhorses and went off singing in earnest.

Ruggiero smiled broadly and looked at Joacim Branco. "Did you recognize it, that song?"

The Portuguese alchemist frowned severely. "I did. These damned Fiorenzeni have not the least respect for genius. Singing the verse of Dante as if it were some trivial ditty." He snorted his disgust as he put the document in the wide sleeve of his houppelande.

"You're offended?" Ruggiero shook his head. "I don't know. Perhaps I'm perverse, but I like it." He gestured for the alchemist to precede him out of the room.

"It is all very well for you to laugh," Joacim Branco said, "but it is typical of these people." He was silent, and when he spoke again, it was on another subject. "The wagons have arrived. I told them to wait in the stables."

"Very good." They were descending the grand staircase now, and Ruggiero looked carefully about. "The largest of the boxes should go into the second hidden room. The others can wait for my master to dispose of as he wishes."

The tall alchemist walked on without speaking, but as he and Ruggiero crossed the courtyard, he said, "I have studied the Great Work all my life, but never have I known of another artifex who slept with his mattress on raw earth, or lined his shoes with earth, or who mixed earth with the substance of his house. Where is the merit in that?"

Ruggiero was unperturbed. "It is a discipline of his own. My master wishes always to remember the earth from which he sprang. All flesh is clay," he reminded Joacim Branco. "It is the earth that nurtures, that sustains him."

Joacim Branco scowled. "I understand that. But the Great Work should transcend earth."

"My master would not dispute that." He stood aside and let the alchemist pass him as they entered the narrow hall that led from the courtyard to the stables.

"It is well that he knows his limitations, and is not filled with pride," Joacim Branco said, somewhat mollified. "I find his austerity excessive, but his intent is good."

"I shall tell him you think so," Ruggiero murmured, and entered the stables.

There were three heavily laden oxcarts in the stables and each was driven by two draymen in Venezian clothing. "Well met, Cristofo," Ruggiero said to the horseman who had been the escort. "How was your journey?"

"About what could be expected," Cristofo answered casually as he swung out of the saddle. "There were two attempted robberies. I tell you, the brigands on the roads are becoming dangerous. We fought them off, of course, and accounted for ourselves successfully. But Sforza of Milano should look to his travelers. Things were better when i Visconti ruled there." He shrugged philosophically. "The athanor is in the second wagon, and we put the jewels there, too. Is it too late to get a meal?"

"No. There is food, if you want to take your draymen to the kitchen. The cook's name is Amadeo and he is expecting you."

Cristofo motioned to the men with him. "We eat," he said laconically.

Ruggiero watched while the men left the wagons; then he told Cristofo where to find the kitchen.

When they were alone with the oxcarts, Joacim Branco began his inspection. He moved from wagon to wagon, lifting lids and handling the various things he found. The athanor particularly delighted him. "I have never seen one better made. Surely we achieve the Egg in this. Ragoczy does well."

"I'm pleased you approve," Ruggiero said, but his sarcasm was lost on Joacim Branco.

"We must start at the next new moon. It would be wrong to wait longer." He touched the bricks of the athanor lovingly, lingeringly. "This is superb."

Ruggiero did not dispute anything Joacim Branco said, but when the men returned from their meal, he made sure it was the largest, earthfilled box that was moved first.

"But the athanor . . ." Joacim Branco protested.

"My master wants his orders followed." Ruggiero spoke gently. "He said that the largest box should be moved first, to his room. I intend to do as he wished."

Joacim Branco hesitated, then came down from the oxcart with the athanor. With ill-concealed annoyance he helped the draymen move the largest box to Ragoczy's room on the second floor of Palazzo San Germano.

T EXT OF A letter from Conte Giovanni Pico della Mirandola to the French scholar Jean-Denis Gastone de Sangazure:

> To that most able classicist and scholar, Pico della
> Mirandola sends Platonic greetings, and asks that

*Gastone de Sangazure remember him to his distin-
guished friends of the Università di Parigi.*

*It has been much too long, my friend, since we have
exchanged letters, and I know that in part blame must
fall to my own laziness. It is to be hoped that this will
remedy some of the trouble and redeem me in your eyes.*

*Fiorenza is much the same, which is to say that it
is always changing. There is a scheme afoot to widen
more of the streets, but that will mean demolishing
more buildings, and the Signoria is reluctant to do so.
There is also the new bridge which everyone wants to
design and build. It will be west of the others, and the
first foundations have been laid, but the bridge itself
will take some time to finish, if only to accommodate
all the discussion.*

*Laurenzo has obtained a number of manuscripts in
French and has set his cousin Demetrice Volandrai to
translating them. If only you were here, you might
have that pleasure. But if Laurenzo's library cannot
lure you from Parigi, nothing can.*

*How I wish you had been with us last week. It was
a pleasant week, with the season just beginning to
turn. On Wednesday Laurenzo decided to explore
some of the ancient ruins on the hills above Fiorenza.
He finds the works of that lost civilization fascinating,
and wanted to search for various artifacts. Agnolo
was not here, for he is still buying manuscripts for
Laurenzo, and has been in Ferrara for more than a
month. But Ficino was available, and I, and that foreign alchemist, Ragoczy. The four of us made up a
party and rode into the hills.*

*At first we found only crumbling walls and a few
stretches of paving with grasses shooting up between*

*the stones. But then, in a curve of a hill, very much se-
cluded and out of the way, we came upon a building,
and though it was roofless, most of the rest was intact
and remarkably well-preserved.*

*You can imagine Laurenzo's delight. He was off his
horse and almost into the building before the rest of us
knew what was happening. Ragoczy was not far behind him, and stopped Laurenzo from entering, reminding him that stone so old is often unsafe.
Laurenzo was grateful for the caution, but decided to
explore the building, trusting that San Cosmo and San
Damiano, who have been the Medici patrons for the
generations, would not fail him now.*

*The building was an odd one, filled with strange
objects we'd never seen before, which Ragoczy suggested might be religious or votive offerings. It was as
acceptable an explanation as any, for the place did
have the look of a temple.*

*After an hour or so, we were prepared to leave
when an incredibly old man, terribly wizened and
filthy, came hurrying over the brow of the hill, yelling
at us, and making gestures in his anger that were as
comical as they were useless. When he had come up to
us, he was quite purple with rage. He called us de-
filers, profaners, sacrilegious fools for entering a temple of the undying thing. I could not follow half of
what the creature said. So overwhelming was his passion that he struck out at Laurenzo with a small club
he carried. Of course there was no way he could have
injured Medici, but apparently Ragoczy didn't realize
this. He moved his horse between the old man and
Laurenzo and told him, quite calmly, to stop at once.*

You would not have believed the change in the old man. In one instant he was as ferocious as Mars, and in the next he cringed and went whiter than his smock. He begged Ragoczy to forgive him and promised to serve him better. He apologized for the state of the temple and told him that there were so few Rasna left that worship had been abandoned.

Marsilio Ficino and I were nearly overcome with laughter. Laurenzo said it was unkind to mock the mad, though he was amused himself. But Ragoczy was very much alarmed. You must understand that the old man had fallen down in complete prostration before him and kept calling him the undying lord, and asking forgiveness because there was no blood on the altar.

At first Ragoczy tried to reason with the old man, but when the fool tried to cut his throat as an offering to Ragoczy, it was too much for the foreigner, and he leaped out of his saddle and forcibly restrained the old man, saying that such an offering was not acceptable to him. He succeeded in calming the old man (he has quite a way, Jean-Denis, for all that he is lacking in height and dresses with monkish restraint), and then urged us to depart before the old man could again become aroused.

Laurenzo commended Ragoczy for his compassion, and Ragoczy suggested that perhaps the Good Sisters at Sacro Infante might be willing to take charge of the old man. They are Celestiane, you know, and often care for the mad. Laurenzo agreed and has written to the Superior of Sacro Infante, though what the outcome will be, no one knows.

I leave for Roma next month, and will stay there until my petition is heard. I will be some little while, I

*think. If there is anything you want from there, such as
books or information, I beg you will send me a list.
I've included a list of books I would like to have, and
if you should discover any of them, pray buy them and
I will repay you with money or in kind. A letter to il
Cavaliere Benedetto Gian-Rocco Fredda da Modena
near Castel Sant'Angelo will find me most quickly.*

*Do not follow my example, Jean-Denis, but let me
hear from you often and soon. I know I have been
shamefully lax, but perhaps your expert example will
spur me to better efforts, though I make no promises.
But in spite of my inattention, you may be sure that this
brings you my warmest friendship and deep respect.*

Giovanni Pico della Mirandola
In Fiorenza, October 1, 1491

*P.S. Tomorrow is the Feast of the Guardian Angels,
and there is a great celebration planned, including a
palio. A race like that one certainly puts Guardian Angels to the test. Two men were killed in the palio last year.*

CHAPTER 6

THERE HAD BEEN rain earlier but now the clouds were
clearing and the people of Fiorenza were ready for the great
palio. All along the tortuous route they waited at windows,
in protected doorways and loggias to see the maddened
plunge of two dozen saddleless, bridleless horses and their
honored riders. Even the Osservanti Brothers were watching

at the door of Ognissanti, their brown cowls hiding antici-patory smiles.

From his vantage place at the end of the course, Laurenzo de' Medici waited and cursed the cold. His knuckles were more swollen than usual and the cold made them ache. He turned to his son, saying, "I'll be glad when you're willing to do all this. Perhaps next year. Then I can have more time for my poetry and library."

Piero shrugged somewhat petulantly. "I don't like palios," he remarked to the air. "I wouldn't be here if you hadn't insisted."

Laurenzo felt anger well up in him, and resisted it. "No, neither do I. But it is Fiorenzan, and we are Fiorenzeni, you and I. Remember that this is a Repubblica, and that the Signoria rules here."

At that Piero laughed. "They're all picked men. They'd do whatever you tell them."

"Perhaps. But if I acted contrary to the good of the city too often, I would be exiled in short order. Make no doubt about it, my son. We rule on sufferance."

"If you're worried, become a Gran Duca under the pro-tection of France. You've been offered it. You can claim it."

Laurenzo di Piero de' Medici looked at his firstborn son as if he was seeing him clearly at last. "I have no desire to be anything but a citizen of Fiorenza. To be a creature of the King of France repels me." He studied Piero's beautiful, haughty face, frowning slightly.

"Oh, well, it would probably be more stupid than this is, so perhaps you're right." He turned away and heard the muf-fled clap of a cannon and the great shout from Ponte Vec-chio. "They've begun."

"Sta bene," Laurenzo said fatalistically and forced himself to smile broadly at Marsilio Ficino, across the Piazza del Duomo.

Ficino returned the smile, and waved. He was in a second-story window, leaning precariously out of it. Even at that distance he could see that Laurenzo's hands were giving him trouble. He frowned a moment, then turned his attention to the narrow streets, listening for the cheer and cries that marked the progress of the race. From the shouts, he guessed that the horses had crossed il Ponte Vecchio and were now turning from la Via por Santa Maria onto la Via della Terme. That treacherous left-hand turn would have casualties, he thought, and had his thoughts confirmed by a sudden outburst of screams.

Three riders were down, one with a broken leg, and two of the horses were hurt. The third struggled to its feet and continued to run with the others. There was no move to stop it, for it was the horse that won the race, with or without its rider.

Where la Via della Terme met la Via de' Tornabuoni the horses had to jog sharply to enter la Via del Parione. It was a dangerous move and five horses collided, two going down in a welter of hooves and tangled legs. One of the riders dragged himself away from the collision, blood spreading over his face where his horse had kicked him. His steps faltered as he got to the edge of the street, and after a moment he fell. The crowd shouted its distress and when all the horses were by, the barrier that blocked the side streets opened and two Carmeliani Brothers pulled the bleeding rider from the street. A little later a small party of butchers came for the animals.

The horses spread out as they galloped across la Piazza del Ponte, and two riders tried to pull one another from their mounts' backs. In the confusion they created one was thrown by his frightened horse and the other had to wrap his arms around his horse's neck to stay astride.

Suddenly the course narrowed again as the race entered

il Borgo Ognissanti. For a moment it looked like the horses would not give way, and there would be a terrific pile-up of mounts and riders. It had happened before, and the danger was very great it would happen in this palio. But at the last moment the rider for the Arte of silk weavers let his mount drop back, and the race thundered down the narrow street.

Above the racing horses, from the safety of second-story windows, the people of Fiorenza shouted encouragement to their favorite riders and hooted at the others. They threw flowers on the competitors, and waved streamers. The sound was echoed and magnified by the straight stone walls until the whole of il Borgo Ognissanti roared like the sea.

Here the street was straight, and here the riders maneuvered for advantage. One of the riders was forced against the wall and he screamed in sudden agony as his knee crashed against a protruding iron grille. His horse reared and the man was thrown.

Another horse tried to move away from the fallen rider and crashed into two more horses. Panicked now, the horses tried to get free of the steep, confining walls. The leader, a sturdy dun horse, bounded ahead, tossing his rider as he broke away from the press of other horses. The rider scrambled for safety, but was caught a glancing blow from a spotted mare belonging to the joiners' Arte. He stumbled and fell.

Horses, riders and spectators all cried out as the rider was trampled by the racing horses. Swerving aside from the broken body, three more horses ran together. There was a scurry of hooves on the stone flags, and then the race continued, leaving two injured horses, one badly hurt, and one dead man in its wake.

Through Piazza Ognissanti they rushed, this time giving no quarter as they plunged into the narrow Borgo once again. Four horses ran against the walls, unable to stop in time to avoid the impact. At the barriers there were cries of dismay as the last of the four horses rolled against the wooden structure, nearly knocking it over.

Horrified at the carnage that had erupted before their eyes, the Osservanti Brothers ran from their church to help the fallen, battered riders.

The palio was stringing out now, with the stronger horses and more capable riders taking the lead. At the sharp turn into la Via degli Orti Oricellari there was only one casualty when a horse, taking the turn too tightly, missed his footing and sprawled to the pavement. The horses immediately behind him scrambled and then resumed their gallop. But now the race was divided into two separate units, one about six lengths behind the other.

The turn into la Via della Scala was steep, and three horses went down, but here there was little hurt done, for though the turn was acute, there was a small plot of open ground and the horses went around those that had fallen.

Ahead was the magnificent bulk of Santa Maria Novella, and the cheering crowds behind the barricades at the piazza in front of the church. The first group of six horses shot past and made the difficult turn into la Via del Moro.

Francesco Ragoczy had not watched the palio. His taste for that kind of sport had worn itself out in the blood of the Roman arena. So he was pleased when the horses passed. Quickly he left the home of his alchemist friend Federigo Cossa and stepped into la Via del Moro.

Shouts around him warned him that something was very wrong, and in a moment he saw the second group of horses come hurtling around the turn, their flanks dark with sweat. Two of the horses were without riders, but by the expression in the eyes of the men still mounted, he knew they were terrified for him.

He turned and pushed on the door, but it was secure and any knocking he might do would be lost in the noise of the race. He sprinted away from the door, reaching for the iron grille over the nearest window.

The horses were rushing nearer and Ragoczy did not waste time looking at them. He climbed up the grille, but was nowhere near high enough to be out of range of the frantic race.

"Oh, Signor'!" cried a voice above him, and Ragoczy glanced up to see hands extended down to him.

He reached up, stretching high over his head in desperation. His fingers almost touched those above him when he overbalanced and fell backward into the street and into the path of the palio.

He heard the gasp of the crowd as the horses came down upon him. He drew himself into a ball and tried to roll free of the relentless hooves. He felt more than saw a horse stop short and rear over him. It was riderless and frightened.

People were shouting now, and someone was trying to climb over the nearest barricade. The horse neighed as it tried to trample the blackclad man underfoot.

The rest of the race was gone. Ragoczy rolled to the side of the street and carefully began to stretch.

A babel of shouts broke out, voices telling him to lie still, to thank God, to be certain he was whole, to get out of the street. He clapped his hands over his ears and shook his head, hoping that this gesture would quiet the people around him. But it did not. There was consternation, and the horse that had tried to kill him came and nudged him nervously.

Ragoczy pulled himself onto one knee, moving slowly to avoid frightening the horse. He reached up and tugged the off-side, pawing hoof toward him, rubbing the fetlock, and when the well-shaped bay head was near enough, he blew gently into the horse's nostril.

"There," he said quietly, hoping that his soft voice would penetrate through the noise around him. "There, you see? I am your friend. I won't hurt you. I won't frighten you." He waited a bit, ignoring the cries and shouts around him. Then, when he was sure that the horse would not bolt, he stood, rubbing the broad neck and talking reassuringly.

Cheers erupted around him, and somewhat startled, Ragoczy looked up. The people were waving handkerchiefs and pelting him with flowers.

Keeping a soothing hand on the bay horse, Ragoczy nodded and bowed slightly and was rewarded with howls of adulation. He said to the horse and himself, "What unexpected glory."

No one nearby heard this sardonic remark. Ragoczy listened for a moment, an ironic smile twisting his mouth. At last he bowed again, and then, with practiced ease, he took a handful of mane and vaulted onto the bay's back.

The tumult grew louder as Ragoczy rode the horse down the street, and with a wave, turned into the last palio street, la Via de' Cerretani. He was by far the last rider to reach il Duomo and the huge civic stand erected there. Already the crowd was surging over the barriers toward the strong sorrel mare that had won the race.

Ragoczy's appearance stopped them, and brought a whispered silence to the Piazza del Duomo.

On the civic stand, Laurenzo de' Medici looked up from making the award, and a certain grimness which had tightened his wide, thin-lipped mouth vanished. "So you aren't dead after all. I had heard you were."

"Appearances are deceiving," Ragoczy said as he brought his horse to a halt by the stand.

"You were unwise enough to venture into la Via del Moro before the race was over."

"Ah, but I didn't know that." He patted the bay before slipping off its back. "Not a bad horse, you know. I was pleasantly surprised."

At that Laurenzo laughed. "As always, you delight me, mio caro stragnero. Let me congratulate you on your lucky escape."

"I gather it was one of the few today," Ragoczy said as he climbed the platform stairs.

Immediately Laurenzo was more serious. "Yes. There were four deaths today, a new record, unfortunately. Even Lionello here"—he gestured to one of the riders who stood near him—"is hurt, though he did stay on across the finish line."

Lionello was holding his arm at a painful angle and the smile he attempted had more of pain than satisfaction in it.

"What did you do to yourself?" Ragoczy asked.

"It is nothing," Lionello protested, eyeing the elegant foreigner with distrust. "I will be better soon."

"No doubt," Ragoczy agreed dryly. "But it would be wiser if you will let me see your shoulder. If you have cut yourself on metal, as I think you have, you must allow me the opportunity to treat you. I have a salve that will ease the pain and prevent any illness or inflammation of the wound."

Piero clicked his tongue impatiently, but Laurenzo met Ragoczy's dark eyes steadily. "On behalf of Fiorenza, I thank you for that."

Ragoczy made a dismissing gesture and turned to Lionello. "Come to my palazzo before the feast and I will treat your hurts. Do not be afraid. I'm only an alchemist, not a sorcerer. You are welcome to bring a friend, if you like." He was plainly amused at Lionello's alarm, and added, "I'm much less of a risk than your cuts are, believe me."

Lionello flushed and stammered a promise to avail himself of Ragoczy's services.

The officers of the winning Arte came forward to get their mare, and a huge shout went up. The bells of Santa Maria del Fiore tolled out their immense joy and the trumpets sounded as a signal to begin the victory procession that would go a few short blocks to la Piazza della Signoria.

Before taking his place in the procession, Laurenzo said to Ragoczy, "I am happy for you, caro stragnero. But I admit that I'm puzzled."

"Puzzled? But why?" Ragoczy asked with utmost innocence.

"I am puzzled because there are three dusty hoof marks on your back, Francesco. They look like direct blows. And so I wonder, though I am glad for your lucky escape."

"Grazie, Magnifico. I was careless." He felt a rush of chagrin as he realized how foolish his bravura had been.

"Sta ben'." Laurenzo nodded to Ragoczy and carefully descended the stairs to the street. Piero followed after him, a dissatisfied scowl on his beautiful face.

"How long will this take? I want to go hunting today." He spoke softly, but Laurenzo turned on him.

"You! Be silent. You will have to forgo your hunting. This is more important. You are a Fiorenzeno, my son. To be a Medici and a Fiorenzeno, you must be willing to give up your hunting once in a while. Younger men than you have been willing to."

Piero's face set with anger. "I know. I have heard all about your diplomatic missions when you were less than twenty. It's not fair to expect me to be you."

Laurenzo looked away from Piero, across the spires of the city. "No, perhaps it isn't."

Then he was gone in the procession while Ragoczy re-

mained on the platform, his face inscrutable, his eyes perplexed and full of sorrow.

TEXT OF A letter to Francesco Ragoczy da San Germano
from a Roman woman writing in colloquial Latin and sign-
ing herself Olivia:

> *To Ragoczy Sanct' Germain Franciscus in Florentia,*
> *or whatever that camp is calling itself these days,*
> *Olivia sends her undying friendship.*
>
> *I have heard from our friend Niklos Aulirios that*
> *you have settled temporarily by the Arno and have for*
> *the time being given up your house in Venezia. Un-*
> *doubtedly you know what you are doing, but you*
> *might consider coming to Roma instead of staying in*
> *Fiorenza, for say what you will about the place, it is*
> *still only a Roman camp trying to be a city. You needn't*
> *remind me of the artists and poets and musicians*
> *there, for Medici is forever sending one or more of*
> *them to the Pope as family courtesy.*
>
> *You wouldn't recognize Roma, my friend; it is all*
> *quite different. The Temple of Saturn that you liked so*
> *much and visited often is now a restored church,*
> *tremendously respectable. Almost no one remembers*
> *its past, and if they do, they ignore it—rather like the*
> *Empress Theodora and her past, which was much*
> *worse than simply being a heathen temple.*
>
> *The Flavian Circus is called the Colosseum now,*
> *and is partly destroyed. That might upset you. Fire and*
> *siege have done a great deal to ruin the city's beauty,*

but I must say that I wouldn't want to live anywhere else. I did try Alexandria for a while, and I spent a few years in Athens, but they are not Roma, and I was not at home there. Roma is the place of my native soil.

Do you remember that first time you came to me? How frightened I was of you then. You wanted to give terror, but instead you gave passion. And it was a little later that you said you no longer wanted to survive on fear. You felt that fulfilled desire gave you a satisfaction you had not known before. I can still see your face, so full of loneliness and anguish. Are you, I wonder, as much alone now as you were then? Don't torment yourself, Sanct' Germain Franciscus. As you taught me yourself, there is delight in this world, and until you die the True Death, life will call to you, and you must answer.

There, I have lapsed into philosophy. I must be getting old. And the reason for my letter is not to share reminiscences but to warn you of the latest developments in Roma.

As I might have told you some time ago, I have again attached myself to the Papal court. In that respect, then, let me inform you that the Cardinals are playing politics again, and Rodrigo Borja y Lara is gaining strength. I have met Rodrigo, and he is a clever man. Beware of him. And if you should ever meet his son Cesare, avoid him at all cost. Cesare is a monster, my friend. He has terrified his sister (though she is a foolish woman and has not an ounce of real courage) and the rumor is that he shares her bed. If that is so, I feel for her.

You know, I have often thought that our condition is unfair to the men of our numbers. We women still have sexual congress as well as the pleasures of our kind, but you men lose the means of that usual satisfaction.

*Is the joy you have enough, I wonder, or do you miss
the other?*

*Once again I am becoming philosophical. Well,
never mind. I won't trouble you with awkward questions any longer.*

*Do send me word, when you have the chance, as to
how it is with you. I think of you often. It would be a
pleasure to see you once more, Sanct' Germain Franciscus, and to have long and possibly even philosophical talks.*

*Guard yourself well, my friend. You always have,
but sometimes I fear that your care makes you vulnerable. I would lose a part of my soul, I think, if you
were to die the True Death.*

As always, this brings you the true affection of
Olivia
On the 19th of October, 1491, Christian reckoning

CHAPTER 7

OUTSIDE THE HIGH vaulted windows rain wept over
Fiorenza, pouring steadily from low, purplish clouds that
jostled through the sky on an east wind. Inside the vast
Chiesa di San Marco there was an uneasy silence. Every
bench was filled and there were people standing in the aisles
along the wall. No one spoke, and the wan light blurred their
features so that they all seemed like dolls made by the same
carver. Incense flavored the air, and the sound of chanting
announced the coming of the Brothers of San Domenico.

The congregation shifted expectantly, and there was a rustling of clothes and whispered words as the somber procession approached. The Brothers wore their black habits with the hoods up, so that their white cassocks showed only at their feet and wrists. One of their number had brought the Fiorenzeni to San Marco, and that was Girolamo Savonarola.

A small, ancient organ played when the monks had finished their chant. The music was sonorous, fatalistic. It joined with the rain in sorrow, reminding the mortals gathered under the great vault that life was short and filled with error and that death was long and the fires of hell burned eternally.

If the congregation could have dictated to the Brothers, they would have skipped over the Mass entirely and listened only to the sermon. But that was not permissible, and so they knelt and made their responses, each hoping that the celebration would be short, unadorned and unaugmented so that they would be able to hear the sermon they hungered for.

Just as the crowd began to grow restless, the celebration reached the sermon, and the people settled in to listen.

The monk who mounted the steps to the oratory was surprisingly small, hardly taller than a twelve-year-old child. He was thin from much fasting, which carved out the planes of his face harshly and served to accent further his lamentably large hooked nose and the large fleshy lips beneath. There was nothing attractive about the man until he fixed his congregation with his ferocious green eyes.

"It is said," he began in a deep, hard voice, "that when Job suffered for the sake of his soul, God rewarded him with plenty for his faith. It is said that God showed him His Glory, and Job knew how vile he was, and from that day he was holy." He stared at the upturned faces, challenging any to contradict him.

"To learn this lesson from the Mighty Hand of God, Job had to lose everything: his wife, his children, his land, his money, his home, the health of his body. He was given nothing to succor him but his faith. And that faith was rewarded, for he saw God in all His Power. Job bowed before the Awful Might of God. As must all men, if there is a grain of piety in them. We should all fall to our knees and confess our utter worthlessness, our unspeakable corruption. We should beg God to forgive our sins, and the greatest sin would be daring to address the Mercy Seat at all." He paused, and when he resumed his sermon, his voice had dropped to one deep tolling note. "We have upon us the great sin of Anger, yet we do not repent. There are those of you who long to thrust a dagger into the heart of your neighbor, and you justify it saying that it is for honor that you do this. What is your paltry honor, your name, when compared to the Honor and Glorious Name of God?"

There was an answering sigh from the congregation, and some of the women clenched their hands in their laps.

"Each day, you see tasks of goodness and charity not done, but you do nothing, saying that it will be done later, or that it is better for others to perform those acts, and you excuse it because you have children who need your attention, or your wants are great this year. But that is the great sin of Sloth, and for it you will toil in hell forever, and fiends shall prod you to do there what you could not learn to do in this life!" He raised his hand, and the moan that had begun in the audience was stilled, so that only the sound of the rain accompanied his words.

"You, *you*, you all are consumed with the hideous sin of Vanity. You deck yourselves in velvets when wool will do.

You buy silks and array your sinful bodies, so that no one will see your utter vileness, your degradation. You let your women paint their faces so that they are a lure to men. In that you get sin and more sin, for women should be quiet and chaste, not flaunting creatures in splendid gowns. If they are beautiful they lure others into sin, and that, too, is on your heads." His voice was growing louder now, and the words came faster. "But you are not content. You steep yourself in greater sin. Vanity will undo you. For which of you has not bought paintings to adorn your walls and scorned humble plaster? Which of you has not desired your fine chests to be carved in pagan symbols, showing fruits and trees and lyres because there are those who follow the damned teachings of the Greek philosophers rather than espouse the Love of Christ and the joys of heaven? Which of you has not brought into your homes objects to incite men's hearts to lust? Statues, paintings, shameful things showing disgraceful nudity disguised as heroes. In that you err, as well, for those are blasphemous things! Diana is the Goddess of the Moon, and she has the same horns as the Devil. Think before you touch her. And Venus, what was she but a harlot who drove men distracted with the splendor of her flesh?"

The people murmured out their shame and an old woman began to sob convulsively.

"You live for the body, not the soul. None of you, not *one*, has ever resisted the urge to cheat at comestio and serve more pies and tarts than you are allowed. You smile when you think of how clever you are. You are clever in Gluttony, not in virtue. To use your thoughts to cheat not only the law of la Repubblica but also God is not wisdom, but the greatest folly! But why do you do it? What drives you to this evil? You all seek to emulate the great Vanity, the great Gluttony, the great sins of Medici, who is filled with so many abominations that the stink of him fills the earth!"

There was an audible gasp and a susurrus of words filled the church. Never before had Savonarola attacked Laurenzo so directly. Immediately interest increased and everyone on the hard benches leaned forward. There was a kind of fascinated fear in many faces.

"Medici's five red balls cannot protect you from the Wrath of God. His usurer's wealth will never buy salvation for him or for any who seek the path he treads now, for it goes down to the depths of hell!"

Several of the young men who had been standing along the side walls had fallen to their knees and had clasped their hands over their eyes.

"Vanity! Fiorenza is stuffed as full of it as a corpse is with maggots. And where there is Vanity, there Envy is also!" Again he paused, an expression of loathing distorting his face. "Envy and Vanity, both great sins, cardinal sins. And you, you nurture them in your bosoms as if they were beloved children. You make them flourish in your hearts like gardens of pleasure. Every one of you is tainted with these sins, from the youngest child to the oldest and most venerable grandfather. Every one of you must burn for these sins unless you repent."

Many of the women were weeping now, and two of the monks had wiped their eyes. It was raining harder, but no one noticed.

"In the lascivious delights of your bed you wallow in Lust! What you caress, what you embrace, is the most pernicious of poisons, for it feeds on the other sins that have come before. Think of those voluptuous sighs and remember that they are the substance of evil. That sweet glutting of your lustful desires draws you forever to perdition."

Some of the men had gone white, and at least one of them cried out at these ominous words.

Near the back of the church, Simone Filipepi turned to his white-faced companion. "Well, Estasia," he whispered with a faint, righteously vindictive smile, "are you listening? Do you hear what Fra Savonarola says? Do you realize that it is your soul he speaks of?"

Estasia made a gesture as if to ward off a blow. "Don't."

"You build up wealth in the world," Savonarola shouted out his warning, "you gather treasures around you in the heat of your Avarice. Possessions are as a malignant disease consuming you. But what is the wealth of the world compared to the riches of heaven, the goods of the Celestial Kingdom? How cheaply you sell your souls. How you will lament your bargains in the next life when all the magnificence of Paradise is denied you for this pale, trivial imitation."

The congregation moaned aloud, caught up in Savonarola's terrible vision. They leaned farther forward, their faces wet, their eyes full of hungry suffering, and they yearned for more, for the release of the monk's castigation.

He did not disappoint them. "I am amazed," he said in another tone, humility making him bow his head. "I am amazed that God has resisted for so long delivering His final blow. We know that the Day of Wrath will surely come, for it has been prophesied from the beginning. We know that on that terrible day, no one will be safe and even the virtuous will plead for mercy before the Throne of God. There is a book, and that book will be read on that day, and every sin, every loathsome thing you have ever done or felt or thought will be known. Think of that. Keep this thought in your heart, if only for one day, so that true repentance may come into your heart, so that you, like Job, will know the full extent of your vileness. Then, only then, will you be saved. You must repent!"

The congregation took up the cry. "Repent!"

"Weep! Weep for your sins! Weep for the thousands who will be flung forever into the heinous pits of hell. Weep for those still benighted and filled with the dung of sin!"

Several people cried out, and many sobbed. Simone grabbed Estasia's wrist and said, "Do you see? Do you understand now? You must repent! You must give up your lovers and your luxuries. Otherwise you will burn in hell and demons will consume your entrails."

"Simone! Let go!" Estasia had risen, and with an expression of horrified revulsion she fled the church, not even stopping to pull the hood of her cloak over her head against the pelting rain.

Simone started after her, but could not bring himself to leave San Marco while his hero preached. He stood at the back, a rapt smile lightening the tears that flowed from his eyes. He felt abjectly vile, utterly disgusting, and at the same time a smug contentment colored this. He sank to his knees, his hands clasped in prayer as he listened.

"The Sword of God is raised high and it will smite the wicked and corrupt, and even the chaste, the virtuous and the just will be brought low. For who will save you on that day, if not God? Where can you turn, but to God? Supplicate, beg, plead on your knees for His forgiveness. You must do it now. There is no time left, for that Day of Wrath is near. I have seen it. I have seen the Sword of God descend on mankind and ravage everywhere. I have seen the world fall apart and beasts trample on its dust. Hear me, Fiorenzeni! You must repent. You can save yourselves if you repent. Cast out the evils and sins in your lives, return to the embrace of the Church and goodness! You must do it!"

The shout which greeted this made San Marco ring like a bell.

"Rise up in virtue and strike down the impious heathens! The red balls will fall. No more Palle! Strike at the head of the evil!"

This time the shout was louder and many of the people were on their feet.

"It is your glorious task to make the first blow. Let there be an end to all sin! No more Anger! No more Sloth! No more Lust! No more Gluttony! No more Avarice! No more Envy! No more Vanity! *No more Vanity!*"

With a roar the people surged to their feet, echoing Savonarola's last cry. There was a general rush filled with strange sound. One old woman had fallen to the floor and lay there drumming her heels. Another woman, this one much younger, clung to her own elbows and gave a series of shrieks from behind clenched teeth. Five young men had pulled off their jeweled collars and were crushing them underfoot.

In the midst of this hysteria, Savonarola cried out, "Repent! The Sword of God is falling! No more Vanity!"

At that the congregation burst out, like the sea breaking through a dike. People ran toward the door and rushed out into la Piazza San Marco.

The rain met them, soaking and chilling them. The mad rush faltered in the puddles and the wet. As if waking from a dream, the people looked at one another and exchanged sheepish smiles and uncertain comments. The momentum of their headlong attack was lost now, and they all began to feel the bite of the cold. Somewhere in the crowd a man sneezed. It was enough. Slowly, and weighted down with rain-soaked clothes as much as the sudden fatigue that came over them, the people left la Piazza San Marco and began their various walks home.

TEXT OF A letter from the Augustinian monk Fra Mariano da Gennazzano to Marsilio Ficino:

> To that most eminent scholar and accomplished philosopher and fellow priest, Sr. Ficino, Fra Mariano sends his blessings and greetings:
>
> I have your message of last week by me, and I pray that you will not trouble your mind anymore. I have seen Laurenzo and I am confident that this current distress his gout gives him cannot last. He has promised me that if this attack should continue he will take the waters and allow himself to be bled.
>
> Of course your concern is that of affection, and I, too, share your worry for Medici. Without Laurenzo, there is no Fiorenza. Certainly we should address God on his behalf, and I will have a Mass said for his recovery. But Laurenzo is strong, and you know that he is in the height of his prowess. He is but forty-two years old, which assures him many more years of life yet.
>
> About the other matter, though, there I must agree with you. The increase in Savonarola's following is most alarming. Arrogance from a monk is always a dreadful thing. We should not seek to place ourselves before our Brothers, but should be humble and prayerful in our work. Neither of these qualities has marked Girolamo Savonarola since he returned to Fiorenza last year.
>
> With the Grace of God, we will not suffer too much from the madness of that Domenicano, but I hope that one of us can convince Laurenzo to address the Pope

on this matter, for Laurenzo has the ear of His Holiness and would get swift redress for his pains.

That disgraceful incident of ten days ago still occupies my thoughts. What a blessing it was that there was rain that day, for otherwise we might have had those misled people running through the city doing all manner of mischief in the name of ending vanity. They cannot see that the greatest vanity is in thinking that they, or anyone else, is wise and holy enough to know God's Will.

But I have said more than I ought. I humbly beg that you will not repeat what I have said in these pages. I will pray for an end of my anger, for it is against all my vows. From Sant' Spirito I send you the affection of this world and the hope of salvation and joy in the next.

Fra Mariano da Gennazzano
Order of San Agostino
In Fiorenza on the 8th day of November, 1491

CHAPTER 8

FROST HAD MADE the air crisp and the sky was winter-bright. Under the trees where leaves had fallen the earth gave off a ripe, pungent smell, like a fruit compote. There was very little wind, so the coolness of the morning was not as noticeable to the six horsemen who rode in their own wind around the crest of the hill.

"Ah, it is beautiful here!" Laurenzo cried as he reined in

near the spiky shadows of a small grove of pine trees. "This is what I needed: the touch of the country again."

Agnolo Poliziano, who hated long rides, grimaced as he pulled up his big Spanish mare. "I wish you'd content yourself with a touch, then. This has been more like a beating."

But Laurenzo laughed. "Come, old friend, admit it. You cannot like anything I like. It could be your favorite dish, and you would scorn it."

"No fear there." Poliziano smiled unexpectedly. "You can't smell, Laurenzo, and you have no idea what food is really like."

Three more horses were pulled up. The first was ridden by il Conte Giovanni Pico della Mirandola and he gestured to the two men with him. "Ficino here insists that Socrates would not enjoy a morning like this, but I think he is wrong. Ragoczy here will not take sides, so we've come to you."

"We discussed that last night," Laurenzo said with a certain inattention. "I thought it was agreed that Socrates was probably not a horseman." He tugged at his gloves and looked back. "Poor Giacomo," he remarked to the sixth horseman. "I should have lent you a sweeter-tempered mount. Never ride Fulmine that way. He must have a firm hand or he becomes fractious."

Giacomo Pradelli, envoy from Mantova, gratefully pulled the tricky roan gelding in beside Laurenzo. "It is not that important, Magnifico," he said, lying heroically. He tried to change the subject by saying, "I have rarely seen land in such good heart. Fiorenza is fortunate, for many reasons."

"Excellent." Laurenzo grinned in sudden amusement. "I will tell Gonzaga that he is most blessed in this representative, and that I will want to purchase more of his library next year." He turned in his saddle to the foreigner on the neat gray stallion. "Well, mio caro stragnero, you have nothing to say?"

"I did not attend your banquet, Magnifico. I do not know what was said. I agree that the land is in good condition, even though some of the crops were spoiled by early rain. What other opinion should I offer?" He brought his horse up beside Laurenzo's. "I saw deer in the hills as we rode here. For all the chill, it is a beautiful morning."

"I am sorry that our tradition excluded you last night," Laurenzo said, and met Ragoczy's eyes.

"No matter. I didn't expect to be included." This was so wholly without rancor or jealousy that the guarded look left Laurenzo's face and Ragoczy went on, "I, too, have traditions which I honor, Magnifico. I don't criticize yours."

"It is an annual event, for those of us who were at the Accademia. Only seven may attend. But I would still like to hear your views. Won't you tell me what you think?"

"About Socrates?" He played with the end of his reins. "You mean, do I think Socrates was a horseman?" He saw Laurenzo nod, and he wondered what to answer. He recalled the ferocious old Greek and his studied slovenliness, his sharp tongue that would put Poliziano to shame, and his eager acceptance of praise. "I haven't read much Plato," Ragoczy ventured cautiously.

"And that, Francesco, is not an answer." The way ahead was steeper and Laurenzo held back, steadying his horse. Then he turned to his riding companions. "Mark this course: down the hill to the spring, jump the log below, then beside the old stone fence to the creek, over the creek and along to Sacro Infante, over the fence and down the slope to the Genova road. Quickly."

It was a treacherous course, and they all knew it. Laurenzo paused only long enough to say to Giacomo Pradelli,

"Not you, my friend. Fulmine would have you out of the saddle on the first turn. Meet us at the Genova road. There is a safe path not far from here. You may ride down easily."

"Let me guide him," Poliziano said quickly. "I hate these stupid competitions, Laurenzo. You know I hate them. Why should I risk my horse and my neck to please you? And if—"

"Very well." Laurenzo's smile was still very bright as he interrupted Poliziano. "But I warn you that I won't stand for complaints from you if you miss the excitement." He waited while Poliziano took Giacomo Pradelli away from the other horsemen, and then gave one loud shout, and the four riders were off down the steep hill.

Two pheasants exploded out of the brush as the horsemen raced past, and their cries filled the morning as they flew into the sky.

Laurenzo cleared the log first, shouting for pleasure as his big bay stallion negotiated the hazardous landing and recovered easily, leaving deep gouges in the moist bank, lengthening his stride as he galloped toward the old stone fence that ran for several leagues through the Tuscan hills.

Il Conte Giovanni Pico della Mirandola followed close on Laurenzo's path, but he was a more reckless rider and his lack of caution cost him as he took his horse over the log, for the showy white mare balked, reared suddenly, lost her footing and then threw Pico back onto the soggy earth around the spring. Muddied and laughing, Pico got to his feet, rubbing at his hip. His wool riding mantle was smeared with mud and his leggings were soaked through. "Go on!" he shouted, and got out of the way of Ragoczy's gray stallion.

Ficino was pushing Ragoczy to a faster pace, his own

dun gelding racing hard to take the lead. "Move aside!" he shouted to the foreigner.

"Pass me!" Ragoczy called back, and spurred his stallion on. His riding style was somewhat different from that of the Fiorenzeni, for his saddle was of a very modified low design, having little support in front of or behind the rider. Ragoczy rode with his stirrup-leathers uncommonly short, in the Persian manner, and as he chased after Laurenzo, he rose in them, so that his body was above the saddle entirely.

Marsilio Ficino broke out laughing at this and kicked his mount more determinedly.

Laurenzo was several lengths ahead, riding beside the stone fence at an easy gallop, his dark hair whipping around his head as he turned back to wave, confident of his lead.

Now Ficino slapped his horse's neck with the end of the reins and yelled encouragement to his dun gelding. Slowly he came abreast of Ragoczy's gray stallion. "Give way, foreigner!" he shouted.

Without a word in answer, Ragoczy shifted his balance slightly forward and his gray bounded ahead. The path was growing narrower, and there was no longer room for more than one horse at a time. Ragoczy did not hesitate. He pulled on the rein, adjusted his weight once more, and steadied his gray over the fence in a stunning display of horsemanship.

In the field, sheep scattered as the gray landed, and under Ragoczy's firm control the horse did not falter, keeping by the fence as he raced to catch Laurenzo.

Ficino had watched the jump in stunned silence. Then he pulled in his dun gelding and let the horse walk the trail. There was no use continuing now, for the contest was plainly between Laurenzo and Ragoczy. He shook his head and let his thoughts wander into the bright, sweet-scented morning.

Ragoczy cleared the creek less than two lengths behind Laurenzo, but his confidence faded as he saw the huge white cloister walls of Sacro Infante of the Celestiane Sisters loom up ahead of him. He could not jump the fence again to Laurenzo's side, for the quarters were far too close for safety. The only alternative was to go around the high convent walls.

"Qual dolor!" Laurenzo called mockingly to him, satisfaction making his smile glow.

Once again Ragoczy did not waste breath in an answer. He prodded his stallion and tugged the rein. Part of him was running with the horse, stretching for the gallop, steadying the pace until the stallion's mad rush flowed like water over the ground. He was almost around the convent when the ringing of a bell startled the gray, and he broke the steady rhythm of his stride. If it were not for Ragoczy's iron control, the gray would have bolted. But the bell stopped and the danger was past. Even though Ragoczy cursed the lost seconds, he knew that there was still time to recover lost ground on the descent to the Genova road. He doubted he would do badly there.

Laurenzo's large eyes grew even larger as he saw Ragoczy round the third wall of the convent, still keeping up with him. He measured the distance between them in a glance, then dug his heels into his horse's flanks.

The last league or so became a scramble, for the hill there was very steep, and the men were both determined. Loose rocks and bits of earth slid down the slope, threatening to upset the horses' precarious footing. Below, on the Genova road, Agnolo Poliziano and Giacomo Pradelli were waiting, and Agnolo wore a large, annoying smile.

In the final rush, Ragoczy forced his gray to a near-run,

and the big stallion overtook Laurenzo's mount, touching the road just moments before the other stallion could.

Both horses were breathing heavily and their coats were dark with sweat. Laurenzo patted his stallion and said, somewhat sourly, "Morello would have beaten you, Ragoczy. He never lost a race."

"Morello?" Ragoczy asked and he took a deep breath.

"He was Magnifico's horse for years," Agnolo explained, delighted that Laurenzo had been beaten at last. "And he may be right, but I don't know. I've never seen anyone ride like that. It's positively heretical."

The breeze had picked up, and now that the race was over, the air felt unexpectedly icy. Laurenzo frowned darkly. "I raised Morello from a colt. I fed him every day, and if I did not feed him, he would refuse to eat. He would stamp his feet when he saw me coming. Not like this beast."

"Come, Magnifico," Agnolo mocked, "don't take it out on the horse. Admit that Ragoczy outrode you." He smiled seraphically at Giacomo Pradelli, and awaited developments.

But Ragoczy was determined to avoid an argument. "Magnifico, if I had not ridden as I did, you would have felt cheated. You've said before that you dislike being flattered. It was an even match, and I think I had a fair amount of luck." He ignored the clouded look in Laurenzo's eyes. "Another day you will certainly best me. It's been many, many years since I've seen riding to match yours." It was no more than the truth, but he did not mention that he measured the years in centuries.

Some of the scowl faded as Laurenzo said, "It is true that I like a good contest."

Poliziano used this to plant another barb. "What you mean is that you like to win."

"Of course." He was about to defend himself when Ragoczy interrupted him.

"He would not be good at competitions if he didn't like to win. That's what made the race worthwhile." Ragoczy hoped that would put an end to the poisonous darts Poliziano was delighting in. "And, Magnifico, you have many more skills than I do."

"Perhaps," Laurenzo allowed, somewhat mollified. He waved to Marsilio Ficino, who had ridden up at last. "The last of our number. I gather Pico has gone back to the villa to change."

"I would imagine so." Ficino looked at the party and sighed. "It's so lovely a day. I saw a few grapes still on the vine. They're past using, but the smell was delicious."

By now, the worst of Laurenzo's temper had gone, and he was able to shrug his shoulders. "I wasn't aware of it." He walked his horse up to the head of the party and looked at his companions. "We're close enough to Fiorenza that I think I'll return today. It's less than an hour to the Porta San Gallo. Ride with me, amici miei, and enjoy the hills."

Marsilio Ficino was pleased to see that Laurenzo's mood was pleasant, and he started to sing, his cracked baritone making his companions laugh. "Very well, then," he said as he broke off, "I don't do it well. You, Laurenzo—you always make good songs."

Laurenzo responded happily. "I haven't made songs this way for a while. Let me think." His horse was trotting now, and Laurenzo motioned the others to keep even with him. "What shall I sing of?"

"Make a farce," Poliziano said quickly.

"Please," Ficino said.

"Love," ventured Giacomo Pradelli.

"And you, Francesco? What would you like me to sing of?"

Ragoczy thought seriously for a moment, and his intent gaze was fixed on the hills beyond them. "Sing about your life, Magnifico. Everything you are stems from that."

"Sta bene," he agreed. "And when I am through, you must sing about *your* life."

"But, Magnifico—" Ragoczy objected, and was cut short by Poliziano.

"Good. The foreigner should sing." He laughed derisively and turned to the others. "Perhaps then da San Germano will be something less of a mystery. Make him sing, Laurenzo."

Although he was irritated by the peremptory tone, Ragoczy knew it was not worth fighting about. "Whatever Magnifico does, I will do my poor best to learn from."

The road was gentle, winding through the lovely hills like a stream, and it descended gradually, so that the way was never steep. There was little traffic on it, and what there was made way for the illustrious party.

"Ah, I have my rhymes, I think," Laurenzo said after a pause. He hummed experimentally and then began to sing. His tenor voice had been roughened over the years, and the melody was simple for that reason.

Fra le dovizie della dolce amor,

he began and quelled the ribald laughter that greeted this opening, saying, "There is no wealth that compares to love, amici miei." He cleared his throat and continued.

Fra le dovizie della dolce amor
lo son perduto, son io sognator.

"I wouldn't call it sleepwalking, myself," Poliziano said.

"I wouldn't call it being lost, either," Ficino said, at his most knowing.

"Let him go on." There was a sharpness in Ragoczy's words, and the others were quiet.

Tuoi nodi diletti mi ferma
Colla febre di gioia mi manca.
Ma più bramo la pace per il mio cor
Or' sanza speranza, e sanza rancor.

Laurenzo's expression was somber as he finished the song. He turned to Ragoczy. "That is my life, mio caro stragnero. Sweet bonds hold me and joy is a fever, but now, peace is too dear."

Ragoczy nodded, and ignored the demands that the others made. He felt the cold of the morning like a finger trace the line of his back. "I see," he said.

"Now," Laurenzo said, shaking off his mood with an effort. "Now it is your turn, Francesco. I have sung a song of my life, and you must sing one of yours."

"What about that homeland you say is so precious?" Poliziano asked, and laughed with the others.

"Sing, Francesco," Laurenzo said, and it was more than an order. For a moment his eyes met Ragoczy's, and the plea in them was plain.

Ragoczy nodded. "I'll need to get my rhymes," he announced. "I will follow your form, I think, Magnifico. But I am not responsible if the song is terrible. I don't usually sing on horseback."

Ficino reached over and gave Poliziano a warning rap on the shoulder. "In that case, we'll be quiet so you can think."

But Ragoczy already knew what the words would be, as he had known even before Laurenzo had begun his song.

His hesitation was for effect only. He sang softly, but the sound of his voice was curiously penetrating.

Io sono stragnero
per sempre ed ancor';
Stragnero della morte,
stragnero dell' amor.

"Is that all?" Poliziano was incredulous. "It's hardly a quatrain. What about that homeland, Ragoczy? How does it compare to Fiorenza? This is insufficient—"

"Be quiet, Agnolo," Laurenzo told him without turning in the saddle. "None of us have the right to ask more." He looked at Ragoczy and there was profound compassion in his brown eyes. "You did not need to say so much."

"You wanted to know what my life is," Ragoczy responded with a shrug. He felt his gray stallion's neck and said in another voice, "He seems recovered. We can pick up the pace again, Magnifico, if you are in a hurry."

Laurenzo nodded and raised his hand. "We go faster," he called out to the other three riders. Then he spurred his stallion and gave him his head down the long way to the walls of Fiorenza.

They entered the city through la Porta San Gallo and reined in as la Via San Gallo became la Via de' Ginori. The city was active and as they neared la Piazza San Lorenzo, Ragoczy called out to Laurenzo. "Should we leave you, Magnifico?"

"No!" His horse was walking easily, avoiding carts and pedestrians out of long habit. "No, all of you come in and share a cup of wine with me. Comestio will be served soon. I know Massimillio will be glad for so many vigorous appetites."

The others greeted this invitation eagerly, but Ragoczy declined. "You must excuse me. It is not my custom to eat at this time of day."

"It is not your custom to eat at all," Poliziano said curtly.

Ragoczy did not respond to this barb. "Perhaps I should leave you with your other guests, Magnifico?"

The sudden rumble of cart wheels drowned Laurenzo's answer, but he repeated himself when the noise was less. "Come in anyway, Francesco. I wish to talk to you."

"Tante grazie, Magnifico."

They swung through la Piazza San Lorenzo and around to the main entrance of il Palazzo de' Medici in la Via Larga. At a sign from Laurenzo the ironwork grille over the great doors was opened and they entered the main courtyard.

Laurenzo came out of the saddle slowly, in an effort to hide the weakness that threatened to overcome him. He staggered as he touched the ground, and to keep his balance, he reached out for the stirrup. A small metal ornament had come loose and it sank its steel prong into Laurenzo's ungloved hand. Quickly Laurenzo sucked away the blood, and turned to his guests. No one had noticed, he saw with relief. He clenched his hand around one glove to stanch the bleeding.

"Well?" Agnolo challenged. "What about comestio?"

"Go with Gabriele there." Laurenzo gestured to his houseman, who had come into the courtyard a moment ago. "He will see that you're fed."

"And you?" Ficino asked.

"I will join you directly, as soon as I have changed my riding mantle for a guarnacca." He started across the courtyard, saying over his shoulder, "Ragoczy, accompany me."

Ragoczy gave his gray's reins into a servant's hands, and followed his host into the arched doorway. They went in silence up one narrow flight of stairs, and they were almost at the top when a bright stain on the step ahead stopped Ragoczy. "Magnifico?"

Laurenzo paused. "Yes?"

"Are you bleeding?" The question hung between them and after a moment Laurenzo resisted the urge to disclaim.

"I cut my hand. It was a foolish blunder—I slipped getting out of the saddle." He tried to make light of it. "I've been riding since I could walk. But I cut myself like a damned novice."

"May I see it?" Ragoczy was only one step below him, and his small hand was already extended.

Laurenzo hesitated, then held out his hand. The glove he held dropped to the stairs. "It's not very bad," Laurenzo said, looking at the cut on the side of his palm. Blood still oozed sluggishly from the wound and his palm was stained with it.

There was anguish in Ragoczy's face. "How long," he said tightly, "has your blood smelled of apricots?"

At that Laurenzo laughed. "Apricots? I don't know. I can't smell. Does it really smell of apricots?"

Ragoczy closed his eyes. "Yes."

Immediately Laurenzo sobered. "Is it a bad sign?"

"It is." Ragoczy forced himself to meet Laurenzo's eyes.

There was no shock in his face, but the acceptance of this hurt him. "I know I am ill, Francesco. I've known for some time. But you, with your salves and alchemical skill, might know what remedy there is."

Ragoczy was silent.

"Ah." Laurenzo nodded. "It is my death."

He could not deny it. Ragoczy bent and picked up Laurenzo's glove.

"And there is nothing you can do." If he felt despair, it did not color his voice. He took his glove and turned it over in his hands, looking at the stained embroidery on the fine green leather. "It's ruined," he said.

"Laurenzo . . ." Ragoczy spoke calmly, though he was filled with desolation and helplessness. "I can make a cordial. It will not cure you, but it will help the pain, when there is pain."

"I have to thank you. Well." He swallowed. "I trust you, mio caro stragnero. I know you have told me the truth. But I cannot help but wish you are wrong." Laurenzo was about to resume his climb up the last few stairs, but stopped and reached out to grab Ragoczy's shoulder with his long, swollen fingers. "What is it, Francesco? What is it that kills me?"

His words came with difficulty. "It's your blood, Laurenzo. It's rotten. It is no longer like blood. And even the power I possess is useless against it."

"Your power. But there may be others with different powers." Laurenzo's brown eyes were bright as he leaned forward. "Perhaps there is one with enough power and knowledge to cure me."

Ragoczy shook his head. "No one can save you." He saw Laurenzo cross himself. "If I had tears, Magnifico, they would be for you. But I have none."

"It would make no difference if you did." He turned away brusquely and went the rest of the way up the stairs alone.

A LETTER FROM Girolamo Savonarola to Andrea Belcore, Superior Generale of the Dominican Order:

> *On this Most Holy Feast of the Presentation, Girolamo Savonarola, Prior of San Marco in Fiorenza, is*

moved most reverently to address himself to his Superior Generale, Andrea Belcore, in Roma:

Most Reverend Father of the Brothers of San Domenico, I pray most humbly that you will hear my petition with a compassionate heart and not turn away from my request out of vain and worldly considerations.

As you know, it has been given to me by God to see visions, and that these visions all warn of the impending Day of Wrath which shall fall upon the wickedness of the world. Because the strength of these visions is such that I cannot deny them, I must beseech you to allow me more time to preach. There is so much in my soul, so much of the Light of God, that it is a torture for me to remain silent.

In this vain and corrupt city, my words are badly needed, for the souls wander in darkness, drawn over the world by temptations and desires. If I am to fulfill that divine mission that I took upon myself when I donned my habit, you must grant me my request, so that the danger around us is known and these unfortunate Fiorenzeni will no longer seek sins as if they were salvation, but will bow instead before the Throne of Glory, and in penitential remorse, confess themselves and be forgiven.

I know well that since His Holiness wed his son to the daughter of the perfidious Medici he has seen the world through Laurenzo's eyes. But I pray most fervently that you will not be likewise blinded and will allow me to preach the truth as I am moved to do. It is not I who makes the pronouncements, but the Holy Spirit, speaking through me. I am the vessel filled by the visions God sends to me. In all humility, I ask that

you do not desert that great Holy Spirit that has cho-
sen me as its medium to be heard in the world.

   In devoted and prayerful obedience, I commend to
you the hope and the spiritual life of

                          Girolamo Savonarola
                          Brothers of San Domenico
                          Prior of San Marco
In Fiorenza, November 22, 1491

CHAPTER 9

IS THIS THE last of it?" Demetrice Volandrai asked of il
Conte Giovanni Pico della Mirandola.

He nodded and took up the loose sheets of closely written parchment. "Yes. I'm grateful you're so fast with the
translations, Donna Demetrice. I doubted that a woman,
even a scholarly woman, could have done so much in so little time."

She raised her brows. "I have nothing else to do with my
time, Conte. Why should I not finish in so reasonable a pe-
riod?"

Il Conte Giovanni laughed and took her hand. "Well, you
know, most women are easily distracted. But you, bella
Donna, are so capable that I am amazed at your skill every
time I see you."

Demetrice's smile remained fixed as she withdrew her
hand. "Since I have neither husband nor family to occupy
my attention, I am grateful that there is so much for me to
do." She rose from her bench in Laurenzo de' Medici's li-

brary and looked toward the fire that crackled in the grate.
Her old gonella was thin and the shawl around her shoulders
did not compensate for that thinness.

Pico was still speaking, his beautiful pleasant face ruddy
with cold and goodwill. "You should have made a superior
scholar, had you been a man. Or a noble. It is a pity your
skill cannot be used to better advantage." He inclined his
head and prepared to leave. "I hope we will work together
again, in future."

"But you are going to Roma, Conte, and I remain here."

"Perhaps you will allow me to make other arrangements." He came closer to her. "Think of it, carina, with my
protection you will have not only the learning you crave, but
other pleasures as well. You are an attractive woman—not
pretty, but not displeasing to me. I could do much for you."

She could feel his breath on the side of her head as he
pressed close to her back, and she had a flash of anger. But
there was no use in making enemies in her cousin's house.
She closed her hands into fists. "I am not at liberty to discuss this," she said in a controlled voice.

"I will speak to Laurenzo, if that is what worries you."
He touched the edge of her jaw and in that moment she remembered another man who had touched her, and she had
been filled with rapture for it. But with Pico it was otherwise. She could feel his lack of force even as he sought to
make a conquest of her. She wrenched away from him and
moved nearer the fire. Her color was heightened, and her
breath came quickly. "Please, Conte, I cannot think of your
offer until I have done all the tasks my cousin has set for me.
After all he has done on my behalf, it would be poor of me
indeed to leave him without anyone to take my place."

"Very well. I am in no hurry." Pico sketched a bow in her

direction, and then with the sheaf of parchments in his hand, he let himself out of the library.

Anger and shame were still warring within her some time later when the door opened and Laurenzo stepped into the room.

"Demetrice, do you have time . . . ?" He stopped as he saw her face. "Tesoro mio, what is it?"

She stopped pacing and tried to smile. "It is nothing. Indeed, I don't know why it bothered me so much—" She came across the room and her heart tightened in her chest as she saw how thin he had become. "Oh, Lauro."

He took her outstretched hands in his. "Distraught, Demetrice? Tell me."

"It's nothing. I should not have taken offense. None was meant. But I cannot bear it when I am weighed and measured like so much sausage." Without thinking about it, she went into his arms. "Lauro mio, I'm frightened."

He smoothed the tendrils of rosy-blond hair back from her face and tilted her head up. "Why, tesoro mio? There is nothing to be afraid of."

There was no way for her to put her fear into words, for to speak the words would make her fright too real. She laid her head against his wide shoulder and said in a small voice, "Do not leave me, Lauro."

"Demetrice." He held her more tightly, as if taking strength from her. Some little while later he said, "Do you remember those beautiful days at the hunting lodge?"

Her laugh was uncertain. "I cannot forget. What a little box of a place it was; barely room for our bed. And the balcony, where we ate. Everything there that was wonderful was part of you, Lauro. I wish we had stayed there forever."

"And I." He lifted her face and bent to kiss her. "That's

another thing I had forgot—how sweet your lips are. Again, Demetrice."

When she pulled away from him she was shaken. She looked at him with luminous eyes. "Sancta Maria, what am I going to do?"

Laurenzo stood back from her, the beginnings of a frown on his brow. "What do you mean, tesoro mio? I am here, and I will always take care of you. Never doubt that."

"I don't." She forced herself to move away from him, to go to the window and look out at the city. "It's been snowing for more than three days."

"Yes." He waited a moment, and then came across the library to her. "Demetrice. Tesoro. Listen to me. Please."

Reluctantly she turned to him. "Lauro. Carissimo Lauro." She looked up into his dear, ugly face and bit her tongue to keep from crying.

"Yes," he said very gently. "Yes, I know, Demetrice. And it is hard for me, too." He drew her away from the window. "But there is time yet. A little time. And I promise I will not leave you alone and friendless in the world."

Demetrice let herself be led back to the bench, and as Laurenzo sank down on it, she held his head against her breast. "Do you remember that morning we rose before sunrise and walked through the woods? I think I would sell my soul to have that time again."

"Demetrice," he said softly. "It is hard enough without this. And your soul is too precious to fling it away so uselessly. It is for your soul that I love you, for without it . . . without your soul, even the greatest pleasures are empty."

"But don't you want that time again?" She managed to keep her voice steady as she asked the question.

"More than you will ever know. And if I could have it

again, it would not be for a few months, but for years." He felt her hands tighten.

"Lauro. Oh, Lauro." In vain she searched for the right words, but they eluded her.

"What do you want of me?" he asked when they had been silent too long.

"I want you to live." Demetrice almost choked on this outburst. She put her hands to her face and moved away from him so that he could not see she wept.

"Demetrice, you must not. For me." He was too tired to follow her across the room. "Tesoro mio, I beg you."

Her cry was full of anguish; she forced her fist into her mouth to stop it. "I can't bear it."

"You must." He caught and held her with his eyes and slowly she regained control of herself. "I am depending on you. How else can I know that everything I value here is safe? Look around you." The sweep of his arm took in the whole library. "I've worked most of my life for this. Who will guard it for me? Who will protect it? Piero? It means nothing to him. Agnolo? As long as it brings him notice, perhaps. Marsilio? He's older than I am, anima mia. But, you say, there's Pico? But he will not be here, he will be in Roma, protecting his own interests. You, Demetrice, you care for these books, and love them as much as I do. You know that they are more than words on paper. You know that they are the very soul of the world. You cherish them."

"But I couldn't stay here, if you weren't . . ." She faltered, and her eyes strayed to the tables and shelves around her.

"Then stay elsewhere. Who in Fiorenza pleases you? Who would you like to live with? Who would you want to learn from?" He asked the questions lightly, his smile almost successful.

"I wouldn't want . . ."

"Demetrice." The name stung her with its sharpness. "I haven't the strength for this. I am asking you to help me. If you are unwilling to, say so."

She saw the force of his implacable will in his face. Slowly she came back across the room toward him, and resisted the urge to embrace him. "What must I do?"

"You must find someone who will care for you. Not marriage, if that isn't what you want. But you need to have a household to live in. I would suggest a scholar, because you love learning. And learning cures many things, tesoro mio. In time, it will cure your hurt." He let his hand fall on her shoulder as she sank to the floor beside him. "Tell me who, then, and I will see that it is arranged."

"I don't know. Perhaps Piero—" She thought of Laurenzo's son and shook her head. "No. I guess not."

The room was darker and the firelight gilded them both. "You should not stay here after I . . . leave."

She tried to think, sifting through the scholars she knew. And then, in sudden realization, she said, "Ragoczy."

"Francesco?" He considered it. "I'll talk to him. He may be willing. He has been a better friend to me than many Fiorenzeni. You will learn much from him."

Now that she had said it, she felt doubts. "Do you think I should? He is a foreigner."

"That may give you greater protection. Do you like him?"

Demetrice traced out a faded outline on her gonella before she answered. "I don't know. There's something about him. He has always been very kind to me, but I feel that he could be very terrible. Perhaps it's because he's not Fiorenzan."

"Perhaps. I admit he is a mystery. But, as you say, he's

kind, and he certainly has a great deal of knowledge. You must ask him to teach you Turkish."

"Does he speak it?" It wasn't really a question, and she was not surprised when Laurenzo did not answer.

"Tell me, tesoro mio: if I had been just Lauro, and not de' Medici, if there were only my face and not my wealth, would you still have loved me?" He was staring into the fire and his hand on her shoulder was tense.

She looked up at him, seeing his lantern jaw, his broken nose, his broad, irregular forehead. Though she tried, she could not imagine him as anything other than he was, but she answered without hesitation, "Of course I would."

He sighed and his hand relaxed. "Poor Clarice," he said, speaking of his wife. "She really didn't like it here. She never forgot she was a Roman Orsini out in the provinces."

"Piero's wife is another Orsini," Demetrice pointed out.

"That's different. Piero doesn't love Fiorenza. Clarice didn't object to my mistresses, but she was infernally jealous of Fiorenza. I suppose it was natural. She died unhappy, and much of it was my fault. Well, it's done." With an effort he pushed himself off the reading bench. "Forgive me, tesoro mio, but I must go. I have to ration my strength. How that irks me."

Demetrice got to her feet quickly. "Lauro, is there much pain?"

He turned to look down at her. "No, not very much. And when there is, I have a cordial. Ragoczy gave it me. The effect is marvelous, I promise you."

She heard the bitterness in his voice and she closed her eyes, fighting for composure.

Laurenzo relented. "No. No, tesoro mio." He turned her face to him. "Go to your foreign alchemist with my blessing. But do not forget me yet awhile."

"Dio mi salva!" she whispered and blindly tore herself away from him. She steadied herself against the trestle table, her hands holding the wood so tightly she feared the table would break, or her hands. When she heard the door close behind him, she turned again, and stared at the door. Though she tried to think, her mind remained stubbornly rooted to Laurenzo.

Somewhat later Demetrice surprised the understeward Sergio by searching him out and asking him to deliver a letter for her.

"Certamente, Donna. Where shall I take it?" He was already pulling off his long apron, and wishing that his winter cloak was warmer.

"Take it to Palazzo San Germano. To Francesco Ragoczy." Her eyes were dry and her hands no longer shook. She handed over the letter and a dolcezza in the amount of two gilli d'or.

"To Ragoczy," he said as he pocketed the little coins. "At Palazzo San Germano."

T EXT OF A letter from Gian-Carlo Casimir di Alerico Circando to Francesco Ragoczy da San Germano:

To his respected friend and illustrious teacher, Francesco Ragoczy da San Germano, at his palazzo in Fiorenza, Gian-Carlo sends his most affectionate greetings.

Your builder who is now embarked for London arrived here a few days ago, and, as you instructed me, I sought him out. Even after two pots of wine he was most reticent. He is calling himself Riccardo, but he isn't yet used to the name, and I gather that his name is Carlo. I prodded him much, but he said nothing more than that a cousin of his had secured him a position in England and that he was going there to take it up. He claims to be from Mantova, but his accent is purest Fiorenzan. You need have no fear that Carlo will betray you. I have seen none of the others, though I have heard from Cola Galeazzo in Genova and he informs me that another builder, called Lodovico, has left Genova for Lisboa. There has been no word from Dietrich Wundermann in Wien yet, but I am sure your third builder will pass through there when the winter is over.

I have taken the liberty of importing a printing press from Cologne. The old Dogaressa has taken an interest in books, and very much wanted a press. Should you receive a letter from her, you will know why.

Your house here has sustained some slight damage in a recent storm. Repairs have been made following your instructions, and the building is once again as sound as you desire. Most of the damage was to the east front, but the roof also took a beating. The foundations are secure as ever, and not one drop of water has ever seeped through.

Your letter of October 10th recommended that I find a new supply of sandalwood, and at last I have. There is a merchant, nominally a Greek, but with more than a touch of Egyptian about him. His name is Darios Kyrillye and his merchandise is of a superior quality. His prices are as reasonable as one can expect. From what I have learned from him, he also has access to certain dyes. If you like, I will find out more.

The iridescent glass you sent to us arrived intact, and I will present it to il Doge tonight, with your compliments. All the glassmakers will be mad to learn your secret.

For the time being I will say farewell. There is much to do before the festa tonight, and the servants need instructions. Should you desire anything more of me, your instructions will be followed most promptly.

Until you return to Venezia and I am once again under your immediate supervision, I commend my work to you, and ask that you will forgive any error I have made.

Gian-Carlo Casimir di Alerico Circando
In Venezia, December 6, 1491, the Feast of San Nicolo

CHAPTER 10

DONNA ESTASIA THREW her silver-handled brush across the room and turned expectantly to her companion.

"But I wasn't finished, bella mia," Ragoczy said, letting her glorious chestnut hair pour through his fingers.

"It's been brushed enough," she said, pouting. Her petulance was unattractive, for it narrowed her large hazel eyes and pinched her ripe-lipped mouth. "You never take off your clothes. I haven't seen you naked," she complained.

"No." He had begun to braid her hair into a single plait down her back.

"Stop that!" She gave an angry toss to her head and her

hair spilled over her shoulders once again. Very deliberately she buttoned the top of her shift.

Ragoczy leaned back, resting against the pillar at the foot of her bed. "Very well, Estasia. What offense have I committed?"

"You do not please me. That's offense enough." Her expression dared him to contradict her.

"And how do I not please you?" There was kindness in his face, and a certain frightening sympathy. "Is it because every time we are together, we make love?"

"We do *not* make love." She started up, and then thought better of it. "You . . . you disgust me."

"You take no joy from me?" he asked, smiling, but the smile was sad and strangely old.

"You know I take joy. And you pleasure more than anyone else. And *it is not enough!*" She fumbled with a few of the jars on her vanity table. "You say you are not a eunuch, but I don't believe it. You won't even let me touch you."

"I told you when we began that I wouldn't. You understood then. Why change now?" He reached out and took her hand. "Estasia, you know what I am. I can't be anything else."

Her shoulders dropped miserably. "Won't you even try?"

Almost reluctantly he moved nearer to her. "But come, bella mia, with whomelse can you be so fulfilled and so chaste?"

"I don't *want* to be chaste. I want to be drunk with your flesh. You treat my body as something sacred that cannot be defiled. But I am a widow, I know what I want. Let me be profane." She clung to his arm. "Please, Francesco. Just once. If you are a man, act the man."

"Diletto, remember what I told you the first time I came to you?"

Sulking now, she released his arm. "Of course. You always remind me. But I didn't know you *meant* it when you said how you would love me. How should I guess that you meant it?"

"You should know because I said it." He pointed to the small, valuable mirror of clear Venezian glass on her vanity table. "Look there. Tell me what you see."

"I won't be distracted!"

"I'm not distracting you. Look in your mirror and tell me what you see."

Angrily she snapped her head around and picked up her mirror. For a moment she looked into it; then, more impatiently she put it down. "Well?"

"What did you see?" His oddly penetrating eyes were on her face. "Tell me, Estasia."

"I saw my face, of course." There was a mulish set to her jaw, and her pointed chin jutted forward.

"And what else?"

"Oh, Francesco, stop this. I don't want your tutoring now. I want your body. I want you to possess me. I want to be vanquished by you."

"What else did you see in the mirror?" His voice was so totally compelling that she answered him.

"This room. What else should I see?"

"And me?" he asked, and waited.

"You?" Some of the color left her face, and she said quietly, "No. I didn't see you."

He spoke softly, his small, gentle hands touching her shift, her arms, her shoulders. "Bella mia, I am not like you. All that is mine to give you, I give you."

"But you do not love me."

"After my fashion."

She shook her head, and some of the terror that had

glazed her hazel eyes faded. "No. You don't burn for me. You don't scorn each hour you are away from me. You've never kept a vigil at my door."

In spite of himself, he laughed. "That was not part of our bargain. You had desires, needs that I could satisfy without danger. Estasia, do me the honor of telling me the truth. I have done what I said I would do, have I not?"

She sniffed. "Yes."

"Thank you." He said this without sarcasm. "Listen to me, bellissima." He was silent until she looked into his face. "If you want me to love you, I will. If you want me to spend the evening talking, I will."

"Really? And what of your needs?"

"I'm not so voracious that I must be slaked at all times." At last he smiled. "I don't require victims."

The cunning was back in her face. "And what if I refused you? Not just tonight, but from now on? What would you do then?"

He was becoming bored with her teasing. "I'd make other arrangements."

"You'd hunger a long time." She was smugly satisfied, and a triumphant glint lit her eyes.

"Do you really think so?" he asked politely, raising his brows. "Well, if I am as distressingly inadequate as you say, it is cruel of me to take your time. I'll remove myself, and leave you to your more conventional lovers."

She snatched at the black robe he wore.

"I didn't give you permission to leave."

It was very still in Estasia's room. The few candles that remained lighted sputtered loudly and the icy wind fingered the windows like spirits in need of warmth. Francesco Ragoczy did not move, hardly breathed. He fixed his gaze on Estasia until she released his clothing. "I didn't mean it that way," she said, sulking again.

"No?" He turned away from her and moved restlessly about the room, touching nothing, seeing very little. "Bella mia, I dislike being played with. You told me you must see me tonight, and now that I am here, you only want to castigate me. Caprice has no fascination for me, bella mia. If you wish to tempt and cajole, do so with another love." He stopped pacing and regarded her evenly from the other side of the bed. "If you tell me to leave once more, I will do so. And I will not return."

Estasia gave a brittle laugh. "How could you think I wanted you to go? It's only that I want full proof of your love. And you have refused to give it. Well, I must be satisfied, I suppose. You have declared that you will take your pleasure as you like, and I know I am foolish enough to accept that." She rose from her vanity table. "But I'm not done with you, Francesco."

As he watched her pull off her shift, Ragoczy knew that he should break with her. "One day, Estasia, you will run out of new sensations. What will you do then?"

Standing naked in the cold, candle-dim room, she stared at him, uncomprehending. "Sensation?"

"Isn't that what you desire?" He had come nearer to her. "You always ask me to do something new, to touch you in a new way, to excite you through a variety of means."

"Oh." She giggled. "That's because you're willing to. And since you don't do—"

He cut her off before she could renew her complaint. "I'm willing to caress you now, wherever you like, in whatever manner you like."

"Any way?" she asked archly, and moved nearer. "Would you bind me to my bed and beat me with lashes of silk?

Would you take me by the hair and hold down my body with yours, a knife to my breast, while you bruised me with your kisses?" She was breathless when she finished speaking, and she leaned forward in a kind of delirium.

Ragoczy was seriously alarmed now. He took her hands firmly in his and forced them to her sides. "No, bellina, I would not."

"But why not, since I wish it?"

"Because I don't want you to be my victim, I want you to be my companion in pleasure." He released her hands. "If you can't accept that, then there's no more to be said."

She sighed, resigned. "Oh, very well, if you won't, you won't. But you will take me to bed, won't you?"

Ragoczy knew that he should leave, that his involvement with Estasia had gone too far. He stared at her delicious nude body, and saw a hunger in her much greater than his own. "Estasia . . ."

She flung herself onto the bed and reached up for him. "I am so anxious for you. Look how I sweat, though the room is cold. See to what desperation you bring me. Francesco. Francesco."

He stood near the bed, but came no nearer. "You have told me I no longer satisfy you. Why do you want me, if that is the case?"

"Don't be tiresome, Francesco," she snapped even as she turned languorously to show him a more promising view of her beautiful breasts and splendidly rounded hips.

Instead of sinking onto the bed beside her, Ragoczy crossed the room to her vanity table. He picked up her mirror and looked into it. "In certain lights, there is a faint outline," he said in a remote way.

But Estasia was out of patience. "I think," she said with a malicious smile, "that I must certainly go to Confession tomorrow. I will tell the priest what has passed between you and me. I will tell him, Francesco, how you take your pleasure, and how shamelessly you have used me. I will say how you have beat me, you have violated me against my will, using a crucifix when you had exhausted your own flesh. Should I," she mused soulfully, "go to the good Francescani at Santa Croce? Perhaps I might go to the Vallombrosani at Santa Trinità. They do not in general hear Confession from women, but they might make an exception for a Confession such as mine. Or," she added after a moment, "God's Hounds! Surely the Domenicani with their especial concern for heresy and blasphemy would be very interested in what I could tell them. But I would have to choose between San Marco and Santa Maria Novella." Her look was no longer languid. She pushed herself up on one elbow. "Think about my Confession before you leave, Francesco."

Through her recitation Ragoczy had stood very still. At last he put down the mirror. "I see," he said evenly. "As long as I come when you call me, and do whatever you ask, your confessions will be ordinary. What happens when you grow tired of me, Estasia? Will you confess then, and let the Church take me off your hands?"

She did not hear the fury in his calm words. "No, I wouldn't do that," she said when she had considered the idea. "It would bring me too much notoriety, and I don't like to have my life too much circumscribed. I had my fill of that as a daughter and a wife. No prisoner was ever more closely guarded than I was, I promise you. I don't want to live that way again." She lay back, her legs somewhat apart, her arms open and inviting. "Do come to bed, Francesco, schiave d'amore."

The word "slave" stung him like a lash and he very nearly hurled her mirror across the room. But if he had learned one thing in his long, long life, it was how to wait. He did not touch the mirror, and after a moment he crossed the room again. "You leave me very little choice. Very little."

Her eyes grew wide in anticipation. "Then you *will* beat me."

"I said I would not." He sat on the bed, his eyes unreadable. "Where do you want me to start? Shall I touch you? Shall I kiss you?"

"Oh, Francesco, don't. You know what I like." She slid nearer to him.

"But you have told me that I no longer satisfy you, so you must instruct me. Otherwise I'll have to bear the results of your displeasure at the hands of Mother Church. So tell me, Estasia, what must I do."

"Santa Lucia protect me," she declared. "Touch me, touch me the way you always have. Put your hands here"— she flinched as his cold fingers closed on the curve of her breasts—"and then do as you always have."

Anger made him rougher than he had ever been with her, and he felt disgust with himself for catering to her demands.

"That's *much* better," she purred as he forced her body to greater arousal. She moaned with delight as he grazed over her flesh with harsh kisses. It pleased her that he took no satisfaction from her, and she made a sound somewhere between a chuckle and a gasp. Suddenly she thrust herself against him. "Do more. *Do more.* I want more."

Grimly he urged on her overwhelming passion, and was not surprised to realize she was resisting her fulfillment. He felt her muscles tighten, and he wondered if she could maintain this new tension for long. As if in answer to this, she cried out as her legs cramped.

"Estasia, shall I stop?"

"No . . . No . . . No . . ." Her face was set in a rictus smile, and then, almost in disappointment, she trembled in violent release. She seized his arms, holding on desperately until she gave a last shudder, and her rapture was ended.

When at last she opened her eyes, she said wickedly, "Next time, I will have you bind me and then you will abuse me. . . ."

"Estasia," he said, moving back from her, already regretting all the pleasure they had shared over the last several months.

"You will hurt me in your lust, and then, unless you have been lying to me, you will enter my body like a man. If you are not a eunuch, perhaps I will not confess." She smiled nastily at him.

"Listen to me, bella mia." There was something in his voice she had never heard before, a coldness that was more than ruthlessness, more than hate. "I have lived more places than you know of in this world. I would dislike having to leave Fiorenza, but rather than be coerced by you, I would."

Her laughter was uncertain. "But you would lose your palazzo, and all your beautiful things."

If anything, this reminder made him more implacable. "I have lost much more than this before. I won't allow your extortion of me. Believe this."

At that moment, seeing his dark eyes on her, she did believe him. "Why, Francesco," she said, with a miserable attempt at archness, "did you think I *meant* what I said about Confession? I think you are not used to our Fiorenzan ways. I shouldn't have thought that a man like you, with all the experience you say you have had, would be taken in by my amusements." She had pulled her blankets up around her throat and she stared out at him with a mixture of fascination and apprehension.

"Of course. I should have realized that this was only sport." His irony was bitter.

"You're being hateful because I scare you," she said quietly. "You don't like to be bested, do you?"

"No better than you do, bellissima." He took a step nearer the bed and she pulled away from him. "I think perhaps that this had better be farewell, Estasia. I'm afraid I am too foreign to enjoy your sport."

"Farewell?" It was as if the word were wholly unknown to her. "You'd *leave me?* Just because I said I'd Confess?" She gathered her covers more tightly around her, and then, quite suddenly, she began to sob. "Oh, how I hate you for this. You can't enter me as a man should, you frighten me, and then you leave."

He stilled his sudden rush of sympathy for Estasia. "Yes. Then you're well rid of me, aren't you?" He went across the room without turning, and opened her window.

"I don't want you. *I never wanted you!*" She was shouting now between ragged sobs. "Get out! *Get out!* GET OUT!" But these last hysterical screams were addressed to an empty window. Ragoczy was gone into the snow-brightened night.

T EXT OF A letter from Simone Filipepi to his brother, Alessandro, called Botticelli:

To his Sandro, brother in flesh and in the Sight of God, Simone sends his prayers and greetings, at this joyous time:

In three days it will be the Nativity, Sandro, and my most ardent wish for you at this time is that your heart

*will be moved at last, and you will see that Savonarola
is right. You have been blinded too long by the riches
and fame of the perfidious Laurenzo. You have allowed
his favor and affection to woo you from the true splen-
dors of this world. I have been on my knees all today,
in supplication before Almighty God, in the hope that
you will at last repudiate the Medicis and come into the
company of those who follow the teachings of heaven.*

*My retreat will end in seven days, and at that time
I will return to Fiorenza. I hope that Donna Estasia
has recovered from her indisposition so that I will not
find too great upset in your home. It is most unfortunate that she should be unwell at the time of my retreat, but the offices of the soul must supersede those
of home and family. You would do well to admonish
Donna Estasia to be more diligent in her piety, for
then she would not be visited with such unpleasant-
ness. Tell her to turn her thoughts away from the flesh,
to the joys of the saints in heaven.*

*A messenger to this monastery has told me that you
are still working on murals in Palazzo de' Medici of
pagan debauchery. Sandro, dear brother, think of the
heavy burden of sin you take on to flatter the vanity of
Laurenzo. To excuse him by reason of his education
and poetry is to fall into grave error. Laurenzo is
damned, and Savonarola has said that he will be in his
grave before the next grapes are pressed. Do not let
him seduce you with his corruptions, for he will take
you down with him to sup in hell.*

*It is my sincerest wish that this finds you well, and
filled with true penitence. I wish you the solemn joy of
the Feast of the Nativity and I commend my familial*

*respects to you even as I commend my soul to God and
the angels.*

Simone Filipepi
*Il Monastero della Pieta, Brothers of San Domenico,
December 22, 1491*

CHAPTER 11

THE HEAVY DOORS of il Palazzo della Signoria swung suddenly wide, and Laurenzo de' Medici stumbled through them into the bright glare of winter sunshine. He swayed unsteadily a moment, and his long-lidded eyes narrowed; then he clapped loudly.

"You! Claudio! My horse." His voice sounded horribly shrill in his own ears, but the young mercenary guard leaped to obey. As he waited, he stared in horror at his hands. They were still shaking, and the joints were grotesquely swollen. Even his elbows and knees were tender and enlarged, and despite Ragoczy's cordial, they hurt when he moved.

"Your horse, Magnifico." Claudio held the sorrel stallion, waiting expectantly.

In that single, terrible moment, Laurenzo feared he would not be able to mount without help. "Grazie, Claudio," he snapped, and took the reins, forcing himself to walk easily. He was close to fainting as he pulled himself into the saddle, grateful that his sorrel stood still despite his clumsiness. It took all his will to tighten his hands on the reins, to pull the sorrel's head around. He let the horse set its own pace through the crowded streets, concentrating on keeping his seat. It was really such a short distance between il Palazzo della Signoria and il Palazzo de' Medici that he was determined to get there without surrendering to the dreadful weakness and pain that washed through him like a tide of fire.

As he neared la Via Larga and his home, he saw that there was a great deal of activity near the door, and too late he remembered that two scholars from Portugal were supposed to arrive that day. He knew it would be impossible to receive them in his current condition, so as he entered la Piazza San Lorenzo, he reined his sorrel toward the church, away from il Palazzo de' Medici.

Pain disoriented him as he came out of the saddle, and for a moment he stood stupidly in front of San Lorenzo, not recognizing the Benedettan Father who came forward, distress and affection in his face. "Mio Laurenzo." He touched Laurenzo's arm as he spoke. "Is there anything the matter?"

"No," Laurenzo said distantly as he mastered himself. "I am in need of prayer, Father. So I came here. My brother . . ."

"Of course," the priest said softly, and led the way into the splendid church of Brunelleschi that Laurenzo's grandfather had donated. There was still some construction going on, but it was away from the main body of the church.

Laurenzo stopped before genuflecting. Agony consumed his legs as he dropped to his knee, and he got to his feet with considerable difficulty. He felt terribly cold and had to clamp his teeth together to keep them from chattering. When he knew he could walk without reeling, he approached the altar. "Strange," he said softly. "I have worshiped here for most of my life, but never, since he died here, have I looked at the altar and not seen my brother lying, just there, bleeding. It was long ago, but as fresh to me as if it had happened yesterday, or this morning."

"I'll leave you alone for prayer, Laurenzo," the priest said, and reminded himself to pray for the health and soul of il Magnifico.

"Ah, Giuliano," Laurenzo said to the empty altar, "how I have missed you. And now, with death plucking at my sleeve, I wish you were here. I could die more easily if you were here. I suppose I am condemned to burn. The prior of San Marco certainly thinks so. Have I been vain, Giuliano, to love learning, and beauty? I am willing to burn for Volterra. It was a despicable act, and my most sincere repentance will not restore that city. If I must burn, let it be for Volterra, not for the things I have loved." He stopped and asked in a lighter tone, "Is that profound faith, or a poet's vanity? Or is it what you used to chide me for—that I have never learned to lose, that even if I am damned for eternity, it must be on my own terms."

He looked up at the vault of the church, as he had often done, and admired the splendor of the building. But neither there nor at the altar did he feel a holy presence. "There's too much Medici and not enough God," he said, and almost laughed at his own effrontery. A line of one of his poems came back to him, a line he had written in yearning and remembered now in despair.

O Dio, o sommo bene, or come fai,
che Te sol cerco e non Ti truovo mai?

All his life he had sought that supreme good, and now, when he wanted it most, it seemed farthest away. He folded his aching hands and began to pray.

Across la Piazza San Lorenzo in her third-floor room of

il Palazzo de' Medici, Demetrice Volandrai paused in what she was saying to look into the street again.

"What is it, Donna mia?" Her visitor came across the room to join her at the window, his black Spanish pourpoint gleaming in the cold light. A narrow ruff of tied lace framed his features, which had been transformed from the courtesy of a moment ago to deep concern.

"There. At San Lorenzo." She pointed down toward the active confusion below them.

"What? There's a mule, which may mean that they have a bishop with them . . ."

"No. There." Her finger moved a little. "It's Laurenzo's horse."

Ragoczy recognized the sorrel once it was pointed out to him, but he said, "He probably has business with the superior there."

"But he said he would be at la Signoria . . ." She stopped awkwardly. "I suppose I shouldn't let it worry me."

Very gently Francesco Ragoczy took her hand in his. "Donna Demetrice, what frightens you?"

She looked away, out the window again. "It's nothing, da San Germano." Her lapse into formality had a different effect than what she thought it would.

"No, Donna, don't cheat your grief." He came closer and his compelling dark eyes met hers. "I know what you fear. And I fear it too."

She wavered between relief and insult, but relief won. "What did he tell you?"

"Nothing. I told him." Ragoczy looked down into la Piazza San Lorenzo again. "Perhaps you're right." He turned back. "Would you like to check San Lorenzo? If we're wrong, and he is fine, and is with a priest, he'll be angry."

Demetrice did not hesitate. "Yes. Oh, yes. I don't care if

he's furious . . ." She went across the little room and picked up a long rust-colored shawl and flung it around her shoulders. "You see," she said in hurried apology, "if he only wanted to talk to the priests, he could have come here, then walked across la piazza. But he didn't come back home."

Though Ragoczy shared her apprehension, he said lightly, "And then again, he may have seen that pack of Portuguese at the door and sought refuge for a moment before facing them." He followed her out of the room, closing the door after him.

"Of course," she said reasonably, and with no confidence in her argument, "and he might have sent the horse back with one of the priests while he went elsewhere. He often goes to the menagerie after a meeting. Do mind the stairs here, they're very steep."

"I will." They hurried down to the second floor, and then took a side stair to the sculpture garden at the rear of il Palazzo de' Medici. "There's no one here today, grazie agli angeli," she said as she opened the door to the small courtyard. "It would be useless to go this way if the sculptors were here." She indicated the door. "If you'll draw back the bolts . . ."

At last Laurenzo raised his head and sighed. "Giuliano mio," he said softly, "do you remember that night we went serenading, and you brought two jars of that strong Spanish wine? It's a miracle we made it home. Our mother was outraged. That was just after Piero was born, wasn't it? And now Piero is a husband." He rubbed his face, trying to clear his thoughts. "Your son is fine. You'd like him. He'll go far in the Church." He leaned forward against the Communion rail. "We hanged most of the conspirators, including the bishop. Sandro's done a splendid mural of it—of the hanging. I wrote some verses for the traitorous swine. But you're still dead, in spite of it. Giuliano." He walked toward the simple tomb of his brother. "I've always meant to have a proper monument built for you. I should have done it earlier. But I'm forty-two years old, Giuliano. How should I know I would have so little time? Do you remember our plan? That when I was thirty-five I'd leave governing to you, and at last devote myself to poetry. Maybe even retire into the country? I haven't done that. I wish now I had." He fingered the plain marble. "Our peace has been expensive, but at least the price was paid in gold, not lives. You were always so lighthearted. It's cold in Fiorenza. I left la Signoria just a little while ago. Giuliano, I could not hold my quill to sign the proclamation for the Nativity festival." Slowly, painfully, he dropped to his knees beside his brother's tomb, and leaning his arms against the stone, he hid his head in the bend of his elbows.

Somewhat later he felt a light touch on his shoulder. Startled more than annoyed, he turned to ask the priest to leave him alone for a little while longer. "Demetrice," he said, very much surprised.

She had prepared herself to see worse, and so was quite composed in spite of the ravaged smile he gave her. "Yes. You have to pardon us, but I saw your horse . . ."

"Us?" He looked around, somewhat dazed. "Ragoczy," he said as he recognized the black-clad figure. "But what are you doing here?"

Ragoczy came nearer. "I had been to see Donna Demetrice about her move to Palazzo San Germano. She's willing to be my housekeeper, and since that consists mainly of keeping track of my books and paying for household supplies, she will have time for her own work, and for your library. I am indebted to you, Laurenzo, for thinking of me." The words were easy and his smile polite, but Laurenzo was not fooled.

"Thank you, amico mio, but you don't have to indulge me.

I am glad you have come. Both of you." He regarded Ragoczy. "I'm not sure why you did. I have thought—forgive me if I am mistaken—that you wanted no part of my dying."

There was silence between them in that echoing church. "Very well, Magnifico. I suppose you have the right." He dragged one of the congregation benches nearer, oblivious of the nerve-shattering sound the wood made on the marble floor. He moved the bench close to Giuliano's tomb and sat on it, his back to the rest of the church. "Many, very many years ago, I watched a cruel . . . amusement. Three people I loved with my life were torn apart. There was no way I could save them or stop their deaths. They died utterly and hideously. I watched them die." He kept his eyes on Laurenzo's drawn face so that he would not think again of the Roman Circus, and would not see it, hear it—and worse, smell it, as he had in his mind so many times in the intervening centuries. There had been worse in those intervening centuries, but he chose not to mention any of that.

"Were they your family?" Laurenzo asked compassionately.

"They were my blood."

"Ah." Laurenzo leaned against his brother's tomb again. He reached up to catch Demetrice's fingers in his own, murmuring, "Mio tesoro." Then he turned back to Ragoczy. "How long ago was it?"

Ragoczy bit back his answer, and said, truthfully, "Less than half my lifetime ago. The memory is vivid still." He went on in a different voice, "I vowed after that I would never again care so deeply for anyone. I haven't always been able to do this, try as I might. The pain of loss is too great. But in time I changed. So I have had pleasures in abundance, but few joys. I have had study and learning, and travel. I have had things of beauty to treasure. And music, always music."

"But alone?" Laurenzo said, and needed no answer. "Your song—I remember. Mio caro stragnero, how sad that you are still a stranger." He tried to rise then, but his weakness prevented it.

Ragoczy was glad to have an end to this uncomfortable intimacy. He got to his feet, saying, "Demetrice, il Magnifico wants our assistance. You get on that side. Take him under the arm, as I do, and we'll help him to his feet. Laurenzo, if you will walk between us, I promise you won't fall. And all Fiorenza will be jealous of the favor you show us." Already he was on one knee beside Laurenzo, his hands in place. He waited while Demetrice readied herself.

"I hate this . . . this weakness," Laurenzo said with quiet venom.

Neither Ragoczy nor Demetrice was offended. "There are times, Magnifico. . . ." Ragoczy said as he nodded. In a sudden, upward pull Laurenzo was on his feet between his companions. "There are times when even the most despised things have value."

Laurenzo was leaning heavily on both of them as he marshaled his strength. After a short silence he asked slowly, "Can I bargain, Francesco? I know there is no hope for me, and little help, either. It's not the pain—your cordial still works well enough for that. But is there a way I can cheat my death, if only for a little while?"

"No one can cheat death forever," Ragoczy said in a strange voice, and gave an odd, bitter laugh. "But there are ways to borrow time, a little time. It cannot be long." He could not bring himself to say how very few weeks his friend had left.

"But there is a way to have a month, isn't there? Or a few days?" His desperation distorted his features.

"If there is anything that can be done, I will do it. Believe this." With a nod to Demetrice, they began to walk with Laurenzo to the door.

"I haven't crossed myself," Laurenzo said as they moved to the back of the church. "I must."

"Magnifico, God knows your condition," Ragoczy said almost angrily. "He knows, and if He is just, as your faith says He is, He will not mind if you don't acknowledge Him at the door."

Demetrice's manner was more calm. "Lauro, you praise charity and tolerance in others. Show the same to yourself."

Laurenzo allowed himself to be persuaded, saying ruefully, "I feel like an old man. My bones ache, my fingers are twisted, I totter along between you. I look on death, and fear possesses me, but there's also a sense of deep relief." He stared down at his hands, and then draped his arms across his friends' shoulders. "I used to have such beautiful hands. They made up for my face, almost. Now look at them. They're gnarled as trees. Well, God *will* teach me humility before my life is over, I suppose."

Ragoczy opened the door of San Lorenzo, and the cold wind poked icy fingers at them, making them shiver.

Through tightened teeth Laurenzo said, "Well, my good friends, you are more than I deserve. But what does that matter now? Come, take me across la piazza. I suppose I must deal with these Portuguese."

A LETTER AND bill from the Arte master to Francesco Ragoczy da San Germano:

Respected Signor Ragoczy, stragnero, the members of the several Arti who have worked on the construction and finishing of your palazzo in the street behind Santissima Annunziata have now completed your work to the letter of your instructions. There is included with this an accounting of charge incurred beyond the amount paid to us in advance.

Most of the work would have been done before now, but as I took the opportunity to inform you, three of the builders left before the work was done and are in fact no longer in Fiorenza, and this occasioned some delay.

We are grateful for the generous thanks you have bestowed upon us. It is not the custom here for men to give every Arte member five fiorini d'or for work, but, as you said, it was not our usual work, and the specifications were unusual. We are appreciative of your gifts.

Your houseman, Ruggiero, had been given the keys and bolts as you requested, and all is in readiness for your reception on Twelfth Night and your tribute to Medici.

If you question the total of the items in the account that comes with this, send word and I will be pleased to review the costs with you.

May the season of Christ's birth be a joyous one for you. It is a pleasure to have so distinguished a stragnero in Fiorenza.

For all the Arte members,
Justiniano Montegelato
In Fiorenza, December 29, 1491

CHAPTER 12

THE JUGGLERS HAD finished their performance and two acrobats were now walking on their hands the length of the loggia of Palazzo San Germano. One of them held blazing torches in his tightly clenched toes, the other balanced full cups of wine on the soles of his feet as he went. They were accompanied by three musicians, one playing drums and cymbals, one with a shepherd's bagpipe, and one plucking on a lute. Their tunes, though simple and purposefully loud, could not penetrate the noise of the gathering.

Since the loggia of Palazzo San Germano was in the Genovese tradition, it did not give ready access to the street, and on this frozen winter day Francesco Ragoczy's guests were glad of the privacy, for it meant extra warmth. Louvers covered the huge window, and they were closed against the snow-laden wind that raged in from the northeast.

The two rooms adjoining the loggia were also filled. In one of them a troupe of French actors performed farces for the guests and in the other great pots of wine were heated on a huge brazier. Amadeo, Ragoczy's cook, supervised this operation, adding a secret mixture of spices to each pot so that the heady smell was almost as intoxicating as the beverage itself.

Ragoczy sat with his honored guests at a long table set up on the broad landing of his grand staircase. He was dressed in a magnificent giornea of black velvet, with slashed sleeves edged in red satin exposing his shirt of shiny white silk. His high-standing collar was edged in red as well, and set off the foreign order of silver and rubies around his neck.

His Russian boots had jewel-inlaid heels that clicked when he walked.

Beside him at the table was Laurenzo de' Medici in a brocaded caftan of dark blue silk that had been sent to him by the sultan in Turkey, and under it he wore a lucco of gold satin. He wore no jewelry, and those who knew him thought he looked fatigued.

". . . but of course the poor foolish girl was a Siciliana, and did not perfectly understand what her master had said." Laurenzo smiled in anticipation of the joke as he leaned toward Marsilio Ficino and the alchemist Federigo Cossa. "So she served the soup in the *chamber pot*!" His laughter was almost as hearty as it had been a few years before, and the merriment around him masked his failing spirits. He reached for his silver cup, when Ragoczy stopped him.

"No, Magnifico. I have a better cup for you." He stood up and clapped his hands sharply, and in a moment Ruggiero seemed to materialize at his side. Ragoczy took a package from his houseman and turned back to Laurenzo. "Magnifico, it is the time for giving gifts, in remembrance of the gifts given to Christ. Other men, too, have given gifts at the Winter Solstice. The Romans made merry and complimented each other at the Saturnalia. In the north many peoples have long given the dark of the year over to festivals and pleasures. Far away in China, there are celebrations now to mark the coming of the sun. So it is fitting that though I am a stranger in Fiorenza, and though my people are not like yours, still your customs go well with mine, and it is a privilege to honor them." He had the attention of most of his guests by then, and he spoke with greater force. "But ceremony is an empty thing if it lacks sincerity. So it is doubly appropriate for me to entertain you now. Fiorenza has been a haven to me, and your affection as welcome to me as rain is to parched soil. On January first, five days ago, you entered your forty-fourth year. In recognition of that, and in honor of the forty-three years you have given to Fiorenza, I present you with the fruit of my Art." He gave the package to Laurenzo with the profound bow usually reserved for princes.

Brows raised questioningly, Laurenzo held the package for a moment. Then he tugged at the gold threads that bound it and pulled the wrapping away from an intricately carved box of inlaid wood and semiprecious stones. He hesitated, enjoying the splendid box.

"Open it," Ragoczy suggested.

"Here?" Laurenzo touched the side of the box where the de' Medici arms were set in jade and polished rubies. He pressed the scalloped shield and the lid moved back to reveal the contents.

There was an awed sigh as Laurenzo removed the cup from the box. It was supported on a base of silver and Fiorenzan gold that had been intricately formed to the letters LAUR MED around the jeweled column holding the cup itself. Redder than the Medici palle, this small bowl seemed to be made of one entire hollowed ruby. It glowed with inner fire, and no wine could match its depth. In silence Laurenzo held it up, turning it in the light, tears of pleasure in his large eyes. When he spoke at last, his voice was husky. "Caro stragnero, I have no words."

This broke the spell and there was applause from the other guests. It was a superb gesture, and they admired it as much as they appreciated the art.

Laurenzo stood suddenly, tipping over his chair as he rose. "Wine! Bring me the best that you have!"

Ruggiero withdrew quickly and Ragoczy said to his guest, "I have an old vintage from Burgundy. My servant is bringing it to you." He turned away slightly, and added, "I have another thing for you, Laurenzo. A thing you requested of me."

Immediately Laurenzo dropped his voice, whispering, "Is it . . . ?"

Ragoczy shrugged uncomfortably. "In this vial." He took it from his sleeve and slipped it into Laurenzo's hot, dry fingers.

"What does it give me?" He held Ragoczy's hand in a surprisingly strong grip.

"Not much, amico. Perhaps a month. The taste is wretched. Drink it with wine or almond milk." He pulled his hand away, and was pleased to see Ruggiero returning with the jug of wine. "Here, Magnifico," he said loudly, catching the attention of the crowd gathered in his loggia. He took the jug from Ruggiero and held it up for Laurenzo's approval. "From Burgundy, you see, from the estate of Saint-Germain."

Laurenzo laughed. "You have something in common with him, da San Germano."

"So it would seem," Ragoczy agreed enigmatically. "It was bottled in 1449, Magnifico, the year of your birth."

"We came in the same year, we will go out the same year." Laurenzo's wide, thin-tipped mouth twisted and he turned away from the guests, covering his sudden despair with an attempt to open the wine.

"Allow me, Magnifico," Ruggiero said, and took the bottle from Laurenzo. With a little knife he stripped out the wax from the mouth of the jar, and with the same little knife, drew out the cork, which he presented to Laurenzo.

"Useless. Let Ragoczy smell it." He handed the cork to his host, who sniffed it perfunctorily before setting it aside.

"Pour some for Laurenzo," he said, indicating the splendid cup.

"And you, mio caro stragnero. You must drink too."

Ragoczy made an odd, dismissing gesture. "I do not drink wine."

"But surely . . ." Laurenzo stopped, and there was something at the back of his eyes that grew bright with understanding. He held out the cup. "Well, whether you drink or not, I will, and gladly." As the fragrant Burgundy poured into the red jeweled cup, he said quietly to Ragoczy, "You don't eat either, do you?"

"Oh, I take nourishment when I need it, never fear," Ragoczy murmured, and bent to set Laurenzo's chair on its legs again. When he stood up again, Ruggiero had put the wine down. "There, Magnifico. A noble wine and a unique cup. A well-deserved tribute to the man who is the heart of Fiorenza."

The guests echoed this enthusiastically, some of the men shouting ribald comments, a few of the women complimenting him with eager smiles.

Laurenzo drank, then put the cup down, satisfaction and fever making his face glow. "No," he said simply, and so honestly that protestations were obviously not expected. "I have some ability as a poet, or so I tell myself, but it is not that which gives the city its life, it is the artists and musicians and teachers who are the true heart of Fiorenza."

Ragoczy gave Laurenzo a wry smile. "They would not be here if you and your father and his father were not willing to pay for them, Magnifico. If artists starve, they leave precious little to the world. If musicians sing their songs to the walls of a hovel, their music dies with their breath." He sat down and motioned for Laurenzo to do the same, saying in an undervoice, "Put a little of the oil in the vial into your wine. A drop or two is all that's needed. If you should run out of it, tell me, and I will give you more. But don't take too much. Whenever you drink, a few drops in the cup will suffice. It won't help you any more to take more than that, and too much of it will very possibly make you sick."

"As you wish," Laurenzo said softly, and brought the vial out of his square silk sleeve. As he dropped a little of the oil into his wine, he smiled appreciatively at Ragoczy's giornea. "You're much more Fiorenzan tonight than I am, Francesco. That velvet was made here, and the cut of your clothes would mark them Fiorenzan anywhere in Europe. The bodice looks molded to you, the mantle and slashings are perfect, and if the skirting is not double-pleated, you may have every stick of furniture I own."

"Well," Ragoczy said with the ghost of a smile, "you, being native, may dress however you wish. But I, being foreign, must not abuse your custom."

"Which is why you have such a preference for Spanish pourpoints, I suppose?" He took another sip of the wine. "This is very good. Little as I like the French, for all that I keep on good terms with them, I admit they have a way with wine. Is it wholly coincidental that the wine bears your name?"

"A conceit, Magnifico. Nothing more." Ragoczy was looking away across the loggia. Near the room where the players entertained were several members of the Confraternità del Bigallo, those influential men whose private charity was helping the poor, providing them with shelter and clothing. Near them were three foreign scholars, Dutch or English by the look of them. All but one of the Signoria were here. Many of the women were lavishly dressed, some in fur-trimmed dresses of velvet with brocaded gauntlets cut so that their fine lawn sleeves could puff through. Near the four officers of the Confraternità della Misericordia, Ragoczy saw Demetrice in earnest conversation with two instructors from l'Accademia. She was wearing the new gonella Ragoczy had given her, one in silk of the most verdant green. A new arrival caught her attention, and she went with a welcoming smile to greet Botticelli, who strolled up to her, still looking lanky in his unaccustomed finery.

"Francesco," Laurenzo said softly, and brought Ragoczy's attention back to the table where they sat. "You need have no fear of me."

"I don't know what you mean," he lied.

"I mean," Laurenzo said with deliberate patience, "that you can trust me. I will not betray you."

"Betray me?" Ragoczy searched for an excuse to leave the table and found none.

"Do you remember that day, last fall, when we came upon that ruin? The one where the old man offered to cut his throat for you?" Laurenzo was idly tracing designs on the white table covering with his forefinger.

"Yes," Ragoczy said through clenched teeth.

"Yes. Do you remember that I went inside the temple?" He didn't wait for a reply. "There were many strange things in the temple, Francesco. Among them a scroll, with writing in a foreign language."

"Was there?" Ragoczy could not ask Laurenzo to abandon his questions without drawing unwanted attention to them. "I didn't see it. What did it say?"

"I couldn't read it. But I did recognize the writing." He paused, then drank the last of his Burgundy, and reached for the jug to pour another cupful. "I'd seen it before."

"Indeed."

"On your arms, Francesco." He looked away, into the gorgeous throng of people. He was almost bored as he went on. "Pray don't embarrass both our intelligences by saying you don't know what I'm talking about. If you wish to keep silent, so be it. But . . ." Here he faltered, staring down into his wine. "The wine and the cup are one jewel. '*Stragnero della morte, stragnero dell'amor*'." he quoted to himself.

Ragoczy felt torn. "My silence," he said awkwardly, "is hard-learned, and there is good reason for it. Believe that. And believe that neither you nor your Fiorenza nor its people stand in any danger from me."

Laurenzo nodded heavily and drank more of the wine. "Sta ben'. I must be content with that." He waved to Botticelli, and motioned him to come to the table on the landing. "Sandro will like this. I thank you for it, Francesco. And for the other."

Sandro was just starting up the broad staircase when there was a commotion behind him and the thick louvers were forced open.

Startled silence fell on the people in the loggia as they turned toward the intruders and the sudden cold that raced through the room.

Ragoczy was already on his feet. "What is this?" he demanded.

In another moment the door, too, was broken open and a band of young men in ash-colored cassocks swarmed into the loggia. Three of them held up a banner proclaiming "*Nos Praedicamus Cristum Crucifxum.*"

"Savonarola!" Laurenzo shouted. "You're Savonarola's followers. What right do you have to come here?" As he stumbled to his feet he upset the red cup, and the Burgundy spread over the white linen tablecloth. "On whose order do you come here?"

"On the orders of the crucified Christ!" said the apparent leader, stepping forward and looking about him with scorn.

"It was Christ Who whipped the moneychangers from the temple, and it will be the spirit of Christ that drives the moneylenders from la Repubblica!" He raised his hand in a kind of Roman salute and the band of young men with him sent up an approving shout.

"Oh, God," Laurenzo muttered, and started around the table.

"No, Magnifico," Ragoczy stopped him. "You are my honored guest. It's for me to deal with this." He vaulted over the table and came lightly down the stairs. "Well, good citizens, what do you want of us? If you were intent on ruining our evening, you have succeeded. You have also ruined my brand-new door, not to mention the louvers. If you wish to pray, pray and be done with it. Otherwise, get out before I summon the Lanzi to deal with you." It was no idle threat. Fiorenza's mercenary troops were paid with Medici gold, and would defend Laurenzo without question.

"I am Mario Spinnati," the leader announced. "I am a follower of the prophet Girolamo Savonarola, who has seen the Wrath of God that is to come. You, with your vanities and your pleasures and your worldliness, will bring damnation upon us. The Sword of God's Vengeances is poised even now over our heads, and only repentance will save us." He opened his arms and set his jaw as if waiting for the nails. "Repent! Make God's suffering your own!"

Ragoczy sighed. "Get out, good citizens."

By now, all of the guests had assembled in the loggia, and two of the French actors had come in from their room, their powdered faces masking their very real fear.

Mario Spinnati shook his head, and he motioned to the other men with him. "We're prepared to deal with you," he said, an expression crossing his face that was unpleasantly eager. At his signal, the men in gray cassocks pulled their hands from the folds of their clothes. They held cudgels, scourges, and two had chains.

Ragoczy never moved, but there was a tension about him. "I must ask my guests," he said, his quiet voice carrying to every part of the room, "to leave, although the festival is not over. Ruggiero, go to the Lanzi immediately."

The men in cassocks were still crowding into the loggia, which was now quite cold. Ragoczy's elegant guests were alarmed now, and two or three of them cast about worriedly for an exit.

"Amici miei," Ragoczy said calmly, his eyes never leaving the hostile group in the doorway, "there are two halls on this floor. Use them." He pitched his voice a little louder as the first murmurs of panic ran through the guests. "Laurenzo, you know where my quarters are. Go there. One of the servants will see you safely out of here." Then, without waiting for comment or assistance, he walked directly up to Mario Spinnati. "You are a sacrilegious coward, to hide your viciousness behind the Cross." Very coolly he slapped the man in the gray cassock.

"*Blasphemy!*" Spinnati shouted, and flung himself at Ragoczy, confident that he could beat the smaller man to his knees.

He was mistaken. As he rushed on the foreigner, Ragoczy ducked under his arm, and rising behind him, grabbed his shoulder, and with a gentle twist threw his opponent to the floor.

"La vendetta d'Iddio!" Spinnati's followers shouted in a ragged cheer, and surged into the loggia, upsetting the long tables of food in their path. Shouts and cries went up from the guests as they bolted for the hallways.

Ragoczy heard his name behind him and turned to see Botticelli near him, his big hands fixed in the collar of one of the cassocked invaders. "Where shall I put him?" he shouted.

"Out!" Ragoczy answered, and jumped aside as one of the men in gray rushed at him, swinging a chain. Amazingly, Ragoczy reached for the chain and let it wrap around his arm. The fine velvet of his giornea was savagely ripped, and the silk camisa beneath it tore under the impact of the chain. But his hand never faltered and as the chain wound the last of its length to his shoulder, Ragoczy jerked sharply and pulled the man in gray off his feet. As he fell to the floor, Ragoczy bent and rolled him aside.

Even the French actors were fighting, but a few of them were taking a painful drubbing for their efforts. In the other doorway, Amadeo stood, his heavy ladles falling like hammers on the men who rushed at him. Tall and cadaverously thin, Amadeo resisted them like a supple pine tree withstanding the full force of a gale.

"Francesco!" The voice was Laurenzo's, and it came from the gallery above. Ragoczy turned just in time to avoid the lash of an iron-tipped scourge. He felt hands reach for him, and for a moment his arms were pinned to his side while the penitent's scourge raked his face.

Sandro was down on one knee, and three of the men in gray rushed on him, sticks upraised. There was blood in Sandro's red-blond curls, and he doubled over, trying to protect himself from the blows.

"Ah, Gran' Dio! for my knives!" Amadeo bellowed as his ladles were tugged from his hands. He brought up his arm to ward off the small whip that was snaking toward his head.

Three more strokes of the scourge had bloodied Ragoczy's face, and the fourth was about to land when his white-burning rage overcame him. In two quick movements he kicked backward and felt bones snap under the sharp blows. As the men in cassocks screamed, he pushed them away with an even jab with each arm. Then he turned to the cassocked man with the scourge. He jumped, and at the height of his jump, he lashed out with his legs, his booted heels crashing on the man's chest and shoulders. As he landed, Ragoczy wasted no time on his tormentor, but launched himself at the men around Botticelli. He kicked out at the back of the knees of the man nearest him, and as he fell, Ragoczy pushed him into his closest fellow penitent. The two went down, arms and legs thrashing.

"Sandro! Roll away!" Ragoczy shouted the words even as he reached for the third man in gray, and grabbed the man's wrist, pulling it high behind him before rapping him smartly in the small of his back.

He had disabled two more of the gray-robed fanatics when a man on horseback forced his mount through the door and dropped the handle of his lance on the floor with a re-sounding crack. When there was not immediate silence, he dropped the lance handle again.

"Stop at once!"

The frantic battle slowed, then straggled into silence. Men broke apart, almost like guilty lovers. There was blood on the new-laid marble and it ran with the upset food.

"Who is master here?" the lancer asked, his horse advancing farther into the loggia.

Ragoczy, his face torn, his clothes ruined, staggered forward. "I am," he said through bruised lips.

"What happened?" the lancer demanded. Beyond the door, a dozen more mounted, armed and armored men waited.

"We were celebrating Twelfth Night," Ragoczy said wearily. "These . . . these citizens"—he made the word a profanity—"not content to honor the laws of their city, invaded my palazzo, threatened and beat my guests . . ." He had to stop a moment as he looked around the wreck of his loggia. "They were," he said ironically, "quite thorough."

But the lancer was incredulous. "These good penitents? They are godly men, Signor."

"So were the Knights Templar." Ragoczy was too disheartened to argue. "Take a look, good sir. Do you see anything here that indicates we *invited* this chaos?"

In the door to the actors' room, three of the Frenchmen held their bruised bodies and moaned.

"If you made a mockery of them—" the lancer began somewhat uncertainly, but was interrupted by a high, slightly nasal voice from the gallery.

"Capitano Amara," Laurenzo said, "believe what Ragoczy tells you."

Ragoczy looked up and saw his friend's drawn, waxen face peer over the gallery railing. "You see, caro stragnero, I would not leave." He almost laughed, but turned again to Capitano Amara. "If you like, I will verify his complaint."

But Capitano Amara hurriedly apologized. "No, Magnifico. I can see how it was. They were maddened by their fervor and could not resist attacking the festival here."

"Something like that," Ragoczy agreed dryly as he helped Botticelli to his feet. "Are you all right, Sandro?"

The big man winced. "I think so. They didn't harm my hands or my eyes. I'll recover."

Laurenzo was coming down the broad staircase now, and Ragoczy saw that he still held the ruby cup. "Capitano," he said silkily, "this was not a matter of religious inspiration, it was an act of wanton vandalism. Any rogue may call himself a holy man, but the damage he does reveals his true nature, does it not?"

Mario Spinnati, nursing a broken collarbone, wanted to

object, but saw the martial light in Magnifico's eyes, and thought better of it. God did not require him to pursue this matter, and to push the fight further would be prideful.

A broken lyra de braccia leaned crazily against the wall. Ragoczy picked it up and its last intact string snapped, and the sound was so poignant that without thinking, Ragoczy hugged the elaborate little viol to his chest.

"Ah, no, Francesco," Laurenzo said as he came up to him. He took Ragoczy's free hand in his, making sure that Capitano Amara saw this gesture. "I will send my servants to clean up this unpardonable shambles."

"It's not necessary," Ragoczy said quietly. He felt a certain disgust with himself for the pleasure he had taken in his rage. He thought he had put that behind him almost a thousand years ago.

"What is it, Francesco?" Laurenzo said, alarm in his voice.

"Nothing, Magnifico; nothing." He looked up at Capitano Amara. "I trust you will get these maniacs out of my home? Immediately?" He sighed, putting one arm across Laurenzo's back. "Come, let me take you to my library. I must bathe, but I will join you there directly." He took a last look at the wreckage and the men in gray cassocks. He nodded to Botticelli. "Come, Sandro. You too. Thank God they didn't get to my inner rooms." He was thinking about the rooms hidden behind the elaborately carved panels on the landing, but Laurenzo saw it another way.

"Your library! At least it's safe." Now that excitement no longer possessed him, he was trembling, and it was not until much later that night that he realized he had taken comfort and support from Francesco's bloody arm across his back.

TEXT OF A letter from Agnolo Poliziano to the medical school at Padova:

> To the esteemed medical faculty of the Accademia Medica in Padova, the Fiorenzeno Agnolo Poliziano sends his respectful request for instruction on a matter in which they are known to be expert.
>
> Good physicians, I have been told that you are more skilled than all physicians from ancient time until the present, and that your knowledge of the illness of mankind is so vast that the disease you have not seen is a mere figment of imagination.
>
> So, good physicians, I humbly desire, as a mere sufferer, that you give me the advantage of your skills and all-encompassing knowledge.
>
> I have a friend—and though you mayn't believe it, this is true, and it is for this friend and not myself that I seek your help—who, for the last year or so has been in failing health. I will describe the course of the illness to you, and from your varied experience you will surely know what ails him and what must be done to save him.
>
> This friend, then, has long been plagued with gout. But until some time rather more than a year ago, he had only few problems, and they were such that they passed quickly. This man is an active man, of intellect and energy. He does not imagine pain where it does not exist. Remembering that, consider this: he has had swelling of his joints, in his hands, elbows and knees most especially. I have not seen him bootless, so I can tell you nothing of his feet. When this swelling occurs, it is painful, and is often accompanied by periods of

great weakness, which have grown worse in the last six months. He has had times when his weakness was such that he could not stand upright or hold a quill. Occasionally now he says he has great knots in his stomach and his bowel, and the agony which distorts his features at such times would touch even your callous hearts. Of late, he has had bruises on his skin and a kind of fever that is sufficient only to dry his body and give it heat. His strength is failing him, and I cannot tell him that I fear for his life, but, good physicians, I do.

Tell me, what is it that has so terribly attacked my friend? What robs him of his strength? What disease or devil of curse has done this? And what will defeat it? What process of your skill will it yield to? If you can tell me this, do so as quickly as you can get a messenger to Fiorenza. Even now I fear that there is too little time.

Do not, I beg you, debate among yourselves, or hold learned discussions on the possible outcome of this disease, or do not decide on some unorthodox way to treat him on the grounds that the new cure is more exciting than the old. If there is medicine, send it. If a surgeon must be sent, send him. If only the Egyptians have skill in this matter, find an Egyptian. But do it quickly. If you spend too long congratulating one another on your perception and knowledge, your expertise will benefit a corpse. If the medical arts know nothing of this disease, do not flock to Fiorenza in the hope of observing yet another death from causes unknown. I would leave my friend some little dignity, and to have physicians hovering about like ravens would rob him of his courage as well as making a mockery of his death.

Respond as soon as may be, good physicians. The time is short. It is already the Feast of the Purification. I want an answer by Easter.

Agnolo Poliziano

In Fiorenza, February 2, 1492

CHAPTER 13

THE LOUVERS HAD been replaced and the marble of the loggia was scrubbed clean. It was more than six weeks since the followers of Savonarola had made havoc of Francesco Ragoczy's Twelfth Night festival. The rooms which flanked the loggia were in good order, one being devoted to music, the other to the reception of guests.

The night was was not too far advanced, but already most of the city was asleep. At San Marco, the Domenicani had finished their chanting, but the Servanti at Santissima Annunziata had one hour to sing yet before their devotional day was through.

Ragoczy sat in his chamber that overlooked the galleried courtyard of his palazzo. He stared out into the night, but apparently did not see the gentle snow that drifted on the north wind. On his lap was an open book, a bound manuscript of poetry written in a singularly forceful hand. With the poetry was commentary in the same hand, given reluctantly. "For," Laurenzo had written some years before, "if the poems have merit, there is no need for this explanation, and if they have not, my additions will not make them any better."

After some little time he closed the book and rubbed at his eyes. The gouges from the penitent's scourge had disappeared from his face, but the memory was fresh enough to give him a momentary twinge. He rose and crossed the room and stood looking out, not into the snow, but into the years that eddied past his eyes thicker than the snowflakes. His face, if anyone had seen it then, was touched with age, making his skin transparent and somehow brittle. He had no more wrinkles than usual, but there was a shadow on him and it turned his face to a skull.

He heard the door behind him open and Ruggiero's familiar footsteps. Without turning, Ragoczy said, "What good am I, old friend? I have one . . . endowment . . . and where I wish most to bestow it, I cannot. Mortality defeats me." The words were spoken in a tongue unknown to any of the scholars of Fiorenza.

Ruggiero answered in the same language, but from the hesitance and cumbersome phrasing, it was plain that he did not speak it natively, as did his master. "You've watched many others die, You-Who-Frees. Why does it pain you so with Medici?"

"I don't know." He was still. "I've seen blood like his before, many times. But often the sufferers were young, and it was unkind to wish them more pain. But Laurenzo isn't young. And there is so much life in him. All I can give him is two months, at the most. I've had something more than three thousand years, and I cannot lend him thirty of them, or three." He put his hand to his eyes. "You think I ought to leave Fiorenza, don't you? Perhaps you're right. Gian-Carlo keeps urging me back to Venezia. But I can't go yet, Ruggiero. I gave my word. It may be foolish of me, but I still honor it."

"I have never found it foolish, master," Ruggiero had reverted to Latin. He came a little farther into the room. "Master, there is a woman to see you."

"A woman? Demetrice? Why didn't you say so?" He turned around and once again spoke in Tuscan dialect.

"No, master, it is not Demetrice. It is Filipepi's cousin, Estasia." His lined face was carefully blank.

"What in the name of all long-forgotten gods does she want?" The words were angry, but his face was sad. He sank his small hands in the loose curls of his dark hair. "What did you tell her?"

"I told her you were busy and it might not be possible for you to interrupt your work." As he spoke, he picked up Laurenzo's book of commentary. "I will say that, if you wish."

"Is she alone?" Ragoczy asked after a moment. He fingered the silver-and-ruby chain around his neck.

"Yes, she came alone. On foot."

"How like her." He condemned her even as he worried. So Estasia's search for sensation had gone to a point where she now openly courted danger. The streets of Fiorenza were not safe after dark for men; for women the risks were much greater. "And I can't send her home without escort. Very clever."

"I can show her to a guest room and put one of the housemaids to sleep there with her." Ruggiero was as conscious of the proprieties as Ragoczy.

"What good will that do? She would only have to say that I had lain with her first, and then summoned the housemaid. Well, at least I don't keep slaves, so my staff can all give testimony in open court. Where is she now?"

"I took her to the small chamber off the inner court. The

one with the two Chinese jade lions in it. I've asked Amadeo to serve her some refreshments. He's been complaining that his work isn't appreciated, so he can apply his skill to Donna Estasia's palate. He was making batter bread in a skillet when I left. Apparently he plans to roll the breads around soft cheeses and sweet boiled fruits." Ruggiero thought a moment. "He is inventive. And he likes cooking."

"Just as well." Ragoczy paced the length of the room. "I'd better see her. She's been . . . unpredictable recently."

Ruggiero preserved his calm. "I gather she is a trying woman. Do you want me to lead you down?"

Ragoczy laughed once. "I don't need a bodyguard, old friend. You say she is in the room with the jade lions. Tell her I will join her directly."

With a slight bow Ruggiero withdrew.

When Ragoczy emerged from his chamber some time later, he wore a red Persian robe that was so thickly embroidered in black that the red showed through like embers in a dying fire. He wore Hungarian heeled boots of black tooled leather and a house gown under the robe of Chinese silk brocade in a black so dense that it seemed a living shadow. He moved with a liquid grace, that made the heavy robe flow behind him like wings. On his breast there hung a polished ruby that shone lambent on the silk.

Estasia had finished the stuffed batter breads Amadeo had made for her, and now she reclined on a low divan of rosewood upholstered in Indian damask. She had opened her long cloak to reveal a camora of sheerest linen. As she heard the sound of the door, she turned and her eyes widened as she saw her host. "Francesco," she breathed, half in fear and half in need.

His manner was disturbingly remote. "I am honored to

see you, Donna Estasia. But do you think it was wise to come here, for the night is cold and the streets are perilous."

She started up, but hesitated. "But I hadn't seen you in . . . a while."

"You told me to leave." He moved across the room but not toward her and she realized how forbidding he could be.

"But you knew I didn't mean it. Not forever, Francesco. I thought you'd be back. Because you need me."

"You are mistaken, diletto." He sat on a strangely carved chair that had once been the chair of a Byzantine emperor.

Flushing, she snapped, "I am not. I know you have to have blood." Her defiance faded.

"Yes. But it needn't be yours." He waited while she tried to gather her thoughts. "Did you come here to see whether or not I am wasting away?"

She shot him a look of hot anger, then smiled with sudden cunning. "No. I came to see your palazzo, Francesco. I have heard so much about it that I could no longer wait for an invitation from you."

He was politely incredulous. "At ten in the night?"

Her titter was the only thing that kept her from screaming in rage. "You always said I should see it. And now that I am here, you want to put me off. I can't come in the day, you know that. I must mind my cousin's house. I wasn't tired and I know you don't sleep much. I was sure you'd welcome me." She was on her feet now, and she came toward him with long, sensuous steps. "Oh, Francesco, I'm sorry for what I said, for the way I behaved. You don't know how much I've missed you. At night I lie in bed and wish for the touch of your lips."

Ragoczy had not moved, and there was such indifference in his expression that Estasia found her desire for him increasing. "At night, don't you want to be with me? I think of you, Francesco. I think of the way your hands arouse me. In my thoughts, you capture me and bind me, all open, so that nothing in me is hidden from you. And then you possess me, assaulting me with your flesh. With *all* your flesh. No matter how I twist in my bonds, I cannot escape you. You overwhelm me, until what I am is only what you will me to be. I succumb to you, I am lifted out of myself." She was next to him now and she pressed the curve of her hip against his shoulder. "Don't you want me, Francesco? Even a little bit?"

Bitterly he realized that part of him did indeed want her, as much to ward off his sorrow as to satisfy his hunger. He rose quickly. "You want to see the palazzo? Come with me." His words were brusque as he swept from the room, not waiting to see if she followed him.

The tour was thorough and swift. He led the way down halls and through rooms, his long stride never slackening. In vain Estasia tried to keep him still, to linger in his music room with his lutes and viols, to pause in his library and hear descriptions of the books and the exotic foreign manuscripts, to tarry in the room with his elaborate bath. He gave short, curt answers to her questions and refused to listen to her rushed enthusiasm. Finally, when they had come once more to the foot of his grand staircase, she grabbed at his arm.

"Francesco, you must stop."

"Very well." He halted and turned to look at her. "I hope that you liked my palazzo, Donna."

Her hazel eyes were bright with tears of chagrin and annoyance. "Yes, I did, no thanks to your manner. Francesco, I will *not* be treated like some disgraceful, cast-off woman who must be tolerated because of the hold her knowledge gives her."

Ragoczy's smile was unpleasantly ironic. "You must forgive me. I thought from our last encounter that's what you were. I wonder how I can have been so strangely deceived?"

"*Stop it!*" She felt ready to drum her heels on the floor. "All right. I was mistaken. I should never have made threats to you. I'm sorry I did." Suddenly her voice changed, and she said meltingly, "If you want me to leave, I'll leave. It's the price I must pay for my foolishness. But, oh, Francesco, if I had it to do again, I would never let you go. When Paolo comes, he only stuffs himself into me, bucks a few times and it's over. He doesn't touch me, or caress me, or set me afire with his lips. And, Francesco, *I'm so lonely.*"

Against all his better judgment, he felt himself weaken to that last miserable cry. Reluctantly he touched her shoulder, "My poor Estasia, we're all lonely."

Her face was as frightened as a child's in pain. "But I don't want to be. I can't bear it. *Francesco!*" She flung herself against his chest sobbing hysterically.

And after a while, the night being cold and empty, he embraced her.

T EXT OF A letter from Francesco Ragoczy da San Germano to Gian-Carlo Casimir di Alerico Circando:

To Gian-Carlo in Venezia, Ragoczy in Fiorenza sends greetings.

I had your letter of December 10 only a week ago. The courier was set upon by brigands and has just recently recovered from the beating he was given so that he could continue on to Fiorenza. I am sending this with a knight in the train of the Papal legation to Aus-

tria, which will be stopping in Venezia soon. That's by Olivia's arrangements.

Tomorrow I am going to the Medici villa at Careggi. Laurenzo has been taken there so that he will recover more quickly in serene surroundings, or that is the ridiculous explanation for the move. When Laurenzo returns to Fiorenza, it will be on his bier. Why must they make this terrible pretense? They are robbing him of his last days in triviality, thinking that it will spare him anguish. If they would but read his poetry, or look into his eyes, they would not hurt him this way. Last week they took his giraffe from the city menagerie out to his villa, so that the animal would cheer him. But Laurenzo is not some child to be diverted with live toys.

In his absence, of course, that Domenicano Prior Savonarola has been declaring that this means the end of Laurenzo. And of course he's right. But la Signoria and the Medici followers all deny it, which is foolish. For now, when Laurenzo dies, Savonarola will sieze upon his death as proof of his prophetical powers, and the Medici court will be jeered by the monk's converts.

Enough of this. It's futile. This brings my instructions to you regarding my villa in that city. First, do not close it. Continue as you have done so well already. This authorizes you to produce another cask of gold and to present it to il Doge with my compliments. Also, I have found a new source of paper, one Helmut Sternhaus in Liege. Order as much as the old Dogaressa wants for her press, and keep her supplied within reason. Use your good sense as a guide. Also, for yourself, purchase and outfit two ships. With your

*experience on my behalf and your own skill, you
should turn them to good advantage.*

*Please commission three murals for the main room
of the villa, one that is allegorical, showing the con-
trast of mortality and immortality. I leave it to you to
choose the artist, but let it be someone with skill and
passion. You may pay whatever is reasonable for the
work. Look for me to return sometime next year. I have
given Laurenzo my Word that I will stay in Fiorenza
one year and one day after his death. If il Doge wants
news of me, tell him that I am still practicing my Art,
and that my especial knowledge is his to command—
that, in case he wants more gold.*

*I thank you for your care of my affairs and your de-
votion. And since on this day Fiorenza is celebrating
the Feast of the Archangel Gabriel, what can I do but
hope that he bring you good fortune and extend his
protection to you.*

Ragoczy da San Germano

In Fiorenza, March 24, 1492
his seal; the eclipse

CHAPTER 14

BEFORE HIS LATHERED, panting horse had come to a full
stop, Agnolo Poliziano was out of the saddle, shouting for a
groom as he ran down the path of Laurenzo's villa at
Careggi. He pounded on the door and cursed at each blow.

"You took enough time, Ragoczy," he said bitterly to the

man who opened the door for him. "Where's Laurenzo? I came as soon as Mass was over!" His small, discontented mouth was more pursed than usual.

"In his bedchamber," Ragoczy said and put a restraining hand on Poliziano's shoulder. "Do not distress him. He has too little time for that."

"Distress him?" Poliziano shrugged Ragoczy's hand away. "Who is here?"

"Fra Mariano is here. He is reading the Gospels to Laurenzo. I think Savonarola is about to leave."

"Savonarola? What's that canting hypocrite doing here?" Poliziano was about to plunge down the hallway, but this news brought him up short.

"Laurenzo sent for him. I think he wants to be sure Fiorenza is safe." Ragoczy had closed the door and now stood leaning against it. "Wait a moment and you need not encounter the Domenicano."

Poliziano considered this, then asked with some difficulty, "Has he Confessed?"

"Yes. And was absolved. And received Extreme Unction." There was strain in Ragoczy's eyes.

"From Savonarola?" was Poliziano's quick demand.

"No. Not from Savonarola."

"It doesn't seem possible," Poliziano said suddenly. "Extreme Unction. He's really dying. Dying?" He looked toward Ragoczy, becoming frightened. "He's forty-three years old. He can't die."

Ragoczy was spared an answer to this as Laurenzo's voice, a thin, reedy travesty of itself, called out, "Is that you, Agnolo?"

Poliziano's eyes flew to Ragoczy's and he stood as if turned to stone. "Laurenzo?" he whispered to the dark-clad foreigner.

"Yes." The word was hard to say. "I'll lead you in to him." As he spoke, he came up to Poliziano and laced his arm through the other's. "Be calm if you can, Poliziano. For his sake, be calm."

"What do you think I am; an inconsiderate fool?" Poliziano asked gruffly as they reached the door of Laurenzo's bedchamber.

That was, in fact, exactly what Ragoczy thought he was, but he said, "No, but you haven't seen Laurenzo for several days and he's much changed. It would distress him if he knew how much."

The door opened from within and a small man in the black habit and white cassock of the Domenicani stepped out. But before he closed the door, he turned back, saying, "If it had been for me to give you Absolution and Extreme Unction, Medici, I would have refused it until you had given up your wealth, your sins and your power. But what's been done is done. And God will judge you with the whole might of His Power. I take comfort in remembering that the hottest fires in Hell burn for traitors."

Agnolo Poliziano had already bunched his fists and was about to hurl both blows and insults at Savonarola when he felt Ragoczy's small hands on his arms and the soft, slightly accented voice say very quietly, "I share your impulses, Poliziano, but it would not be kind to Laurenzo."

"No," Poliziano admitted, and opened his hands again. "But it galls me, Ragoczy. One day, if God is truly just, I will see that monk flayed."

Apparently Savonarola overheard this, for he turned and his bright green eyes glared at Poliziano. "Another worshiper of the Antichrist," he said measuringly. "Think of the Wrath of God, sinner, and tremble." With a deliberate force, he pulled the door closed behind him and marched away toward the front of the villa, one of his pitifully narrow shoulders hitched higher than the other. He did not look back.

Ragoczy paused a moment and then opened the bed-chamber door, standing aside so that Poliziano could enter ahead of him. "Another friend, Magnifico," he said softly.

The hangings around Laurenzo's bed had been pulled back, and Laurenzo, wearing a thin lucco, was propped up by pillows. He was painfully thin and his skin stretched over his bones with dreadful tightness. There was two days' stubble on his face. His wide mouth gaped in an agonized, happy smile and he tried to raise an arm in greeting. There was a smell about him, sweet and rotten, like fruit that was over-ripe.

Poliziano clapped his hands to his eyes and gave one strangled sob. He moved drunkenly toward the bed and fell to his knees, his head buried in the pillows that raised Laurenzo.

"No, no, Agnolo, bellissimo," Laurenzo said in his ruined voice. "No, don't weep." With considerable effort he put his hands on Poliziano's shoulders, trying feebly to lift him. "Agnolo, you must not. It's too hard for me if you do."

From his place by the door, Ragoczy turned his eyes to Marsilio Ficino, despair in them. Ficino nodded helplessly, moving away from the foot of the bed. As he came to the door he whispered to Ragoczy, "I must leave. Laurenzo told me to escort Savonarola back to Fiorenza. I'll be back as soon as possible."

The Agostiniano Fra Mariano looked up from the Gospels he held open on his lap, and for a moment the gentle murmur of his voice stopped.

"Yes, Brother, I'm going," Ficino said shortly, and let himself out of the room. The door closed with a hollow sound.

At last Poliziano raised his head and turned his grief-reddened eyes to Laurenzo. "Why did you let him say that?" he demanded incomprehensibly.

But years of friendship with Poliziano had taught Laurenzo understanding. He answered, "What are his denunciations to me now? If Fiorenza is safe, then his gestures cannot hurt me. Agnolo, he has hated me so long, you mustn't begrudge him his moment of venom." He had sunk back on the pillows; even those few words exhausted him.

Ragoczy crossed the room silently and took up Ficino's place at the foot of the bed.

"But damnation, he as much as cursed you!" Poliziano had got to his feet and there was a militant glare in his eyes. "Let him say one word about this, *one word*, and I'll have him hanged from the clock tower."

Fra Mariano got to his feet. In a quiet, stern voice he said, "Poliziano, if you have no respect, have courtesy enough to be silent for those who do." When Poliziano had turned abashed eyes on him, he nodded once, and resumed his seat.

"But, Laurenzo," Poliziano said after a moment, keeping his voice as low as his emotion would allow, "I know the man. I tell you, it will be all over Fiorenza in two days that he refused you absolution, unless you let me throttle him now."

Laurenzo seemed not to hear, but in a moment he took a slightly deeper breath. "It doesn't matter, Agnolo. Truly, it doesn't matter. If Savonarola was right, I will dine tonight in hell on brimstone. And unless Satan restores my sense of smell, it will make little difference to me." His laugh grated once, then stopped as his body contorted with pain. He breathed deeply, trying to hold the pain at bay.

In the far corner, two physicians exchanged worried glances, and debated pulverizing more precious stones to feed il Magnifico. Laurenzo's own physician, Ser Piero Leoni, turned away, utter despair in his face. He crossed himself and began softly to pray.

When he could speak again, Laurenzo went on, more weakly, "If, on the other hand, God is just, and . . ." He took his lower lip between his teeth for a moment. ". . . and has read my heart, then perhaps . . . He will send me to Purgatory. Until my errors and sins and evils are burned away. . . . Does Christ open His arms in anguish or compassion? Laurenzo the Banker or Laurenzo the Poet. Which one is worthy? And of what?" He caught sight of Ragoczy at the foot of the bed. "Mio caro stragnero."

"Magnifico." He was mourning already, and the word was thick with the tears he could not shed.

"Come closer. It's too dark to see you well." He waited until Ragoczy stood near his head. "If you were God, Francesco, what would you do with me?" His voice was only a thread now and he groped for his silver crucifix.

"I would love you, Magnifico."

Poliziano turned suddenly and flung out of the room. The door slammed and the room was silent.

Laurenzo held the crucifix to his lips, and as Fra Mariano once again resumed his reading, Laurenzo murmured the familiar verses of the Passion with him, occasionally breaking off as his little remaining strength waned. It was not long before the crucifix fell from his hand and the silence in the bedchamber stopped even the sacred words of Fra Mariano. Then Laurenzo groped slowly, achingly for his crucifix.

Ragoczy dropped swiftly to his knee beside the bed and carefully held the crucifix for him.

"Grazie, Francesco," he breathed, and put one hand over Ragoczy's.

For some time there was only that pressure, feather-faint,

and the almost imperceptible rise of his chest that told Ragoczy that Laurenzo de' Medici had not yet died.

A bell sounded from the monastery at the crest of the hill, a call to Vespers and the special services of a Passion Sunday. No one in the bedchamber gave any indication of hearing it.

Under his fingers, Ragoczy felt a last flutter of breath that became a faltering sigh, and the lean, swollen hand over his was limp. Ragoczy pulled the crucifix away and rose to his feet. As he kissed the crucifix, Fra Mariano stopped reading for the last time.

"Should we get a mirror?" one of the physicians asked in a frightened undervoice.

"No." Ragoczy took Laurenzo's hands, folded them over his breast and returned the crucifix to him. Mercifully Laurenzo's long-lidded eyes were closed, for Ragoczy knew that he could not bear to see them glassily flat, untenanted. As the others in the room crossed themselves, he copied the gesture automatically, and then, as Fra Mariano began his prayers for the dead, Ragoczy bent and kissed his friend for the last time before leaving the bedchamber, the hall, the villa at Careggi.

The twilight bloomed around him, new stars littered the sky and a soft breeze redolent with flowers and the freshness of spring carried away the cloying, fatal sweetness. Ragoczy stood by the fountain while his horse was brought to him. The opulent beauty of the season was arid and desolate to him, the laughter of the fountain a cruel mockery.

When the groom brought his horse he swung into the saddle without a word, spurring the gray to a gallop before he was out of the villa's court. He rode recklessly, forcing his stallion to greater speed as the night deepened.

He was halfway to Fiorenza when he heard the first grieving note as the funeral bell at Sacro Infante began to toll.

Text of a letter from Donna Demetrice Clarrissa Renata di Benedetto Volandrai to her younger brother, Febo Janario Anastasio di Benedetto Volandrai, at the estate of Landgraf Alberich Dieter Fritz Grossehoff near Wien:

To her brother Febo in this time of sorrow, his sister Demetrice sends her blessings and sympathy.

You have, by now, heard that our beloved kinsman Laurenzo di Piero de' Medici died on April 8. He had been ill for some time, and though it is hard to lose him, we must thank God that he has been spared further suffering. And, Febo, he did suffer. We all hoped for a miracle, prayed for it, but there was none. His physician was so overcome that he has thrown himself down a well. The Church has refused him Christian burial for this act, but Ser Piero Leoni deserves better.

Laurenzo was brought to San Marco to lie in state before being buried in his own Chiesa di San Lorenzo. It was strange to see him there, not for the death, but because of the animosity that has long existed between the prior Savonarola and Laurenzo. Yet that is where he was taken, his catafalque draped in red and gold brocade, his Last Attendants in white. His funeral and monument were very simple, for no one knows how to honor him. The whole city is in mourning still, every one in black or red.

Yet I can't believe he's really dead. I have grown so used to him, to his vitality, that Fiorenza still seems full of him. Everywhere I turn I see him—in the sculpture and frescoes that make the city beautiful, in the widened streets and new buildings. I am still working on his library, and I find I must catch myself often, for

I will read a manuscript and will find a passage that he would like for its beauty or its learning, and without thinking, I will want to call out to him.

The Saints in Heaven be thanked for Francesco Ragoczy! Without him I could not endure my life. He has been much affected by Laurenzo's death, and I have heard, but not from him, that he was there with Laurenzo at the end. He has made no public show of grief except to dress in black—which is no show at all, for he has always done so. He does not weep and when I have thought I would be overcome with mourning, he has given me courage. But I think he is more afflicted than even I am, for his suffering is silent, as if to speak it would be more than he could stand.

I am now a resident of Palazzo San Germano, Ragoczy's home. I serve in capacity as housekeeper, but his houseman Ruggiero does most of the work as well as managing the staff. Ragoczy has no slaves, but hires all his servants, which is an added expense, though he insists that his household be run on that basis. Apparently he has tremendous wealth, for the palazzo is amazingly rich, and he was able to have it built in little more than a year.

Febo, my dear brother, I have yet to make arrangements for your education. I realize Laurenzo had promised that he would provide you the funds, but Laurenzo is dead, and from the rumors I hear, his bank has suffered unfortunate losses. I have decided to ask Ragoczy if we can make some adjustments in what I earn so that you will indeed be able to go to Paris at the end of the summer. But this may not be possible, for I have no demands on Ragoczy. You may rest assured that I will not barter with my body. If he takes me as his leman, it will be for devotion, not for payment. When I know more, I will write to you again. I am sending this with the Fiorenzan merchant Arrigo Niceli Perrigolo, who is traveling beyond Wien into Poland.

Pray for the soul of our good, generous kinsman, Febo. Without him, you and I would be beggars today. If that thought will bring him one step nearer the Mercy Seat, I will sing it every hour of the day.

Meanwhile, do not despair. You will have word from me before the summer, I promise, and if the thing can be done, I will see that you have money for your studies in Paris. You are too great a scholar to be forbidden that opportunity. I will do my utmost for you, the Saints be my witnesses.

As always, this brings the affections and duties of your sister,

Demetrice Volandrai

In Fiorenza, April 29, 1492

PART TWO

Francesco Ragoczy da San Germano

> *Io son stragnero*
> *per sempe ed ancor';*
> *Stragnero della morte,*
> *stragnero dell' amor'.*
>
> I am a stranger
> always and ever;
> Stranger to death,
> stranger to love.
>
> —FRANCESCO RAGOCZY

TEXT OF A letter from Pietro Delfino, the Superior-Generale of the Camaldolese monks of Santa Maria degli Angioli in Fiorenza, to His Holiness, Innocento VIII, in Roma:

> With deepest humility and the most profound reverence the Superior-Generale of Santa Maria degli Angioli sues for the gracious attention of the Pope, His Holiness, Innocento VIII, Heir to San Pietro, Vicar of Christ on Earth.
>
> I most piously beg to bring to Your Holiness's attention a situation which has arisen in this Tuscan city of Fiorenza. While it is true in the past that Papal ire has been directed at this city surely it was out of worldly malice and not holy charity that your predecessor used us so harshly. We have always been sincerely devoted to the True Faith, and mere political concerns are of little importance to sincere Christians, or to such strict monks as we of the Camaldolese Order.
>
> It ill becomes a monk to speak against any other man or woman in Orders, and I have searched my soul for sin and error most rigorously, and I beseech Your Holiness to vent the whole weight of Papal wrath upon me if I do this for any reason but the purity of belief and the Glory of God.
>
> Your Holiness, there is a prior in Fiorenza, a member of the distinguished Brothers of San Domenico. He is a preacher, and is gathering a very large num-

ber of converts around him. He has taken credit for the great misfortune suffered recently by this city, the death of Laurenzo de' Medici, who, though a worldly man and surely stuffed with sin, at least had the virtue of loving his city and defending it. This prior, then, has taken credit for Laurenzo's death, not as a murderer, but from having knowledge of that event given directly to him by God. It shames me to tell Your Holiness that there are many sufficiently blind and misled who believe him, and who are struck dumb with terror at his ravings.

This is not Christianity, this is not the Way of Christ. Your Holiness, Savonarola is sent to test us, to see if indeed we are weak and faithless enough to be deceived. Though many people wander in error from the Light of the Lord, some have courage to resist the temptations of this godless man.

Before Fiorenza is lost to the pagan worship of false prophets, before those souls for whom we pray always have forsaken the salvation which the Son of God purchased so dearly for them, Good Holy Father, intervene here and cast that man from the bosom of the Church, for surely there we nurture a viper who could poison us all. Put him to the test before the Office for the Congregation of the Faith, and see what your good Inquisitors might do. They are his fellow Domenicani. If he is in the right, they will discover it. If he is not, then the secular arm must enforce the penalty for blasphemy, for to speak as if from the Mouth of God and to tell lies is the greatest blasphemy known.

Your Holiness, my good Brothers have heard of your recent indisposition. We are giving time to spe-

*cial prayers for your speedy recovery, through the
Grace of God, His Son, the Holy Spirit and the Gracious Intervention of the Blessed Virgin.*

*In the name of Christ Who died for us and Who is
Risen in Glory, I most humbly submit to your judgment and welcome your chastisement should I be
fallen in error.*

> *Pietro Demo*
> *Superior-Generale, Camaldolese*
> *Santa Maria degli Angioli*
> *In Fiorenza on the Feast of the Visitation, July 2, 1492*

CHAPTER 1

THE SECOND SCREAM was louder than the first and brought
Sandro Filipepi upright in his bed, sleep banished completely by that sound of bubbling terror.

He swung out of bed, shoving the hangings aside as he
moved, and reached for the candle that always stood on the
small table by the window. A third scream almost made him
drop the flint from his clumsy fingers, but he forced his attention to the light, and in a moment the spark touched the
wick, and he was no longer in darkness. He hesitated only
long enough to find a camisa and pull it on over his head before he took up his candle and hurried into the hall.

Farther down the corridor, Simone's face appeared, a
study in fright and disapproval. "It's Estasia," he said unnecessarily and condemningly.

"I know." Sandro brushed past his brother, shielding the

candle flame with his hand. When he got to her door, he knocked once out of habit, but the renewed shrieks told him she could not hear. He waited long enough to test the latch, then forced the door open with a sudden blow from his arm and broad shoulder.

Estasia's room was faintly illuminated in the single candle's light, but it showed Sandro the wholly disordered state of the place. Bedclothes were strewn about and cosmetic pots thrown against the walls to break and spill their contents on the furniture and floors. The bed hangings were torn down on one side, and on the other, Estasia pulled at the draperies and screamed. Her night rail was in tatters and her body was marked with deep scratches. Tangled hair framed the terror in her face as she twisted against the hangings to turn toward the door.

"Estasia," Sandro said as calmly as he could when he had taken in her disordered state. "Don't be frightened, cousin."

"Satana! Satana! *Apage Satanas!*" She raised her hand as if to ward off a blow, then her fingers curved, and talonlike, they raked her breasts as she keened, her teeth set tightly, her face distorted with pain and fear.

Sandro came a few steps farther into the room, his rough-hewn features set with worry. "Estasia, you mustn't."

With an incoherent cry, Estasia wrenched herself out of the hangings and fled across the room to crouch in the farthest corner, her hands over her face.

A quick glance around the room revealed the candelbrum tossed under Estasia's vanity table. Sandro bent to retrieve it, and as soon as it was upright again, he lit the two candles that were still whole. Putting his candle down beside the other two, he bent low and tried to approach Estasia.

"No! No! Proteggimi! God have mercy upon me. Deliver me from the fiends of hell. Sweet Lord, it is You I want. Forgive my defilement. Make me pure again. I pray You, I beg you . . ." Her words tumbled out in breathless desperation as she pressed close to the wall, eyes averted and wild. "Save me, save me, save me, save me, save me." Again she tried to cross herself, and again her nails gouged mercilessly at her soft flesh.

By now Sandro was near enough that he could grab her wrists. "Estasia, you must not hurt yourself this way," he said firmly as he reached for her.

"Salva me, fons pietatis!"

In the next instant he was almost knocked over as Estasia lunged at him, her hands set to scrape his face with her long nails. He slid backward, shocked and quite sobered by this attack. The next approach he made toward her was considerably more cautious and he had grabbed one of her soft pillows. Just before he reached for her, he thrust the pillow into her arms, and then, as she tore frantically at the pillow, he pinioned her arms behind her. He was strong, with the untiring strength of a painter who must spend hours doing meticulous brushwork on huge, high walls. The tendons stood out on the backs of his hands in ridges and his big shoulders were as taut as those of men twenty years his junior.

Estasia lashed out with her feet and twisted, breaking away from her cousin with shrieks of panic. "Save me, dear God, sweet, kind God. I am vile. I know I am vile. But take me out of hell, I beg you." She dropped to the floor, moaning. "Oh, God, take me out of this hell. Don't abandon me. Don't leave me here alone. Save me. Take me to You. Embrace me with Your love. Save me. Save me." She began to sob, great spasms shuddering through her body. "I want only You. Don't leave me, God. I will put all sin behind. Just don't forsake me. Please. Please. Please. God, don't leave me in hell. I repent. I promise I will do only as You com-

mand. But there are fiends here, and they torment my body."
She cried out as her own right hand lacerated her cheeks.

Sandro stood unsteadily and watched Estasia as she
writhed on the floor in the shards of broken jars and their
cosmetic contents. "Estasia," he tried again, moving closer,
but not close enough to warrant another attack. "Stop, Estasia. Wake up. You are not in Hell, and I am not a demon."

She ignored this, pulling herself along the floor, her
wretchedness evident in every aspect. "Take me, God. Save
me. Deliver me from the fiends of Hell who assault my
flesh. Wrap me in the wings of angels. Heal me with Your
touch, with Your look. Let me be one with You. Save me.
Save me. Unite me with Your Hosts in Grace." Languidly
she rolled, and supine, she reached up yearningly, inviting
an embrace.

Thinking that the worst of her fright was over, Sandro
once again moved closer to Estasia. She smiled up at him
and as he bent to lift her, she wrapped her arms around his
knees and pressed her face against his thighs. "I am Yours. I
worship You," she whispered against his legs. Anxiously she
lifted his camisa, and her exploring hands moved upward.

"Ah!" she cried and her hands became talons. "You're a
man! You're sent to tempt me."

The touch of those long nails on his genitals filled Sandro with icy, numbing fear. As quickly as he could he broke
free of Estasia's hold, stumbling in his haste.

She was already on her feet, rushing toward him, her
hands ready to strike. "Fiend! Fiend! Tormentor!"

Sandro moved quickly around the end of the bed and
quickly pulled down the last hanging. As Estasia rushed at
him, he wrapped the heavy fabric around her. The binding
was crude, and the knots clumsy, but they held Estasia in
spite of her violent convulsions. It took some little time for

Sandro to wrestle her onto the bed, and longer still to quieten her.

When at last her hysterical outbursts had deteriorated into hiccups, Sandro sat on the side of the bed. He had opened a window and the night smells of high summer filled the room, sweetening the reek of spilled perfumes and ointments.

"Protect me, God. Save me," Estasia muttered as she tried to roll off her bed.

"Estasia, listen to me," Sandro ordered her, much of the kindness gone from him. "What's wrong, Estasia?" He asked the question he'd wanted to avoid for a little while yet. "Are you with child? Is that the reason for your fear?"

Her laughter at this was hideously shrill. "With child?" she gasped. "With child?"

But Sandro was quickly losing patience with her. "You have had at least two lovers in the last year. It's not impossible."

This stern common sense had no effect on Estasia. She let out another high wail of laughter, and then regarded her cousin coyly. "I don't want a child. I want . . . I want . . ." Her face contorted and she would have cried out if Sandro had not slapped her once.

"I won't have this, Estasia!" He waited while she stifled her impulse to scream again. "You thought you were in Hell. If not for pregnancy, then why?" His rugged face softened with compassion. "Don't be frightened of me, Estasia. Tell me what the matter is, and let me help you."

She twisted away from him. "I *was* in Hell," she insisted in a small voice. "I was in Hell and devils hurt me while I burned. They flogged me with silken lashes. They took me with members like burning clubs." She swallowed and a shiver ran through her.

"Estasia, if there is sin on your soul, go to church and confess it. Free yourself of the fires of Hell."

Again Estasia laughed, this time in a sensuous purr. She rolled as far as her wrappings would let her. "And tell the priest what the fiends do to me? The poor priest, he won't know what I'm talking about." She inhaled sharply, pleasurably. "It was a nightmare. It terrified me. I thought I would be destroyed. It was *wonderful.*" She stretched a little and smiled.

There was a sound at the door, and Sandro turned his head. "Yes?"

Simone, severe and righteous, stood in the doorway, and with him was an apprehensive young Servanto Brother. "I heard what our cousin was suffering, so I have brought help for her."

"That was good of you, Simone," Sandro said, resisting his first impulse to snap at his brother. He stood reluctantly and stared down at his cousin's lovely, demented face. "Perhaps you're right," he said wearily. "I don't know what to do for her." He nodded to the Servanto Brother. "Would you like to be alone with her?"

The monk could not have been more than sixteen years old, and his immaturity showed in the eager, apprehensive glance he gave Estasia. "I . . . I don't . . . Is she violent?"

"Not at the moment. She was earlier," Sandro admitted, with a comprehensive glance around the room.

As if in contradiction, Estasia screamed. "A priest! Oh, God, save me!"

The Servanto Brother stared at her in alarm and clutched his breviary more firmly. "Buona Donna," he began, and was cut short by another of Estasia's shrieks. He turned helplessly to Simone.

"She is suffering pangs of sin," Simone announced with

deep satisfaction. He shoved the monk a little farther into the room. "If only she will Confess, these visions of Hell will vanish."

"Visions of Hell?" the young Servanto asked, and repeated the question to Sandro.

"That is what she said." Sandro was tired of the atmosphere of excess that surrounded Estasia now. He frowned. "Don't encourage her, Brother," he said to the Servanto. "And you shouldn't either, Simone."

Estasia had begun to sing; the tune was popular and the lyrics she set to it remarkably lewd. As the three men watched, she wriggled nearer to them and began to move her tightly bound hips in a slow, sensuous counterpoint to her song. She interrupted herself to say, "At least the fiends of Hell know what to do with a woman. Simone, you're useless—you're constipated with religion. Sandro, ah, Sandro, if you had been willing, I would never have needed other lovers. You paint such lovely, lovely nudes, surely it would have pleased you to come to my bed. Take off this stuff you've bound me with. Look at my breasts. They're like ripe fruit. Touch them. Take them in your mouth and taste the sweetness."

"Stop this, Estasia," Sandro said as he walked slowly to the door. He could see a blush on the monk's face and the formal indignation on his brother's. He sighed. "If you want to deal with her, Brother, I would appreciate it. Who knows? Confession might help."

"I . . . I will try, Signor. But if she really is possessed of devils . . ." He stopped and set his jaw. "Devils are for the Domenicani. Our Order is for praises."

Sandro gestured helplessly. "You must do as you think best, Brother. But if she screams again I may throttle her."

With that, he shouldered his brother aside and went down the long hall toward his bedchamber.

"You must exhort her," Simone said in a steely voice as he glared at the monk. "Listen to her. No woman who is chaste and modest would sing that way."

Estasia heard this and laughed. "The words don't frighten the boy, Simone," she said mischievously. "It's what the words *do to him*. Sandro may have no use for my body, but I wager the monk does." She tried to find a position where she could see the young monk more clearly. Her hazel eyes brightened as she realized that he was good-looking and fairly athletic. "Does your body know what I want, monk?" she teased. "Exhort me *all* you like. I'll be *happy* to learn of you."

Simone stopped her suggestive words. "Where the Devil is, pain will cast him out." He trod across the floor, bits of broken jars crunching underfoot. He reached down and took hold of her tangled chestnut hair. Harshly he jerked her head back, pleased at her gasp. "There, you see? She's not so willing a servant of the Devil now." He tightened his hold on her hair and Estasia strained to save herself from Simone's abuse.

The Servanto Brother was at once shocked and curious. He came nearer the bed and looked down at the woman there, seeing how thoroughly she was tied in her own bed hangings. "Don't hurt her any more, Signor," he said after a moment.

"We must not be gentle with Satan," Simone admonished the young monk.

"But we must not judge until we know that it *is* Satan we punish. To do otherwise is prideful." For all his youth, he was shrewd enough to see the distorted satisfaction in Simone's stern face. He directed his attention to Estasia, making a gesture to dismiss Simone.

But Simone was not going to leave immediately. "You cannot be alone with her, Brother. What if she were to become violent again?"

"She is well-confined, Filipepi," the monk said gently. "If there is trouble, I will call. Surely you won't be so far away that you cannot rush to my defense?" He had a pleasant moment of victory as Simone lowered his head, crossed himself and backed out of Estasia's bedchamber. "My dear sister," the monk said firmly to Estasia as he knelt by the bed, "I am Fra Enzo, from Santissima Annunziata. You are in distress."

Estasia ran her tongue over her lips. "Oh, yes. And you must help me, Fra Enzo."

He nodded and clasped his hands together. "Tell me your affliction and together we shall pray for guidance of your soul."

A half-turn brought her even nearer to the monk. "Fra Enzo," she whispered, "you can do so much for me. I have faith that you can."

Fra Enzo was young enough to be flattered by this, but he did his best to maintain his dignity. "We must ask for the help of Heaven." He began to recite the First Psalm, his eyes closed, his voice rich with sincerity.

"I know a better way to worship," Estasia said softly. She lay back and waited for Fra Enzo to give her his attention.

When he finished the psalm, Fra Enzo opened his eyes and smiled earnestly at Estasia. "You have heard Holy Writ without terror and cries. The Devil, if indeed he holds you, is very weak. Tell me what happened and be free of the toils of Hell."

Estasia's half-smile was disconcerting in the soft light. "Very well, Fra Enzo. You must forgive me . . ."

The monk was alarmed, and reprimanded her gently. "It is not I who will forgive you, sister. It is God Himself Who will forgive your errors."

"But through *you*." The tone of her voice was disquieting. "Shall I tell you what I thought the fiends of Hell *did* to me? Shall I tell you what their lusts were?" She laughed. "They possessed me . . ."

Fra Enzo was on his feet. "Sister, it is neither fitting nor decorous for you to speak this way. If the Devil himself were holding you, you would find my presence a torment. But you don't. And you think because I am young and that my face is fair to you, that I am foolish enough to be lured by you." His indignation rose with his voice. "I have had to endure this before. You think because my face and form please you that my vocation is a lie. I am a monk because that is all I have ever wished to be. I take pleasure in my vows, and in chastity, poverty and obedience. You won't trick me, Donna." He turned abruptly and stormed out of the room, his young face deeply flushed.

Simone, who had been waiting near the door, drew himself up in haughty surprise as Fra Enzo came up to him. "What has happened, good Brother?"

"That woman is no more possessed than I am," he said with asperity. "To think that men like you are fooled." He did not pause, but went quickly out of the house.

When Sandro had once again secured the door, he came back to his brother. "Well, Simone, what now?"

"We must get a Confession from her. Obviously, the Servanto was too young to understand in what peril her soul stands. His advice was good: we must take her to the Domenicani."

Sandro's expression was filled with disgust. "Let well enough alone, Simone. You are as bad as she, feeding her illusions this way."

"The Devil," Simone said, growing very solemn, "is the father of lies. Take care that you do not admit him into your heart through such misguided tolerance."

"Santa Chiara protect us." Sandro sighed. "As you wish. If in the morning Estasia still desires to Confess, by all means, take her to Confession, just so long as there is an end to this nonsense." Sandro hesitated before adding. "That includes your nonsense, too, Simone. I won't have any more discord in my house. I have too many commissions to complete, and I can't work with you and Estasia nettling each other." He put his hand on Simone's shoulder to soften his rebuke. "You know that artists are difficult. So, if it will make it easier for you, pray for me."

There was icy disapproval in Simone's angular face. "You are the master here. Of course I will do as you wish."

"Simone, don't . . ." He stopped. It was useless. He went past his brother into Estasia's bedchamber once more. "Cousin?"

The voice that answered him was flat, hard and practical. "You may untie me now, Sandro. My nightmare is over. I'll be sensible. Who knows? I may even go to Confession, if only to keep peace in the house."

Sandro approached her bed and saw that there was no more voluptuous passion in her posture. Her vixen's face was set and her hazel eyes regarded him coldly. "Move nearer, Estasia. Let me free you from those bonds." She responded in silence, waiting patiently as Sandro loosened the knots he had made in her bed hangings. At last the chore was done and he stood back. "I'll send in the two slaves tomorrow to clean up. You needn't trouble yourself with the chore."

"Thank you." Her tone was absolutely colorless.

Although he had started for the door, Sandro stopped. "Are you all right, Estasia?"

"I'm quite well," she said in the same emotionless voice. "You need not fear I will repeat my unfortunate scene tonight."

Those words, so sincerely uttered, should have reassured Sandro, but instead he wondered what next she would do. If it was not nightmare that disturbed his household, what else might it be? And when?

He found no answer, and no peace for the rest of that warm summer night as she closed her door behind him.

TEXT OF A letter from Leonardo da Vinci to Francesco Ragoczy da San Germano:

> *To the alchemist Francesco Ragoczy da San Germano, Leonardo sends his thanks and greetings from Milano.*
>
> *You must forgive the inelegance of my script, but as I am left-handed, I usually simplify the matter and write the other direction. I have heard from Botticelli that you have the knack of writing with both hands equally well—and I would assume, in either direction. I wish I were as fortunate as you. I think I could cut my tasks in half with such a talent.*
>
> *Let me thank you for the dyes and pigments you were good enough to send me. I particularly like that*

blue, which you say will not fade when mixed with oil or prepared in an egg tempera. I have tried the latter and am in general quite pleased with it. But I wish it—and the others as well—were faster-drying. You must have heard by now how impatient I become and a faster-drying paint would please me very much indeed. If you have any particular knowledge in your skill that would make it possible to speed the drying of paint, but with no loss of depth and color, I would become your apprentice, I promise you.

It is the ultimate frustration of an artist's life that nothing he ever produces is as superior, as excellent as the image he has of it in his mind. I don't know if it is as true in your particular discipline or not, but I have found over the years that nothing I have done—nothing—is as fine as the vision from which it sprang. I hate to say a piece is finished when it is less than I know it could be. That is one of the reasons I like building the various engines I have a certain reputation for. With an engine, it is always what it ought to be, and works fairly much as expected. An engine can be finished, but art, never.

I am sorry to hear that all is not well in Fiorenza. There is nothing I can do beyond expressing my regret. And that must be enough. Our mutual friend Sandro is much troubled, and I understand that of late he has had conversation with you. It may please you to know that he takes comfort in your knowledge and remarkably wide experience. He tells me that you have been to India, and have seen temples as vast as the center of Roma. How fortunate for you. If I were not bound to Sforza and my other patrons, I think I would ramble the world over.

Perhaps, if you are ever in Milano, you will visit with me, and tell me some of the tales that have so enthralled Sandro. And if you have any other colors, paints, dyes, pigments or varnishes, I would deeply appreciate it if you would share them with me. How rare it is to find someone who not only loves art, but understands the colors and tools behind it.

Be kind enough to extend my greetings to Botticelli and those friends of Medici who were there when I was. I wager Magnifico is much missed. Even I, in Milano, miss him. I thank you again, a thousand times, for your gift. This should reach you quickly, for it comes with the herald of Il Moro to that young man who will never replace his father. Well, the world could never endure true excellence for long. Look to yourself, then, Ragoczy, as I will look to my own safety. And with that warning, I will send you my respects and all such.

L. da Vinci
Unfortunately in Milano, September 15, 1492

CHAPTER 2

GASPARO TUCCHIO HAD been waiting almost an hour and he was becoming annoyed. He had walked through the cellars of Palazzo San Germano, but since he had helped build them, there was little to surprise him, and nothing he wanted to criticize. At last he settled in the room adjoining the kitchen and listened to Amadeo sing while he made the pastry for the meat pies that would feed the household at prandium.

Ruggiero found him there and began with an apology. "It's truly unfortunate that you had to be kept waiting."

"If it's because you've decided that now my Arte brothers are out of Fiorenza that you no longer need to honor the contract we all signed . . ." He had risen and now he thrust his thumbs into his wide leather belt.

"Of course not," Ruggiero said quellingly. "There are some minor matters that had to be attended to before I could devote my attention to you." He did not mention that the minor matter was a complaint brought by one of the Domenicani from San Marco, and was little more than a veiled threat. "Often a visit from the Domenicani is longer than others."

"Them!" Gasparo almost spat in disgust. "What do they expect of decent men? I attend Mass, I take Communion, I know the Credo, the Paternoster and the Ave Maria. I honor the Saints on their feast days and I don't blaspheme. Beyond that, it's up to them. It's useless for them to carry on so. That prior, the one at San Marco. He's too arrogant by half." Gasparo stopped abruptly, his brow clearing. "Well, it's no concern of yours, is it, good houseman?"

Ruggiero was secretly relieved to hear such sentiments from Gasparo, but he maintained his reserve. "The Brothers spend so much time thinking of heaven that they assume we must all do the same." He motioned to the door. "Come, I want to review the accounts with you."

Gasparo nodded, but was not willing to let the matter of the Domenicani go quite yet. "Life everlasting! They tell us that's the reward for suffering and dishonor in this world. Well, I have given the matter some thought," he said in a louder tone as they came up the back stairs to the second floor. "I have thought about life everlasting. I don't think I'd like it much."

Pausing on the stairs, Ruggiero said, "Not like it much? Now, why is that?"

"Well, if it is to be the same thing over and over—praising God and sustained by the glory of Heaven—a few weeks of that, let alone an eternity of it, would drive a man distracted. Now, I understand that the Turks are promised women and pleasure in heaven, and that's more to my liking. Damn it, Ruggiero, if I weren't a faithful Christian, I'd turn Turk and hope for a plump little angel with a bouncy behind." He laughed at this, but stopped when he saw the black-clad man at the top of the stairs. "Eccellenza," he murmured respectfully.

"Oh, come, Gasparo," Ragoczy said as he extended his hands to the builder. "Fiorenza is a Repubblica. What do I need with title here?" As he had the first time they met, he touched cheeks with Gasparo, then stood back smiling. "So you think you would not enjoy eternal life?"

"I would not!" Gasparo covered his embarrassment with bluster.

"Eternal life," Ragoczy mused and stood aside for Ruggiero and Gasparo as they walked down the hall. "Perhaps we aren't supposed to enjoy it?"

Gasparo threw up his hands. "If we can't enjoy it, then why do we tolerate the struggles of this one?" He was not quite as overbearing toward Ragoczy, and there was a defensive gleam in his heavy-lidded eyes.

"The next room, Ruggiero," Ragoczy said, then remarked lightly, "I have an old friend . . ."—he nodded at the words—"yes, she is a very old friend. And she would tell you that you are being philosophical, Gasparo. You must meet her one day."

"If she is in Fiorenza, I will be glad to know her." For an instant he imagined himself with the rich men and their splendid ladies, and he grinned uncomfortably.

"She is, sadly, in Roma. But who knows? One day she may come here." They had gone into a small room on the second floor, one with long tables and various measuring devices. There were three kinds of clocks, each inaccurate in its own way; there were brass scales with any number of weights, ranging in size from something hardly larger than a pea to a great shining spool that was bigger than a melon; there were other weighing tools, including one that dropped from a beam and was made of highly polished wood; there were counters, some that were familiar to Gasparo, like his own tally stick, to little frames with beads strung in them; there were devices that measured distance, time, shape, weight, bulk, every kind of quantity that could be reckoned. Gasparo whistled involuntarily.

"Please take one of the chairs," Ragoczy pointed to an elegant chair of rosewood, a far more sophisticated piece of furniture than any he had ever seen before. Gingerly he lowered himself onto it, and waited, wondering if it would collapse.

Ruggiero had gone to the far end of one of the tables and had gathered up three leather bags that clinked when he moved them. These he handed to Ragoczy, and then he withdrew to the door.

"There is gold in these pouches, Gasparo, in the amount we agreed upon last year. I want you to open each of the bags and count the coins there. Then I will seal them, and you will put a mark on the seal, just as it says in the contract. If you wish, you may come with me when I deliver the pouches to the various messengers who will deliver them.

But you may be assured that they are all honest merchants and priests."

Gasparo almost blinked as he watched Ragoczy. "There's no need . . ." What was it about the elegant stragnero that so unnerved him? Gasparo wondered as he held his hand out for the first of the pouches.

There was a suggestion of a laugh in Ragoczy's voice. "You are well within your rights, and your obligations, to question me, and to demand proofs."

"But, Eccellenza . . ." He took the pouches, and opened the first, counting the gold as it spilled into his hand. "Yes, it is correct, of course." He waited while the pouch was sealed, and then he drew a cat's paw in the hot wax. He touched the second pouch, and opened it somewhat carelessly. Three of the fiorini fell to the floor, and Gasparo dropped to his knees to pick them up. "Sorry, Eccellenza. A clumsy mistake . . ."

"Tell me," Ragoczy said, ignoring Gasparo's predicament, "have you heard from your Arte brothers?"

At last Gasparo had gathered up the coins. Puffing a little as he got to his feet, he answered, "Yes, I have heard from them. Giuseppe has taken a Polish wife and says he has learned more in bed than anywhere else. He likes Krakow and is working on a new church there, doing parts of the ceiling. He enjoys it, having never done such ornamental work here. Carlo says that London is cold and that the English are strange. He has seen the King once, and finds him lacking when compared with Laurenzo, who was only a banker."

"The Tudors are new to royalty. Tell Carlo to forgive them," Ragoczy murmured. "And Lodovico?"

Now Gasparo frowned. "Lodovico is dissatisfied. He does not like Lisboa after all, and may go into Spain. The work he has been doing is not to his liking, and he complains that his skill is not appreciated. I don't know what to suggest, Eccellenza. If there is someone in Spain whom you know and who might be willing to transfer funds for him, it might be best for him to go there."

"And when he becomes bored with Spain, he will go into France, and we'll have to arrange matters once again." Ragoczy sighed. "But I suppose it must be done. Very well, I agree. When the pouch is sent, there will be a note that will introduce him to certain persons in Spain. He will have to go to Burgos first. After that, I will do what I can to see that he is happily settled."

Gasparo had finished counting the coins in the second pouch and waited to affix his sign to the hot wax. When that was done, he stared lugubriously at the third pouch, then opened it. "Well, I know you are generous, Eccellenza . . ."

"I have asked you, amico, not to give me a title." Ragoczy set his eclipse seal above Gasparo's mark.

"I don't give it to you," Gasparo growled. "You have it. It clings to you like a halo to a Saint. There are fools who do not know remarkable men when they see them." He stopped talking to finish his counting. "The amount is correct," he said with unaccustomed formality. "All three pouches are what you have said they would be."

Ragoczy nodded and sealed the third pouch. "You should have letters from all three men before the end of the year. If you do not, come to me and tell me. If for some reason I should not be here, send a messenger, one you can trust, to this man in Venezia. His name is Gian-Carlo Circando and the messenger should find him in a new palazzo not far from Piazza San Marco."

Gasparo stared at the parchment that Ragoczy handed

him. "Why will he do this?" he demanded, suspicious once again.

"He will do this because I employ him. He's an honest man, and has managed my affairs there most honorably."

"Now, now," Gasparo said with a gesture, "don't bristle up at me, Eccellenza. If you say the man is honorable, then he is, and that's an end to it." He got to his feet and stretched. "Your palazzo turned out quite well. Everyone talks about it."

"Mille grazie," Ragoczy said as he handed the pouches to Ruggiero. "If that is so, much of the credit must be yours, Gasparo. If you and your builders hadn't done such a superb job, it would not have been the success it is."

Gasparo was prepared to disclaim even as he flushed with pride, but there was a knock at the door.

"Yes?" Ragoczy called out somewhat sharply, motioning Ruggiero to answer the door.

Demetrice stood on the threshold, two heavy leather-bound books in her hand. "Excuse my interruption, San Germano, but I have a few questions about these books."

The sharp look faded from Ragoczy's face. "Come in, Donna Demetrice. I am just settling a matter with this good man, Gasparo Tucchio, who is a distinguished member of the builders' Arte."

"Bontà Donna," Gasparo muttered politely.

"Donna Demetrice is looking after my library as well as running my household," Ragoczy explained, for though it was no disgrace for a man to house the woman for whom he had a devotion, he was not anxious to have that stigma attached to their relationship. "What is it, my dear scholar?"

She offered the books to him. "What language is this? I don't know it, and I have no title I can list it for."

Ragoczy went to her and examined the books. "They are

manuscripts in Persian, but an older version than is used currently. This one in red leather is the chronicle of conquest long ago, some five hundred years before Christ. And this one in the dark brown binding is a religious tract, dealing with the gods of Egypt as well as India and Persia." He handed the second back to her, but held the first for a moment. "The Persians were very warlike then, and their methods were cruel."

Demetrice opened the book and stared at the unfamiliar script as if the intensity of her gaze might bring her understanding. Then she sighed, closed the book and took back the other. "Well, I will list them with your other foreign books, and note their age. If Laurenzo had known you had these . . ." She stopped very suddenly. "I will see you in the library after prandium," she said in another tone, and let herself out of the room.

In the silence that hung in the air after Demetrice's departure Gasparo fumbled with the wallet that hung on his belt. At last he looked at Ragoczy, and felt a strange compassion for the stranger in black. Before he could stop the words, he said, "Don't blame yourself, Eccellenza."

"What?" Ragoczy fairly snapped the question, then went on smoothly, "I stopped blaming myself more years ago than you can imagine, my friend. But I have never grown used to my . . . impotence, for want of a better word." For a moment he both heard Estasia's taunts and saw the grief Demetrice had sealed away in her soul. He turned suddenly and went to the small scales, removing another stack of gold coins as he glanced back at Gasparo. "You have a fee as well, Gasparo. I think that you will find this is sufficient." He scooped the coins into a wooden box and handed it to the builder. "I have taken the liberty of adding a ring which I hope you will honor by wearing."

Gasparo stammered. "Eccellenza . . . I do not . . . I don't think . . . You can't mean—"

Ragoczy cut him short. "Gasparo, amico, it would please me to have you accept this. There is so little I can do by way of thanks for the office you fill for me. Take the ring, *prego*."

For a moment Gasparo was still. He looked toward Ruggiero, but the houseman's expression told him nothing. "Eccellenza," he said in a choked voice, "if ever I were to call any man master, it would be you. I will wear your ring, and proudly." He pinched the bridge of his nose to keep from crying. "I am your man until death, Francesco Ragoczy." And Gasparo Tucchio, of the builders' Arte, who had never bowed to any man, dropped to his knee like a *cavaliere* and kissed Ragoczy's hand.

TEXT OF A letter from Piero di Laurenzo de' Medici to i Priori della Signoria:

> *To the honorable gentlemen of i Priori della Signoria, Piero de' Medici sends his greetings and regrets that he cannot deliver them in person.*
>
> *Your summons came as I was preparing to leave for the country and it is unfortunate that I could not delay my departure so that I could speak to you myself and make an end to this misunderstanding at once. For that reason, I am sending this to you by the hand of my cousin Giuliano, who will leave Ambra this afternoon so that you may have this message first thing in the morning, and need not fuss any longer.*
>
> *But let me address myself to your grievances. First, you claim that I am not attending to the business of Fiorenza. Rest assured that the city is very much in my*

*thoughts. Our bank, as you yourselves have often
pointed out to me, has, thanks to Henry Tudor, come
to an unhappy pass, and requires much of my time. My
father left it in a terrible state which it appears I must
remedy. For that reason, Medici funds will not be
available civically as they have been in the past. I realize that I promised several of the artists who are
beautifying Fiorenza that my family would pay them,
but I don't think it will be possible now.*

*Your second complaint indicates that you feel I
should not deal with either His Holiness Alessandro
VI or with the King of France. How am I to manage a
business that is international if I do not negotiate with
these men? You say that you fear they will get the better of me. Surely I can understand your worry about
the Pope, for he is a Borgia and a Spaniard, but why
does France concern you? His Majesty has no hold on
me, and if he chooses to honor me and my house with
gifts, there is no harm in my gracious acceptance. You
think that because of my youth that I will be duped by
these men. I may be young, good Priori, but I am not
a fool. I will remind you that my father was my age
when he undertook to guide la Repubblica.*

*While we are trading disappointments, I would like
you to know that I consider your condemnation of my
recent additions to our bank impertinent. If I am to re-
coup our fortunes, I must furbish up our building.
Also, I thought you would agree that Federigo Cossa,
the alchemist, had gone beyond the bounds in charg-
ing that ridiculous amount for the wholly inferior gold
he made for me. What choice had I but to exile him?*

*This lack of leadership you disparage would be
less of an issue if you would support my decisions. I*

cannot work if I find my path impeded by you tedious old men. You have always obeyed my father's instructions, and there is no reason why you cannot now obey mine. In future I will expect you to follow my lead.

At present I plan to remain in the country for perhaps ten days. I want to see the harvest brought in, and when that is done, I will return to Palazzo de' Medici. If necessary I will stay here a few days longer, for there may be an opportunity to do some hunting, and I have had little chance to hunt these last few months.

Look to see me, then, in the first week in November. I will call upon you, and I hope I will find you in a more tractable mood. Until then I commend myself to you and request your assistance and good wishes for the accomplishment of my duties.

Piero di Laurenzo de' Medici
At Ambra, Poggio a Caiano, October 23, 1492
P.S. Your threat of formal censure means very little to me. My father, you will recall, was excommunicated, and it made no difference to him. If he could ignore a Pope, why should I fear you?

CHAPTER 3

THE WIND THAT ruffled the trees was heavy with the promise of rain. From the crest of the hill it was possible to see all of Fiorenza laid out far below them, like a huge toy. The dark clouds had robbed the buildings of color, which made it seem more unreal, like the images in a dream.

Demetrice reined in first, her dark green cloak flying behind her. She had hiked up her wool skirt and was riding astride as Laurenzo had taught her when they had gone to his hunting lodge. Her high boots were better suited to a boy, as was the embroidered three-cornered cap that held her rosy-blond hair in place.

There was the sound of hooves and Ragoczy pulled in his gray beside her roan mare. Today he was wholly in black: no red or white or silver marred the perfect ebon of his clothes. From Russian heeled boots to French gloves to soft Spanish hat, he wore black. It may have been for that reason his face appeared more pale than usual.

The clouds, purple-bellied, pushed through the sky, blotting out the last of the sunlight. Demetrice shivered and pulled her cloak around her.

"Are you cold, amica?" Ragoczy asked as he leaned in his saddle to catch the end of her cloak for her.

Her face had been wind-buffed to a rosy shine, but she said, "No, Francesco. It doesn't matter." At last she looked down at the city. "It's so small."

"It's the distance," he said in a strange tone. "Distance is deceptive."

She heard the odd note in his voice and turned to him. "What is it, Francesco?"

He looked away then, saying, "Nothing, amica. It's nothing."

"That's not so," she said gently. "But I won't press you." With a tap of her heels she set her mare trotting, and did not wait to see if Ragoczy followed her.

In a few moments he had caught up with her, and there was a certain firmness in his expression. "It's not safe for you to ride off that way," he told her when he was near enough to be heard.

"Why do you say that?" She was still watching Fiorenza far ahead. She shuddered as the city darkened.

"Because it isn't safe for anyone to ride alone. The brigands are raiding much nearer Fiorenza than they used to. Some of them apparently used to be part of the Visconti household, for their victims say that they have seen the badge, silver with a blue serpent devouring a red child. That means they are very likely organized much as they were when they were part of the Visconti household. For that reason alone they're dangerous. And renegade soldiers are not . . . kind . . . to women." He held his horse near hers, and watched her face.

"You say that, and you're not even armed." She scoffed to disguise her sudden fright.

"Am I not?" He dropped his reins and crossed his hands to his sleeve cuffs, drawing two poignards into view. "I'm not quite that innocent."

"No, you're not," she admitted. She looked away as he restored the long knives to the sheaths in his sleeves. "Fiorenza isn't the same anymore." It was hard for her to speak of Laurenzo's death, but Ragoczy knew what she meant.

"Yes, it's changed." He studied the city through narrowed eyes. "It isn't just that, amica. Look at it. It's stopping. The crops have been poor for three years, there isn't as much foreign trade in textiles as there used to be. The English market is almost gone, now, and the Arte della Lana is feeling it. And nothing new is happening. See, there, on the east side of the city? There are two new buildings that are unfinished and have been unfinished for almost a year. There are many like that. Fiorenza should be a running stream, not a stagnant pond. Or," he added as he thought of the religious fervor that was spreading through the city, "a floodtide. Well, that's for the future."

Demetrice looked up at the clouds. "It's starting to rain. Look at the hills there. We'll be soaked."

Ragoczy nodded. "Demetrice, I promised you, you have nothing to fear from me."

Until he spoke the words, she had not known he sensed her disquiet. "I'm not sure I understand."

He sighed. "Yes, we will be wet before we get home." Then he relented. "I don't know how much Laurenzo guessed about me, or what he told you. But I told him, and I tell you now, that you are in no danger from me. Or at least, I myself am not dangerous to you." He saw a loosening in her expression and it was enough for him. "Come, Donna mia, we'd better race now or we might as well look for soap."

Demetrice almost smiled as she jabbed her heels into her mare's flanks and followed Ragoczy down the road toward San Miniato al Monte.

Rain was falling heavily by the time they rattled over il Ponte Vecchio, and as they made their way through the heart of the city they were already starting to shiver as their clothes soaked through.

In the stableyard at the rear of Palazzo San Germano, Ragoczy drew in his horse and came out of his odd light-weight saddle in time to help Demetrice dismount. As he reached up for her, she smiled down at him. Her cloak dragged at her shoulders and her clothes were pasted to her body by the rain. From under her neat wilted cap, her soft hair straggled over her face like seaweed.

"Come," he said to her, and took her by the waist. Although she was almost as tall as he and burdened with soaked clothes, he lifted her easily and set her on the flagging beside him.

Her eyes met his for an instant, and there was inquiry in hers, and a startled pleasure. Ragoczy's dark, enigmatic eyes warmed to her, but he moved away quickly, and taking her hand, led her toward his palazzo while grooms came from the stable to collect their horses. "You're cold, amica. I will tell Ruggiero to heat the bath for you. I don't want you to take a chill."

"And you?" she asked a little breathlessly.

"When you are done, I'll bathe." He glanced at her and the beginnings of amusement lurked in his wry smile.

"But you're as cold as I am."

He held the door for her to pass through. "It doesn't matter, Demetrice."

She was about to object, but realized that he wasn't listening to her. He opened a second door and they were in the courtyard. "Stay under the upper gallery. You shouldn't get much wetter." He had followed his own advice, and moved under the overhang of the second floor. His boots rapped sharply on the mosaic tiles, a counterpoint against the sound of the rain. He moved quickly, like a shadow in the forest, only the sound of his voice and the crisp report of his heels revealing him. "I will have to go out tonight for a time. Don't be concerned. Amadeo will see you have prandium soon. If you like, I will have him prepare a soup as well as a pie. In this weather, you may want it. After that, use the time as you wish. You're welcome to any book in my library. Don't be concerned if I am not in until quite late."

Demetrice had followed him, but interrupted him. "San Germano!"

The urgency of her call brought him to a halt, and he

came back toward her, frowning. "What is it, amica? What's wrong?"

Now that she had decided to talk to him, her throat was suddenly quite dry and the words came out almost cracked. "I would . . . I would like to learn from you."

"Learn what?" He was truly baffled.

"Whatever it is you study in those hidden rooms of yours." The words were out. She waited, trying to hide her apprehension, not daring to look at his face.

"And what do you know of hidden rooms, Demetrice?"

"I . . . I have seen you. I have watched." She might as well confess the whole, she thought, and said in a rush, "I knew that there was some secret to this place. I knew you had secrets you didn't share with anyone. So I decided to find out. I stayed up late at night. I followed you in the halls. I have seen you enter those hidden rooms. There is a door upstairs and one behind the landing of the grand staircase. I think that there is one on the upper gallery somewhere, but I haven't found it."

Ragoczy did not look angry. His expression was neutral, but his compelling eyes measured her. "Is there anything else?"

"Yes." She said this in a small voice and absentmindedly began to twist the thongs of her wallet that was tied to her belt.

He came nearer, and there was a great deal of gentleness in his face now. "What is it, amica mia? Don't be afraid of me, I beg you." He did not touch her, and there was a sense of dread cold in him as he watched her.

The dark under the gallery hid the worry in her face, but she still did not dare to look at him. "I have watched you at other times."

"Yes?" He was certain now of what she would say, but he

knew he could not stop her, and he knew that he didn't want to stop her. He waited, resigned, for what Demetrice found so difficult to tell him.

"You went out a few days ago. I remember that you left a lantern lit in your bedchamber. I kept in my chamber, but I listened for you. It was less than an hour to dawn when you came back. I saw you walk along the gallery. The light from the lantern . . ."—here she finally dared to look at him—"I saw you in the light, San Germano. There was blood on your lips."

"Ah." It was an effort of will not to turn away from her, but he sensed that if he did, he would lose her trust and might never again recover it.

"Before he died . . . Laurenzo told me about you, about what he guessed."

"He didn't guess: he was sure," Ragoczy said, remembering the evening of his Twelfth Night festa, which had ended so disastrously.

"Yes." Demetrice looked at him apprehensively. "Was he right, San Germano?"

Why was it always so difficult? Ragoczy wondered. Was it that he hated to be feared? Was it that admitting the truth would set the final seal on his loneliness? "What did Laurenzo tell you?"

"He said you were more than an alchemist. He said that you were immortal. . . ."

"Not immortal. Not quite." The words were quick, harsh.

"He said you were . . . are . . . a vampire." When he gave her no answer, she went on recklessly, "He said that the Church was wrong, and that your kind are not demons or cursed of God, that you are not like Satan. He said that you are something else entirely."

"He was right," Ragoczy said softly. He stood still a moment and listened to the rain. "Demetrice," he said almost dreamily, "I told you before and I tell you now that you stand in no danger from me. No danger whatever. No one and nothing in Fiorenza is endangered by me." He stopped and considered. "Or if there is harm, it is not my intention."

Before she could stop herself, she said, "But I saw blood . . ."

"I had it from one who was willing to give it. Beyond the Porta San Frediano."

"Not Donna Estasia, then?"

"No."

Demetrice was surprised by the jealousy she felt as she spoke Estasia's name. She stopped thinking of Botticelli's cousin as she gathered her courage again. "What happens? When you . . . drink?"

He desperately wanted this conversation to end. "Most of the time, very little. There is a pleasant dream, a sweet satisfaction, and in the morning some lassitude because a little blood is gone." He recognized the skepticism in her face. "No, amica mia, I am not the ravenous thing you think me. You could fill the ruby cup I gave Laurenzo with what I take from the living. But just the blood is not enough. It will keep me . . . alive . . . but it is not enough. So when it is possible, I have intimacy as well. It is not only the blood that nourishes me. It is nearness, pleasure, all intense emotions. Only those who come to me knowingly are . . . tainted by me. Only those who accept me as I am will be like me." He turned away from Demetrice.

"San Germano, if someone comes to you, can you give them your life?" Her voice was very small and filled with anguish.

"Yes, most of the time." He knew what question would follow, and braced himself to answer it.

"Then *why didn't you save Laurenzo?* Why did you let him die? He was your friend, San Germano."

"I know." He moved away from her, his eyes closed as the pain of loss welled up in him afresh. "I didn't save him because I couldn't. There was nothing I could do."

"You didn't even try?" Her hands were fists now, and her clear amber eyes shone with anger and tears.

"Demetrice, Demetrice, believe me, if there had been the slightest chance, I would have risked anything to make him . . . live, even his eternal hatred."

"But why didn't you?" She was beseeching him. All her anger was gone.

He spun around on her. "*Because I couldn't!*" He steadied himself and went on with fearful intensity. "Understand that. I could not save him. And every day he suffered, I searched, I hoped for a way. But it was his blood. To be . . . changed, the blood must be clean. Laurenzo's was so diseased that it killed him. Oh, I could have shared blood with him. It would not have hurt me. But it would have made no difference. None."

The rain was falling harder, making a sound like an army marching in the distance. The afternoon had grown much darker. In the courtyard the mosaics were no longer visible through the splashes.

When she could speak, Demetrice said, "I didn't realize." She faltered, finding the words too trivial. She came through the gloom toward Ragoczy. Silently she held out her hand.

He looked at her, his dark eyes questioning. Then he took her hand in his, wishing that he were not wearing gloves. He nodded. "Demetrice, amica, you are welcome to stay with me. But if you would rather not, I will provide you money or a dowry. If you stay here, I promise you I will not touch you, will not seek you out, even as a dream."

"I don't want money, and I don't want a dowry. But," she

said, her interest kindling, "I would like to study with you. I want to learn what it is you do in those hidden rooms. Will you let me learn from you?"

"Very well." He pulled her nearer, his dark eyes compelling her as much as his insistent hands. "Be my student, then, and welcome. And be my friend, Demetrice. Not my lover, my friend."

She held back from him, still uncertain.

"Do I frighten you?" He had not intended the words to be so revealing, but his despair could not be disguised.

"No," she said quickly. "You have never frightened me." It was almost the truth.

"Not even now, knowing what I am?"

She could no longer read the expression in his eyes, but she knew they searched her face. "You've said you won't harm me, and I believe you, San Germano. If you were to cast me out for imposing this confidence on you, I would not fear you. But I would certainly be angry," she added with a smile.

Kindly, gently he drew her into his arms and touched her cheeks with his. "Demetrice, do you know what it is not to be loathed?"

There was nothing she could say in answer, but she felt a deep sympathy for Ragoczy, and realized what his question must mean. She returned his embrace briefly.

But it was Ragoczy who stepped back first. "Come," he said in quite a different tone. "It's icy here. You must have a bath or you will take a fever."

Demetrice accepted this, and admitted to herself that she was chilled through the bone. She made no demur but followed him into the hall, glad to have the warmth of the palazzo around her, and the awakened comfort of the friendship of Francesco Ragoczy da San Germano.

TEXT OF A letter from il Conte Giovanni Pico della Mirandola to Marsilio Ficino:

> *To his friend in Fiorenza, Marsilio, Pico sends greet-*
> *ings in Plato from Roma.*
>
> *You must be the first to hear of my good news. The*
> *Pope has at last granted me an audience for my peti-*
> *tion. Who would have thought that Rodrigo Borja y*
> *Lara, of all men, would be willing to hear me? But it*
> *may be that I will have the infamous ban against my*
> *work lifted at last. Pray for me, Marsilio.*
>
> *I have seen Cardinale Giovanni (and I must have*
> *heard a thousand times now the pun about Giovin'*
> *Giovann'; and grown heartily sick of the witticism).*
> *Of course Giovanni is young, and of course it is obvi-*
> *ous that the seven tasthes on his hat have not aged*
> *him or given him an old man's wisdom. But he is very*
> *much a Medici, and a Fiorenzan to the marrow. If you*
> *think that the Orsinis look down on Fiorenza, it is*
> *nothing compared to the way our young Cardinale*
> *views Roma. But he is clever and he will learn. He is*
> *also ambitious and likes to lose even less than his fa-*
> *ther did. Laurenzo might not like what his son is doing*
> *here, but he would be proud of him, nonetheless.*
>
> *There are some very disquieting rumors in Roma,*
> *however, about what Piero has done to Fiorenza. The*
> *ambassador from Genova has been hinting that Gen-*
> *ova would be interested in acquiring Pisa and*
> *Livorno, which would be disastrous for la Repubblica*
> *Fiorenzena. Unless Piero takes control of the bank*
> *from his Tornabuoni uncle and stops leaving statecraft*
> *to that other Piero, Dovizio da Bibbiena. It's all very*

well to have a secretary to copy out letters and to or-
ganize appointments. But it is more than enough if
they run the state. It would have been better if Piero
had had a Fiorenzena to wife. Alfonsina is much
worse than Clarice ever was. It's past help now.
They've been married almost three years. Not even a
"Borgia" Pope would annul that.

This was the first year we didn't gather on November 7 to honor the birthday of Socrates. I felt very
empty on that day. It was not only that I am here in
Roma, but it was the knowledge that no such meeting
occurred in Fiorenza. I have very often missed Laurenzo, but never more than that day just a month ago.

I am sending a few poems with this, and since it
will be carried by Cardinale Giovanni's messenger, I
am confident that it will reach you in good time. Do, I
ask you, read them and when you have had time to
consider their merit—if any—send me word. Your crit-
icism has always been of great use to me.

Be kind enough to greet all my friends in Fiorenza
in my name. I hope to return as soon as Alessandro
grants my petition. In the meantime I commend myself
and all my work to you.

Giovanni Pico, Conte della Mirandola e Concordia
In Roma on the Feast of San Ambrosio di Milano,
December 7, 1492

CHAPTER 4

THE GREAT NAVE of Santa Maria del Fiore was almost full, the benches crowded, and many people sitting huddled on the floor. It was a terribly bright, cold day and a shattering wind carried the breath of the snow-clad hills into the city and the cathedral.

Since Savonarola had been granted the right to preach in the cathedral, his followers had grown in number and it seemed that this day they were all determined to hear the ferocious little Domenicano speak. It was a holy time of year, and that promised fervid sermons. The service was unbearably long, the Mass seeming to go on forever. The congregation murmured and joggled and rustled as each person tried to endure the ritual before Girolamo Savonarola could speak to them. Finally there was an impatient hush and an expectant shuffling as people sat straighter, hoping for a better view of the angular little man walking stiffly toward the oratory of the cathedral.

Simone Filipepi glared at his cousin Donna Estasia, sitting woodenly beside him. "Listen to him, cousin," he hissed in her ear. "His words will reward your patience."

Estasia had hated the whole thing. From the moment that morning when Simone had almost dragged her from the house, to the long wait as the cathedral filled, it had all seemed hideous. Her head ached, she was cold, and the three hours they had sat on the hard bench so that they might be near Savonarola when he spoke seemed to her the height of folly and a waste of time. She let her thoughts stray back to the night before. Ettore, her new lover, had been a disappointment. He had been clumsy, too hurried, and when he had taken his pleasure, he had hurried away from her, making some flimsy excuse about needing to be fresh in the morning. Not for the first time she scolded herself mentally for having been such a fool about Ragoczy. She had been capricious and it had cost her the pleasure she took with him.

Around her the people leaned forward as the incongruously big, harsh voice of the prior of San Marco began to fill the cathedral. "With a sorrowing, humble repentant heart," he announced, "I have prayed. I have prayed that the destruction that is to come will not fall while Fiorenza is yet so ripe with sins."

This awful pronouncement was a most promising beginning. The congregation strained to hear more.

"Oh, Fiorenza, you must repent while there is still time. My visions tell me that the time is short. Fiorenza will be as a desert, laid waste and barren. It is not my voice that tells you this, it is the Voice of God that speaks through me!"

Simone shot a look at Estasia, and seeing the wanton, arrogant smile she wore, whispered, "You are vile! *Vile!*"

Savonarola leaned forward in his oratory, his bright green eyes snapping with purpose. "Dress yourselves in humble white, for purity, O Fiorenzeni. Plagues and war will come to destroy you if you do not repent. I have seen the Sword of the Wrath of God over this city, and it came with the storm and devastation followed."

This is what the people had come to hear. A few of the congregation cried out for mercy and shouted they had repented.

"The early Christians, who gladly wore their martyrs' crowns, lived in simplicity amid the corrupt luxury of Roma. They knew that the truth lies only in the words of Christ, in the Gospels and Testaments. They, who had the power of an empire around them, turned away from the fallacious teachings and accepted the Will of God."

Estasia sighed and looked around the cathedral, a smile

in her eyes as she saw handsome men in the crowd. There was one, obviously rich, perhaps from Pisa, by the cut of his clothes. As he glanced her way she signed to him, and hoped he would seek her out after the sermon.

"You have fallen away from this. You read the heresy of Plato and Aristotle, and think that you can entertain their notions as well as the Teachings of Christ. You are deceived. Plato and Aristotle even now rot and burn in Hell!" He held up his hand to quiet the muttering in the congregation. "They are in Hell! I have seen it through the Grace of God. And you, you read their works and congratulate yourselves when you understand them. What you understand is the way to perdition!" This time he let the groan run its course.

The young Pisan saw Estasia and nodded to her, a soft, sensual anticipation warming his features.

"You read of the forbidden excesses of the friends of Socrates, of congress between men, which the Testaments most strictly forbid. The Word of God commands that sodomites be burned alive. What prideful folly to overlook that command." He saw some of the men wince and others bristle at his words. "Yes, you resist. You are rank with corruption and you revel in your perversity. You are like the Romans of old, who killed good Christians and today shovel coals in Hell and bemoan their fate."

Simone saw the exchange between Estasia and the young Pisan nearby. He grabbed her hands roughly. "You're no better than a whore. Learn to live in humility. Learn to despise the flesh."

"Oh, Simone." Estasia sighed petulantly, and pretended to give the preacher from Ferrara her attention.

"How you emulate those Romans, and take pride in it. You have horse races, and gamble on the outcome. If there is to be salvation, the palio must end. Every one. You bet on ards and dice and all manner of disgusting sport. You caper more lasciviously than any pagan at festival time, and give yourselves over to the monstrous sins of the flesh at carnival. You paint your women, and you allow even holy art to show the Mother of God as simpering, jeweled and scented as a harlot in the court of Caesar." He pointed to a new Madonna recently added to the cathedral decorations. "See here? See? Her eyes are not humble and pure. Her countenance is bold, inviting, and the hand at her breast fools no one. It is not to nourish Our Lord, but to pervert the minds of this congregation."

Every eye turned to the Madonna, and there was a murmur of horrified agreement.

"Is it any wonder that the most respected matron in this city still bedecks herself in paint and struts abroad in indecent splendor. And think of those degraded women who truly follow that life, who are terrible in their lusts. Any woman of this city might be a prostitute, wallowing in the rankness of desire. You have seen them. You have touched them. You are contaminated by those bits of rotten meat with eyes!"

This time the wailing was almost overwhelming. Savonarola stood still, his hand upraised. Then slowly, deliberately he brought it down, pointing out various members of the congregation. "You have sought out lewd women for unnatural pleasures!" he declared as he singled out a slender young woman sitting modestly with her family. She shrieked and put a hand to her suddenly pale face, denying it as tears welled in her eyes.

"You . . ." Savonarola next picked out a woman of more than forty years. "You have decked yourself in man's clothing, and against all the laws of the state and God, you have traveled abroad without shame."

There was spirit in the woman, for she shouted back.

"What am I supposed to do? Wear petticoats and be raped by brigands?"

Savonarola ignored this, and his baleful glance settled on Estasia. "You, you wanton, luxurious, depraved! You are channel of iniquity. What death lurks in that fair body. Vicious carnality fills your thoughts. And for that you will be punished in Hell forever. You will be penetrated in every orifice by the minions of the devils and you will bear in every part the seething offspring of Satan. Your flesh will rupture and run and the decay of your soul will fill all Hell with its stench!"

Estasia blinked and shook her head mechanically. "No. No."

But the congregation was howling for more, shouts rising from the general roar as guilt and remorse overwhelmed them.

"Look upon her!" Savonarola shouted. "You and she are alike, Fiorenza! Fair, fair, temptingly fair, you conceal your rottenness beneath a facade of the most voluptuous pleasures. But see her!" He leveled both hands at her, and Estasia tried to twist away. "See how her face contorts. See how she writhes. The Devil has seized her by the hair! She spreads her legs and moans like the whore she is! But who among you could endure her now?"

Estasia had fallen to the floor, where she clutched at the ankles of people near her. She was whimpering, pulling at her bodice so that her breasts were exposed. Methodically she began to scratch the rounded flesh, her nails leaving deep bloody tracks in her skin. "I repent! I repent! Have pity! Have pity!"

Wholly embarrassed by this turn of events, Simone tried to drag Estasia to her feet, but as he touched her, she screamed. "Estasia, control yourself!" he ordered her, pulling his hands away from her. "You're disgracing yourself!"

Savonarola's voice rose above this. "How long

iorenza? How long before God sickens entirely of you?
How long before your corrupt loveliness offends Him beyond all tolerance and love? You walk on the brink of eternity and you flirt with chaos!"

Her bodice was almost in shreds and her hands now
clawed at her face. She sobbed convulsively through tightly
closed teeth. The people she touched shrank away from her
and some of them prayed.

"You see that woman touched by the Chastening Hand of
God, yet you dare not look too closely. But it is you who
might next be touched! Repent, O Fiorenza. Prostrate yourself at the Throne of Mercy before the Wrath of God over-
whelms you!"

As Estasia tried to get to her feet, she was twitching and
her face wore a distorted expression of hopelessness and
dissatisfaction. She clasped her hands and raised them heavenward. "Help me! Help me! Spare me!" She began to draw
herself forward, knocking over the bench before her and
keening as the rough-hewn wood tore at her arms.

"Repent! Repent! O Fiorenza, look upon this woman! See
how she is robbed of everything, how she grovels before the
might of God! Come! Come! Come up, woman, and repent!"

Estasia had fallen again and as the tightly packed people around her tried to make way for her, or to escape her
terrifying presence, they kicked her, and her shoulder
began to bleed. She put her hand into the blood, then
reached out.

Even Simone balked at that. He wanted desperately to
leave the cathedral, but he had a greater desire to remove Estasia as well. He tried once more, vainly, to reach her, and
found his way blocked by kneeling, praying, weeping
Fiorenzeni. "Estasia! Cousin!"

She did not hear him. She was crying out now, high, thin

sounds like an animal carried off by an eagle. There wer
bruises on her face and arms, and as Simone watched
shocked, two young men reached out for her and grabbe
vindictively at her breasts, taking a strange pleasure from
her revulsion and pain.

Apparently Savonarola saw this as well, because hi
voice rose in fury. "Why do you seek after such filth? If yo
indulge the joys of the senses, you condemn your souls t
everlasting torture."

Estasia had almost reached the altar and the Dominicar
serving Mass glanced at one another in distress. None o
them wanted to deal with this demented woman, an
Savonarola was still in the oratory, addressing the congrega
tion.

Their worry was removed when a small woman in th
white habit of the Celestiane Sisters pushed her way throug
the crowd and took hold of Estasia.

Twisting, wrenching, her face wet with tears and bloo
Estasia screamed as the nun held her. Then, in an entirel
different voice she began to curse, to call every form of ob
scenity and blasphemy on the little nun in white.

Nothing that the congregation had hoped for could hav
exceeded this. It was shocking. It was horrible. They wer
scandalized and delighted. The Nativity had threatened to b
incredibly dull with no festivals and only religious proces
sions to mark the day, but now the artist Botticelli's cousi
had given them royal entertainment and they were anticipat
ing a delirious season.

The nun pulled Estasia closer to her, shielding her from
the eager, outraged Fiorenzan citizens around her.

"Would every one of you want to emulate that pitifu
creature?" Savonarola raised his fists to the vault of th

cathedral. "Forbid it, God! Rather strike down this city, this world, than to let us be so degraded!"

Suor Ignata held Estasia closer to her and said, "Pray for tranquillity, my sister. God will answer you if you ask for His Peace."

There was a great deal of excitement in the cathedral now. Some of the women had fallen on the floor and were crying out to be saved. Men were weeping, their hands clasped in prayer. Others had begun to sing hymns as the Domenicani moved among them, blessing those who asked to be blessed, comforting those who wept.

"Think on your sins! This is the last hour God will grant you. After today, there is no chance. Repent! Repent!" Savonarola's eyes were fever-bright and there were some who looked on his affliction as another sign of his blessedness, his uniqueness.

By now the shouting had become so loud that there was almost no way to hear the prior speak, and a great many of the congregation abandoned themselves to the excitement of repentance.

"My dear child," Suor Ignata said in her low, musical voice, "don't be distressed. We will help you. My Sisters and I will take you into our community. Be calm, my child, you will be cared for."

If Estasia understood, or heard, she gave no sign of it. Her head was thrown back and her eyes were glazed, unseeing. She made garbled sounds that might have been words, but no one heard them clearly enough to make them out.

Simone wrung his hands in distress, then fell to his knees and began to pray rapidly, as if the speed of the prayers would hurry an answer. He deliberately ignored his cousin so that her shame would not fall on him.

Suor Ignata pulled Estasia aside, and at last succeeded in

leading her from the cathedral. "There, my child," she sai
in the same voice she used for the imbeciles who were care
for at Sacro Infante, "you need not be frightened. I am Suo
Ignata and I am taking you to my Superiora, Suor Merzede
We'll look after you. Never fear. You will be cared for."

The convent's rough cart was drawn by two yoked oxe
and Suor Ignata drove them with the exasperated ease of th
farmgirl she had been. Three of the other Celestiane nun
were in the back of the cart, their practiced care at last calm
ing Estasia's outbursts.

"What will her family do?" Suor Stella asked in an urge
undervoice as the nuns left the city through la Porta all
Lanza.

"I hope," Suor Ignata said with some asperity, "that sinc
they have so singularly failed her, they will let her stay wit
us until God heals her mind again. But we must leave that
God and to the persuasive powers of Suor Phidia and Sig
nale. I hope that they find her family reasonable."

Somewhat later Sandro Filipepi was interrupted at hi
work by two Celestiane nuns who knocked timidly at hi
door. Ordinarily Simone, Estasia or his houseman Valeri
would have answered. But Valerio was gone to visit his in
valid sister, Simone had locked himself in his room to med
itate and pray, and Estasia had not yet returned from th
cathedral. Sandro hated to be interrupted when he worke
but there was no help for it. He wiped his brush and gave
last critical scrutiny to the Orpheus, thinking again that h
should have finished it for Laurenzo. But it had been
minor commission, and Laurenzo had never rushed him
Now Ragoczy had offered to buy the work and Sandro ha
accepted, knowing that the foreigner would not mind th
Orpheus had Laurenzo's face.

The knocking grew louder and Sandro hurried from h

studio to the door. He stared at the two white-habited women who faced him, and swallowed the congenial curse he had been about to utter. "Good Celestiane. What may I do for you?" He stood aside and motioned them into the wide hall.

"I am Suor Phidia, from Sacro Infante," the older of the two, a strong-faced woman of forty, announced.

"Your presence honors my house," Sandro responded automatically, feeling bewildered.

"I gather that you haven't yet spoken with your brother," Suor Phidia said as she looked around.

"My brother returned from the cathedral more than an hour ago. He's still at his devotions. If it is necessary, I will interrupt him, but his is a fervid soul . . ."

Suor Phidia gave her younger companion a speaking look. "And your cousin, Signore Filipepi?"

"She is still at the cathedral." He thought for a moment that Estasia had done something foolish. If she were with child—for a woman her age might well bear children, and it was true that Estasia had at least three lovers—she might have gone to the Sisters in the hope that they would help her. But none of her lovers would refuse to acknowledge a child of their getting. They were honorable men, and Estasia was of good family, not some trull to be cast off after a night of debauch. He stopped his wandering thoughts, and turned his attention to the nuns again.

This time the younger nun spoke. "I am Suor Signale, Signore Filipepi. I am afraid that your cousin has suffered a . . . misfortune."

Sandro closed his eyes. He had feared something might happen to Estasia. He had seen that overly bright shine in her eyes and knew that her emotions sank and soared erratically. "What happened?"

Suor Signale smiled compassionately and grasped the wooden rosary that hung from her high, wide belt. "Your cousin, Donna Estasia della Cittadella, while at the cathedral, suffered a kind of seizure. It occurred during the sermon, and she was much moved by the words of Savonarola. Unfortunately, your brother was unable or unwilling to come to her aid, and so our Sister in Christ, Suor Ignata, approached her, and got her safely out of Santa Maria del Fiore."

"I see." They were from Sacro Infante, that hospital convent where the mad, the incompetent and the childish were sent. He thought of Simone, and for the first time in some years he found he was dangerously angry with his brother. Simone annoyed him often, but this went beyond the bounds of religious severity. If Simone had one spark of the faith he professed, he would not have shirked his duty to his cousin.

"Signore Filipepi . . ." Suor Signale began.

"I am sorry, good Sister. My thoughts were wandering. I ask your forgiveness. Tell me: what has become of Estasia?"

Once again Suor Phidia took over. "With your permission, good Signore, we are taking her to Sacro Infante. We have some skill in nursing those in distress and it would please us to have this opportunity to give charity as Our Lord commanded us."

Sandro was dangerously near smiling. The nun had put it so neatly that any denial would seem not only cruel but also unchristian as well. "She is a widow, and her father is dead. If I have any authority over her, it is slight. But if you think it wise, by all means keep her with you until she is calmer. I haven't the time or the capability to deal with her properly, and I fear my brother would find it difficult to give her the sort of care she must need."

"Where did her husband live?" Suor Phidia asked, concerned now that there might be objections from Estasia's husband's family.

"In Parma. It's unlikely that they would interfere with your care. You must understand, good Sisters, that my cousin was married to a merchant a great deal older than she, and the object was to unite two commercial houses. It was the marriage that mattered, not her widowhood. Her husband's nephew runs that business now, and her half-brother. That was why she asked to come to me in the first place. She has no children and her life was most restricted there. She asked to come here only because there was no other way for her to break free of the limitations which had been imposed on her, all to protect a business partnership."

The nuns once again exchanged glances, and Sandro wondered if it was because of what he had told them, or because it meant that Estasia might be willing to part with some of her widow's settlement in appreciation of the nuns' work on her behalf.

Suor Signale nodded. "I see. It is often so with women who have no children and are possessed of strong appetites. We will do all that we can for her, and with the help of God, she will be whole again."

With a gesture that might mean resignation and might mean encouragement, Sandro inclined his head to the nuns. "I know that if anything can be done for her, you and your Sisters will do it."

"It is a pity that she has no religious vocation," Suor Phidia murmured, and waited for Sandro to respond to this obvious invitation.

"No, I am afraid that the religious life offers too little . . . stimulation to Estasia. All the religious vocation has been used up by my brother, I fear." He regretted his facetious remark as soon as he said it, and so he added, "Your pardon,

Sisters. I am still somewhat dazed by what you've told me. I didn't mean what I said."

Suor Signale had bridled, but Suor Phidia had heard such remarks, and very much worse, many times before. She smiled gently. "If you wish to see her, come at the end of a week. We will be able to tell you more about her, and we can discuss any arrangements that might be necessary then. If there is some man who is devoted to her, pray ask him to come with you. The affection of those we care for is a great solace to those afflicted as she is."

"As you wish, Sister. I will come to you in a week. But if there is any change in her, either to the good or to the bad, I want to know of it. Send a messenger to me and I will come to your convent as fast as my horse will bring me."

At that show of concern, Suor Signale's reserve vanished. "Ah, you are good, Signore Filipepi. I knew that a man who has shown the Virgin in all her purity and love would not turn away from his cousin."

There was a pause, and all three realized that there was nothing more to say. Sandro was the first to recover from the silence.

"Well, good Sisters. I am anxious to hear of my cousin. And I thank you with all my soul for what you have done. Estasia will thank you, too, one day." It was difficult to say the last.

"I will pray God for that," Suor Phidia said, then turned to Suor Signale. "We must not stay. It will be dark in two more hours, and we must be at the convent for our prayers." She looked once more at Sandro. "You may be certain that all of us will care for her with all the skill at our hands, and the love of God to guide us."

Sandro nodded, and said the necessary inane farewells. He was grateful when he had closed the door behind the nuns, grateful to them for what they had done, and grateful that they had kept him occupied until the worst of his anger had passed. He turned away from the door and went down the hall, thinking as he went that Simone had a great deal to explain.

TEXT OF A letter from Lodovico Sforza, called Il Moro, acting Duca di Milano, to Charles VIII, King of France:

To the Most Illustrious and Christian King, Charles VIII of France, the uncle of il Duca di Milano, who has the honor to act for his nephew in all matters of government, sends most respectful, obedient greetings.

It has come to the attention of il Duca that Your Majesty has long had claim to the Kingdom of Napoli, Jerusalem and other parts of the world, which Your Majesty has been reluctant to pursue. Certainly the weight of royalty is formidable, and those who are burdened with it have much to bear. Yet my nephew is uneasy in his mind, for if one ruler is lenient in his reign, all rulers must carry the burden of that leniency.

Let me urge you, on behalf of my nephew, to regain your hold on Napoli and other estates. It would bring order once more to il Re Ferrante's realm, for you must know that Napoli falters under his weak rule. Think what Napoli would be, once again under the stern, loving hand of France.

As one who has seen the chaos that is here in all of Italia, I am convinced that you must act, if only for our

*benefit. Since such an expedition would impose on you
to benefit us, I have made certain inquiries so that the
cost would be borne in part by those who would reap
the results of your concern. There is a bank in Genova
which would be willing to extend to you, through myself, the amount of one hundred thousand francs to
offset the cost incurred by Your Majesty should you
decide to assert your rightful claims in Italia. The
payment of the money to the bank would fall on Milano's shoulders, as would payment of the interest,
which has been guaranteed at fourteen percent.*

*Most sincerely I beseech Your Majesty to mount what-
ever expedition seems prudent and to come to Milano so
that you can more fully assess the situation in Napoli.*

*I would also like to mention that the political situ-
ation in Tuscany bears watching most closely. If, as it
has been said, Fiorenza is the compass of Tuscany,
then there is a great deal of misfortune coming. Laurenzo has been dead for almost a year, and despite all
his protestations, his son Piero has shown himself to
be disinclined to take up the obligations left him by his
illustrious father. There is also a wave of religious excitement in that city, and it has had some startling ef-
fects on la Repubblica. Your Majesty may be needed
there, to guide and supervise the course of that state.*

*With the profound wish that Your Majesty will con-
sider most carefully all that I have said in this letter,
on behalf of my nephew, Gian Galeazzo, il Duca di
Milano, I pray heaven will bless Your Majesty and all
your endeavors.*

> *Lodovico Mauro Sforza*
>   *for Gian Galeazzo Sforza, il Duca di Milano*
In Milano, February 18, 1493

CHAPTER 5

JOACIM BRANCO HELD his bleeding hands up to ward off the blows which continued to fall on his back and sides. Beside him his apprentice Narciso Boscino groaned as the long cudgels pounded his shoulders and arms.

Biagio Spinnati chuckled as his solid kick drove the tall Portuguese alchemist forward onto the flagged street. His somber guarnacca was spattered with blood, and this displeased him. He motioned to his companions. "Ehi, Ugo, Clemente, leave that one. He's almost out, anyway. This one." He kicked Branco again. "Get him on the back. Break his legs."

Ugo complied immediately, and the first blow he gave Joacim Branco made the alchemist double up, gagging suddenly as pain exploded through his bowels.

"Look at him," Biagio cried, and wet his lips with his tongue. "He's going to foul himself."

Joacim Branco had got to his knees and his long arms were wrapped tightly across his stomach. The pain in his guts ravened like a mad beast. He fought to control himself, and was absurdly pleased that he did not vomit.

Clemente Sprezzando came away from belaboring Narciso and gave Branco a last resounding blow across the neck and shoulders. He crowed with delight as the alchemist fell unconscious at his feet.

"I wish their master was here," Biagio said breathlessly. "I'd pay him back for what he did to Mario."

The other two were already tiring of the game, but Clemente asked, "Was he the one who broke your brother's bones?"

"Yes. May God damn him forever!" He gave Joacim one last vicious kick. "And now that Mario's become a monk, he can't take vengeance for himself."

"Well, we've done it for him," Ugo said, proud of himself.

"In part." There was a grim set to Biagio's mouth as he moved away from the two alchemists. "Maybe they'll die," he mused, then changed his mind. "No. I want them to tell Ragoczy. I want him to know what's in store for him."

This brought a sour smile to Clemente's dissolute young face. "You could write a message and nail it to his door. That palazzo of his has three big wooden doors. Paint the message on it."

"Or carve the message in. 'Godless foreigner,' perhaps." The idea obviously appealed to Biagio. He turned the matter over in his mind, and started out of the narrow alley near the public granary where they had waylaid the alchemists.

"That's not a good way," Clemente warned. "It takes time to carve a message, and if you got caught, Ragoczy could take us to court. He might be a foreigner, but la Signoria would take his part then. They'd have to."

Even Ugo agreed. "But it would be great, hacking up that big carved front door. The two side doors aren't nearly as good. The front one has those scenes from ancient times."

Biagio was reluctant to turn away from the plan. "We could throw stones at the door. Some of them would be sure to damage it, and unless the alchemist came out immediately, he could never find out who had done the damage."

They were walking toward la Via Porta Rossa, the alley behind them. It was not entirely safe to be abroad at dusk, but none of the three minded. They had never been approached by desperate men, and secretly they were disappointed.

"Do you think the old alchemist will tell his master?"

Biagio shrugged. "Who knows? He'll have to tell him something. But he doesn't know us."

Clemente frowned. "He might identify us if he sees us."

"Who'd believe him?" Biagio grinned. "I'm going to San Marco. They will want to hear what we've done."

It was several hours later when Joacim Branco had come sufficiently to his senses to be able to make his way through the silent streets to the side door of Palazzo San Germano. He was almost too exhausted to knock, and when he did, he despaired of ever being heard. Before he could lift his arm a second time, there was the sound of bolts lifting, and in a moment Francesco Ragoczy faced him, his lucco of embroidered black velvet almost making him look like a habited monk.

"Branco!" he said, horrified, and clapped sharply. "Ruggiero! We need help here." He had already reached to support the Portuguese alchemist, and his small hands searched out the worst of his hurts swiftly and gently. "Who did this?"

"I don't know," Joacim Branco mumbled through smashed lips. "They waylaid Narciso and me. I think Narciso is dead."

"Where?"

"In an alley. Off la Via Porta Rossa. Near the Medici bank." Ruggiero had appeared as Joacim Branco said the last. Ragoczy never turned away from the battered man as he gave instructions to his manservant. "Ruggiero, take Araldo and Pascoli, go to the alley off la Via Porta Rossa near the Medici bank. Narciso Boscino lies there beaten, and perhaps dead. Bring him back here immediately so that we may tend to him."

"I will."

"Be sure you take weapons with you. There may be more

trouble. Short swords should do." He had caught Joacim Branco's weight as he neared fainting again. "Close this door. I'll take Branco to the chamber at the end of the court-yard. It's closest." He had an awkward moment as he lifted Branco into his arms, because the Portuguese was a head taller than Ragoczy. But an instant later he held the injured man like some strange, outsized infant. He waited long enough to be sure Ruggiero knew his instructions, then car-ried Joacim Branco to the bedchamber at the end of the hall that opened onto the courtyard.

He had just put the man down when Masuccio and Gualtiere hurried into the room. Both were understewards and were not wholly prepared for what they saw.

"Christ and the Angels!" Gualtiere gasped as he saw the bleeding, bruised legs where the torchlight fell on them.

Ragoczy spoke with asperity. "Never mind oaths and prayers. I need basins of water, clean cloths, and herbs. . . . I'll get them later. But water and cloths, quickly. Quickly!" He was pulling Joacim Branco's long robes off him, but in several places blood had matted the cloth to his wounds, and resisted the gentle tugging.

Gualtiere had seized the opportunity to escape and had gone for basins of water, but Masuccio stood quite still, pet-rified by what he saw.

"You've tended broken bones before," Ragoczy snapped, wanting to bring the understeward out of his shock.

"Not like that," Masuccio whispered.

If Ragoczy had not been so worried for Joacim Branco, he would have given a few sharp, pithy words to Masuccio, but it was a luxury he could not afford, nor could Branco. So he said, "Get me clean cloths. Immediately."

The sound of swiftly retreating footsteps told Ragoczy that Masuccio had gone, and in a few minutes other steps approached. Without turning, Ragoczy said, "We have to soak his robes off and open wounds. Start with the left arm: it's the worst. Be very gentle."

"Certainly," said Demetrice Volandrai. She came to the side of the bed and Ragoczy saw that she carried a tray with a basin, clean rags, and a pair of shears. She still wore the countryman's smock she had donned to work in Ragoczy's hidden alchemical laboratory, and her crown of braids was covered with a simple kerchief. "I gather you need my help."

There was a spark of admiration in his eyes. He was glad she was so composed, and hoped that dealing with the hideous damage done to Joacim Branco would not prove to be too much for her. "Yes, I do. Or rather, Joacim does. But he's badly hurt. If you can't face that, you'd be more help in the kitchen."

"Which is to say, no help at all." She had put the tray down and came to stand beside him. For a moment only her features reflected her revulsion, and then she mastered herself. "What must I do?"

By this time Ragoczy had pulled away as much of Branco's clothing as he could without causing greater hurt. "Where the cloth has adhered to the wounds, you must soak it loose. Don't hurry. It takes time. Do this as slowly as necessary. Change cloths often. And make sure the water is warm but not hot. Also, there is a compound—you can find it in my laboratory, in the herb cabinet. It's got the Eye of Horus on it. Put a handful of that in the warm water and it will help prevent infection."

She nodded. "I'll be back quickly. Where should I begin?"

Ragoczy's attention was once again focused on Joacim Branco, but he said somewhat remotely, "Start with the left arm. Be very careful. His bones are broken on both sides of the elbow."

"Will it ever heal, Francesco?" She was in the door, but she turned back to ask the question.

"If you mean, will it mend, yes, after a fashion. But if you mean will he ever use it again, and will it be strong, I'm afraid it's extremely unlikely." His words were crisp, and tinged with anger. "Fortunately, Joacim is right-handed, and the cuts on his right arm will heal cleanly."

Nodding in acceptance of this evaluation, Demetrice left the room, bound for the herb cabinet in Ragoczy's hidden laboratory.

Ruggiero did not return for more than an hour, and when he did arrive, Araldo and Pascoli carried Narciso's stiffening body between them.

"What is it, old friend?" Ragoczy asked in his native tongue. Residual fury burned in Ruggiero's eyes. He answered in Latin. "I went to la Loggia dei Lanzi, I went to il Palazzo della Signoria, I went to Santa Maria del Fiore, I went to Santissima Annunziata. No one, no one was willing to hear my complaint or take the body for burial. I wanted to make sure the authorities knew what is happening in the streets of Fiorenza. But no one cared. No one listened."

Araldo and Pascoli were more frightened than exhausted, and Araldo had courage enough to say, "Master, one of the Domenicani said that Narciso was under a curse for practicing forbidden arts, and that his death was an Act of God."

Ragoczy raised his finely drawn brows. "Act of God? With most of his ribs kicked in and his skull broken?" He was growing angry, but said, "My temper is not aimed at you, my stewards. You've done everything and more that I could have asked of you, and you have done it well. Be good enough to carry the body into the reception room off the loggia. It's only a few hours until dawn, and I'll go to la Signoria as soon as the day's session begins. The matter will be cleared up quickly." He wished he was as confident as he sounded.

"And Branco?" Ruggiero asked as the two understewards carried Narciso's body to the front of the palazzo.

"Badly hurt. Do you remember that physician we knew in Constantinople? The one they burned for sorcery?" He shook his head again as he thought of the waste of the man's life and skill. "I wish we had him here now. I've been trying to recall how he dealt with the kind of break Joacim has. You don't happen to know what he did, do you?"

"You mean Leoninas?" Ruggiero frowned. "He held the bones together with fine wires. But that's all I remember."

Ragoczy made a gesture of exasperation. "I've racked my brain trying to think of what to do, but nothing seems to work." He indicated that his manservant should follow him back to the bedchamber where Joacim Branco lay. "I'll want clothes set out at first light." He touched his embroidered velvet lucco. "This is quite ruined, I'm afraid."

"What will you wear?" Ruggiero knew that he was dirty himself, and asked, "If you are going to be busy here, may I bathe in your tub?"

"Of course," Ragoczy said impatiently. "But draw fresh water for me at first light. I'll want to bathe before I dress."

Ruggiero again considered the matter of clothing for his master. "Do you have any preference in the matter?"

"I'm going to la Signoria. Make it something impressive."

So it was that some time before eight of the morning clock, Francesco Ragoczy da San Germano, in full black barbasillio and red professorial cap from la Universidad de

Salamanca, strode into il Palazzo della Signora and demanded to talk to i Priori.

The guard who stopped him asked what his business was.

"I wish to bring to the attention of the Console the dreadful conditions of their streets after dark. Last night one of my colleagues was badly beaten and his apprentice killed by three young men. It happened only a few steps from here."

The guard looked confused, and began to say in an overly concerned way, "It's true that there is danger abroad at night, and for that reason it was most unwise for your colleague to venture out. Now, while it's lamentable that his apprentice should have been killed, you can't be—"

But Ragoczy cut him short. "Buon Signore," he said icily, "are you going to announce me to the clerk, or are you going to talk forever?"

Bristling, the guard defended himself. "You can't just march in here and demand to see the Console. Only Fiorenzeni have that right. You must ask for a time to address them—"

"Show me to the clerk, Signore, or I will turn around and shout it through the city that I will pay five hundred fiorini d'or for the capture of the men who hurt Magister Branco and killed his apprentice, who was a Fiorenzan."

The guard hesitated. He knew the foreigner's reputation well enough to realize that he would do exactly what he threatened to do. Authority and prudence warred in his heart. Prudence won. He lifted his pike from Ragoczy's path. "The clerk is in the reception chamber, Ragoczy."

"Thank you," Ragoczy said sweetly as he entered il Palazzo della Signoria. He walked up the stairs quickly, sensing the new hostility around him. The other men in the governmental building were reserved, and a few of them made soft comments about the foreigner.

The clerk's reception room was crowded, and Ragoczy resigned himself to a long wait. He folded his hands into his square sleeves and fixed his eyes on some distant point far beyond the windows.

More than an hour later the clerk looked up, ready to motion to Ragoczy, when a merchant in somber clothes moved forward. "I am a Fiorenzan. By right I should be taken first."

"But he has waited longer," the clerk objected mildly.

"Let him wait!" He turned to Ragoczy, real hatred in his face. "Foreign alchemist! Godless heathen!"

Ragoczy brought his attention back from the distant hills. "I admit to being an alchemist, and certainly I am foreign. But I am not a heathen, and as someone who owns land in Fiorenza, I have the same rights as you, my friend."

"I am not your friend!" the merchant exploded, his round face taking on a dark hue. He came nearer to Ragoczy. "You should not be allowed in this city. There should be laws against it. You contaminate the place, and for you, we all face destruction."

Though he was fairly certain now that the merchant was a follower of Savonarola, he asked, to make sure, "And do you disapprove only of me, or of the whole of Fiorenza?"

"God alone approves. It is not for me to approve, it is my lot to obey the will of God."

Ragoczy nodded wearily, and motioned to the clerk. "Since it would be useless to try to conduct my business with this man present, I will wait until he is through. And then, I trust, you will allow me to present my complaint in full?"

The merchant glared at him. "I know you, Francesco Ragoczy. You damned Palleschi!"

This had obviously been intended to provoke him, but Ragoczy laughed outright. "If you mean I stand by Medici

Palle, you're right. Laurenzo was my friend." He stopped abruptly.

"You're proud of it?"

"Signore," Ragoczy said to the merchant, "you have business with the clerk. It is so urgent that you have insisted that your dealings precede mine. Very well. But get on with it. My business is also urgent." He turned back to the window, oblivious of the fierce scowl the merchant directed at him.

When at last the clerk was willing to hear him, Ragoczy had thought out the matter completely.

"You have a complaint?" the clerk asked, starting to prepare another parchment.

"I do indeed. Ordinarily I would ask to address i Priori themselves, but it appears that I can't. Therefore, I will leave my complaint with you, and trust that the Console will hear of it soon enough."

Gradazo Ondante tapped his quill and stood a little straighter. "It's my function to see that all complaints are heard by the Console."

"I'm aware of that." He forestalled any objection to this remark by getting immediately to the matter. "I am Francesco Ragoczy da San Germano, by rank, Conte." He had never used his title before in Fiorenza. He saw the officious clerk's eyes widen a little and his attention was caught. Ragoczy went on. "I have a palazzo on the north side of the city, near Santissima Annunziata. I conduct various experiments—"

"Many of which are contrary to Fiorenzan law," Gradazo Ondante interrupted him, but with a self-deprecating smile.

"Fiorenzan law is strangely pliant in some matters. And I have," Ragoczy went on, not allowing Ondante to sidetrack him, "the honor to count several distinguished alchemists among my associates. One, Magister Joacim Branco, has come from Portugal to Fiorenza to continue his studies. He took an apprentice some months ago. Last night, Signore Ondante, Magister Branco and his apprentice, Narciso Boscino, were attacked by three young Fiorenzan men, well-dressed and educated in their speech. They beat Magister Branco until his bones were broken, and they killed Narciso Boscino. It was not an accident that they did. Both his skull and his ribs were broken."

Gradazo Ondante paled at this. "When did it happen? And where?"

"Last night, at dusk. The place was an alley off la Via Porta Rossa. Magister Branco heard one name, Clemente. He did not know if other names were used, being then too much in pain to understand what was being said."

"And the apprentice is dead?" Gradazo Ondante held the parchment before him as if it could ward off such bad news.

"He is dead. He lies in my palazzo. It is unfortunate that no church would accept the body last night. I feel it necessary to mention that Narciso Boscino was Fiorenzan. His father is an apothecary and has a house in la Via della Primavera. If you find it difficult to pursue the matter for me, then I am sure you will for Signore Boscino."

The parchment rustled as the Clerk Ondante gripped it more tightly. "I will report this to the Console."

"That is your duty," Ragoczy agreed.

"Beaten, you say, and bones broken?" He was clearly worried, and found it increasingly difficult to meet the foreigner's penetrating eyes. "The Portuguese?"

"Pray send some official physician to my palazzo and let him testify to the extent of Branco's injuries."

"And Boscino killed?"

"The body lies in my reception room. He should be in a

church. There are prayers that should be spoken for the repose of his soul."

The clerk nodded rather distantly and said, "Yes. Of course. It will be seen to. We'll send a messenger to his father—"

Ragoczy interrupted him. "I have taken that liberty. My understeward Araldo carried the news to Signore Boscino at first light. It would be better to send a priest."

"Certainly." The clerk was more distressed now. "It will be seen to. You may be assured of that."

"When?" The question hung in the air between them, almost a visible presence.

"When?" the clerk repeated. "Ah . . . Soon. Yes. Soon."

"Today?" Ragoczy suggested.

"Yes. Perhaps. Soon." With those gasped words, Gradazo Ondante fled the reception room.

As Ragoczy walked back toward Palazzo San Germano, his thoughts were as dark as his frown. It was rather more than a year since Laurenzo died, and the city seemed stunned without him. He watched two young men in the robes of the Università di Pisa, the braid down their backs indicating they studied law. Both the young men were apprehensive, one of them glancing uneasily at the tall spire of Santa Maria Novella, a few blocks away.

He was so preoccupied with the unhappy students that he failed to notice the five or six youngsters who followed him. Then a pebble struck his shoulder from behind, and he spun around.

"Antichrist! Antichrist! Antichrist!" the boys shouted as Ragoczy faced them. "Foreign Antichrist!"

"What . . . ?" Ragoczy was more startled than frightened. "What is this?"

The next pebble struck his forehead, drawing blood.

At the sight of this victory, the boys began throwing more pebbles, as well as anything else that came to hand—dung, bits of fallen roof tiles.

As he turned once more, Ragoczy noticed that the two Pisan law students were nowhere in sight. He was also aware that the few people in the street were encouraging the boys, and a few made the sign against the evil eye.

More boys rushed to join Ragoczy's tormentors, and as they ran through the streets, he tried to evade them, ducking down ancient narrow streets and racing through busy corners. Once he nearly upset a butcher's stall, and paused only long enough to toss a few coins to the butcher, who immediately stopped cursing.

Then he saw the elegant bulk of Brunelleschi's San Lorenzo ahead, and he ran into the church, almost knocking against the elderly Benedettan Brother who stood near the door to aid the sick and the infirm into the church.

"Forgive me, Brother," Ragoczy said, and was about to explain when the crowd of boys rounded the corner and set up a cry at the sight of their quarry.

The monk put his hand on Ragoczy's shoulder briefly. "Go in, my son. They dare not enter here." And he folded his arms over his chest and took up his stance in the center of the door.

Ragoczy was grateful for the rest, for though he was not out of breath, the long run had awakened his ancient fears again. He walked down the nave, remembering the last time he had been in San Lorenzo. Then the church had been draped in black and all Fiorenza dressed in mourning.

Outside, the boys railed at the old monk, howling for the blood of the foreigner. Inside, Francesco Ragoczy sat down on the unadorned tomb of his friend, and waited.

TEXT OF A letter to Francesco Ragoczy da San Germano from Olivia:

> *To Ragoczy Sanct' Germain Franciscus in Fiorenza,*
> *Olivia sends her lifelong affection.*
>
> *I had your letter of May 12 in good time, and I am indeed sorry to learn the rumors we have heard here are true. This is not the first time we've seen this happen, old friend. It was you yourself who told me that hatred and destruction are easier than love and creation. You and I have seen more than our share. I can tell, from what you choose not to say to me, that you fear for everything you love in Fiorenza. Be sensible, then, and return to Venezia. There is art there, and music, and joy. You will not be stoned in the streets, your associates will not be beaten. Or come to me in Roma, where you have revisited too infrequently. We will visit all the places we knew when we met. You will see for yourself how the city has changed of late. And if you like, you may have an audience with the Pope (though I advise against it. Rodrigo Borgia is rapacious, and the cost of such an interview would be high. His Holiness Alessandro VI, may God or someone bless him, has been using his office to enrich himself and his family).*
>
> *It will take a great deal to make this Borgia Pope turn against Savonarola, but I agree that it would make everything easier. If I learn anything about it, I will surely let you know. I have heard that the Camaldolese prior in Fiorenza and one of the Francescani are unalterably opposed to Savonarola. So, too, is the Agostiniano Fra Mariano, but it is expected of the latter, since he was one of the Medici favorites.*

Dear Sanct' Germain, it hurts me to read your letter. You have so much loneliness and despair in your words. Yes, I realize you said nothing of those feelings, but after all this time, I know you as I know the lines of my palms or the sound of the Tiber. For the sake of your friends, spare yourself this anguish. Return to your Carpathian mountains, if you can avoid the carnage there. Play music again. If you can't leave Fiorenza, take that student of yours—Demetrice, I think you said her name is—take her to you. Share your life with her. Love her. You say that she has your secret and honors it. You say that she is intelligent. If she mourns for Laurenzo still, as you do, your pleasure together will soothe her heart. And yours, Sanct' Germain. I promise you that. I was in mourning when we first met, and when my terror was gone, I went into your arms more eagerly than ever I have gone to others before or since. Why do you lock yourself away when the greatest wish of your heart is to be open, to be loved without lies or pretense?

Yes, and now you're out of patience with me. If more than a thousand years cannot buy me a few privileges with you, you're impossible.

Send me word, my dear, if you should have need of me. As long as I have earth in my shoes, I am at your service. I owe you so much, and there is so little I can do to redeem that debt, now or ever. But what I can do, I will. You have only to ask. And do not, I beseech you, debate too long whether or not you need help. When the time comes, if it comes, send me word.

Now I must hand this to Cardinale Giovanni's messenger, who will carry it to Fiorenza. And I will leave for Palazzo Borgia, where tonight they are keeping the

*Feast of Moses the Prophet in what they fondly think
of as Roman style. If only they knew. I'm wearing this
silk gown that is somewhat in the fashion of Byzan-
tium and tied with cords in the old Greek way, and I
have been assured that this ridiculous costume is most
authentic.*

*Be kind to yourself, and be on guard for your
safety. And if you can, spare yourself more pain.*

With my love and my life, this comes from

Olivia

In Roma, September 4, 1493

CHAPTER 6

OCTOBER HAD TURNED hot and Fiorenza shimmered in the
afternoon sunlight. On the streets, almost no one moved, and
these few men abroad were bowed with the weight of the
heat.

Sandro Filipepi had spent a disturbing morning with la
Priora di Sacro Infante. Suor Merzede insisted that Estasia
should remain at the convent for another month. It was the
third such extension la priora had required, and Sandro was
beginning to be profoundly worried. A letter sent to Estasia's
relations in Parma had not helped him, for they had authorized Sandro to act in their stead and trusted that he would
do whatever was best for Estasia.

On impulse, as he came through la Porta alla Lanza, he
turned eastward, toward the tall rounded bulk of Santissima
Annunziata. The walk was not pleasant, and he realized he

was not anxious to speak to Ragoczy. But he knew that he owed it to his afflicted cousin. Crossing la Piazza San Marco, he was struck for the first time by the paradox of that little square. On the north, San Marco, the Domenican church and convent that had housed Fra Angelico, Beato Antoninus and now Girolamo Savonarola. On the south side of la piazza, surprisingly still on his hot afternoon, la Galleria dell'Accademia, that remarkable school where Plato and Aristotle were as revered as the lives of the saints, where Greek and Latin were taught, where the things Savonarola most despised flourished.

A frown creased Sandro's craggy face. Perhaps Simone was right, and Savonarola would save Fiorenza. But he could not trust the little Domenican Prior. The learning and the love of human endeavor taught in l'Accademia appealed to him more. He walked through Piazza San Marco, and soon turned on the flagged lane to Palazzo San Germano.

The sound of the knocker was solemn, and Sandro was startled by the gloom it created in his mind. He was almost ready to abandon the idea of seeing Ragoczy when he heard footsteps, and in a moment, Ragoczy himself opened the door.

"Botticelli," he said with a genuine smile as he held the door open. "Come in. It's sweltering out there."

In spite of himself, Sandro warmed to this welcome. He went through the door into the loggia and sighed. "It *is* hot. I didn't realize how hot." He wiped his flushed face with his loose outer sleeve and stared enviously at the flowing caftan of Persian taffeta Ragoczy wore. "I wish I had one of those."

Ragoczy responded promptly. "Give my houseman your measurements and I will have one made for you. What color would you like? You needn't wear black as I do. There is a splendid blue and a shade like ripe peaches, almost the color of your hair."

"It's not necessary, Conte," Sandro said, suddenly diffident.

"Conte?" Ragoczy repeated the title. "This is Fiorenza, amico, and a Repubblica. You've called me Francesco before. Why say Conte now?"

Sandro turned away. "I don't know. But I haven't seen much of you, and lately there's been ... trouble ..." He stopped, not knowing what to say.

Ragoczy finished for him, his voice soft. "I know, Sandro. They're calling me Il Conte Stragnero now, aren't they?"

"I have heard that," Sandro admitted with difficulty. "But, truly, Francesco, nothing is meant by it. It's the fear, that's all." He felt miserable talking this way to his foreign friend.

"That's *all*? What is there worse than fear?" With a gesture he invited Sandro into his reception room off the loggia. "What may I get you? Amadeo is very good with wines and fruits." He had already clapped his hands, and Ruggiero appeared in the doorway.

"I'm sorry I was busy at the back of the courtyard, master. I would have opened the door." He nodded to Botticelli. "It's an honor to see you again, Signore."

"And you, Ruggiero," Sandro said automatically.

"Fetch our guest whatever Amadeo thinks is worthy of his art," Ragoczy told Ruggiero.

"If I fetch all that, master, Signor Filipepi won't be able to leave until late tomorrow." His smile was genuine. "We've had few guests of late. I'm certain you know why."

"Yes." Sandro sighed, and sank into one of the Turkish chairs away from the windows. "Bring me whatever you

wish, so long as it is cool. My mouth is dry as tinder. I've
walked to Sacro Infante and back today, and in this heat, I
feel my years."

There was a moment of silence; then Ruggiero bowed
and withdrew and Ragoczy studied his guest, saying in a
colorless way, "And how did you find Donna Estasia?"

"I don't know." His expression was complicated, drawing from his real concern as well as his irritation. "One day
she is better, much like herself of old. Then she is charming
and speaks of nothing but home and how much she would
like to return to us. And on another day she lies in her little
cell and whimpers, saying that she sees her own damnation,
and then she will speak to no one, not Suor Merzede, not
me. And on some days she welcomes her damnation, and
what she says terrifies me. She was like that today. She
clung to me and cried out as if we lay together. The good
Sisters all behave as if she has done nothing outrageous,
but . . ." He stared across the room toward the windows
where Ragoczy stood, a shadow against the distant glare of
the day.

"Why did you seek me out today, Sandro?" The question
was gentle as he turned to face his guest.

"I . . . I'm not sure; I truly do not know, Francesco."

"Because, perhaps, that I was Estasia's lover, once?"
There was no shame in taking an unhindered widow to his
bed, but he knew that Sandro had been trapped between his
brother's austerity and his cousin's sensuality. He went on,
"That was over some time ago. She tired of me, I think. I
know I could no longer please her."

The relief in Sandro's face was amazing. "That's it, at
least in part."

"And you were wondering if ever she behaved then as

she does on occasion now?" He had come nearer Sandro and his eyes were compassionate.

"I don't mean . . . You needn't . . ."

"Who has a better right?" Ragoczy chose another of the Turkish chairs, a few steps from Sandro's, and sat, using the time to think.

"If you'd be willing . . ." He stopped. "Most men wouldn't mind, not Fiorenzeni, but now, things are different. It's not seemly to talk of the sports of love . . ."

"You mean that the Domenicani are getting stronger and that they take a dim view of the pleasures of the body." He said this harshly, recalling other times he had seen the Brothers of San Domenico come to power, and the havoc their fierce Christianity wrought. "I'll answer your questions, Sandro, whatever they are. I doubt if either of us will run to San Marco afterward."

This time Sandro almost smiled. "You're right, amico. Why I should be so uncertain . . ."

Ragoczy could think of several excellent reasons for Sandro's uncertainty, but kept them to himself. "What do you want to know?"

"Anything. I can't account for what's happened to her. Someone must know—"

"As you wish." Ragoczy cut Sandro short before he could begin another convoluted apology. "It was shortly after I came here that I had the pleasure to meet Donna Estasia. It was on a Sunday afternoon, one of those splendid days at Palazzo de' Medici, when Laurenzo had most of the talents in Fiorenza under his roof for a meal and entertainment." He stopped, and a feeling very like physical pain filled him. "Do you remember those afternoons?"

Sandro, too, was moved. "Yes, I remember."

"You had come, and brought Estasia with you. You and

young Buonarroti were off somewhere having a delicious argument about the relative virtues of sculpture and painting, and Estasia was bored. She didn't read very well, spoke only Tuscan and had few interests beyond her home and womanhood. So I spoke to her, since I was a stranger then, and knew no more than half a dozen of Laurenzo's circle. She was glad to have someone to talk to, someone as foreign as I, someone as unknown. She asked me to withdraw with her for an hour or so, and when we were alone, loosened her bodice to let me fondle her breasts."

On the afternoon this had happened, Sandro would have been pleased to learn of it, and would have felt no embarrassment. But that was almost three years ago, and now he shifted awkwardly in the Turkish chair and gazed out through the windows rather than meet Ragoczy's eyes. "I see."

"She asked me to come to her bed a few months later, and you know that I did." He looked at Sandro's uncomfortable face. "It was not quite what you think. She took no risks with me."

Quickly Sandro turned to look at him. "No risks?"

"I gave her pleasure after my fashion and in my way, as she knew I would, and I took mine of her, but I promise you, never in the manner most men use women." He stopped, and said easily, "I'm incapable of it."

Sandro's skin was fair, and for that reason blushed all the more brightly. "You needn't—"

Again Ragoczy stopped him. "I'm telling you this so that you will understand Donna Estasia somewhat better, and perhaps be able to help her more. She was not willing to accept my . . . limitations, after a while."

Ruggiero came into the room then, with an engraved golden tray holding a tall ewer and a single glass cup.

"Amadeo has made a sweet in the Muslim manner. It's called a sherbet. It's quite cooling."

Sandro was grateful for the interruption, and gave Ruggiero all of his attention as the chilled fruit pulp was poured into the cup and honey mixed with it.

"Will you want me soon, master?" Ruggiero asked when Botticelli had been served.

"I don't think so. If you would rather return to your work."

"I would." He inclined his head to Ragoczy, then added as an afterthought, "Donna Demetrice is working with me. The task should be finished soon." He was reluctant to say more about the shipment of alchemical compounds which had arrived that afternoon from Modena.

"That's fortunate. I will call Araldo if I need anything."

Ruggiero nodded and was gone.

"I haven't seen Donna Demetrice in some time," Sandro mused.

But Ragoczy would not be sidetracked. "When you leave, if you like, we can go through the court and you may have conversation with her then."

Reluctantly Sandro nodded. "You're right. This must come first." He took a little of the sherbet, savoring the mixture. Then he put the cup down and regarded his host carefully. "What happened between you and my cousin, Francesco?"

"For a while we enjoyed each other. I thought that was all she wanted—a safe, exotic foreigner who was willing to satisfy her flesh . . ."

"But you said that you are not able . . ."

Ragoczy smoothed the front of his house gown. "There are other ways, amico mio, and for a time they were enough." He paused, wondering how much Sandro needed to know. "I was mistaken about her. I didn't realize that she had other expectations." He left his chair and once again went to stare out into the pale afternoon. "She didn't want me because I was foreign and safe. She wanted me because I offered her a new sensation. And when that sensation was exhausted, she demanded more. There was nothing more I could do."

"Could or would?" Sandro asked shrewdly, his discomfort all but gone.

"If you must have it, would. I won't give that excitement that takes its pleasure in hurt." He had spoken curtly, and he said, to soften the blow, "Sandro, no one lives who could be all the things your cousin demands in a lover. It's not her error. It's not anyone's fault. There is no sin, no matter what Girolamo Savonarola says. But as long as she has such needs, she will be unhappy. With time, she may be rid of her trouble. But I can't do more than I already have. She's angry with me. Because I failed her too much." As he said this, Ragoczy picked up the little Greek flute which was lying on a chest under the window. He held it, his fingers on its simple stops.

"I see." He had more of the sherbet. "She has refused to Confess. She says that the devils torment her flesh when she tries to pray, and that she can't ask for forgiveness."

"I'm sorry." Ragoczy at last came to stand near Sandro. "Botticelli, protect yourself. She is a woman obsessed. Without meaning to, she might do you great harm."

"She might do the same for you."

Ragoczy shrugged. "Just fuel to the fire. Anything is believed of a foreigner. I'm prepared to leave, if I must. But you"—he touched Sandro's arm—"you live here. You work here. This is your home. It would be easy for her, without any such intention, to destroy you, amico. So be on guard."

The warmth and affection in Ragoczy's voice startled Sandro. He put the cup down, rising as he said, "I will. And I am grateful to you. You told me . . . so much you needn't have."

"Would you like to see Donna Demetrice?"

Sandro nodded, accepting that this difficult interview was at an end. "No. She must still be busy. I will call another time, if you'll have me." There was an awkward moment, intensified by what they had said; Sandro made a resigned gesture and cleared his throat.

"Of course," Ragoczy had started to move to the door, but Sandro caught his shoulder with one big paint-stained hand. He pulled the smaller man around and touched his cheek with his own.

Ragoczy was still, and then, in his soft, slightly accented manner, he said, "Thank you. For your humanity."

Sandro was somewhat taken aback, and frowned, suspecting some sarcasm or bitterness, but as he followed Ragoczy to the huge door at the loggia, he realized that the foreigner's thanks had been genuine. He tried, as he stood in the door, to respond somehow, but Ragoczy had become remote.

"Come next week, and Amadeo will make a banquet," he said in a rather formal way.

Sandro was chagrined. "I'm afraid I can't then. Simone is keeping a fast, and I have agreed to keep it with him."

The ghost of a frown clouded Ragoczy's eyes a moment. "Very well. Come when you want. You are welcome." He was about to close the door, but he added, "There are many things to be on guard against, Sandro. Don't be deceived."

"What do you mean?" Sandro's rough-hewn features grew tight with worry.

"Nothing," Ragoczy said, then relented. "We lose as much to affection as we do to hatred, amico mio. Remember that." Then, with a kind gesture, he turned away to hide his face.

TEXT OF A letter from Gian-Carlo Casimir di Alerico Circando to Franceszco Ragoczy da San Germano:

> To his excellent and deeply respected teacher, Francesco Ragoczy da San Germano, in Fiorenza, Gian-Carlo in Venezia sends his urgent greetings.
>
> I have had word from Luis Santiago y Choranes that the builder Lodovico is not satisfied with his work in Spain and desires to go into France. I will, if you wish, write to Reynard Puydouce and request that he act as your agent in this matter.
>
> But I am very much afraid that this will not serve. This is the second change the man has made, and nothing we have arranged has suited him. He did not like building villas in Lisboa, he hasn't liked working on two big churches in Spain. He has indicated that he doesn't want to do anything else, and he is not willing to settle on a farm.
>
> This is contrary to your instructions, but I would like to hire an assassin to deal with the man. He cannot be managed any other way. If you delay taking his life, he will bring you nothing but trouble. You have said that you will not make light of your oath. But you do not make light of this man if you have him killed—you recognize him for the danger he is.
>
> If you are willing to authorise it, I know of a man, a Genovese, who will do the thing for a hundred gold ducati. He comes highly recommended and is known to be both discreet and honest. No one who has hired him in the past has ever been blackmailed by him, and none of them were ever implicated in any murder he undertook.

This message may be long in reaching you, for the winter storms have been very severe, and travelers have spoken of nothing but trouble on the road. It has been so bad that even the brigands have not been about much. I will send this with a party of monks going to Ferrara, and then hope that it will be sent on from there.

Your recommendation that I buy leather goods from Poland was excellent. I have a large order in your warehouse and there is a great deal of interest in the boots. The heels, as you remarked, are particularly desirable for horsemen and might indeed start a fashion. I plan to order more when the spring comes and passage to Krakow is possible again.

The shipment of resins from Egypt has been taken by pirates and it will be at least a year before I can get more for you. I am at present trying to find other sources, but so far my inquiries have led nowhere. If you know of a merchant who can supply the resins, other than the Egyptian, let me know.

Il Doge has granted you the right to build the extra rooms you requested onto your palazzo here. As you guessed, the seven pounds of gold speeded the petition to il Doge in good time.

Send me word of you as soon as the weather allows. The news we have here of Fiorenza is almost all bad. Anything is believed now that the Domenicano Savonarola is risen so high. Until I hear from you again, I commend myself and all my work to you.

        Gian-Carlo Casimir di Alerico Circando
In Venezia, January 18, 1494
The Feast of i Santi Piero e Paolo

CHAPTER 7

Piero de Medici had just come in from a fine ride through the hills around Fiorenza. His face was flushed, his eyes bright, and his smile almost erased the petulance from his mouth. He strode through the reception chamber of Palazzo de' Medici, calling for wine and some of the sweets that Massimillio made for him and that were his favorites.

"Pardon, Signore," said one of the understewards as the new slave was sent running to the kitchen.

Piero stopped, "What is it, Sergio?" He already showed an annoyed frown. "I want to change."

Sergio nodded, but said, "There is a physician to see you, master. He was sent by la Signoria. He's been waiting all morning."

"What does he want?" He wanted to be patient, remembering for a moment how generously his father had given his attention to every messenger and fool la Signoria had foisted off on him.

"I don't know, master. He didn't choose to tell me." Sergio stood aside, as if waiting to lead Piero into the little room off the larger court that Laurenzo had used for his study, and Piero now avoided whenever possible.

"Oh, very well." Piero's sigh was exaggerated so that Sergio could not miss it. "A physician, you say?"

"Yes, master. He has addressed la Signoria, and i Priori felt that you should hear what he has to say." He held the door for Piero and followed him across the court. "If you will recall, there was a note ten days ago about the physician . . ."

"That?" Piero scoffed. "One of those Padovan medicals

who is forever giving warning of this disaster or that. As bad as Savonarola, finding doom in every raindrop."

Sergio walked faster so that he could open the door for Piero. As he did, he announced, "Piero di Laurenzo de' Medici. This is Aenea Ermanaricco."

The man in the formal scholar's lucco rose respectfully, his somber face and intelligent eyes revealing a certain disappointment. "God give you good day, Medici," he said with full courtesy. "I had the honor to meet your father some years ago."

He could have said nothing worse to Piero. "Yes. My father seems to have known everyone in the world, if I'm to believe the petitioners who come here." He strolled across the room to the unused writing table. "There's something you wish to discuss with me? About some tale you told la Signoria?" He sat on the edge of the table, one leg swinging negligently, showing his mud-spattered boots and patterned calzebrache as well as his contempt.

"Signore de' Medici, you've fallen heir to a tremendous responsibility. And you are, if I may say so, very young to shoulder so great a burden."

"Indeed? And yet, my father, whom you met, or so you say, was no more than twenty-one when he assumed that same responsibility. So you see, it runs in the family. We have power early in life, and learn to deal with the burden while we're still strong and eager, and we don't wait until we're old and doddering to lead the state." He smiled sweetly, his light-colored hair framing his face like the bright halos of Botticelli's angels.

"Yes," Ermanaricco's brows drew together. "Have you read the material I presented to i Priori?"

Piero's smile was more of a sneer. "I glanced over it, but it really didn't seem important. Perhaps you'd be willing to explain it to me while I wait for my cook to prepare a little food for me?"

This time the physician hesitated before answering, and there was deepening worry in his face. "I'll try, Signore. But allow me a little time with you."

"You have it," Piero assured him mendaciously. "Begin, good physician. I'm certain you'll amaze me."

Ermanaricco bit his lower lip, then began. "If you have read the report, then you will know that last year there were three cases of plague in Fiorenza. And there were more cases in the houses beyond the Porta San Frediano. In all, seventeen souls returned to God from the visitation of the plague."

"Who were these people?" Piero asked, trying to remember anyone he knew who had been ill.

"For the most part, wool carders. It would appear that some degree of infection came with wool into the city. There is always some vermin with the wool, and it is currently believed by the faculty of the Università di Padova that much infection accompanies vermin."

Piero laughed. "How far the study of medicine has come, when learned men are reduced to studying vermin."

The physician would not be provoked. "If medicine is to save anyone, there must be nothing we will not study," he said sharply, then resumed his explanation. "There is a great deal of concern now about the coming summer. Plague is always worst in hot weather, and I am very much afraid that if nothing is done, then there will be more infection this year."

"And you want me to do something?" Piero demanded, and his dangling leg stopped swinging. "You come to me for that?"

"There is no one else, Medici," the physician said gently.

"Fiorenza has always looked to your family to lead them away from danger."

"What danger?" Piero asked. "You can't tell me that, can you? You say that there may be a plague, and it might come this summer." He waited, then shook his head. "No, Ermanaricco, that's not enough. What kind of plague is this? Black plague? The pox? Swine plague? Or is this new?"

As Piero mocked him, Aenea Ermanaricco's serious face had turned grim. "It is a kind of swine plague. The unfortunates who become infected by it succumb to putrescent humors and an infusion of blood."

If this picture upset Piero, he gave no sign of it. He was on his feet now. "I'm not frightened, physician. But tell me, what am I do to in order to prevent any Fiorenzan from dying of putrescent humors?"

Although he realized he pleaded in vain, Ermanaricco said, "You must pull down all the old houses where there is a great deal of filth, and where too many people live close together. You must build more privies for the poor and you must see that all wells are cleaned, and that everyone who works carding wool is examined by physicians to detect any sign of illness at least once a week."

Piero's expression was frozen. "I see. And of course, you think that I will pay for this?" He paused. "You ask Fiorenzeni to tear down their houses for nothing? You ask physicians to examine wool carders once a week out of charity?"

The physician pulled at his dark pleated gown. "It would be worth it, Medici."

The little room was cool and the noise from the courtyard was muffled, and there was as much privacy there as anywhere in il Palazzo de' Medici. Piero was glad of it, for it allowed him a chance to do some plain speaking. "Are you aware of the situation in Napoli? Do you know what Fer-

rante's death will mean to Italia? Do you? And did you know
that Il Moro Sforza is wooing the French king into Italia to
conquer us? Did you know that? The King of England
seized our bank in London, and to this day, we have recovered none of the money he took from us. Henry Tudor has
said that he will not give back one English farthing. He has
stolen over eight thousand fiorini d'or. Or hadn't you heard?
Siena and Genova both want to take Livorno away from
Fiorenza. Does that matter to you? Well? And you expect me
to worry about a handful of wool carders who might fall ill
this summer?" He crossed his arms over his chest. "Come
back again, in June, and tell me then if there is any sign of
the plague, and perhaps then we can arrange to pull down
buildings and clean wells."

Ermanaricco's face was still now, and he looked as if he
had been struck. "It will be too late. Your citizens will be
dying by then. The only way to stop the plague is to prevent
it from getting a hold in the city."

"Then let me suggest that you go to the priests and ask
them to pray. Ask the Virgin or San Cosmo e San Damiano
to help you. But they haven't done very well by our house
recently."

"If you will not help," the physician said slowly, "then
tell me who might. You can busy yourself with your hunting
and your festival and your whoring. That's your choice. But
I must do whatever I can to prevent this plague."

It was Piero's turn to be insulted. Color stained his face
and his full mouth was rigid. "Talk that way, Ermanaricco,
and you will find yourself talking to the walls. Stone walls."
He walked to the door and turned back. "I want to hear no
more of this. If the old men at la Signoria want to believe
you, that is their affair, but I will have no more of you. If you
try to speak to me again, I will have you thrown into prison

until you are no longer dangerous." He clapped his hands loudly and Sergio appeared beside him almost instantly. "I suppose you overheard."

Sergio was silent.

"I said, I suppose you overheard."

The understeward ground his teeth, but he answered, "A few words, master. Only a few."

"Well, they were nonsense," Piero snapped. "If you parrot this madman's predictions around, you will find that neither I nor any of my friends will employ you. Then you can join those foolish Domenicani and prate of doom." He turned on his heel and went back across the courtyard.

For a few moments Aenea Ermanaricco was still; then he drooped in his robes and gave Sergio a resigned look. "You did hear?"

"Yes," Sergio admitted. "I'm sorry, physician."

He shook his head as much from disgust as worry. "Don't be sorry for me, steward. Be sorry for those poor people who will die this summer. They deserve your pity, not I." His fists clenched and he released them with an effort.

Sergio hesitated a moment, then said, "I don't know if I should tell you this, physician. But Magnifico's cousin, Donna Demetrice Volandrai, is still in the city, at the house of the foreign alchemist."

"Palazzo San Germano?" Ermanaricco asked. He had heard something of the foreigner, most of it respectful, but in these fear-clouded days, it was hard to know what to believe. "What could she do?"

"Well, she is a scholar. She might be able to speak to some of the others, and they might be able to talk to my master . . ." His words trailed off uncertainly and he thrust his hands into the deep pockets of his apron.

"Do you think it likely?" He opened his hands again.

"Well, I am desperate enough to try even that. And it is good of you," he added ruefully, "to help this madman."

There was sadness in Sergio's face. "Piero is not very much like his father." He held the door open, prepared to escort the Padovan physician from the house.

"He's not," Ermanaricco agreed, and picked up from the reading table a parchment, which he rolled and tied with a wide ribbon. "I'll take your advice and try my luck with the cousin. Or do you think il Conte will prevent me from seeing her?"

Sergio had not yet grown used to hearing Ragoczy called il Conte, and so he did not respond at once. "He's not likely to stop you. I know that there have been things said about him recently, but they're not accurate. He's foreign, but he was Laurenzo's friend."

The physician considered this. "I'll see what he says. If Donna Demetrice Volandrai will help me, you will have my gratitude for every life that is spared." He swept past the understeward and out into the larger courtyard of Palazzo de' Medici, and without waiting for Sergio, made for the entrance with a long, swinging stride.

Text of a letter from Febo Janario Anastasio de Benedetto Volandrai, brother of Donna Demetrice, to Marsilio Ficino written in classic Greek:

> To his most revered master and beloved scholar, Marsilio Ficino, his former pupil Febo di Benedetto Volandrai sends his greetings and affections from the estate of Landgraf Alberich Grossehoff, near Wien.

As you see, illustrious master, I have not yet left here to continue my studies, but it is a great joy for me to tell you that at the end of August I will quit my post here and journey to Paris, where I will enroll at the Université at last. I have been in communication with three of the great scholars there and I am assured that I will be welcome. Also, the great English University at Oxford has assured me that I might find a home for myself at Balliol College there.

I cannot tell you how much this pleases me. It has been a kind of purgatory here, for though I have enjoyed teaching the Landgraf's sons, there are few men here who love scholarship as I do, and I yearn for the company of intelligent men, and the good conversation they have, the fellowship and the understanding. It is the greatest delight of my life to be entering, once again, into the company of men of learning.

This opportunity, this realization of dreams, my sister, Demetrice, has made possible. It was she who sent me the necessary funds, and provided me with letters of introduction which she said were the gifts of Francesco Ragoczy, who is, I understand, her benefactor. She claims that he is nothing more, except her teacher, but I must confess that the only blot on my happiness is the fear that perhaps she has compromised herself for my sake. I realize that Ragoczy was a friend of Il Magnifico's, but Laurenzo has been dead for almost two years, and his effect has lessened. Surely this foreigner might by now have made arrangements other than the ones originally concluded with Laurenzo.

Certainly my sister could not sell herself to such a man, but she might, however, misguidedly, take a lover

*of less worth than her own. There is some rumor, I
have heard from Poliziano, that Ragoczy is titled, but
we have all seen strangers who claim titles for their
aggrandizement. If he is indeed a Conte, then Demetrice may count herself fortunate to have won his devotion and to have gained his protection. But if he is
some adventurer, she may be hardly used and find herself deserted and friendless.*

*In short, my dear, respected master, I am of two
minds about this sudden fortune of mine. If indeed the
gift comes freely, and if indeed this Ragoczy treats my
sister with honor, then my satisfaction is unmarred.
But if Demetrice has been foolish for my sake, send me
word of it, and I will do what little lies in my power to
remedy her disgrace. Otherwise, I will leave for Paris
with a glad heart.*

*Of course I realize that her tale of being a student
of Ragoczy's is a gesture to me, so that I need not feel
she is forgetting her education. Well, if he allows her
the use of his library, she will have a chance to read
and her learning will not be wasted. You may not believe this, dear Ficino, but when we were younger, she
was thought to be the better student of the two of us.
That didn't last, but some part of her nature still finds
pleasure in study, which is rare in women. Undoubtedly she should have found a husband and been a
mother, but since she seems destined to remain unmarried and has no vocation for the Church, it is just
as well that she plays at scholarship. Laurenzo, you
may remember, credited her with great intelligence,
and she took an absurd satisfaction in this praise.*

*What, by the way, is your opinion of the news out
of Spain about the land to the west of us, far across the*

*ocean? I have heard a little about this new discovery,
but I am inclined to discount it. The Spaniards are
greedy for more land, and for power. It would be like
them to claim they have found a new world if only to
solidify their position in Europe.*

*Write to me here, or in Paris when you can. I con-
fess that I am hungry for news and the words of my old
friends. Only Demetrice's letters come regularly since
Lucio Facciabianco went into Orders.*

*With my love and respect, I commend myself to you,
dear master, and pray that your skills entrusted to me
will be a credit to you when I am in Paris.*

                              Febo Volandrai
On the Feast of Benedetto di Subiaco
March 21, 1494, near Wien

CHAPTER 8

SUOR MERZEDE HAD just begun the Agnus Dei when there
was a disturbance at the back of the chapel. The assembled
Celestiane nuns persevered through the prayer until the
noise became too great. With patient resignation the familiar Latin words straggled to a stop and Suor Signale stepped
out of the choir to look to her unfortunate charge.

Estasia shrieked as the nun touched her. "No! Nothing
holy!" She twisted violently, crouching low as Suor Signale
approached her once again. "No, nothing holy! I won't have
it!"

Suor Signale eluded Estasia's flailing hands and long fingernails, saying gently, "Dear Estasia, don't be troubled. If you will come with me, you may be comfortable once again."

By this time Suor Merzede, Superiora of the Sacro Infante convent, had come to join Suor Signale, and said in an undervoice, "She's getting worse."

"Yes, she is," Suor Signale agreed in an undervoice, then tried once more to calm Estasia. "No, my dear, don't be troubled in this way. Pray to God to forgive you. He is the beginning of tranquillity."

It was doubtful that Estasia heard her at all. She had fallen to her knees and wailed in a hideous voice. "The Devil is tempting me. See how he tempts me!" She threw herself backward. "See how he uses me. *See what he does to me!*" Her skirts were flung back and she spread her thighs.

"Oh, dear." Suor Signale sighed. "It will take time, Superiora. I'm afraid these seizures don't pass quickly. In a moment she will say that a thousand devils are ravishing her." The nun crossed herself. "It puts me out of all charity with her." It was a terrible admission for the nun to make.

"What God sends you, accept gladly in His name," Suor Merzede admonished her, but gently. "See if you can persuade her to Confess. I know you have before," she said resignedly. "She has resisted. But we must not be remiss in our faith because others wander." With that she turned once again and motioned to the assembled nuns to resume their prayers.

The gentle petition of the Agnus Dei filled the chapel as Suor Signale moved nearer to Estasia.

"No! No! *No!*" The cry rent the prayers, but the nuns paid no attention, their voices keeping up the words in a steady rhythm. Estasia flung herself to the stone floor and began to pull off the old gonella she wore.

"Now, sweet Donna Estasia," Suor Signale said, a certain asperity creeping into her tone. "You must not demean yourself this way. Ask God to give you strength to resist."

Estasia struck out at her, her hands like claws, her hazel eyes livid with hatred. "You shall not touch me! It is not for you to touch me. I don't want you. I want the other. See where the demons come. See how they stretch out their hands to me. See how they caress me, how they burn my flesh with their touch." She was almost naked now, and she lay supine, her legs apart, her head flung back. "No man, no one has done this to me. Only the demons can gratify my senses. They fill me everywhere." Her breathing slowed, sighed. She panted deeply. "Deeper! Deeper! Your seed burns me like vitriol. Your members are hot as furnace hooks." Her body tensed, spasmed, she shouted terrible blasphemies, and then fell back heavily, her face slicked with sweat, her body quiet.

Suor Signale had watched this with annoyed detachment, and recognized the end of the episode. She was relieved that it had taken no longer. Other times Estasia had writhed for hours, bruising herself, digging wounds into her flesh with her fingernails. This seizure had been as brief as it was intense, and Suor Signale was glad it was over. She knew from past experience that it was these times immediately following her erotic fits that Estasia was the most tractable, the most cooperative.

Gathering up Estasia's discarded gonella, Suor Signale reached gently for her suddenly lethargic charge. "Buona Donna, cover yourself. It isn't seemly for you to be naked in chapel. For your duty to the Good God Who loves you, treat yourself with the respect that is due to one of His creatures."

"Uum?" Estasia turned to the nun, and realization flooded her. Her eyes grew bright, and she looked down, sickened, at her voluptuous body, and then at the other Celestiane Sisters who continued their devotions.

"It happened again?" she said, anguish in her tone, her eyes filling with tears. "The devils came again?"

"You are better now," Suor Signale assured her, attempting once more to draw her from the chapel.

"Oh, good Sisters," Estasia cried aloud, "how can you bear one such as me? Why do you not abandon me to my fate? Leave me on the mountainside where beasts will tear me to pieces! I don't deserve your kindness. I deserve your wrath, your curses." She cried, great racking sobs drowning the gentle sussurus of prayers.

"Donna Estasia," Suor Signale said firmly as she took the weeping woman by the shoulders, "control yourself. If you are so filled with shame, think of the outrage you are committing at this moment." Inwardly the nun was horrified at her own outburst, but it seemed to have a calming effect on Estasia, who shuddered and clung suddenly to Suor Signale, making tiny gasps against her coif.

"I am unworthy. I am unworthy. I am unworthy," Estasia murmured with the same intensity that the nuns used in their repeated litanies.

Suor Signale clenched her hands on the beads of her rosary and admonished herself to be charitable. "Donna Estasia," she said, pulling her tightly locked hands away from her habit, "you are not doing as well as you should. It is unwise of you to remain here. You are in need of rest and reflection." A thought occurred to her. "Have you eaten today?"

Estasia shook her head. "I have no taste for food. I want only to think, to beg God to forgive me, so that I can confess my great errors. So many sins. So many, many sins." She gave the nun a sly sideways glance. "Do you envy me my sins, Suor Signale?"

"No," the nun answered brusquely. "I envy no one their sins."

"But you would have liked mine," Estasia persisted. "I had a *great many* lovers, some of them very rich, some of them very beautiful men. They were all intoxicated with me. They made themselves drunk with my body. Only I could satisfy them. Don't you ever wish, in the dark of the night, when you lie alone on your bed, that you had a lover who would so possess you that you were yourself no longer?"

Suor Signale controlled her sense of outrage. "The love that fills me, Donna Estasia," she said with asperity as she held open the door to the chapel, "is the love of Christ. It is not a love of the body, but a love of the soul. It does not pass when the tryst is over, when the heat of lust is spent."

Estasia laughed as she left the chapel beside Suor Signale. "You poor creature. What do I care if I am damned, so long as the devils in Hell cannot resist me." There was a merry light in her face as she reached the door of her cell a few steps beyond the cloister. "If lust is a sin in Heaven, it must be a virtue in Hell." She giggled. "Therefore I will be virtuous."

Suor Signale blocked Estasia's way into the cell, and there was a quality of light to her face made more penetrating by the white gorget, coif and wimple that framed it. "Listen to me, Donna Estasia. You will send yourself to eternal damnation with your loose words. Eternal damnation! You think that you will be satisfied by demons because they assail you with pleasure, hideous pleasure now. But how do you know what will become of you? And how many times can you be ravished and still feel anything? Hell numbs you, and even the keenest agony would be preferable to the unending, intolerable numbness. There is no passion, not even the passion of hurt there. Hell is boredom, Estasia; it is satiety. Glutted in every sense, you will be without strength, without joy, without anguish throughout eternity, forever repeating that which brought you joy and terror, but finding neither. What is to be gained? Why do you persist in your error, when you know it can avail you nothing? Make Confession. Be taken into the Church again, and share in the joy that exalts the spirit and fills the soul. You wanted to know if I ever missed a lover. What lover can lift me up as the love of Christ does? What pleasure of the body compares with the transcendent bliss of the soul?" She stopped abruptly and turned away from Estasia. "Forgive me, Buona Donna. I didn't mean to speak to you in this way. It is immodest of me, and improper."

Estasia was staring at her, and at the nun's apology she shook her head as if waking from a dream. "No. You were right to speak to me thus. It's wrong of me to revile you, when *I'm* the one in error." She stopped, then turned away from Suor Signale, saying, "Do you *really* feel so transported? Is the love of Christ so wonderful?" The words were helpless, almost childlike.

"Oh, Buona Donna!" Suor Signale's lustrous eyes filled with tears and she reached to embrace Estasia. "There is nothing in the world that comes near it. The greatest pleasures are pale in comparison. You think of your lovers and of the ravishment of devils, but they are nothing, nothing at all. Christ is all glory. His Mystery, His Splendor! There are no words to tell you what terrible sweetness fills my heart at the thought of Him."

The cell was plain, whitewashed on walls and ceiling, the floor flagged with natural stone. The narrow bed had a straw-filled mattress and two blankets. There was no pillow. Over the bed hung a simple crucifix, and at the moment, light touched it, making the wooden figure glow with the warm tones of life. A small chest held Estasia's few belongings and also served as a chair. One candle stood on the chest. Until that moment the room had seemed unutterably ugly, but now, with Suor Signale's words sounding in her like a call to battle, the cell was transformed. Dazed, Estasia walked into the cell and rather absently took her gonella once again, only to lay it aside before she stretched out on the comfortless bed.

"Donna Estasia . . . ?" the Celestiane nun asked uncertainly, dreading another seizure like the one in the chapel.

"I am well, Suor Signale," Estasia assured her in an odd, remote tone.

"But you must eat a meal yet, Buona Donna."

Estasia opened her eyes a moment. "It is not mortal bread that will nourish me now," she announced, and closed her eyes again.

When she had shut the door of Estasia's cell, Suor Signale hastened to the chapel. The last of the prayers were being recited, and Suor Signale said them rapidly, not thinking too much of the significance of the words. Her thoughts were still on Donna Estasia, and the more she thought, the more worried she became.

"How is she, Suor Signale?" Suor Merzede asked when the ritual was over.

Suor Signale answered honestly, "I don't know. She's calmer than she's ever been, and that should make me grateful, but I don't trust it. She might do something . . . much worse." Without knowing what she did, Suor Signale tangled her hands in her rosary and began to move the beads automatically through her fingers.

"Do you think she could go home?"

"If she remains as she is now . . ." Suor Signale broke off, frowning.

"You have some concern, Suor Signale. Tell me what it is." The Superiora rarely gave orders, but this was plainly one of those occasions. She waited while the nun gathered her thoughts.

"If she would only Confess. Then perhaps there would be no more of this reveling with demons. Perhaps they are demons, and they do assault her as she claims. And perhaps they are mere dreams, and she visits them on herself." She hesitated, knowing she was perilously near heresy.

"Go on," Suor Merzede encouraged her. "If you are in the wrong, God will mete out your punishment. But if you are right, it is your duty to speak so that the soul of Donna Estasia may be saved."

"As you wish, Suor Merzede," Suor Signale said against a sudden tightness in her throat. Her eyes closed as she composed herself, breathing a prayer for guidance before she said, "Donna Estasia had many lovers after she became a widow. It's common knowledge. And it was rumored that she satisfied them in many ways, including some that are contrary to the teaching of the Church. If that's so, then she may long for those carnal acts, and being unable to achieve them any other way, entrusts them to the demons of her mind." She gave her Superiora a defiant stare. "I think she wants the demons. I think she enjoys them."

"And that's why you fear her calm now?" Suor Merzede nodded as she considered it. "I have seen this before, once or twice. The women were not usually young and beautiful. But it is possible." She gazed pensively at Suor Signale. "Her cousin Sandro Filipepi comes tomorrow to see her. What do you think?"

"He should see her," Suor Signale said promptly.

"And should he take her home?"

This time it took Suor Signale some little time to answer.

"No. I think that until she Confesses, it would be better that she remain with us."

Suor Merzede nodded once more. "I believe you're right, Suor Signale. I pray God gives me the words to persuade Filipepi. There will be trouble enough if she remains here. But should she go into the world again, who knows what would happen?"

Suor Signale crossed herself and joined her hands and began to pray. After a moment, when Suor Merzede had left her, she dropped to her knees, and as her rapture grew, she swayed deliriously and then fell forward onto the floor.

Text of two identical letters from il Conte Francesco Ragoczy da San Germano to the clerk of la Signoria, Gradazo Ondante, and to Ippolito Andrea Cinquecampi, officer of i Lanzi, written simultaneously with the left and right hands:

> To the most respected clerk of i Priori and Console/To the excellent Capitano Ippolito Andrea Cinquecampi, il Conte Francesco Ragoczy da San Germano commends himself and asks that you will consider this report and act upon it accordingly.
>
> Yesterday, being the Feast of San Giocoppo, I had occasion to be away from my palazzo for many hours. Owing to the holiness of the day, I dismissed all but one of my servants so that they might spend the time in devotion appropriate to the honoring of the Apostle. The remaining servant was my houseman, Ruggiero, who is known to you. He, being an honest and

industrious man, was busy with household accounts in a room where I keep such records, toward the rear of my palazzo. I wish you to realize that Ruggiero is not a young man, and his labors are as much as he can accommodate.

The day being holy and the city of Fiorenza at its devotions, I thought my home and property safe. But as it turned out, this was not the case. A person or persons unknown to my servant broke into the house. They subdued my houseman at the points of their swords and they bound him in the stable while the man who surprised Ruggiero and his companions ransacked my palazzo. Apparently they were after coins and other such materials, for they went to the room where I keep my scales and other instruments of measurement. They took three of the scales, most of the weights, and a certain amount of gold which was there to be weighed.

Also, they took two manuscripts bound in leather and written in a tongue they cannot possibly understand. The loss of that manuscript is a major one for me, far exceeding the worth of the gold.

In the process of robbing my weighing room, they broke several of the instruments, and I invite you to send your agent or come yourself to assess the damage that was done.

I am abashed with the need to remind you that members of my household have suffered at the hands of unknown Fiorenzan rowdies before. Magister Branco is still not recovered from his beating. And now, this second intrusion makes it necessary and I once again request that you enforce the laws that govern la Repubblica. If for some reasons you are unwill-

ing or unable to do so, I will be forced to seek other remedies.

Let me assure you that I look forward to receiving you or your agent at the nearest possible hour. I am certain that if you are willing to examine the evidence you will see that there has been an injustice committed here.

In happy anticipation of the mutually satisfactory conclusion of this lamentable affair, I am honored to sign myself

                               Francesco Ragoczy da San Germano
In Fiorenza, May 1, 1494

CHAPTER 9

BECAUSE THE DAY was hot, the stench was worse. Fiorenza was plum-ripe with gutter smells and a slow, insidious rot that ate away the old buildings near the river. Heavy, low clouds moved sluggishly through the sky, and occasionally a discontented snarl of thunder echoed through the hills.

There was little traffic on the street and only one ferry moved over the river. Everyone that could be inside was, and there were services in four of the churches to pray for rain. Even the massive doors of il Palazzo della Signoria were closed and the Console had adjourned to hear Girolamo Savonarola preach. A few stalls were set up in il Mercato, but almost no one came to buy, and the vegetables and meat wilted and stank in the enveloping heat. In the buildings of l'Arte della Lana the looms were still and many of the weavers were in church with the masters of the city. Only one of the silkmakers was busy today. In defiance of the order of il Prior di San Marco, Buovo Frugatti kept shop, and the spinning and clickings of his silk looms were strangely loud in the humid afternoon.

Ragoczy had changed from his Persian caftan to a guarnacca, for the short, flared garment was not only more typically Fiorenzan, it was cooler, being made of black-dyed Egyptian cotton. The slashed sleeves today revealed only Ragoczy's well-muscled arms, and not his usual fine white silk shirt. He had substituted Venezian silk hose for the standard calzebrache, and his boots were ankle-high and heeled after the Hungarian fashion. The wallet tied to his broad black leather belt was quite large, and at least half its contents were forbidden substances under the stringent new regulations affecting physicians and apothecaries.

"But I want to help you, San Germano," Demetrice protested as he went into the courtyard.

"You will do that by staying here."

He tried to move by her but she blocked the way, and her jaw was set with determination. "If it is dangerous to me, it must be dangerous to you."

"Must it?" He met her eyes, a certain anger behind his flippancy. "You're mortal, Demetrice. Disease can strike you down as surely as it killed Laurenzo. But I have died once, and no disease can touch me. Destroy my spine, and I will die the True Death. Chop off my head or burn me or pull me limb from limb, and I will perish at last. No disease will do that. So you will stay here, if you would please me."

Her arm still blocked his way. "There are other dangers. Or have you forgotten so soon what happened to Magister Branco?"

"I haven't forgotten," he said softly. "And if that's your

best argument, then think what might befall you if you were with me and I was attacked. The Palleschi are as much targets for mischief as strangers like me, especially now with the Medici house in such disorder. And you are known as a Palleschi, aren't you?"

For the first time she did not answer at once. "Yes, I'm a Palleschi. It's an honor to be a Palleschi!" Her jaw came up again. "Let me maintain that honor, San Germano. When Laurenzo was alive, he never refused to aid his city, no matter what the danger. If Piero won't uphold his family, then let me."

Ragoczy knew it would be a simple matter to push her out of the way and leave Palazzo San Germano without her. Yet he did not want to cheat her. "Is this a debt, then?" he said kindly.

She nodded, and her amber eyes met his directly. "It's a debt."

"Are you certain there is no other way you might pay it? You still have much to do with Laurenzo's library." As he spoke he felt himself weaken. "He would not ask you to walk through fire, amica mia."

"I would have done it if he wished it." At last she lowered her arm blocking Ragoczy's way. "He wouldn't have to ask me. Just as he didn't have to ask you."

"Yes." Ragoczy looked at her, seeing worry lines around her eyes that hadn't been there two months ago. "Do you understand that the people are dying of swine plague? Do you know what it's like?" He looked beyond her. "I've seen it many times. In Roma, in Egypt, in my homeland. It is a terrible way to die. And there is little anyone can do to save the victims. Syrup of poppies will lessen the pain and poultices sometimes will help. But beyond that, all we can do is offer help to ease dying."

Demetrice looked at him and her expression was solemn. "If you will wait a few moments more, I will be ready to go with you."

Ragoczy capitulated. "Very well, Donna mia. I will wait for you. Wear something that you can burn when we are through, and be sure that you discard the garment before we come into the palazzo. I will give you a solution to wash with, and you must use it when you cast aside your garment. Otherwise you may carry infection in to the servants."

"I will do whatever you think I should. You have only to tell me." She paused, as if she were about to say something more, and then she turned and hurried into the palazzo.

When she returned she wore a sensible gonella cut off just below the knees and tied at the waist with three stout cords. Her rosy-blond hair was tucked away under a linen cap and she had put high kitchen boots on her feet.

"Will this do?" she asked. There was nothing provocative in the question and her manner was briskly impersonal.

"It will do very well indeed. Where did you find the kitchen boots?"

"They're mine. I've had them since before my father's death. You'll see where the cloth tops are worn. I won't mind giving them up, if that concerns you." She fastened her wallet to her belt and watched him. "Shall we go, San Germano?"

He had thought to attempt to dissuade her, but he knew now it would be useless. He shrugged, but warned her, "If there is too much danger I will send you away. And you must not seek to argue with me then."

Demetrice was glad to agree to that stricture. "I'll do it."

He almost smiled. "Good. I'll be in no mood to brook opposition." Then he stood aside and they walked out into the street.

As they passed San Marco they could hear chanting and occasional outbursts of prayer. The frightened cries blended with the singing in a terrible harmony. Ragoczy felt his body tighten as he listened to the sounds.

"What is it?" Demetrice asked, seeing his discomfort.

"I was . . . remembering." Plainly he did not want to discuss the matter.

"Remembering what?" Demetrice persisted.

"Many things," he snapped. Then, as they crossed to la Via Larga he relented. "I've seen all kinds of delusions. I was remembering what happened shortly after the Domenicani were founded, and what they, in their zeal, did to the Cathars."

"The Cathars?" Demetrice frowned. "I don't know if I've heard of them."

"The Albigensians, if you prefer." As they went past il Palazzo de' Medici, Ragoczy said, "Piero hasn't given orders to pull down the old buildings where the plague is yet. He'll regret it."

"I've heard of the Albigensians. They were heretics."

"No," Ragoczy snapped. "That's the verdict of the Domenicani. Before they, in good faith, destroyed the Cathars, they explained that it was because the Cathars were heretics. That was not the Cathars' opinion, believe me." He shook his head. "It isn't the time to discuss this."

"But will you, later?" She had to hurry to keep up with him, and as her breath grew short, she realized that his breathing was even and there was no sign of sweat on his face in spite of the heat of the day and his quick pace.

"Perhaps." He was silent then, and shortly they came to la Via degli Arcangeli. It was a narrow, mean street, and the old buildings crowded close together, touching one another as if taking strength from the presence of other equally an-

cient wrecks. There were sewer smells here, and the scent of
rancid food. But the stranger odor of sickness was stronger
than any other, and its putrid touch lingered on the air, its
corrupting flavor masking all other smells.

Ragoczy saw that Demetrice had whitened. "It's worse
inside," he warned her. "If you go in, you must breathe that
fetor. If you can't, I'll escort you home."

She shook her head and bit her lip. "No. I'll stay. I'll
manage."

"If that's what you want." He went to the third house
from the corner. It had a black stripe painted on the door, and
beyond, there was the sound of weeping. Ragoczy knocked
once, twice, and then called out, "Cuorebrillo, it is
Ragoczy."

It seemed that no one had heard, and Ragoczy repeated
his knocking. This time there was a breaking off of sobs, and
a scuffling and scraping indicated that they would be admitted.

Sesto Cuorebrillo was twenty-seven years old and looked
fifty. His soft brown hair was already frosted with white and
his face was gouged deeply with the marks of pox and sorrow. He stared at Ragoczy with red-rimmed eyes, then,
dumbly, held the door open.

"I have brought more help with me, Cuorebrillo,"
Ragoczy said as he stepped into the dark, filthy room. "This
is Donna Demetrice, who does me the honor to be my student."

Cuorebrillo glared at her. "As she honored Laurenzo?
Well, you are too late. Annamaria died this morning and Lu-
grezia is failing too fast." He wiped his face with a dirty
apron and crossed himself as an afterthought. "Come this
way."

"What of your wife, Sesto? And your other children?" Ragoczy was gentle, but he demanded an answer.

"Feve is not well, and has laid down to mourn. Cosmo, Gemma and Ermo have been taken to the good Cisterceni Brothers at San Felice until the danger is over, or until we are all dead. Only Ilirio is left. He's too young to be taken away. Without his mother, he will die because we have no money for a wet nurse."

"Take him to la Casa Ospedale delle Madre," Demetrice said, knowing that the home for nursing mothers and foundlings rarely turned anyone away. "Take the infant and your wife there."

Sesto scoffed. "They will not admit anyone from a house visited by plague. It endangers all the others." Bitterly he turned away, and started back into the house. "Go away. Go away. Leave us to our ends. Go away."

"Cuorebrillo," Ragoczy said, and though he had not raised his soft, low voice, the name carried as if it had been shouted. "Take us to your wife. I promise you we will do her no harm."

"Per tutti angeli! Let us die peacefully! Leave her alone. She's had too much of sorrow." Quite suddenly Sesto brought his hands to his face as he wept.

Demetrice went up to him. There was neither revulsion nor fear in her as she took the poor man by his shoulders. "Signore Cuorebrillo, do not abandon hope. It is a great sin to forget the Mercy of God. Surely your wife must be given every chance to live. If we do less than that, then we're worse than wolves ravening in the fields. We know that it is wrong to let her suffer, but wolves do not. Let us see her. If there is nothing else to do, we can at least pray for her together."

The low, ill-lit room was filthy and the thick, fetid smell

like a blanket pressed to the face. Sesto raised his head slowly and looked around the room. "Buona Donna, the rest of the house is no better."

"With your family so ill and yourself worn beyond endurance, I'd be much troubled if it were otherwise." Demetrice nodded philosophically. "If Our Lord could touch lepers without fear, what is a little dirt to me?"

Sesto stared at her as if she was mad, but turned and led the way down a narrow hallway, remarking as he went that the floor sagged but probably wouldn't break.

Ragoczy went behind Demetrice, pointing out to her white patches on the old wooden walls. "There, do you see? These buildings should have come down a long time ago. Laurenzo mentioned that he'd wanted to take down these hovels and make new houses for the poor beyond la Porta Santa Croce. It's a shame there was not time enough to see it done."

Up ahead of them Sesto had stopped at a doorway, and as he motioned to Ragoczy and Demetrice, he lifted the thin, torn curtain that covered the opening. "Feve, sposa," he said in a small, heartbroken voice, "the foreigner has come again. There is a woman with him, the one you said was so pretty when il Magnifico came back from the country with her. We were fishing for our supper and we saw them ride by."

It was doubtful that his Feve heard any of this babble. She lay on a hard bed in blankets soaked with sweat and urine. Her eyes were distant and glittering with fever, her hair lay in great matted tangles on her pillow, and she trembled under the three thin blankets though the room was stiflingly hot.

Demetrice paused on the threshold to cross herself, and to school her features to show none of the dismay that filled her.

282   *Chelsea Quinn Yarbro*

Through parched and blistered lips, the woman on the bed croaked out, "Buona Donna . . . You must . . . not . . . I'm dying . . ."

Ragoczy had come into the room behind Demetrice and his first glance told him that there was very little hope of saving Feve now. But he opened the wallet he carried and brought out a small glass vial. If he was upset by the surroundings or worried about the woman's condition, there was nothing in his calm, assured manner to show it.

Taking Ragoczy for her model, Demetrice went to the side of the bed. "You are not to despair, Feve," she said evenly, and turned to the door where Sesto lingered. "We'll need water."

"Don't take it from the old well," Ragoczy cautioned. "Leave the city on the east and take fresh water from the Santa Croce spring."

Sesto's eyes widened, then narrowed. "That will take a great deal of time. You might do anything while I'm away."

Ragoczy straightened up and regarded Sesto silently. Then he said, "Cuorebrillo, if this plague is in the city, then your wells may be contaminated. There would be no benefit in giving water from wells where the disease lurks. Therefore, you must get your water from uncorrupted springs. If you go to i Lanzi, you will get the loan of an ass and two barrels. That way you will not have to return for a few days and there will be fresh water for you, and for the others who live in these disgraceful hovels."

"But we have been forbidden to work on this day. Savonarola himself has declared that all must pray and worship for salvation from dawn until sunset." Sesto was genuinely concerned, for there were new and unpleasantly punitive laws affecting those who were lax in their religious exercises.

"For how long," Ragoczy mused, "has it been a sin to succor those in need? Undoubtedly I am mistaken in thinking that feeding the hungry and comforting those in distress are acts of charity."

Under this rebuke Sesto squirmed. He nodded, but said with a finger upraised in warning, "If i Lanzi will not give me the ass and the barrels, you can fetch the spring water, stragnero."

As soon as Sesto was gone, Ragoczy held up his vial. "Here, Demetrice. Give this to her. Moisten her lips with it, and then, when she can swallow, tip it down her throat."

"What is it?" She took the vial as she asked and unstoppered it, turning a little of the clear liquid onto her fingers. These she touched to Feve's lips.

The woman sobbed. "I can't . . . My mouth . . ."

"More on the lips," Ragoczy said crisply and moved the two feeble rushlights nearer the bed.

Demetrice did as he instructed her, ignoring Feve's futile attempts to force her gentle hands away.

"Now. Not too fast." Ragoczy watched as Demetrice poured the shining liquid down Feve's throat. Feve gasped, coughed and for an instant seemed to choke on the fluid. Then she swallowed deeply, and sighed.

"What is it?" Demetrice asked again, not taking her eyes from Feve. "What does it do?"

Ragoczy shook his head, saying somewhat obscurely, "The process is something like the others you have learned. The liquid is for healing. If the body is not too much harmed, it can stop some diseases. It begins very humbly," he added in a different voice, "as moldy bread. It is transformed into a white substance, and then, through another process, into that clear liquid."

Only Demetrice's raised brows expressed her surprise,

and with it, a kind of apprehension. Before she could stop the words, she asked, "And would it have helped Laurenzo?"

"No."

She recognized that cold, remote tone, and knew that she should say no more, that her first question had been unwise. "But didn't you give him some medicine in a vial . . . ?" She broke off as Feve began to cough. A swift, worried glance at Ragoczy told her that there was no great danger to Feve yet.

Easily, smoothly, he said, "I gave him two vials, one was a cordial for pain, the other . . . the other a compound to . . . to buy a little time. It was all I could do. You credit me with more skill than I have, Demetrice, if you think that I, or anyone, can restore blood that is rotten. No one has a cure for that. This"—he nodded toward Feve "—occasionally can be treated. But the other, no."

"I'm sorry, San Germano," she said, and there was a heightened color in her face to punctuate her apology, "I had no right. But I hated so to see him die . . ." Again she stopped. "If it hadn't been for you, I don't know what would have become of me."

Ragoczy looked down at the neat row of vials in his large wallet. "We'll wait a bit and give her some more of the fluid. If that greenish cast has left her skin after that, she will have a good chance to survive —that is, if Sesto can get some decent food for her. One of the charitable Confraternitè should be willing to help. If she doesn't improve, we'll know that we've done all that we can." He joined her beside the bed and looked down at Feve. There was a strangeness in his face, both infinitely sad and infinitely distant, as if he looked down the centuries with sorrow.

Demetrice had never seen an expression like this before, and it frightened her. In spite of herself, she shrank from his hand as he laid it on her shoulder. Immediately she felt ashamed and she said with difficulty. "That . . . that was not what you think."

"You have no idea what I think," he said, and turned away.

Lightning was pricking the dusk-thickened clouds by the time Sesto returned. He kicked open the door with a shout and in a few moments there was the rumble of a barrel being rolled into the hall.

"I have brought you spring water," Sesto announced as he came to the doorway. Under the grime his face was gray with fatigue and he leaned against the rough frame as if every muscle in him ached.

"Excellent," Ragoczy said, and looked down at Demetrice. "If I bring you water, will you wash Feve? Until she's clean again, there will be no chance for her."

Demetrice nodded. She was determined to atone for her earlier mistakes, which had in her mind by now taken on the importance of disastrous and irremediable blunders.

Already Ragoczy had turned his attention to Sesto. "I will need your largest basin and fresh cloths. And there must be other blankets to put on the bed. If you haven't any clean ones, go to the priests at Santa Maria del Fiore. They have such things. Tell them it is an emergency."

Sesto nodded, somewhat numbly. "Why don't you go?" he asked.

"Because I am a foreigner, I am a landholder, and it is known that I am ineligible to receive charity." Ragoczy put his hand to his eyes.

"But they know you're working with the sick . . ." Sesto sighed and gave up. He went into the hall and was almost at the door when a high, thin cry came from the depths of the house. He stopped abruptly. "Ilirio! He's awake. He's alive."

With more strength than he knew he had, Sesto pushed the second barrel aside and stumbled into the main room of the house.

In the corner was an old, rockerless cradle, and in it, Sesto's son cried, twisting in his swaddling bands. His infant face was screwed into a reddened, enraged mask. Eagerly Sesto reached into the cradle and lifted Ilirio out, crooning to the child as he carried it back to the room where Feve lay.

"What is it?" Ragoczy asked, frowning as Sesto came into the squalid room once more. "We need those blankets."

"It's Ilirio," Sesto said, holding up his squalling son. "He's hungry. He wants the breast."

"No." Ragoczy stood ready to block Sesto's way.

"But he's hungry. He must have milk." Sesto held up the baby and said to Demetrice, "Buona Donna, it is as I say."

"I know he's hungry," Ragoczy began, attempting to explain.

A particularly loud burst of thunder blocked out Sesto's objection and set the baby to screaming. Sesto busied himself tending his son, and then renewed his arguments. "Don't deny him. He could die if he has no food . . ."

"If you let him nurse when his mother is so full of sickness, he will most surely die." The words were harsher than Ragoczy had intended, and Sesto glared at him while Ilirio shrieked.

"The prior of San Marco said that God will save the mother who holds her infant to the breast. He says it is holy, and holy things drive out all ill. It is heresy to deny this, Savonarola says."

Instead of answering this with anger, Ragoczy shook his head slowly. "Believe what you want, Cuorebrillo. Believe that demons have poisoned your well, believe that this is a judgment upon you, believe that a woman giving suck is proof against disease." He stared down at Feve, and knew that the woman who lay there in torment would not survive the night. "You have all believed that, and in the last eight days, more than fifty of you have died."

One of the rushlights winked out and Sesto stared at it, and murmured, "Libera me, Domine."

At this point Demetrice decided to interfere. She pushed herself to her feet and wiped the sweat from her face. "It's very hot, and I must bathe your wife, Signore Cuorebrillo. If il Conte Ragoczy says that your wife is too ill to nurse your baby, then it is true. Get me water and blankets and cloths so that I may finish my work."

To Ragoczy's surprise, Sesto stopped arguing. "As you say, Buona Donna. But what of the child?"

"You must take him to Perpetua della Porta San Nicolo. She will nurse him until your wife is well." Already Demetrice was working on the guttered rushlight to see if there was sufficient oil to make it burn again.

"And how will I pay her?" Sesto was quickly becoming angry. "I am a poor man. I have no gold."

"But I do." Ragoczy untied the small purse that hung beside his wallet. "Do as Donna Demetrice instructs you."

Sesto looked from his fainting, shivering wife to his crying child, then took the purse. He started to say something, changed his mind, and with Ilirio still in his arms, rushed from the room. A few moments later the street door slammed shut behind him.

Demetrice let out a long sigh, then resumed her place beside Feve. "It will be good to be home," she said to Ragoczy as she adjusted the soiled blankets over the stricken woman again. Feve moaned and plucked at the thin brown wool fitfully before she began to cough once more.

"We won't be home for some time yet," Ragoczy said, a

hint of a smile in his eyes at her use of the word "home."
"When we are through here, there are still three other houses
to visit. In this terrible heat, the disease will spread rapidly."

The last burning rushlight began to falter, giving out a
few sputtering flames before it started to fade.

"There won't be any light without it," Demetrice said,
more to herself than to Ragoczy. "I'll need light."

"I'll bring you more lamps." Ragoczy said, and left the
room, to return a few minutes later with four tallow candles.
The rushlight was only a small blue spark in the corner of the
room, and he thrust one of the twisted straw wicks into the
brightness. There was light in the room again, and Ragoczy
set the candles about the room.

"Where did you find them?" Demetrice asked rather absently as she studied Feve, who had begun to toss restlessly.

"One was under their Madonna shrine, and the others
were in the main room. They'll give you a few hours of
light, but then we'll need something else."

"Will we be here that long?" Demetrice said in an undervoice.

As he had done many times that afternoon, Ragoczy went
to the sick woman, touched her forehead, her hot, dry hands,
the side of her neck. "I don't think so."

"You should fetch a priest, then," Demetrice told him,
then bit her lower lip to stop from weeping in vexation. She
was losing her battle for the life of Feve Cuorebrillo, and she
hated losing.

Apparently Ragoczy understood, for he reached over and
touched her arm affectionately. "I know, amica mia. And it
never gets easier. Never." Memories crowded in on him of
the many times he had been unable to save those who came
to him.

A peal of thunder deafened them for a few moments, and

then it was quiet again. Demetrice said, "She will need a priest, San Germano. Look at her."

"No priest will come. Yesterday Savonarola declared that the plague is of infernal origin, and that it is a damnable act to give Last Rites to those who are dying."

Outraged, Demetrice got to her feet. "He can't mean it. This woman deserves better." She was almost too angry to speak, and she took an agitated turn about the small room. "This is unforgivable. It's infamous!"

"That may be, but it is also the law." Ragoczy hesitated, then pulled two stoppered silver bottles from his wallet. They were both quite small, of exquisite workmanship, and each was marked with the Cross. "Here. This is consecrated oil, and this is holy water. You take Communion regularly and have Confessed just two days ago. Mark her forehead for her. That way, Sesto need not know."

Demetrice nodded, then knelt before the silver bottles in Ragoczy's hands, crossing herself and closing her eyes to pray. When she was done, she took the bottles and reverently approached the bed.

When Sesto returned he was drenched by the downpour which at last signaled a break in the weather. The blankets he carried were also soaked, but by then they were no longer necessary.

TEXT OF A LETTER TO Piero di Laurenzo de' Medici from an unknown person:

> To Piero de' Medici one who wishes him well sends warnings:
> Charles of France covets your land, Medici. His expedition into Italia is for the purpose of gaining

strength and holdings, not to restore peace. You think
that he will not harm you, but I tell you that he will see
you driven from your home and will install those who
are compliant and willing at the head of your government.

If you act at once, you may avert disaster. Beware
of enemies. Remember that Savonarola favors the
French, and regard his advice with caution. Remember that Il Moro, Lodovico Sforza, has borrowed large
sums of money from Genova and is working for your
downfall. Remember that your father refused titles
from the French so that he might retain his independence and the independence of la Repubblica Fiorenzen.

Heed this well and act quickly. Or be exiled and
disgraced forever.

A friend from the north
July 10, 1494

CHAPTER 10

THE CROWD THIS hot summer morning had been disap-
pointingly small, and Savonarola had castigated the entire
congregation for the lack of fervor the Fiorenzeni were
showing him. His threats of the dire fate awaiting the lax
worshipers were enough to make three women faint, and he
felt somewhat mollified.

He lingered at Santa Maria del Fiore to have a few words

with i Priori, for many of the city's dignitaries were alarmed about the coming of the French.

"You will see," he told the apprehensive men who had gathered around him, "that this Charles of France is a godly King, not a man of flesh and coin." He was pleased to see how soberly i Priori were dressed. No more bright-colored guarnacche with embroidered edges, no more brocades. The men wore the lucco, which was not unlike a cassock, and all were made of simple, dark-dyed wool. Aside from the collars of their office, none of the men wore jewelry. Even their shoes were plain, having no slashings or elegantly turned-back linings. He considered the matter then decided he would mention this new mode. "It is gratifying to see you have put vanity behind you and are turning your thoughts to other concerns. To see men of your station and responsibility forgetting their dignity and strutting like peacocks is always distressing. But now, in your simple garments and humble manner, at last your true worth may be seen, not for the display you make in the world, but for the excellence of soul you show to God."

One of the officials smiled at this praise, and was instantly rebuked by Savonarola. "It is not fitting for you to be pleased. You should strive only to be pleasing to God. If you take pleasure and pride in this, then I have failed and you are surely damned to burn forever in the deepest pits of Hell."

At last the clerk of la Signoria dared to address the little prior on another matter. "Reverend Domenicano, though you are not given to think of these considerations, it is necessary that we have your opinion on what is to be done with the Franchesi in Italia. Are we to wait here? Are we to welcome them? You tell us that Charles is a godly man, but if his army is not?" Gradazo Ondante glanced at the other men uncomfortably. With the full force of the sun on him, his lucco of dark wool was intolerably hot. He saw that the others were suffering in the same way, and wished that the small man in the Domenican habit would show the same human distress.

The oldest of the delegation, a man who had served the Console for many years, added a few words to Ondante's questions. "We are concerned, Buon Prior, for the safety and security of this city, of la Repubblica Fiorenzen. It would be a simple thing for Charles to defeat us with arms, and then we would be isolated. Siena would not come to our aid then, nor Modena, nor Milano, certainly. We might be crushed."

Savonarola studied them, his green eyes smoldering. "If you are worried about your fate in this world, I am filled with shame. This world is nothing. It is Heaven that matters. All else is vanity. You say that you fear we will be crushed. I tell you that unless there is repentance, reform and acceptance of what God sends to us, then the heaviest, most utter ruin that might be visited on us will be too light to make amends for the gravity of our sins."

"But," Gradazo Ondante persisted, "if the state is destroyed, how then do we serve God? If my life preserves the life of Fiorenza and her citizens, that's nothing—"

"A prideful boast, Ondante. Remember it when you come to Confession."

For the first time Gradazo Ondante found he was out of patience with Savonarola. "It was not said in pride—"

"God alone knows how it was said. Be sure you Confess it, for to question God is heresy." He looked at the men around him and met their uneasy glances with a challenge, "Don't attempt to bargain with God as if He were a rival merchant. That way lies disaster and the Vengeance of God that waits for all who deny Him and who live their lives in sin."

One of the Console coughed and tried to motion the others aside, but Ondante was determined. "All that you tell me may indeed be so, and for it I will suffer eternally. But for the moment it is my responsibility to help keep la Repubblica in order, to keep it whole and prosperous. If I don't do that, I have failed in the task given to me in life, and God admonishes us not to shirk responsibility. If it is appropriate that we make the first gesture to the Franchesi, then let us do so now. But if we bring war onto us, then every one of us should be cursed." He didn't realize how heated his voice had become until one of the others pulled at his sleeve and murmured a few words to him.

Savonarola had given him a measured glance for the latter part of this outburst, and he said slowly. "You have given me a great deal to think on. Yes. I will send for you when I have decided what action should be taken to discipline you." With a curt nod he dismissed i Priori and stood waiting until the men had moved away from him.

He was about to join the group of monks waiting to return to San Marco when he saw a white-habited nun coming toward him. He had seen Suor Merzede, Superiora of Sacro Infante, perhaps a dozen times in the last four years. He disliked the serenity of the Celestiana, he found her confidence inappropriate to her calling. But he refused to let these conflicting feelings trouble him. He assumed his most forbidding expression and waited until the nun had come and made a proper reverence to him.

"Greetings in the Name of the Father, the Son and the Holy Spirit," Suor Merzede murmured as she kissed Savonarola's outstretched hand. "I pray you will hear me out, good Prior."

"Well? What is it?" He knew that this response was far

from gracious, and he hurriedly made the sign of the Cross as a gesture of amends.

Suor Merzede blinked at this Turkish treatment, but she had long dealt with monks and knew that their ways were often harsh. She folded her hands into her sleeves and said, "It has been more than a year since you were last at Sacro Infante. We've had the care and counsel of Fra Milo, but my Sisters and I long for your guidance. Many of our charges, too, yearn to hear your prophecy. The mad and infirm are as much in need of salvation as the prosperous and tranquil of mind—it may be that they crave your ministration even more in their loneliness and affliction than others do, who have the benefit of daily recourse to your teachings."

Savonarola regarded Suor Merzede with suspicion. He moved back a step or two so that her slightly greater height would not be noticed. As he did so, he remembered that the nun was one of an ancient and distinguished Pisan family, and it seemed to him she had lost too little of her aristocratic manner in her convent. "There is too much for me to do here, Suor Merzede. It is true that all those in despair deserve the comfort of Scripture. But madness—that may be otherwise, for madness is often caused by demons."

"Then who but you should cast them out?" Suor Merzede said swiftly. "Blessed Savonarola, listen to me, if not for the sake of the habit I wear, then for the sake of the wretches kept at Sacro Infante. Every day our Sisterhood sees the terrors of Hell reflected in the eyes of those we care for. We know what it is to fight endlessly for the smallest of victories. It is a victory when a simple man learns to mend a pan. It is a victory when a boy who has done nothing but stare at the walls for three years asks one morning for a piece of bread. Each of these little, little triumphs we offer to God in our love. But there is so much more we could do, and because we are few and our charges are many, those other triumphs are lost, perhaps eternally. You, good Prior, you could give us new courage and help us renew our determination to battle for our tiny successes. And certainly your words will stir the hearts of all who hear them."

As he cast an anxious glance over his shoulder toward his waiting Brothers, Savonarola said, "It might be possible, Suor Merzede, but not just at present."

Skillfully Suor Merzede concealed her annoyance. "There is another reason I ask you to come to Sacro Infante."

"Yes?"

At il Palazzo della Signoria its famous bell, la Vacca, named that for its mooing tone, began to toll, indicating that the Console had gathered to meet. Savonarola felt a certain satisfaction in knowing that they were meeting to discuss what he had said only a few minutes before.

"We have a charge, a certain Donna Estasia della Cittadella, who has been with us for some time. She would seem to be possessed of the very devils you mentioned. But of late she has said she would like to Confess so that her soul will be free from sin at last. She has fasted much, and tried to pray, but declares that until she has received Absolution, she cannot hope for redemption."

Somewhat absently Savonarola nodded, forcing his concentration back to what Suor Merzede was saying. "Then provide her with a priest."

"She has said," Suor Merzede said, meeting the monk's green eyes evenly, "that she will confess to no one but you, for it was your exhortation that first brought her to awareness of her sins. She had declared that if you will not come to her, she cannot Confess."

"It is vain and prideful in her. If she is truly repentant, she will Confess most humbly to anyone who in the function of his office hears Confession." He was about to turn away, but Suor Merzede's next words stopped him.

"That's what we told her, and we brought Fra Milo to her. She promised obedience to the decision to have him hear her. But as soon as she tried to speak, devils seized upon her, and she tore her shift from her body and threw herself with lascivious abandon on the crucifix that stands to the side of our chapel. She used it as she might want to use a man. Fra Milo was horrified, and when Donna Estasia was restored to her senses"—she did not mention that this was done with a sharp slap—"she herself cried out in her suffering, demanding that she be walled up to be an anchorite where she could harm no one, and would have only herself and the demons for company."

"Donna Estasia . . . Donna Estasia . . ." Savonarola turned the name over in his memory. "Was she the one who disrupted my sermon, some time ago? The one who exposed her breasts and tore at them?"

"Yes. She was brought to Sacro Infante that day and has not left since then. Her cousin Sandro Filipepi comes to see her often, but she despises his company now, and swears that she doesn't want to talk to him out of shame for what she has done in his company."

One of the monks approached to find out why Savonarola was being delayed by the Celestiane nun. He was quite near when his prior made an abrupt gesture that sent the monk scurrying back to his Brothers.

"She says that demons seize her: what then?" He nibbled his lower lip furtively though his eyes were haughty.

"They impose on her. There is much carnality, much sensuality. But it terrifies her, and she struggles to escape. She is convinced that if the demons possess her, your strength and your righteousness must prevail and bring her at last to salvation." Suor Merzede had seen the flash of interest her mention of Estasia's complaint had caused, and she could not help but wonder if indeed the prior was as uncorrupt as everyone claimed. She quickly banished this dreadful thought from her mind, and sternly ordered herself to beg her bread and water for a week.

"Always before the demons have prevailed?" Savonarola asked, measuring something in the distance with his bright eyes.

"Yes. You are her last hope. She insists that if you will not hear her, if you will not fight for her, she will find a way to take her own life to be free of these terrible visions."

"For that sin she would surely be damned forever to the greatest of tortures." He said the last word slowly.

"We have told her that, but she insists that if you cannot save her, then she knows she is damned anyway, and she might as well dispatch her soul to Hell rather than risk contaminating others with her devils." Suor Merzede still thought that Donna Estasia was being capricious to demand that Savonarola himself be her confessor, but she had prayed that the beautiful young widow might be restored, and occasionally allowed herself to hope that once redeemed, Donna Estasia might desire to be of help to Sacro Infante. It was an unworthy thought, but she could not banish it.

"If I hear her Confession, it will be written and proclaimed in public. The Confession must be complete. No detail overlooked, no shameful act left unrecorded. If she still wants to Confess to me, send me word and I will come with a secretary. And if this is a hoax, she will pay dearly for her heretical tamperings." He did not pause to see what effect this announcement would have on Suor Merzede. With a quick motion he turned and strode away to join his anxiously waiting Brothers, so that only they saw the strange smile on his fleshy lips.

TEXT OF A document of commendation issued by the Console of la Signoria:

By the order of i Priori, la Signoria and the Console, I, Gradazo Ondante, clerk of la Signoria, am mandated to issue notice of thanks and commendation to il Conte Francesco Ragoczy da San Germano, stragnero, residing in Fiorenza.

For in the unfortunate time of plague which has recently claimed two hundred thirty-one Fiorenzeni souls, this Ragoczy did, with the assistance of Donna Demetrice Clarissa Renata di Benedetto Volandrai, succor the sick and dying with no regard for his safety or his expenditure. Further, he did, of his own will and volition, offer to victims of the plague such articles of need as blankets, other bedding, candles, and foodstuffs, which often he himself distributed.

For in the time of plague, he compounded or caused to be compounded a miraculous substance that saved many from the jaws of death, and with that compound and others, rid many houses of all trace of plague, thus serving not only the unfortunate victims, but the city at large with his protection.

In acknowledgment of this splendid service and selfless devotion to the good of Fiorenza, this official commendation is published so that all will know of Ragoczy's good works and his amazing skills.

Executed by order of i Priori, la Signoria and the Console, this day, August 23, 1494, by my hand.

Gradazo Ondante
clerk

CHAPTER 11

GASPARO TUCCHIO WAS out of breath by the time he got to the courtyard of Palazzo San Germano. While he tugged at the bellrope he gulped air, cursing when he had the energy to do so.

When at last Araldo came to the gate, Gasparo glared at him from under his heavy brows. "What took you so long?"

Araldo raked a glance over Gasparo in his rough builder's clothes. "Do you have business with anyone in this palazzo?" He was still too young to carry off his haughtiness well, and Gasparo lost his temper.

"Do I have business?" he mocked. "Let me tell you, cockerel, that if you don't bring me to your master at once, it will be the worse for him and the worse for you. If one of the servants is to throw me out, have it be Ruggiero, for he has that authority, and you do not!" His big hands clung to the wrought-iron grille that opened into the courtyard. "I laid the foundation of this building, puppy. And I'll pull this gate off its hinges if I have to."

Gathering what little was left of his dignity, Araldo unlocked the gate and held it for the older man. "I didn't know," he muttered as a kind of excuse. "We must be cautious."

"Good. There's reason to be cautious. Now, where's your master?" Gasparo was ready to expand his argument. He stood squarely in front of Araldo, hands on his hips, his badger-gray hair brushed by the wind that smelled of harvest.

Araldo began to explain why it was that Ragoczy could not see him when the door to the house opened and Ruggiero stepped out into the courtyard. He wore a houseman's gown, but over it had tied a long apron with many pockets, and in one hand he carried a ring of keys.

"Ah! Ruggiero!" Gasparo waved and trod across the mosaic tiles to Ragoczy's manservant. "I've got to see il Conte. Immediately."

Ruggiero met Gasparo and touched cheeks with him. "I will be pleased to lead you to him." Ruggiero was wholly unperturbed by Gasparo's sudden appearance and his insistent demands.

"Then tell that young upstart that," Gasparo demanded, his temper still ruffled. "He tried to keep me out. As if he could."

Ruggiero regarded Araldo a moment. "Is that true?" he asked the young man.

"I didn't . . ." Araldo flushed to the roots of his light brown hair. "With all the trouble and the theft and . . . And he's only a builder."

Gasparo took instant exception to that. "I am a member of my Arte, and proud of it. And my father was before me. He was one of those who raised the dome of Santa Maria del Fiore. Who are you, a houseman without an Arte, to cast aspersions on me? And if," he went on, not giving Araldo time to reply, "you think that working for a foreign noble grants you the right to act as if your blood were the same as your master's, then you're mistaken. There's no man in Fiorenza who is as fine or as good or as . . . knightly as your master.

Learn from him, if you want to know how to treat others."
He turned on his heel and stalked across the courtyard.

As Araldo twisted the lock in the gate, he said to Ruggiero in a fierce undervoice, "Why did you let him talk to me that way? I had the right to keep him out. Ragoczy said so."

"He said, in fact, that you were to be cautious in whom you admitted. But he didn't tell you to refuse our friends. We must cherish our friends, Araldo; there are so few of them."

On the other side of the courtyard, Gasparo called to Ruggiero and gestured his impatience. "Where is il Conte?"

Ruggiero had left Ragoczy and Demetrice in the hidden rooms behind the stairs, rooms that Gasparo had helped build. "He is at his studies," Ruggiero said cautiously.

"Ah! Good. I know where to find him. You needn't lead me." The old builder stepped through the door into the hallway. He paused to give the building his critical consideration. He could not approve of all the oddities of design, but on the whole it was very nice. The workmanship, he congratulated himself, was superb, and anyone who saw it would never know that the palazzo had been built in little more than a year, roughly a quarter of the time that was usually needed for a building of this size. But he refused to linger. With one last proud nod, he entered the loggia and moved toward the stair. It had been a while since he had been there, and it took him a few moments and a false start to find the hidden latch amid the complicated wood carving. Then he found the bough of fruit with the apples that were guarded by a dragon, and he knew which one to turn.

The first of the three rooms behind the stair was empty and almost dark. One solitary candle burned on a huge wooden chest that had several bands of iron around it.

Gasparo blinked and stumbled as his foot struck a low

bench. He shouted as he tried to move away from the obstacle, and was tripped by another wooden form, probably a stool, because it turned over with a dreadful clatter.

In the next moment there was light in the door, and Ragoczy, a lantern in his right hand, a sword in his left, stepped into the room. At that moment his neat, stocky body seemed huge, and there was something sinister, forbidding about him.

"Eccellenza!" Gasparo cried out from where he had fallen. "It's Tucchio. I must talk with you."

Immediately the menace was gone, and Ragoczy, his sword cast aside, had come across the room, his hand extended to his friend. "Gasparo," he said as he pulled Gasparo to his feet. "Buon' amico. What ever possessed you to do that? If you had tried to come into the laboratory, you would have been killed."

"Killed?" Gasparo was brushing himself off, but this stopped him. "How, killed?"

Ragoczy gave him a rueful, charming smile. "Since the palazzo was broken into, I have taken certain . . . precautions. There is a notched crossbow rigged to the door. Be grateful that you fell, Gasparo." He took the builder by his shoulders and touched cheeks with him. "It must be very important, whatever brought you here." He motioned Gasparo to go past him into the laboratory.

"Well, it is," Gasparo said defensively, then found himself in a brightly lit room filled with strange glass flasks and many instruments he had never seen.

Most puzzling of all were the two brick structures in the middle of the laboratory. Each sat in a large box of sand, and each looked like a brick beehive with a thick iron door in its side. At the moment, Donna Demetrice Volandrai was bending over one of them, making some minor adjustment in the rounded top. Without turning from this delicate task, she said, "San Germano, close the door. I can't keep the heat even if you don't."

Obediently Ragoczy closed the door behind Gasparo. "Accept my apologies, magistra."

Still Demetrice did not turn. "It's all very well for you to tease me," she said with asperity that was belied by a slight smile, "but if we get dross instead of gold, what then?" She made a last-minute shift of the bricks, then stood back, putting one hand to her rosy forehead. When she turned, she was startled to see Gasparo.

"We have a visitor," Ragoczy explained, mischief in his dark eyes. "Don't be worried: Gasparo was one of the four who built these rooms. He has sworn a Blood Oath not to reveal what is here."

Demetrice sank onto one of the nearer chairs. "I didn't doubt your wisdom or your choice," she said, but there was still no real rebuke in her tone. "It will be another two hours before the crucible can be moved again. I'm going to ask Amadeo to make me a meal. What time of day is it?" she asked as she pulled the linen cap from her head.

"Roughly midafternoon. Never mind whether this is prandium or comestio. Get something to eat." He had crossed the room to her side and gently touched her shoulder with one small hand. "You're wearing yourself out, amica mia."

She made an effort to shake off her fatigue. "No, I've been too lazy the past few months and I'm paying for my sloth now." She got to her feet. "I will leave you to talk with this builder." She nodded to Gasparo. "May I bring you anything when I come back? Amadeo has some very good preserves just now. I could bring some served over cheese?"

Ragoczy said with some amusement, "Bring whatever

you think would please Signore Tucchio. But in good quantity." He stood aside to let her pass, and as she got to the door, he added, "Mille grazie, Demetrice."

"Niente," she responded, and went out of the room.

"An excellent woman. Superb. Delightful," Gasparo said, letting his enthusiasm grow. "You are a fortunate man, and if she does not have your devotion, you are a fool, Eccellenza." When Ragoczy said nothing, he went on. "I know, since that foolish Domenicano has taken the reins of Fiorenza, we're not supposed to have pleasure of the flesh. We can't wear fine clothes, we can't eat good foods, we can't sing anything but hymns, we can't go anywhere but to church. And we must not touch women but for their fecundity. Fools! Asses!" He glared at the foreigner in black. "That's not why I came."

"I didn't think it was." Ragoczy motioned Gasparo to a chair of bent wood and tooled leather. "Sit down, Gasparo, and tell me what the trouble is."

Gasparo approached the chair cautiously, then dropped into it as if he was afraid it would bolt from under him. "I have had word, Eccellenza."

"From whom? About what?" Ragoczy had put down his lantern and busied himself with one of several stands of candles. A slight breeze from the high, hidden windows moved the flames and carried the warm scent of harvesttime into the room.

"From a builder I know who now lives in Francia. He writes to me occasionally. He's a good man. He sent me an earlier message, but the man carrying it was killed by brigands on the road to Genova. He didn't learn until June that I hadn't got the message, and he sent me another as quickly as possible." Now that he had got to Ragoczy, Gasparo was finding it difficult to tell him the news, for he feared

Ragoczy would vent his anger on him. And Gasparo would not find it in his heart to blame him if he did.

"I'm sorry to hear about the messenger, but that isn't what brought you here, is it?"

Apparently Gasparo didn't hear him. "But what can you expect with the Franchese King coming into Italia, bringing men-at-arms? The brigands used to be soldiers. What else do they know but killing and pillage?" He leaned back in the chair and sighed.

"Come, Gasparo, whatever you have to say cannot be that horrible. We'll agree that the roads are becoming more dangerous than ever, and that someone should do something about the brigands, though, of course, neither of us can. And I'll be glad to assure you that you speak to me in confidence." Ragoczy had brought another chair into the center of the room, and now he sat near Gasparo. "What has Lodovico done?"

Gasparo jumped visibly. "Santa Chiara, how did you know?"

Ragoczy shook his head. "Who else would perturb you this much? We know that Carlo is happily settled, and Giuseppe is doing very well for himself. And Lodovico had said he was going into Francia. Tell me: did you ask your friend there to seek out Lodovico, or what?"

Shamefacedly Gasparo said, "Yes. Here I am, an honorable Fiorenzeno, and I ask a Franchese—a *Franchese*, Eccellenza—to find a Fiorenzeno for me. To spy on him." His big hands locked together in his distress. "Do I think Lodovico is capable of betraying his oath? Why else would I ask Alain to seek him out?"

"You arranged it because it is you, Gasparo, who are a man of honor, and it is your honor alone that keeps you from condemning Lodovico now." Ragoczy leaned forward and his compelling eyes fixed on Gasparo's. "You are bound by your oath, and you want to keep it. That's a trust worthy of a Pope. But you are loyal to your friend, and it pains you to have these suspicions. Am I right?"

Gasparo nodded. "Yes. You're right. How could I have been so mistaken about Lodovico? You understand, Eccellenza," he went on, coming to grips with his news at last, "Alain found Lodovico, and spent a few nights drinking with him. And then Lodovico departed. He said he was coming back to Fiorenza. He said he knew of a rich man who had many secrets in his palazzo, and that it would be an easy matter to steal them. He said he was tired of living in foreign lands and being scorned for the convenience of a man who was not even a Fiorenzeno, let alone Italiano. Alain tried to find out more, and in his letter he tells me that Lodovico wants gold, a lot of gold, so that he can at last have the pleasures and happiness that rich men know." Gasparo scrambled out of the chair and paced the length of the room. "He means to come here, Eccellenza. He means to rob you, or worse."

"Yes. I realize that." There was something in Ragoczy's calm that angered Gasparo.

"Is that all you have to say? Does it mean nothing to you that a man is going to try to rob you, perhaps try to kill you?"

Ragoczy paused to reach out and pinch a guttering candle. "Yes, it means a great deal to me. It means much more that you warned me. I am very much touched that you were able to keep faith with me. If you had not been able to, I couldn't blame you."

Gasparo snorted. "I took a Blood Oath." To emphasize this he slammed his broad hands down on the nearest table, and the candles jumped at the blow.

Slowly Ragoczy rose from his chair. "Blood Oaths are broken every day, amico mio, in a thousand ways. Think of the Commandments we all break out of habit. Your loyalty is rare, and I treasure it as much as I treasure . . ."—his smile was tinged with a kind of self-mockery—"my soul."

With a deep sniff which he managed to turn into a cough, Gasparo faced Ragoczy. "Well?"

But Ragoczy was busying himself with the opalescent contents of an oddly shaped glass flask hung over a low-burning lantern. He gave Gasparo a quizzical look. "Well what?"

Gasparo straightened his shoulders. "I'm ready. Whatever your punishment is, mete it out. I deserve it. I should not have chosen Lodovico, and we both know it."

As he took the flask and moved it gently so that the strange liquid swirled in it, Ragoczy said. "Of course we know it. But I thought I made it clear that I don't hold you responsible. I'm very grateful. You've done all that anyone could or would do. That's enough. I'd be a fool to ask more. And often I've had much less."

"You mean there is no punishment?" Gasparo said, incredulous. He had seen even the fairest of masters whip a man for much less.

"No. Why should there be? Would it change anything?" At last he set the flask aside and turned his full attention to Gasparo. "If you hear any more, I would like to know of it, and as soon as possible. I suppose it's too much to hope that Lodovico will contact you, but if, perhaps, he does, find out what you can."

"Of course, Eccellenza." Gasparo nodded vigorously before he started toward the door.

"And if you learn through the other builders, oh, anything that bothers you, tell me that as well. It's inconvenient that

Lodovico chose this time to come back, but I suppose it was inevitable." He came across the room to Gasparo and put an arm across the builder's burly shoulders. "I am very much in your debt. If there is any way I might be of service to you, tell me, and you have my word that it will be done."

Gasparo was about to make a stumbling explanation as to why this wasn't necessary when the door opened once more and Demetrice came back into the room. She carried a tray with slices of light-colored cheese and a bowl of fragrant chunks of preserved fruit. There was also a jug of wine on the tray, and a piece of meat pie.

"Amadeo thought this might be to your satisfaction, Signore Tucchio," she said as she held the tray out to him. "There is a little table in the alcove there, and if you set the books on it aside, you'll find it a pleasant place to eat. I've had many meals there." As she spoke she moved across the room to the alcove and nodded toward the leatherbound books that covered it. "Just stack them in the corner."

"Certainly. In the corner." Gasparo hurried to Demetrice's assistance, pulling the huge volumes into his arms.

Laughing, Demetrice set the tray on the table. "There. You can look out that lozenge window there. You can see San Lorenzo and Santa Maria Novella if you lean forward a little." She stood beside the table until Gasparo was settled. "We'll be working, but don't be disturbed. Nothing very terrible is going on just now."

Gasparo nodded his thanks and pulled out his knife to eat.

When Demetrice came back to the two beehive-shaped athanors, Ragoczy said to her very softly. "Elegantly done, amica mia. You're a marvel."

She grinned frankly at his praise. "All Fiorenza knows that foreign noblemen have no manners." Her light, bantering tone left her a moment as she added, "You deserve some courtesy, if only from me. You've been kind to me when no one else was willing to be. And whether it is for Laurenzo or for me, I thank you."

Ragoczy's dark eyes met her amber ones, and there was an enigmatic expression in them that she couldn't read. "At first, amica mia, it was for Laurenzo. But no longer." Then, before she could ask him any questions, he picked up one of the flasks. "This needs more of the oil from Madras added. You'll find it in the chest there by the hearth."

Demetrice almost fled to the chest, and by the time she had found the oil, she had regained her tranquillity.

It was somewhat after dark when Gasparo Tucchio at last left Palazzo San Germano. He had been well-fed, and the wine was the best he had tasted in many days. Ruggiero had engaged him in a game of chess, and Gasparo had played lavishly and lost with joy.

A low mist had come up from the Arno and it gave the whole city a pale, unreal splendor, like a kingdom seen in dreams. It also lent an insidious chill to the air, as Gasparo discovered when he was a little way from Palazzo San Germano. He wrapped his arms over his chest for warmth and listened to the chanting from Santissima Annunziata. It was not much past the ninth hour, and if he walked quickly, he would be home before the mist penetrated his clothes.

As he neared the river the mist grew denser, rendering the buildings around him almost invisible. Gasparo listened intently, but there was little to hear except the soft murmur of the Arno.

He turned onto a street he was reasonably sure was la Via Tornabuoni. It would take him to il Ponte Santa Trinita, and from there over the river to his little house behind Santo

Spirito, where the Agostiniano Brothers marked out the night with prayers and psalms.

As he neared the bridge he heard uncertain footsteps and laughter accompanying slurred words. There were two women, Gasparo decided, and three men. If they were discovered together, particularly if they were as drunk as they sounded, then they would be publicly denounced by Savonarola the next time he preached. Gasparo felt a twinge of anger at the prior of San Marco, and a touch of pity for the men and their companions. For a few minutes Gasparo stood in the fog, an innocent eavesdropper, as the men and women sported together and in their disordered way debated where they should go to enjoy one another. At last the party drew away in the fog, and Gasparo realized with a start that he was bitterly cold.

Now he moved quickly and his old bones ached. He saw the bridge ahead, a strange, dark shape in the white mists. It was a welcome, though insubstantial presence, and Gasparo stepped onto it with a certain ill-defined relief.

The few buildings that clung to the bridge loomed over him in the dark, and the sound of the river was louder, almost like thousands of footsteps, following him as he crossed the bridge.

When he had almost reached the south side of the Arno, Gasparo stopped, cocking his head. In spite of the cold he willed himself to remain silent, to keep from shivering while he listened. For a moment it seemed to him that there was indeed someone following him, creeping stealthily nearer along the bridge. But as he forced himself to hear every sound, Gasparo could distinguish nothing but the noise of the river.

He had just started walking once more when he felt a hand on his shoulder. Frightened and angry, he turned to give his assailant a blow from his clenched fists. But before his arm was raised high enough to strike, there was a thrust below his ribs, and a sharp, hot pain spread swiftly, crazily through him. Bewildered, he took the knife by the handle and tried to pull it out of his chest. And then he dropped his hands. It was too much work. As Lodovico approached him, Gasparo opened his mouth to tell him something. But blood ran out and he could no longer speak. He felt a strange lassitude come over him as Lodovico lifted him, and slowly, so slowly, raised him over the edge of the bridge and let him fall lightly, drifting through the fog.

Long before his body splashed into the river, Gasparo Tucchio was dead.

TEXT OF THE Confession of Donna Estasia Catarina di Arrigo della Cittadella da Parma, made to Savonarola and published in Fiorenza on the Feast of the Guardian Angels, October 2, 1494:

> *In the name of God the Father, Christ the Son and the Holy Spirit, Amen. This is the Confession of the heinous sins and crimes committed by Donna Estasia della Cittadella, widow of a merchant of Parma, given of her own free will and in her own words, without additions, commentary or embellishments.*
>
> *Gentle Savior, Holy Son of God, grant that my Confession is whole, without any interest beyond the expiation of sin and the redemption of my soul.*
>
> *For many months I have been visited by devils, and they have led me to great wrongs. It is the fault of my flesh, which is too easily roused, and which I have vowed to master with fasting and scourges. I have made*

my body the house of sin and men have wallowed there. In my vanity, I have been happy to be beautiful, desirable, a woman to be looked at with lust in the heart. I have reveled in the wanton pleasures of lascivious congress, joining my flesh with the men who have pleased me. What temptation there is in the flesh, the loathsome, sensuous flesh that lures us all to desecration, to the delirium that drowns the songs of the angels.

All but one of my lovers have Confessed and have repented their debauchery, and for that reason they should not be shamed by me, though I desire to be free of the stench of my filthy liaisons. The five men who have made peace with God are forgiven in Heaven and will sin no more. And theirs were sins common to all of you, the bestial ruttings of animals, sating themselves in their passions on my body.

In deep humility and utter self-abasement, I beg those good men to forgive me for the transgression we shared. I urge them to forget the tangle of our limbs, the frenzy of coupling, the sweat, the sounds, the cries we made in the act. Their thoughts should never again dwell on the languorous sighs and the trembling flanks pushed together in heat, the taut sinews, the perfumed nights in silken sheets.

The devils that torment me do not visit them, and it is just, for it is my sin that brought them to their error, and their repentance shows me the way to the Mercy Seat.

Whether the other lover was a devil or a man, I cannot say. He was a foreigner, a rich stranger who chose, for some unnamed reason, to live among us. He was a man of great wealth, and for that worldly consideration, such is the venality of Fiorenza that all accepted the stranger and did him honor.

*He came to me first three years ago. He had seen
me once, at a distance. We had exchanged no word.
But I knew that he desired me and that he would not
be satisfied until he had possessed me. He importuned
me later and I denied myself to him. He swore a great
oath then, declaring that he would ravish me if he had
to kill my cousins to do it.*

*I dreaded the man. And I feared that he would
bring my other lovers to some hurt, and so I refused to
see them again. I hid in my cousin's house and feared
to go abroad because I dreaded finding that foreigner
waiting, stalking me as a cruel lion stalks the baby an-
telope. Whenever I saw his splendid black clothing, or
heard his soft, accented words, I was ready to swoon
with terror. But there was nothing I could do to escape
him. There was no place in Fiorenza safe from him,
for he was an alchemist, and privy to all sorts of forbidden secrets that gave him powers none but the
holiest of men could resist.*

*At last I could not fight his will. He chose a night
when Sandro and Simone were away and forced his
way into the house. Though I tried to defend myself
against him, he prevailed and at last bound me to my
own bed. He was of enormous proportions and he tore
my body with his virile member which he thrust into
me mercilessly, spending his seed many times that
night. He beat me cruelly with whips of silk, and
forced me to anoint his member with holy oil before he
used me with unnatural brutality.*

*But this was not enough for him. He came again to
my bed, and ravished me in ways I dare not describe,
save to say that sinful men sometimes use boys as he
used me. He told me then that his seed would not fill*

me with child, but with devils, that my flesh would be a temple for devils. How much I despaired then, and how my tears fell when I was alone and none could see them.

Then I hoped to be rid of his passion. I tried to Confess, but the devils he had put into my body gagged me and caused me such torture that I could not endure the holy words the good priest said to me.

When he came to me the next time, he gave me a vile drink, and I was not in my senses while he rutted over me. But when I was again able to think and see, imagine my horror, my complete end of hope as I realized I had been carried to a church, and there in the dark, with black candles burning, my lover had bound me to the altar.

It maddened him when I pleaded with him to kill me, but to spare the sacred objects and building from this depraved, profane use. He silenced me by renewed violations of my body, laughing when I could not keep from screaming.

When at last his member was depleted, he gathered his spilled seed into the Chalice and forced me to drink of it. Then he took the crucifix from the wall. It appalls me even to think of this, let alone describe it, but I must tell you or the devils in my flesh will overcome me once again. He used the crucifix on my body as he had used his gigantic member. I was too shamed, too horrified to cry out, and later, I was driven to madness by the infamy of the acts he had forced upon me.

Devils have taken my flesh, used my body, and all at his instigation. He has caused my thoughts to turn away from the joys of Heaven and to worship at the torments of Hell.

I have been forsaken by God for my lusts and my sins, and unless there is more power in the Lord God than there is in the foreigner's devils, I am damned for eternity.

Pray for me, good Prior. Pray for me and drive the devils out of my flesh. Chastise me! Show me my vileness! If it will drive out the devils, flay me with knives! I will endure humiliation, exposure, odium, calumny. Scourge me! Beat me! Cast out that foreign devil, for it is he who commands the demons in my body. I will spend the rest of my life on my knees if only to be free of him.

Most heartily I repent my sins, those committed knowingly, and those that were forced upon me. I admit my transgressions and my errors. I accept the judgment made on me and will gladly perform any Act of Contrition demanded of me. In anguish, in humility, in total submission I await your decision, blessed, blessed Girolamo Savonarola. I offer my sin-ridden soul to you—you who have never been corrupted in the flesh, have mercy on me. See my suffering and save me. Save me! Save me!

Verified as a correct and exact transcription of the Confession of Donna Estasia Catarina di Arrigo della Cittadella da Parma, taken at Sacro Infante September 29, 1494.

Girolamo Savonarola
Prior di San Marco
Domenicano

CHAPTER 12

In flagrant disregard of half of the sumptuary laws in Fiorenza, Massimillio had prepared a subtiltie of liver paste which he had molded in the form of a wreath of laurel leaves, reminding of the friendship Poliziano had shared with Laurenzo, and he had colored the wreath black with a paste of mashed pepper and juniper berries. Within the wreath was the name Agnolo Ambrogini Poliziano.

There was little mirth at Palazzo de' Medici this last night of September. Poliziano's death a few days before had shocked the few remaining Medici stalwarts, and now there were more rumors about the advance of King Charles of Francia.

Piero sat at his high table with Ficino and a handful of his Medici and Tornabuoni relatives, and from his immoderate laughter and the anxious looks his wife cast him from her place at the women's table, it was plain that he had drunk more wine than was good for him. He signaled one of the servants to bring him more of the liver-paste laurel wreath, then he refilled his cup.

"Is that wise?" Ficino asked with the audacity reserved for senior scholars.

"Plato says even Socrates got drunk. It's in the *Symposium*. When I was a child, Poliziano tried to teach that to me, and when I wouldn't do the translation, he beat me. Well, he's dead now. Too bad. He was younger than my father was."

Ficino gave Piero a look half of sympathy, half of disgust, then turned away from his young host.

Near the foot of the men's table a musician played melancholy songs on his lute. He paused to say to Francesco Ragoczy, "I see you can't eat either."

"No. I can't." He smoothed the front of his black velvet giornea and adjusted the silver links around his neck that held his order in the sign of the eclipse.

"Agnolo was a sharp-tongued devil, but he was a brilliant scholar. His poetry was good, too." The musician ran his fingers down the strings, making a light, plaintive sound. "Young Buonarroti will miss him the most. Agnolo always loved his work and encouraged him. He could be like that, you know."

Ragoczy looked up at the musician. "I know." Quite suddenly he rose and moved away from the dining tables. He stopped by the chest where the food was set out and glanced toward Massimillio, who hovered in the doorway. "It was well done, Massimillio. A wonderful tribute."

The cook's eyes were moist. "I have served the Medici household for most of my life. But how much longer? Even now Piero hints that he has little use for me, and there are few in Fiorenza now who would want me. There is little use for Palleschi in this city."

"As one Palleschi to another," Ragoczy said as he nodded toward the design of red balls, the famous Medici palle, that were carved into the doorway, "it will not always be so. The Medici and Fiorenza are linked together, and they will be separated only when one or the other is dead."

Massimillio sighed. "If it were so, I would have nothing to fear. But la Signoria mutters about us. If Savonarola has his way, there won't be a Medici left in Fiorenza."

Ragoczy nodded slowly and looked over the forlorn banquet. "If you should decide to leave, there is a man in Genova. His name is Arturo Peligrino. Go there, if you must leave Fiorenza, and say that San Germano sent you to him."

The huge cook studied Ragoczy's face, as if doubting the words, or fearing mockery.

With an ironic smile, Ragoczy looked up at Massimillio. "Signore Peligrino lives in la Via della Diva Marina. He is a merchant who buys and sells jewels and spices. He won't turn you away, you have my word on that."

"How do you know?" Massimillio blurted out.

"Because I own his ships. And because, unlike myself, Peligrino loves good food." Ragoczy picked up one of the juniper berries that garnished the liver-paste wreath and squeezed it between thumb and forefinger. The little berry broke and its sharp scent freshened the air. With a final reminder to Massimillio to remember Arturo Peligrino in Genova, Ragoczy left the banquet room and wandered through the familiar halls of Palazzo de' Medici. He smiled sadly at the beautiful statues, the paintings, the furniture. There were many things with the LAUR MED, marking them as Laurenzo's.

Though there was no particular pattern to his wandering, Ragoczy came at last to the library. He stood at the door, wondering if he should go in. Laurenzo had loved his books with a tenderness that Ragoczy valued and shared. And bitter, harsh-tongued Poliziano had often turned affectionate and delighted in the company of books. Would there be ghosts in the library? Ragoczy asked himself. Would the room be full of Laurenzo and Poliziano? His hand was on the door latch when the sound of his name made him turn almost guiltily.

"Francesco," Botticelli said again as he hurried toward him. He was still in his cloak and the spattering of rain dampened his clothes. His boots were muddy and he was slightly out of breath.

"Sandro," Ragoczy said, turning to touch cheeks with the tall painter. "I didn't know you'd be here."

"I didn't know it, either," he said as he shrugged out of his cloak. "Sergio said that you were not with the others, and I thought I might find you here." There was a certain distraction to his words and worry scored his rough-hewn features into a medieval mask.

"What is it?" Ragoczy asked, sensing that Filipepi's concern went beyond mourning for Agnolo Poliziano. "Are you well?"

Using the corner of his cloak, Sandro blotted the rain from his hair and face, then leaned heavily back against the wall. "Oh, Gran' Dio. I don't know how to say this."

"Say what?" There was a stab of worry in him now. "Is Demetrice well? Have they found Tucchio yet?"

Botticelli shook his head and made a complicated gesture of mingled annoyance and grief. "No. Demetrice is fine. You've seen her more recently than I have. Tucchio is still missing. No, that's not it." He took a deep breath. "I wish it were Demetrice. Or Tucchio. I wish it were anything but . . ."

Then Ragoczy knew. "Estasia?"

"Yes," Sandro said through clenched teeth. "I've just come from Sacro Infante." He moved swiftly, grabbing Ragoczy by the shoulders in a powerful grip. His golden eyes were intense as he leaned toward Ragoczy. "Do you swear on your eternal soul, on your eternal soul, stragnero, that you told me the truth about what passed between Estasia and you?"

It would have been a simple matter for Ragoczy to break free of this grip, but he accepted Sandro's desperation and made no effort to get away. In a level voice he answered. "I swear it was the truth. I swear it by my life, by my blood and by my immortal soul."

"Did you beat her? Did you defile her in church?" The hot, relentless eyes bored into Ragoczy's.

Ragoczy stifled the laugh in his throat. "I did no more or less than I told you before. I never entered her body as a man. I pleased her as best I could in my manner, and she pleased me. I will swear that by anything you like. I have no reason to lie. And if my pride demanded that I lie to you, it could be easily disproved. Estasia herself . . ."

The strong fingers released him and Ragoczy stood back from Sandro as he said, "Estasia has Confessed."

"Confessed? Confessed what?"

"Today, to Savonarola himself. I was there. I heard her. There was more blasphemy in her new piety than ever there was in pagan rites. And Savonarola listened to it, believed it, hoarded the horrible things she said like a miser counting gold. He wanted to believe her. He wanted her to lie about herself." He met Ragoczy's dark eyes with pain. "He wanted her to lie about you, Francesco."

So it had come at last, Ragoczy thought, and knew that he had been waiting for it. His small, beautiful hands clenched and he forced them to open. "What did she say?" he asked softly.

Botticelli's eyes sickened. "It was foul. Disgusting."

"What did she say?" Ragoczy asked again, and something of his calm communicated itself to Sandro.

"She talked of sacrilegious acts, of being violated on a church altar . . ."

Ragoczy turned his face away, as if to avoid a blow. His dark eyes filled with anguish. "What else?"

"Isn't that enough?" Sandro demanded with sudden violence.

"*No.*" The word was barely a whisper but it struck home. "Not if I must defend myself against her accusations."

"Defend yourself?" Sandro said, and ran his fingers through his tawny hair. There was white in it now, and it fell in loose curls like an askew halo. "Christo e San Dismo! You can't defend yourself, man. That's what I'm trying to tell you. She's branded you satanic, Francesco. You've got to leave. Now. Tonight. They'll arrest you tomorrow if you stay."

"Satanic?" He frowned. "What did she say that made me satanic? Your first questions—is that what she's said? That I raped her on a church altar? Truly? As her Confession?"

"Yes."

"And the Confession? Was it public?"

Sandro nodded, looking very tired now. "It's to be published on the Feast of the Guardian Angels." He looked up at the ceiling, studying the carved and painted beams, but forced his mind back to his foreign friend. "Do you need help?"

Ragoczy's rather vacant expression changed at once. "No. No. I will manage. It would be bad for you if it became known you helped me. You must not let anyone know you came to me this evening."

Botticelli could not meet his eyes. "I'm shamed, Francesco. That one of mine should do you so intolerable a wrong . . ." He slammed his fist against the top of his thigh. "Let me make amends."

"How?" Ragoczy asked without condemnation. "If there ever is a way I might need your help, be sure I'll ask for it. It may be that I'll need friends in Fiorenza."

"Then count me one," Sandro said quickly, his intensity returning. "No matter what occurs, I will be your friend."

"But not publicly," Ragoczy warned. "It may be dangerous to be my friend, once this Confession is known." His glance traveled along the ill-lit hall to a bronze statue. There, frozen in the metal, a seated Daphne was already sprouting limbs and leaves as a gloriously nude Apollo reclined to embrace her, forever too late. Laurenzo had loved it, and recently Piero had asked Ragoczy if he cared to buy it.

"That's true," Botticelli admitted. "But it may be known that I came to find you." He was somber, and then he chuckled. "If you give me a blow on my face, I will be able to say that I tried to apprehend you, we fought, and after striking me, you fled. My report will take some time to give." Then the mischief was gone from his eyes. "I need to do this to aid you. For my honor."

"As you wish." He gave a last look to the library door. "I should have gone in." He recalled then the first time Laurenzo had entertained him, and how he had brought Ragoczy to the library as the afternoon sunlight filled the room with golden splendor. He was delighted that Ragoczy shared his love of books, and he had said as he fingered the gilt-and-leather binding of a volume of Dante Alighieri, *I have had seven children from my wife, and others elsewhere. But these are my best-loved children, the children of my soul.* Laurenzo's smile then had given his ugly face a beauty that Ragoczy missed now with an intensity that was close to pain.

"Francesco?" Sandro ventured, alarmed.

"It's nothing," Ragoczy said, not knowing how desolate his eyes were. With an effort he pushed his memories aside. "There's not much time, is there?"

"No." Botticelli studied the backs of his hands, and said, as if he were talking of the weather, or a bit of unfounded gossip, "There will be a warrant for your arrest issued. It may have been given already. It will come from la Signoria, but it is on the order of Savonarola. He needs you, or someone like you, so that he can reveal more danger to the people. If it weren't you, it would be someone else."

"Of course. But do you know, Sandro, I wish it weren't me?" He touched cheeks with the artist. "I thank you again for the risk you took for me. I will not forget what you've done."

Botticelli looked somewhat relieved, as if his guilt were lessened. "When do you go?"

"Soon." He studied Sandro's lived-in face a moment. "Are you sure you want me to strike you?"

"Yes, of cour—" He was silenced as Ragoczy's fist slammed into his cheek. His ears rang, his vision clouded and wavered as he staggered backward, arms flung out to keep from falling.

By the time he had steadied himself and overcome his dizziness, Ragoczy was gone.

T HE WARRANT FOR the arrest of il stragnero il Conte Francesco Ragoczy da San Germano, issued to i Lanzi by the Console, i Priori and la Signoria:

> By the consent and order of all the government of Fiorenza, i Lanzi are mandated to seize and hold the perfidious diabolist known as il Conte Francesco Ragoczy da San Germano, and to deliver him up with all speed to the officials of la Repubblica for prosecution as a notorious blasphemer and heretic. All precautions to prevent his escape or his suicide must be taken. This Ragoczy is guilty of atrocious crimes

> *against the State and God and it is essential that he*
> *feel the full weight of the law, temporal and spiritual.*
>
> *With the full authorization of the Console, i Priori,*
> *and la Signoria*
> September 30, 1494

CHAPTER 13

THE LANTERN WHICH she held aloft shed a dim, ruddy light over Demetrice's face as she came through the hidden door and said, very softly, "They've gone."

Ragoczy turned to her as he finished adjusting his heavy riding mantle. "Did they believe you?"

"Of course. There was no reason not to. I let them search the rooms and they found nothing." She put the lantern down on the nearest chest and sank onto a low stool. "I was frightened, San Germano. I've never seen any of the lancers like that." She pressed her hands together to stop their trembling.

"Demetrice," Ragoczy said in a different tone as he stopped tugging on his heavy leggings, "if you're frightened, then come with me. You'll be safe in Venezia. Think carefully. I don't want to leave you in danger."

She shook her head and turned her face up to him. "San Germano, how can you understand? This is my home. Fiorenza is where I live. I would die away from it."

"I understand," he assured her. "More than you know."

"You're very old, aren't you?" she asked, not really hearing what he had said to her. "It must seem foolish to love this city so, or to want to stay here."

Ragoczy reached for his riding boots, and before pulling them on, he held them up and tapped the thick soles. "Do you know what's in them?" he said, and there was a command in his tone that caught her attention and held it.

"No." Her face had lost some of its fear and there was the familiar spurt of curiosity in her eyes.

"Earth," he said shortly. "My native soil. Without it I would be unable to cross running water or walk in the sunlight for fear of being burned as you would be by hot metal. Don't tell me about the pull of home. I know it. I have known it for more than three thousand years, in lands you know nothing of. The earth is my life as much as blood is." He took one of the boots and began to tug it on.

Demetrice watched him, her face serene, her eyes troubled. "They think you killed Gasparo Tucchio," she said at last. "They think you made a pagan sacrifice of him."

"Of course," Ragoczy said with disgust. "They'll be saying every filthy thing they can about me in a few days."

She was alarmed now and reached out to touch his arm. "Oh, no, San Germano, not after what—"

He cut her short, placing his fingers gently on her lips. "And you must let them." He spoke softly, and the gravity of his expression defied contradiction. "Donna mia, if you defend me, you will be in danger. Condemn me with the rest. I ask you to do this for me. Agree with those who vilify me."

Her eyes searched his face. "But why, San Germano?"

"Because, cara," he said as he pulled on his other boot, "if they are willing to believe that I am diabolic, that I desecrate altars, that I cause demons to attack women, they may never discover what I truly am. A sacrilegious ravisher is a bogey to frighten children and give adults a few moments of titillation. But a vampire? A vampire is a dangerous, hideous, voracious thing that will kill them all in their beds." Impulsively he reached out and took her face in his small hands. "Demetrice, you have trusted me until now. Will you trust me again?"

She felt a sting behind her eyelids and she blinked to stop the tears. "If that is what you want, San Germano."

For the first time he kissed her mouth. It was a swift delicate kiss, their lips hardly touching. Then he straightened up and reached for his large leather wallet that lay open on the chest. As he tied it to his belt, he said, "I've made arrangements to have Joacim Branco moved to Siena. There is an alchemist there who is willing to look after him. He will need more care than you will be able to give him, if God's Hounds get after you."

At this mention of the Domenicani nickname, Demetrice flinched. "They will leave me alone, I think. They have too little to gain from me. I'm not notorious. I'm not important." She rose and was secretly pleased to find that her knees were steady and her hands no longer shook.

"That may not be enough," Ragoczy warned her. His wallet was secured, and he reached into the chest, drawing out two long poignards, which he tucked into the sheaths in his sleeves. "I will want to hear from you every month. Ruggiero is making out a deed even now that will give you title to this palazzo until such time as I myself return to claim it. There is money enough in the coffers in the measuring room to keep taxes paid and to allow you a few servants. I'll sign the document before I go."

This was too confusing for her. "Wait," she objected, then was silent as she saw how weary he looked. "Are you able to travel? You seem tired."

"If you were my age, you'd be tired, too," he said with a poor attempt to cheer her. "No, you deserve an honest answer. I am able to travel, though I'm . . . hungry. Well, that will wait. My need isn't urgent." He tugged his cloak from a peg by the door and motioned her to follow him.

Demetrice stood her ground and she barely flinched as she spoke. "If you are, as you say, hungry . . . you need not be."

Ragoczy stopped in the act of opening the hidden door. "Ah, sweet Demetrice." There was a gentle, sad rebuke in the words. "I don't ask that of you. Look at you. Your mouth is white with dread. You're as malleable as a marble statue." He came nearer, but not so near that her fear overcame her. "Amica mia, I take blood from those who want me. You make yourself an unwilling sacrifice. I'm grateful for the gesture. I know what it costs you to face me now. But no."

"No?" Demetrice's eyes widened, and she found herself on the verge of anger. "If you think I will not satisfy you . . ."

Carefully he took her hands in his. "No, Demetrice. I fear that I will not satisfy you." He gave her no time to consider this, but went back to the door, drawing her after him. "There are papers yet to sign." As he led her onto the landing of the grand staircase, he secured the door carefully. "I think it would be wise," he said as he regarded the hidden door, "if you change the entrance system for the door. And lock all entrances but this one and the one through the kitchen ceiling. The palazzo will probably be searched again."

"But why?" She climbed the stairs beside him. "Surely you don't think that the Console would allow the Lanzi to come here again? There would be no point to it."

"If Girolamo Savonarola wants this building searched

again, it will be searched. If he wants its contents, he will try to seize them. That, in part, is why the land will be deeded to you."

She regarded him through widened eyes. "But women cannot own property. If there is real opposition, la Signoria will authorize sale of the property."

They had reached the top of the stairs and Ragoczy gestured her toward his own chamber. "This is a provisional deeding. You are acting only as my agent and representative. Unless I refuse to pay taxes, neither la Signoria nor Savonarola can claim this building."

Her face was dubious, but she said, "If you're sure . . ."

Once again he stood aside for her as they entered his chamber. "Donna mia, I am not certain that the Emperor Caligula is not at this moment a haloed angel. But knowing what I do of Caligula, if he's an angel, Heaven is not what I've been told it was. Be calm, Demetrice. If the laws of Fiorenza are so overset as to take this place away from you and me, you may be sure you will have warning, for much worse will have occurred already."

As he closed the door to his chamber, Ruggiero came from the alcove where Ragoczy's writing table stood. He held a parchment document in his hand. "It's ready, master. Your signature and that of Donna Demetrice are all that's needed."

Ragoczy made his signature with his left hand, then gave the quill to Demetrice. "There," he said, pointing to the place prepared for her name. While Demetrice read the parchment, Ragoczy spoke to Ruggiero. "Are you ready, old friend?"

Ruggiero nodded. "I leave tomorrow at noon, on the road to Pisa, and, I hope, misdirect any pursuers. From Pisa I will go to Modena, then to Milano, and on to Venezia. It must be a quick journey, and at Pisa I will hire guards so that I and your goods will not fall victims to brigands." He repeated these instructions in a flat voice, like a student repeating a lesson.

"Do you think you'll be able to leave so soon?" Ragoczy made a gesture to include the furnishings of his room. "You have a lot to take with you."

"I will leave at noon," Ruggiero said evenly. "If I am detained by la Signoria, I will use the Papal summons Olivia sent you. Even Savonarola dares not deny that."

"Not yet," Ragoczy allowed. "Very well. Do as you think the wisest." He took the finished document from Demetrice as she finished sanding her signature. He rolled the deed, bound it with ribbon and reached for his wax and seal. In a moment he had affixed his eclipse crest to the seal.

Ruggiero took the deed, holding it carefully while the wax cooled. "Your horse should be ready, master," he said in a carefully neutral tone. "It's the Turkish stallion. He's in good form, and he's strong. You'll be many leagues from here before he'll have to rest."

"The Turkish stallion," Ragoczy approved, then turned again to Demetrice. "Cara, you can still change your mind."

She shook her head. "No. I do want to stay." She looked toward the dark windows. "And you must be gone soon. It will be dawn in little more than an hour."

He nodded. "I want you to send me monthly reports. There will be scholars and monks journeying between here and Venezia, and they will carry messages. Brigands don't attack monks and scholars very often—it's not worth the trouble. If you have need of me, send for me and I will come. If there is no one you can trust with a message, go to Sandro Filipepi, and he'll see that I hear from you."

Demetrice shrugged. "If that's your wish, I'll do it, but

you're worrying needlessly. What could possibly happen to me? I have your generosity and the strength of the Medicis to protect me."

Inwardly, Ragoczy felt that neither of these assets would be of any use if she were marked by Savonarola, but he said nothing. Loyalty like hers always humbled him, and he refused to help destroy it. He went toward the door, then turned back to her.

"San Germano? What is it?"

"I don't want to leave you." There was so much feeling, so much compassion in his words that she blinked in amazement and took an involuntary step forward.

Very softly in the distance there was the sound of sheep's bells, jingling as the flocks were led into the hills.

It was enough. Demetrice shook her head and hung back. "No. It's too late. You must go."

Ragoczy met her amber eyes. "Don't break faith with me, Donna mia."

"I won't." She managed a bit of a smile, and then added, "You said something about angels earlier. Do you believe in them, then?"

"No." He turned his head sharply as the sound of the bells came again. For the last time he looked at her. "I believe in you, Demetrice. And that is enough." He left quickly, his boots striking the marble floor like small explosions as he hurried through the silent palazzo to the stable.

Demetrice stood in the window, watching the sky turn from slate to silver to rose, listening to the sheep bells, and church chimes and the distant birds. Once or twice she thought she heard the receding thunder of a running horse, but there were so many other sounds that she could not be sure.

TEXT OF A letter from la Signoria to Girolamo Savonarola, Prior of San Marco:

With reverent humility, i Priori della Signoria send their greetings to Girolamo Savonarola, Prior di San Marco, and beg that he will approve the measures i Priori and the Console have taken after much prayer and discussion.

First: should the efforts of the foolish Piero de' Medici to placate the Most Royal Charles of Francia come to naught, we of la Signoria would count it most wise to banish him, his family, and all his kin from la Repubblica, for they are most impious and dangerous.

Second: in the event that the same King Charles is the ascendant in his dealings with the unfortunate Piero de' Medici, there should be measures taken to ensure the welcome of his Gracious Majesty to Fiorenza, and a good welcome for his troops. This would assure King Charles of our good faith as well as guarantee that Fiorenza would not suffer from mistreatment at the hands of the Franchesi soldiers.

Third: that fast days should be made mandatory, and strictly observed. The suggestion that you were willing to make to us, that there should be a squadron of young men who would see that these new measures are observed and respected is in every way desirable, and i Priori are more than willing to form such a group. It will provide good and holy works for our young men, and will ensure that the law is carefully and regularly observed.

Fourth: the Lanzi should be empowered to act on behalf of the religious leaders of Fiorenza as well as on the orders of the civic government. Heresy, as you were good enough to remind us, strikes not only at the Church, but at the State, for a state that is not founded on the fear of God, that does not adhere to the teaching of the Church, is doomed to destruction in this world, and utter damnation in the next.

Fifth: that those associating with suspected heretics, magicians, alchemists, and other Godless men should be put under observation, their right to travel revoked, their Confessions recorded and questioned for error, their houses searched and whatever is profane and sacrilegious seized. Further, those who continue to consort with known blasphemers should be imprisoned and examined by your most pious and excellent Domenicani, so that their souls may be saved.

Sixth: the harboring of criminals, heretics, and other desperate persons will be punishable with the same severity as the crime for which the person harbored is punished. Lenience in matters of the law, as you have pointed out to us, has brought Fiorenza to the dreadful pass that now threatens her very existence.

Seventh: those openly questioning or scoffing the new laws should be shown their error and made to recant their views in public Confession.

We seek your guidance in these matters, as in all matters, and we pray that through your wisdom and the justice of i Priori and the Console, our lives, our Fiorenza and our honor will be preserved, if it is the Will of God.

> G. Ondante
> clerk, la Signoria

In Fiorenza, October 12, 1494

PART THREE

Donna Estasia Catarina di Arrigo
della Cittadella da Parma

> *Su! Su! Sorge coll' aurora!*
> *Brillo è l' eternità!*
> *Gloria splenderà!*
> *L' ombra della vita spentò in un' ora.*

> Up! Up! Rise with the dawn!
> Shining eternally!
> Glory resplendent glows!
> And in an hour, life's shadow is gone.

—SUOR ESTASIA DEL MISTERO DEGLI ANGELI

TEXT OF A letter from Marsilio Ficino to the Venezian poet Cassandra Fedele:

To his admired colleague and respected friend Cassandra Fedele, her old adviser Ficino sends greetings from Careggi.

It's been too long since we have exchanged letters, and though I realize this is more my fault than yours, still I find myself anxious to hear from you, to learn what you are doing. Your recent works have been true inspiration for me at a time when little else can move me to any emotion but sorrow.

As I sit in this underground room at Laurenzo's old villa, I am caught up with my memories. It was just three years ago that Piero and his family were exiled. It was three years ago that young Conte Giovanni Pico della Mirandola died, though he was little more than thirty. To have his death follow so soon on that of Agnolo Poliziano's was a great blow to me. So here I sit, the last of them, waiting for death to reunite us. A terrible thing for a priest to say? You'll recall that Socrates chose death, and Our Lord welcomed it. I feel as if I have outlasted my time, and that I am over-due to leave this world. What good am I? I am forbidden to teach, my friends are dead or far away and my works gather dust in locked chambers.

I went into Fiorenza last week, which was a mistake. You would not know the place now, Cassandra. There is no joy there. Even the grave delights of wor-

ship are gone, and though the churches are full, there is fear and desperation there, not solace, wisdom and triumph.

You no doubt see now why I write so rarely. What I have to tell you saddens me, and my heart is too full of sorrow already. Tonight, if Laurenzo were still alive, if Fiorenza was now as it was six years ago, there would have been a feast to celebrate the birth of Plato and we would have spent the night in the pleasures of philosophy and good fellowship.

Now, those sons of Pierfrancesco de' Medici call themselves Popolano, as if they are shamed by the memory of Cosimo and Laurenzo. Fiorenza calls them traitors, but it was Cosimo and Laurenzo who glorified the city while Pierfrancesco's line had paid to have Botticelli's murals of the Pazzi conspirators destroyed, and Laurenzo's verses defaced. I never believed it would come to this, that Fiorenza would so soon forget the family that loved her, and filled her with all the beauty of the world, gave her the treasures of learning and art to adorn her.

The young Flemish scholar I told you of last year, de Waart, has had to flee, for he is under suspicion of being an alchemist and irreligious. As strict as the laws were made two years ago, they are now even stricter. They have fallen heavily on all of us—not just de Waart, but every man of learning. Educated men are suspect, and that kind young woman Demetrice Volandrai, whom Laurenzo loved so dearly and who has been living in the palazzo of il stragnero Francesco Ragoczy, has been imprisoned on some ridiculous excuse. Apparently it has been decided that it is sinful for a woman to be able to read Greek.

This religion is like a plague, sweeping everything before it, robbing the city of life, of hope. If I were not so old, and so weary of life, I think I might leave Fiorenza, dear as she is to me and much as I have loved to live here. It is agony to see her brought so low, that she is powerless and despised everywhere when once she was a beacon to all the world.

I have sought consolation in philosophy and in the practice of my faith, but I am overcome. I have been a priest for more than twenty years, and now, when I most desire the strength of my vocation, I am weak and filled with doubts. I see Girolamo Savonarola standing at the center of Fiorenza, defying the Pope and his excommunication, and I remember that Laurenzo also refused to accept such a Bull, and I wonder, is it that I loved Laurenzo and fear Savonarola that makes it seem that Laurenzo's act was one of enlightened courage and Savonarola's one of arrogant pride?

There. I made a vow not to burden you with this, Donna Cassandra. You have too gentle a heart to have it weighted down with my despondency. But every time I take my quill in hand, grief possesses me and I am helpless to deny it. You may seek to cheer me, if you like, but I feel now as if my heart was a cinder, and that it will never glow with fire again. Perhaps Suor Estasia del Mistero degli Angeli is right, and it is in heaven only that hope, joy and glory reside. That's what her visions tell her, and I, like San Tommaso, find only doubts.

Before I trouble you more, I will say farewell for a time. When my mind is less oppressed I will write to you once more, and tell you the beautiful sights I have

*seen, and the pleasure I have in learning. In spring the
countryside will be beautiful, and there will be fewer
brigands, perhaps, to assault travelers. Certainly
there will be some happiness in the world, if it is only
a new flower in the hills or a barnyard full of chicks.*

*I commend myself to your kindness, and thank you
again for the fruits of your talent. This, with my blessings, and my most genuine affection.*

Marsilio Ficino
At Careggi, near Fiorenza

November 7, 1497

CHAPTER 1

OUT ON THE Gran' Canale the moonlight spilled in silver
profusion, touching the gentle waves with a diamond luster
that shone against the dark tarnish of the night. The moon
lent its color to the golden front of Ca' d'Oro, and dappled
the fine marble of the great houses and palazzi, and in the
back canals, where there was squalor and poverty, the
moonlight hid that meanness in its gauzy deception. As
sometimes happened in winter, the night was clear and calm
and for once the Feast of the Circumcision was not marred
by gales and rain.

The courtyard of il Palazzo del Doge, unfinished as it
was, still rang with the laughter and music of the great celebration as the great, glittering throng surged from one elaborate room to another, here to drink wines from every part
of the world where Venezian ships sailed, there to hear

singers from Spain and Denmark. Il Doge himself, Agostino
Barbarigo, strolled among the guests in his splendid official
garments, the large gold buttons undone so that his simple
black gonnetta showed against the elaborate brocade. He
was a good host, his dark eyes and bristling beard as arrest-
ing as his cap of office.

In one large salone with the walls the same smoldering
blue as the sea at high summer, il Doge Barbarigo came
upon a lively discussion between the foreign Conte
Francesco Ragoczy and a young sea captain, Ulisso Viviano,
and he paused to join in.

"But if there is a New World in the Atlantic, and not just
another side of India, we Veneziani should exploit it. Think
of my name, Ragoczy. I was destined to go there. There is
no place in the world that interests me so much as the New
World and it would be a great pity if Spain alone were allowed to have it. Think. It would take no more than three
ships for the first voyage, just enough to get there and see
for ourselves what it's like. I already have a trusted crew
who have gone everywhere with me. They are eager for the
chance to have such an adventure. You have two ships in
port right now, and in a month, another will arrive. I promise
you a good return on your investment."

"Do you?" Ragoczy's face was polite but his eyes were
bored. This was the third time Viviano had accosted him
with plans for the New World.

"Of course. Think of it. Jewels. Gold. Spices. Two or
three voyages and our fortunes are made."

"Unless you should be killed, or the ships not survive the
seas, or the foreign people not want you there." Ragoczy
shook his head.

"What you mean, Viviano," il Doge interrupted, "is that
your fortune would be made. Ragoczy is rich already, and no

thanks to you. Or have you forgotten that you lost one of his ships two years ago?" He turned away from the young captain and regarded the foreigner with an appreciative eye. "The gold you've given the state for the adornment of la Scuola di San Giovanni Evangelista would outfit half a dozen such expeditions." He took Ragoczy's hand in his and pulled him away from the aggrieved Viviano, remarking as he did, "He's fairly honest, and he's ambitious. You could do worse things than finance him. The matter with your ship was more misfortune than bad judgment." He had brought Ragoczy into another, smaller room that was still being completed. Half-finished murals filled the walls, and the carved wainscoting was not entirely in place. Il Doge gestured to the murals. "What do you think? I like the style, but I admit that I wish I had your friend Botticelli here to do some of it."

"Ask him then." Ragoczy had done little more than glance at the murals.

"I have. He refused." Il Doge sighed and gestured fatalistically. "What is it, Francesco? You're not yourself tonight."

Ragoczy shook his head, then changed his mind and answered the question. "Tonight, had things been different in Fiorenza, Laurenzo would be celebrating the anniversary of his birth. He would have been forty-nine. And instead, Fiorenza is in the sway of Savonarola, who is fighting with the Pope as he grows in power."

"Have you had word from Fiorenza?" Barbarigo asked, taking a professional interest in political gossip.

At that, Ragoczy's frown darkened. "No. And I should have."

"Well, the winter is severe in the mountains. Perhaps the message is delayed. I've had two messengers killed since

September and the merchants say that it isn't safe to travel. But I have need of your advice, Ragoczy. You come from Transylvania."

"Yes. But many years ago." He rarely made a secret of his homeland, particularly when there was so much disruption going on in that part of the world.

"Did you know Matthias Corvinus?" Il Doge was too offhand, and Ragoczy knew he was leading up to a much more important question.

"Not intimately. I saw him once or twice. He was a courageous man. His second wife brought him to Napoli often, for she loved her own country. He was liked in Roma, and those I knew in Fiorenza who met him regarded him with respect. Why?"

"Well, Matthias often suggested that Venezia and Hungary should make common cause against the Turks. He had some powerful arguments to put forward—not just the demands of a threatened king, but reasons that would be advantageous to both our countries. Now that Matthias is dead, I have sent certain messages to Ulaszlo and have had no answer. I don't understand. I know that the messages were delivered, but Ulaszlo is silent."

"What did you want of him?" Ragoczy wondered aloud as he turned away from il Doge.

"I invited him to come to Venezia, to take part in a council that might be mutually advantageous. You'd think—"

Ragoczy snorted. "King Dobre? Do something on his own? If his Austrian masters think it might be beneficial, you may be sure he'll take part in your council. But remember that he's Austria's toy. Dobre, Barbarigo, means assentgiver. He earned his nickname."

Il Doge shook his head. "I feared it might be that. Well, I'll send one more message, and if there is no response, I'll try dealing with France, though there's less reason for them to help us." He looked at the unfinished murals once more. "I hope I live long enough to see them complete," he said softly before he turned and walked to the door. There something more occurred to him and he turned back to Ragoczy, saying, "Do you know la Donna Cassandra Fedele? She's a poet. Her work is read quite widely. She's recently had a letter from Fiorenza. Perhaps she'll be willing to give you news of your friends there." He glanced over his shoulder. "She's here tonight. You ought to seek her out."

"Grazie, Signor' Doge. Perhaps I will." As he said it he very much doubted that he would actually speak with the distinguished old poet, but to his surprise, she sought him out somewhat later in the evening.

She was a delicately boned woman, of great dignity and a strange, deceptive fragility, and when she spoke, her low, musical voice was the most beautiful sound in the world. "Ragoczy," she said as she came up to him. "You are il Conte Francesco Ragoczy, aren't you?" Being so remarkable a woman, and not young, she was allowed certain social freedoms denied many other Venezian women. She rarely flaunted her unique independence in the world's face, but she found it useful to be able to converse with men at will, instead of waiting for a properly chaperoned and constrained moment.

"Donna Cassandra," he said with a moderate bow. "I am very honored that you know me. I have for many years known who you are, and have admired your work. Poliziano first acquainted me with it."

"Ah, Agnolo. I miss him very much." She drew a deep breath and said more briskly, "I've been hoping for the opportunity to speak to you." She drew her arm through his, and added in her most polite tones, "I have never learned how you manage to look so completely elegant in plain black. The rest of us are got up like peacocks, and you out-shine us all."

He adapted his mood to hers. "Well, this plain black, as you choose to call it, is sculptured velvet, and the slashes are edged in silver and red. It is not quite as plain or as severe as you seem to think. And my Order," he said as he touched the silver-and-ruby chain where the eclipse medallion hung, "is not precisely inconspicuous."

She smiled her approval. "Very good. Did you learn that in Fiorenza? I've heard that the conversation there used to be remarkably audacious."

"No," he said, adding outrageously as she led him to a window alcove somewhat away from the celebration, "if I were to tell you where I learned that, you wouldn't believe me."

Donna Cassandra Fedele sat down and indicated that Ragoczy should do so as well. "I am concerned about Mar-silio Ficino. You know him, don't you?"

"Somewhat." It was a cautious answer and Donna Cas-sandra accepted it as such.

"I have had a letter from him. It disturbs me very much. He sounds so much unlike himself, despondent, fearful. You know more about Fiorenza than I do. I wonder if you will read his letter and tell me what you think."

Ragoczy studied her fascinating, lined face. There was no duplicity there, and no guile. He nodded. "Very well. When would you like me to call on you?"

"You need not go to that trouble," she said brightly. "I brought the letter with me, for I hoped to see you, or someone from Fiorenza." She reached into the small old-fashioned purse tied to her belt, and pulled out the tightly folded parchment. This she handed to him, saying nothing, waiting while he opened it and read.

Before he had finished, Ragoczy's dark eyes were burning and his face was white. At one point his small hands tightened convulsively, crumpling the fine parchment. Startled by his own violence, he put the letter onto his knee and smoothed it carefully, not seeing the words as his fingers covered them. "I'm sorry, Donna Cassandra. I wrinkled your letter. I didn't mean . . ."

Her flinty old eyes were sympathetic. "You know these people, Ragoczy. Their misfortune must alarm you."

"Demetrice," he said, and for a moment he saw her as he had seen her last, her face filled with light. "In prison." Ragoczy disliked anger. He knew what it did to others, and over the centuries had grown to despise what anger made him capable of doing. The anger that filled him now was welcome as rain in time of drought, as the warmth of a fire in midwinter.

Donna Cassandra's sharp old eyes studied him, and as he rose, she nodded to herself. "Do you wish to leave?" She received no answer to this question. "Il Doge seeks to honor you tonight, at the midnight meal. If you leave before then, you will offend him."

"I never eat." Ragoczy held out the letter to her. "I must thank you, Donna Cassandra. The news is bad, but you have relieved my mind. At least now I know what I must do, and with whom I must deal." He touched the chain that hung across his chest and traced the eclipse device with his fingers. "Your letter was written on November seventh. Have you had any word since then?"

Before she answered, Donna Cassandra folded the parchment and once again tucked it into her purse. As she looked up, a French musician with a lute in his hands bowed to her.

"I have set two of your verses to music, Donna rispettata," he said in poorly accented Italian. "I would be honored to sing them to you."

Ragoczy knew the musician was talented and at another time he would have wanted to hear the songs, but now he gave Donna Cassandra an impatient nod and she met his eyes with understanding.

"You honor my verses too much," she told the musician. "And I want very much to hear your work. But here it is crowded and there is too much talk to disturb you. Come, if you will, to my home tomorrow and we will spend a pleasant hour together."

The musician bowed deeply. "You overwhelm me," he declared, and turned away to find his companions so that he could boast of his triumph.

"Have you had any word?" Ragoczy repeated when the musician was gone.

"No. But there is a man here in Venezia," she said, and there was a measuring quality to her words. "He arrived two days ago. He came through Fiorenza late in the year. I believe he'll be here tonight, but a little later. He's Polish, a student of languages, and has been in Roma for more than a year." There was a slight malicious smile on the poet's face. "I don't know how he fared there, but if his Italian is any example of his prowess as a scholar, he'll need more than the libraries of Roma to teach him anything." She broke off. "No. It's not the Polish scholar who annoys me, it's the arrogant Borgias. He has been praising them, and I dislike that."

"I'll seek out this scholar when he arrives." There was a grimness about his mouth as he spoke. "I'll need news of Fiorenza. As recent as possible."

Donna Cassandra gave a short, canny laugh. "Unless I am badly mistaken, you're about to leave Venezia again. Do not be away for so long this time, Ragoczy. I'm an old woman, and there is little time left for me. I do hate spending it among fools. You're an intelligent man, and there are lamentably few intelligent men in this world. I enjoy your conversation, when you're willing to speak. One day you must tell me what you think of the ruins that were discovered near Udine last spring."

He knew he owed her a great deal, so rather than give her a curt response, he said, "The ones at Casa Sole?"

"Yes." She stared out at the milling, gorgeous crowd. "Most of them neither know nor care about the ruins. The people are dead and buried who built it, and what can it mean to them that their homes are brought to light. But you know it is important."

"Well," Ragoczy suggested with a shrug and an air of nonchalance that was belied by the glitter at the back of his eyes, "if the name is any indication, there was a temple of the sun there once."

"Or," Donna Cassandra said as she watched Ragoczy, enjoying the restlessness she saw in him, "it may mean the house of the unique one."

"Another temple, still." Ragoczy dismissed it and looked about the room. "You must excuse me, Donna Cassandra. You've been very kind to me, and it is impertinent of me to leave you so rudely, but I see Gian-Carlo at last and there's much I need to say to him." He bowed swiftly, his formality as minimal as was possible on such a grand occasion.

"Yes, of course. I will hear about this when you return. And be sure you speak to the Pole." She waved him away reluctantly, then turned her keen eyes to a young couple who thought their meeting was unobserved.

Gian-Carlo acknowledged Ragoczy's wave with one of his own and came through the crowd to meet him. He was resplendent in a short Venezian giacchetta of turquoise silk shot with gold thread, which was worn above particolored silken hose of turquoise and white. His camisa, which puffed through the slashes in his tightly fitted sleeves, was of ostentatious gold silk and his codpiece was fastened to his belt with shiny white ribbons. He wore a tall velvet cap on his soft brown hair and at the moment his face was bright with wine and pleasure. He grinned at his mentor. "Francesco," he said a great deal more casually than was polite, "I wondered where you'd got to."

Ragoczy took Gian-Carlo by the elbow and whispered to him, "I must talk to you. Now."

The unfamiliar brusqueness of this command bewildered Gian-Carlo, but he willingly followed Ragoczy to a smaller room where games of chance occupied one group of men at a large table. There was a degree of privacy in that room, and Ragoczy added to it by drawing Gian-Carlo toward the farthest corner.

"It's disrespectful of me to say it, but you look terrible. Francesco. Your face is the color of chalk. Are you ill?"

"No. It would not matter if I was." He watched Gian-Carlo through narrowed eyes, wondering how much of a risk this beautiful man of thirty-three was willing to take for his teacher. He knew that Gian-Carlo was honorable and sincere, but would he, faced with the threat of imprisonment or death, keep faith with Ragoczy? Not if he knew the whole of Ragoczy's secret. Once or twice he had thought to tell Gian-Carlo what he was, and trust that their friendship would survive the telling. But at the last he had always drawn back, and now he dared not put Gian-Carlo's loyalty to the test, either with the truth or in asking him to come to Fiorenza. Even so, the question he asked startled the young

Veneziano. "Do you know where I can get clothes made for me in less than a week?"

Gian-Carlo scowled. "Have Attilio do it. He does all your clothes, doesn't he? He's pretty fast."

"No. Not Attilio. He'd question too much. Who does your clothes?"

"I get the cloth from Eugenio, mostly, and Sabina Nimbue makes it up." He moved uneasily. "Francesco, what's this all about?"

Ragoczy did not answer that question at first. "Would she make up clothing for me? Quickly? In a week? I'll need a fair number of garments, in the Hungarian style. And in colors."

"Colors?" Gian-Carlo said, scandalized. "You never wear colors."

"I'm going back to Fiorenza in ten days." This announcement, given as it was in an offhand way, stunned Gian-Carlo.

"But they'll arrest you." He thought, fleetingly, that Ragoczy was mad or drunk. But he knew Francesco never touched wine, and that he was frighteningly sane.

"Only if they know who I am. I will return as . . . my nephew, I think. Come to claim his inheritance. That has a probable ring, doesn't it? My heir would go to Fiorenza if there was a valuable piece of property involved, wouldn't he? My hair is shorter, and if I speak Italian badly and wear bright colors in the Hungarian style, there are few who would question me. Not enough of my old friends are there still. Only Sandro . . ." He stopped. Why hadn't Sandro sent him word of Demetrice's imprisonment? He realized that had been worrying him since Donna Cassandra had shown him Ficino's letter. Marsilio had said nothing about Sandro, so he had assumed the artist was well, but it might be that

Botticelli, too, had fallen into disfavor with the stringent new regime of Fiorenza.

"Francesco?" Gian-Carlo's reluctant interruption pulled him away from these new and unpleasant thoughts.

"I will see you have my measurements. Deliver them tomorrow to Sabina Nimbue and tell her that I will require the garments in eight days. Price is no concern. She may charge me whatever she must to do the work. If she has to hire more needlewomen, tell her that I will pay their wages and give them five gold ducati a piece for every garment finished in seven days or less."

Gian-Carlo shook his head. "I'll do it, if that's what you want, but you're taking your life in your hands if you return to Fiorenza. How long do you think you'll go unrecognized? Your housekeeper . . . what's her name? She'll know you in a moment."

Ragoczy's face darkened. "She's in prison. That's why I'm going back."

"In prison?" Gian-Carlo scowled and it took him a moment to collect his thoughts. "If she's in prison, all the more reason for you to stay away. She may have denounced you already. They're not very kind to alchemists in Fiorenza recently. What was she sent to prison for? Perhaps she deserved it."

At that moment Ragoczy hated Gian-Carlo, and along with the instant of fury, he realized with a certain humor that Gian-Carlo had not offered to go with him or to go in his place. He felt his hatred leave him, and he said very gently, "If you were the one in prison, would you still feel that way?" He did not expect an answer, which was just as well, for Gian-Carlo flushed scarlet and could not meet Ragoczy's dark eyes. "Gian-Carlo, I must go."

"Yes." He muttered the word. "But will you take someone with you? If not me, Ruggiero? You must not go into that viper's nest unguarded. They might imprison you as well, even if they believe that you're your own nephew."

Ragoczy shrugged. "I doubt it. They have nothing to gain from that, but they might not let me stay there very long. That's just as well. If I'm to free Demetrice, it must be done quickly."

"Francesco," Gian-Carlo said with clumsy kindness, "have you considered that it might not be possible? That she might already . . . that perhaps . . ."

"That perhaps she's already dead?" Ragoczy suggested harshly. "Yes. I've considered that. I understand there is a scholar who is to attend this celebration sometime tonight who has recently been in Fiorenza, and I hope he will give me news."

Gian-Carlo gestured to the crowd in the adjoining room. "One scholar in all this? How will you find him?"

At that Ragoczy's humor returned a little and he almost laughed. "I understand he's Polish. It won't be difficult."

"I see." Gian-Carlo had already accepted the fact that Ragoczy was determined to return to Fiorenza, and decided not to try to persuade him to do otherwise. His own misgivings were still strong and he wished he had the force of argument on his side, for he liked Ragoczy and was anxious to learn more from him. But he inclined his head in elegant capitulation, thinking as he did that although he knew Ragoczy was the shorter of the two of them, the foreigner always contrived to seem to be the taller. "Tell me what you want made and give me your measurements in the morning. You said colors? Do you have any choices?"

"The brighter the better. And of Hungarian cut. If it's possible, at least two of the rondels should have the pearl embroidery which is still fashionable. Use my store of pearls if you must. I want it to seem that I'm part of the Hungarian court."

There was a tacit understanding between Gian-Carlo and Ragoczy that the Veneziano would ask him no questions concerning his background, but now Gian-Carlo's curiosity overcame him. "You have been away from your homeland a long time, haven't you?"

"Yes. A long time." Then, abruptly Ragoczy was himself again. "Gian-Carlo, see that I have those clothes. Tomorrow I will need to arrange for money, and I must send a message to Teodoro in Cavarzere to meet me in Chioggia with horses in ten days. I'll need a good mount. I want to make Ponte-lagoscuro the first day and Bologna the second."

At this brutal suggestion Gian-Carlo blanched. "San Filippo, you'll kill your horse! It's impossible to do in twice the time."

"Teodoro must arrange for changes of mount for me along the way. I still have horses at Pietramala, don't I?" He had left such matters in Gian-Carlo's hands the last year when it had seemed unlikely that he would return to Fiorenza for some time.

"Yes. Dionigi Fano at Il Bosco has them. There are four mares and two stallions."

"Good." Ragoczy rubbed his hands in anticipation. "What color are they? Is there one that isn't gray?"

"There's one white mare."

"I'll want her." He saw Gian-Carlo's shocked face and he relented a little. "If I'm going to survive the viper's nest, as you call it, I must at least confuse them. Just as I never wear colors, I always ride gray horses."

"A message will go to Teodoro at first light." Gian Carlo put his hand to his eyes. "Bright clothes, heavily embroidered, in eight days. Horses ready for you between here and

Fiorenza, and you want the white mare from Dionigi Fano."
He rolled his large blue eyes upward, as if appealing to
heaven for comment.

"Very good," Ragoczy approved. "And now I must try to
find the Polish scholar. When I have spoken with him, I
must leave. Tell Riccardo to have the gondola here in an
hour."

"I will." With a last, resigned sigh, Gian-Carlo strolled
away, his brilliant smile masking the icy dread he felt.

TEXT OF A letter from Antek Kazielawa to Francesco
Ragoczy da San Germano, written in Polish:

> To the distinguished gentleman Francesco Ragoczy da
> San Germano in Venezia, Antek Kazielawa sends his
> greetings, and gives himself the honor to relate to Sr.
> Ragoczy what he saw and heard while he stayed in the
> Toscana city of Fiorenza.
>
> Journeying north from Roma, where I had contin-
> ued my studies of antique languages, I arrived in
> Fiorenza at the end of October and was anxious to
> learn more at the library established by Cosimo de'
> Medici, who was called Pater Patriae. It was most
> disheartening that the Medici family is in great dis-
> grace in the city so that even the books gathered by
> Cosimo and the Magnificent Laurenzo are held in
> contempt and suspicion. With the aid of several
> Francescani Brothers from Santa Croce—who are op-
> posed to the new order, if I have understood them cor-
> rectly and it is not just more of the rivalry between the

*Francescani and Domenicani—I was at last granted
access to those books of ancient scholarship which
are the topics of my life studies.*

*Over the years I have so often heard the praises of
Fiorenza sung that my disappointment was all the
greater when I discovered how far removed from her
former glory Fiorenza is today. Where before all I
heard was talk of the splendid art, the elegant conversation, the wonderful entertainments, the high learning,
the delights in all things philosophical and graceful, to
find the city so somber, so glum, and practicing an austerity more in line with the lives of the Saints than the
Spartans, I fear I was too deeply shocked to understand
at first that this was not typical of Fiorenza.*

*Much can be blamed on the poor wool and textile
trade, which has fallen off very much of late, and perhaps it is true that poor crops have made fast days
more necessary. There is also a certain unrest which
is the heritage of the French. But most of the unfortunate erosion of scholarship and the equally lamentable decline of the arts comes from the new religious
fervor that had taken control of almost all the people.*

*While I was there I saw many religious processions,
but the strangest of all was of Domenicani Brothers
who danced through the streets, garlands on their
heads, singing hymns and beseeching God to visit them
with His Holy madness. All the while their prior, one
Savonarola, who has been excommunicated, marched
with them and exhorted them to pray and to accept the
presence of the Spirit of God. No one attempted to stop
this prior, though it is a sin to hear him.*

*It was at the height of this strange procession that
Suor Estasia del Mistero degli Angeli was called by*

Savonarola to come forth and speak of her visions.
Even the monks who had been dancing paused and
were rapt in the glory of her words. She was faint with
fasting and there were scourge marks on her face
(which is all of her that could be seen, for this pious
woman covers her hands as well as the rest of her
body, so that she cannot seek contact with any but the
Most High), but she spoke with an elation that wholly
entranced her listeners. Then she began to sing a new
hymn, and the monks took it up, and were soon dancing as if in a trance. All those who saw this fell to their
knees in awe, and Savonarola called upon all of
Fiorenza to bear witness to the Power and Might of
God. As Suor Estasia finished her hymn, she fell at
Savonarola's feet, which she kissed with the greatest
devotion before she swooned, and had to be carried
away by her Celestiane Sisters, who have their convent
a little way beyond the city walls. Since Suor Estasia
has brought Sacro Infante so much fame, the Sisters
have had to build another wing on their hospital where
they minister to those who are not whole in their
minds. The Superiora, one Suor Merzede, has observed that there seems to be more madness in the
world, not less, and for this Savonarola rebuked her
severely and has suggested that since Suor Estasia has
shown the greatest evidence of grace, it is she and not
Suor Merzede who should head the convent. But there
Suor Estasia begged the Prior di San Marco to forgive
Suor Merzede and to recognize her good works.

Those who saw and heard this and were not moved
by this outpouring of the Mystery of God were later
denounced and made to confess their errors before all
the people who filled Santa Maria del Fiore, their

cathedral. Public penance was imposed on them and various Domenicani Brothers were sent to harangue the few who denied the holiness of the day.

While I was there in Fiorenza, I was twice visited by a troop of young men, not yet of an age to be bridegrooms, who entered my quarters and searched for vanities and other religiously proscribed objects and texts. It is their custom to do so, and they have been given authority to enter everywhere by i Priori and la Signoria, who are governors of la Repubblica Fiorenzen, but who are much influenced by the Domenicano Girolamo Savonarola.

Recently those who will not submit to the new rule have been subject to more persecution than they have felt before, and I gather that for some time their treatment has been harsh. The accusation of heresy is being made and it is the intent of the Domenicani to try and judge all those who have had that offense laid at their door. Many have been detained in prison, but as yet there has been no further action taken against them (or, rather, there had not been when I left Fiorenza, which was just after the Feast of San Nicolo in early December), and it had been agreed to defer the matter until the Holy Season of Christ's Birth had been celebrated and those facing accusation have time for reflection on their errors.

I trust that this account is acceptable to you. Your Polish is so excellent that I've assumed you read it as fluently as you speak it. If I was in error, you have only to tell me and I will render this into Latin. It is not common to find a man in Italy who speaks Polish as well as you do. Most of the time Italian or Latin is spoken, and those of us with foreign tongues must do as

*best we can to be understood. It may be that because
you are a foreigner, too, you have so much sympathy
for my position. I admit that Italian often bewilders
me, since it lacks much of the order of Latin. Is it because you travel that you've learned my language?
Forgive the question. I know it is not appropriate of
me to ask.*

*If there is any more information I might give you,
Sr. Ragoczy, I beg you will do me the honor of coming
to the house of Lino Vazzomare near San Gregorio. I
assure you that it has been a pleasure to serve you in
this matter.*

*Antek Kazielawa
In la Serenissima Venezia*

January 4, 1498

CHAPTER 2

IN THE END it took Ragoczy six days to reach Fiorenza, a
speed that would have been good in the summer and was
amazing in the dead of winter while snow blocked many of
the roads and ice made all travel precarious. One of the fourteen horses Ragoczy rode between Chioggia and Pietramala
had split his hoof on the muddy gravel of the old mountain
trail Ragoczy had used for a shortcut, and he had had to kill
the animal before walking three hours through a numbing
sleet to a little village where he had found warmth and a
mule to carry him to Pietramala.

Ragoczy demanded a great deal of even his tremendous

strength, and he was feeling worn when at last he came through the pass in the mountains and looked down on the tan walls and red roofs of Fiorenza shining in the wan, slanted light of a winter sunset. He knew he had to hurry or the gates of the city would be closed to him and he would have to seek shelter in one of the monasteries in the hills. He pulled on the reins and the white mare responded slowly, making a soft, distressed whicker as she began the descent to the valley.

"I know," Ragoczy said as he patted her neck. "And you have done well. There will be food and rest for you inside Fiorenza's walls. You deserve it." He shifted his weight and once again was glad for his lightweight Persian saddle.

Only la Porta Santa Croce was open, guarded by three lancers carrying Swiss pikes, waiting restlessly for their duty to end. Church bells were still sounding vespers, and by law, until the last of them had tolled, la Porta Santa Croce could not be closed.

The stranger on the white mare attracted more than the usual attention from the guards, for he was elegantly attired in a cloak of green Russian brocade lined in marten fur, and his high boots of golden leather had jewels embedded in their heels. His fur cap was Hungarian and a golden loop dangled from one earlobe. When he reached out his small hand to the captain of the gate, he was seen to be wearing embroidered gloves and a sleeved cote of Russian leather dyed a dark green.

"Name?" The captain studied the stranger covertly, his curiosity piqued by the fine clothes and arrogant carriage of the man on the white mare.

"I am Germain Ragoczy. I come from Hungary." The white mare shied away from the captain's pike and Ragoczy controlled her with skilled ease. "Please step back, soldier. You frighten my horse."

The guard captain was not used to being addressed in that manner, and even as he did as the stranger ordered, he found himself both hating and envying the grand hauteur of Ragoczy's manner. To vex Ragoczy, he decided to ask a few more questions. "What is your business in Fiorenza, Ragoczy?"

"I am here to claim my uncle's estate," Ragoczy responded, deliberately mispronouncing a few words.

"Your uncle, if that's what he was, left this city under threat of arrest," the captain informed the newcomer with a certain air of smugness.

"Where is my uncle's palazzo, soldier?"

There was a flicker of anger in the captain's eyes. "I said that your uncle left here under threat of arrest."

Ragoczy nodded. "Very likely. Where is his palazzo?"

"To the north. Near Santissima Annunziata." He pointed toward the dome of the Servanti church, though it was dwarfed by the huge dome of Santa Maria del Fiore. "It's deserted, though. No one lives there now. You'll be alone there."

"Deserted?" Ragoczy feigned outrage. "My uncle said that he had left someone in charge of his palazzo. Tell me where I may find his agent. This is inexcusable."

"It's not my place to answer that," the captain said with an unctuous smile as he stood aside to let Ragoczy pass, thinking as he did that he would have to inform i Lanzi and the young men of la Militia Christi that the nephew of the demonic Ragoczy was in the city. He stood while the doors were pulled to and barred; then he knelt with his men and prayed, as the new laws required.

Riding along the darkening streets, Ragoczy looked in

vain for the statues that had been the delight of Fiorenza. The pale stone walls were cold, the windows unadorned, and no brightness relieved this bleak prospect. One banner caught his eyes as he rode past San Marco, a white banner lettered in red that proclaimed *Nos Praedicamus Cristum Crucifixum.*

When at last he reined his mare in at the gates of the courtyard of Palazzo San Germano, he saw other lettering, this on the walls, accusing him of Satanism, of desecration. At that moment he admitted to himself that he was filled with foreboding. He had not believed that Fiorenza had changed so much, or that Savonarola truly had the political strength to defy Papal authority. But he knew now that he had underestimated the Domenican prior. Fiorenza was utterly his and he ruled as surely and as unofficially as Laurenzo ever did. For Fiorenza, Savonarola's excommunication was proof of his godliness and his willingness to accept martyrdom at the hands of a corrupt and venal Pope.

Slowly, his body heavy with fatigue and years, Ragoczy came down out of the saddle and led his mare toward the stable at the side of the palazzo. He ignored the crudely drawn insults, and the figures that went with them, huge horned men with tails and enormous, erect phalluses. He thought ironically that Estasia had accused him of what she had wanted him to be, which was impossible, but had neglected to say what he in fact was. Pushing open the stable door, he saw that there had been rifling there. Most of his tack was gone, and one of the wagons had been stripped of all harness and metal.

"Come, Gelata," he said, tugging gently on the rein and pulling the mare into the stable. He had settled on the name when he had first seen her standing in a frosty field where her color blended almost perfectly with the sparkling ground. Reluctantly she followed him into the stable and looked around, her curiosity revealing her distress.

Ragoczy looped the reins over a saddle rack that was now empty, and made quick search of the stable. There was some grain, enough to give the mare tonight, but tomorrow other arrangements would have to be made. He found a shovel near the back of the stable, and with it he began to clean out the stall nearest the palazzo wall, since this would be the warmest part of the stable. He worked steadily, his face impassive, his movements mechanical, until the stall was cleared; then he looked into the loft above for straw. Luckily some still remained and from the smell was not too musty. Ragoczy forked the straw down to the stall, and spread it out, a new bed for his Gelata. At last he led the mare into the stall, removing her saddle and bridle before bringing her grain and water.

When he was sure that mare would eat, he left the stable and went through the connecting door to the courtyard. In the dark he was unable to see what, if any, damage had been done to the courtyard. He hoped that his mosaics were still intact, but refused to waste time looking for torches now. There would be light in the morning.

As he entered the hallway to the front loggia, his boots sounded absurdly loud in the empty building. The palazzo was cold, for no fires had burned there since November. A smell reminiscent of mushrooms hung on the air and dust marred the shine of the floor. In the loggia the chairs were overturned and the elaborate hangings were torn or missing altogether.

Nothing in his expression revealed his fury at this wanton destruction; he had seen worse before. Ragoczy strode quickly through the loggia and turned to the stairs. On the landing he touched the heavily carved wood paneling and was relieved to discover that the interior lock was in place. He went back down the stairs and in a short while was descending into the kitchens.

There had been little damage here, and most of the utensils were still in place, still clean and waiting for Amadeo to return. Ragoczy wondered what had become of his cook, but the thought was fleeting. It was more important to build up a fire in the stove so that the mildew would be got rid of. He set himself to that task, and when the kindling at last began to smolder, Ragoczy leaned back against the huge cook's table and sighed. He waited while the fire took hold of the wood piled in the stove, and then he added more wood. He was confident that there would be heat for several hours as he closed the grating and checked the flue one last time.

The concealed entrance to his hidden rooms had gone undetected, and he opened the door carefully, in case the crossbow trap had been set. There was no ominous twang as the spring released the quarrel, no wood-shattering impact as the quarrel ripped through the door. Ragoczy went into the dark stairwell and began his slow climb to the hidden rooms above. He found the unlit stairs oppressive, though his eyes saw better in the night than most. That he should return to his own palazzo like a thief, stealing into the rooms, not daring to light a candle! At the top of the stairs he entered the antechamber that adjoined his alchemical laboratory. This room was his own private retreat, and everything as he had left it. The monastically hard bed stood against the far wall, its narrow mattress lying on a thin layer of earth. There was a small chest containing a few articles of clothing and other accessories. And on the wall near the door was Botticelli's Orpheus that was a portrait of Laurenzo. As Ragoczy struck flint and steel to light the candle, he found himself staring at the picture. Again he asked himself why Sandro had not written to him, and the answers that crowded his mind distressed him.

With the candle in his hand, Ragoczy inspected the laboratory, and found that it was in order. On one of the long tables were several sheets of parchment filled with notes in Demetrice's neat, sloping hand. She had advanced in her studies, Ragoczy realized as he read over the records. The beginning of a smile pulled at the corner of his mouth, and quickly faded as concern for her took possession of him once again.

As he paced through the laboratory, Ragoczy wondered what had happened to his servants. Araldo, Pascoli, Gualtiere and Masuccio had been sent money late in autumn, and had accepted their fees. And Amadeo should have stayed on. Had they been imprisoned as well, or had they fled Fiorenza? He could not ask directly, of course, but there had to be some way to find out what had happened.

Little more than an hour later, Ragoczy had pulled off his gorgeous clothes, and in his familiar severe black caftan, he slept on the good earth that had nurtured him for more than three thousand years.

TEXT OF A proclamation given by Girolamo Savonarola, Prior di San Marco:

> *To the devout citizens of Fiorenza:*
>
> *As the glorious season of Lent comes upon us, it is fitting that all pause and reflect on the great sacrifice that God's Son made for us. And as it is good that we emulate the love of God, it will be appropriate that*

*our observance of this most holy time be observed
with the most religious practices.*

*To that end, there will be several events at which
pious men may demonstrate their faith. Let every one
of you search your hearts and examine your conscience so that these solemn festivals will truly reflect
the humility and submission to God's Will which must
surely be the strength of the state in this world, and the
path to grace in the next.*

*On February 19 there will be a day of public expi-
ation of sin, wherein those who have erred will Confess and will beg forgiveness of Almighty God before
the citizens of la Repubblica Fiorenzen. They will kiss
the feet of those they have offended and will wear
about their necks signs designating their sins. These
they will wear through the entire Lenten fasts until
Easter Sunday.*

*From February 24 through Good Friday, the Mili-
tia Christi will be empowered to inspect any and all
houses in the city, and to seize all vanities and sacrilegious objects, texts, paintings, as well as all items of
bodily adornment not acceptable to good Christian
life.*

*On March 4 there will be a Bonfire of Vanities,
wherein all these items will be burned to signify our
rejection of worldly vice. Those who have resisted the
admonitions of the faithful of God would do well to
give up their venal trumperies and consign their excesses to the flames. What is a piece of molded brass
that damns you but the reflection of the Devil? Its
beauty is a lie, a vile seduction away from the stern
glory of God. Search your hearts and be sure that God
will judge you without excuse.*

The great festival of Lent will culminate on March 10, when those who have been accused of heresy will stand before the citizens of Fiorenza and either acknowledge their errors or accept the fate they in their pride have chosen. If it seems harsh, remember that they themselves have chosen eternal flames in the life that is hereafter, and that it is only fitting that they embrace those flames in this world. If the exhortations and examinations of the Domenicani Brothers cannot bring them to recant their heinous impiety, then it is truly the duty of the beloved of God to cast these pernicious souls from them as we would cast away a viper or would kill a mad dog.

Pray for guidance, Fiorenza, so that this purging of vanity may indeed be complete and sincere, so that God, who reads your hearts and from whom nothing is hidden, may at last turn upon this city and see it as a shining light of faith where before the idolators' pagan fires burned.

By order of Girolamo Savonarola, with the consent of la Signoria, i Priori and the Console, January 18, 1498.

CHAPTER 3

THE MORNING WAS not far advanced when Ragoczy left Palazzo San Germano. Ice glittered treacherously on the flagged streets and Ragoczy walked cautiously, his high boots of bright blue tooled leather cracking the ice as his heels struck. Today he wore a heavy woolen sleeved tunic of periwinkle blue lined in ermine. Each of the sleeves and both the front and back panels were edged in elaborate gold- and pearl embroidery. Instead of a gathered camisa, he wore a simple square-cut monte with a standing collar. His cap was of fur-trimmed velvet and he still wore one gold ear- ring. He knew he attracted attention as he walked toward la Via Nuova. The somberly dressed Fiorenzeni watched his progress and whispered among themselves. He held his head arrogantly and pretended to ignore the stir he was creating.

When he turned into la Via Nuova he made a point of looking about as if not knowing which house to choose. At last he walked uncertainly to Sandro Filipepi's door and knocked.

The wind off the hills was touched with snow, and when the door was opened by Simone, he shivered before he saw the elegant foreigner on the doorstep.

"Please," said Ragoczy in commanding accents, "is the painter called Botticelli here?"

Simone disliked the stranger on sight. He was too for- eign, too colorful, too elegant to be in Fiorenza. Everything that had corrupted Fiorenza before the godlike Savonarola shone in the man in blue.

"This is his house," Simone said grudgingly, "but Signor' Filipepi is at prayers." Simone was ready to close the door, but could find no excuse for shutting out the visitor, who plainly was not going to leave.

"At prayers?" It wasn't really a question. Ragoczy thought of his last talk with Sandro, and found that there was a cold fear in him. "When would he be available to speak with me? I have business with him. I am Germain Ragoczy."

The name got all the reaction he hoped it would. "Ragoczy? You dare show yourself in Fiorenza?"

Deliberately Ragoczy made his accent heavier. "Yes. I understand that my uncle did not make himself liked in Fiorenza." He crossed his arms and stared at Simone. "I am here to settle his estate, and for that I must speak with the painter Botticelli."

"Come back later," Simone said, and started to close the door.

Somehow, and Simone never quite knew how, the stranger stopped the door and without any obvious force stepped into the small entryway, letting the door swing shut behind him. "You will tell him that I am here, and that I wish to talk with him. In private."

Short of throwing the stranger out bodily, there was little Simone could do. "I will tell him," he muttered. "In Fiorenza it's considered inexcusable to force your way into houses where you have not been invited."

Ragoczy raised his finely drawn brows. "Indeed? And yet I am told the youths of the Militia Christi do it every day. Strange how one may be misinformed." There was a faint sneer in his smile as he watched Simone hurry toward the large room at the rear of the house that had been Sandro's studio for several years. Left alone, Ragoczy glanced around the walls, remembering that often Sandro hung his latest commissions here as a display until their owners claimed them. What he saw startled him. Gone were the soft, sensuous paintings of wonderfully human gods and goddesses. Gone were the lyric sketches of men and women working, playing, fighting, laughing. Instead the walls held deeply religious works, the Virgin, Christ, martyred saints at the moments of greatest travail. Ragoczy frowned. This wasn't the bright, easy style of three years ago. Now the paintings were dark, hesitant, strangely introverted. He paused by a large painting on finely sanded wood, depicting the martyrdom of

San Sebastiano, and realized, with a pang, that the agonized face and tortured body all transfixed with arrows were those of the artist.

"My brother will receive you." Simone had returned silently and took a certain degree of gratification when he saw the visitor start at the sound of his voice. "I see," he added with a satisfied expression, "that you are admiring Sandro's work. He has certainly done much to glorify God of late. Before, as you may know, he spent his time in the vain expression of venal pleasures. But this"—Simone nodded approvingly—"this is worthy of the name of art, for its sole purpose is the praise of God."

The chill Ragoczy had felt as he approached this house had little to do with the weather, and it increased as he watched Simone point out the various new works. "You see here, this new painting of the Virgin accepting the Holy Spirit into her? See the modest humility of her downcast eyes, the manner in which she covers her body so that the holy moment is not rendered profane by her pleasure or her flesh? Sandro didn't always paint so. For many years he indulged his senses and led men to lust and error with the nakedness of pagan deities. If you will follow me, I will take you to him." Simone turned quite abruptly and stalked off down the hall without waiting to see if the foreign visitor was behind him.

Ragoczy kept pace a few steps behind Simone, his thoughts racing. From what Simone had said, it was possible that Sandro had succumbed to the teachings of Savonarola, but perhaps it was that he had not wanted to antagonize the fierce little Domenican. He was still apprehensive as Simone held open the door to Sandro's studio and announced, "Ragoczy."

Sandro looked up from the wide table where he had

spread out a number of preliminary sketches. Three years had aged him. There were more and deeper lines in his craggy face, and his tawny-red hair was paler now, some of the loose curls being almost white. He gave Ragoczy a piercing look, then put down two of the sheets of paper and came around the end of the table. "I'm Sandro Filipepi," he said, touching Ragoczy's outstretched hands but not his cheeks.

"I am Ragoczy," he said, looking around the room.

"Simone said you were here about your uncle." He was plainly anxious to return to his work. "You resemble him, you know."

"So I have been told." He cast a significant glance at Simone. "Signor' Filipepi, if I might speak with you alone?"

Aside from one brief questioning look, Sandro accepted this, saying to his brother, "Simone, I'm certain you have duties that require your attention. When Signor Ragoczy is ready to leave, I'll call for you."

Simone drew himself up in indignation, turned sharply and punctuated his departure with a slam of the door.

For some few moments neither of the two men said anything; then Ragoczy indicated the sketches on the table. "May I look?" he asked.

"Go ahead." Sandro stood out of the way, remarking as Ragoczy picked up two of the sheets and held them up, "I can't make up my mind. If you've got any ideas, I'd be glad to hear them. Your uncle had a good eye for art. I hope you do, too."

Holding the sketches so that the white winter light fell on them, Ragoczy studied the swiftly drawn charcoal lines, the quick studies of hands and faces twisted with fear. "What are you planning?"

Sandro rubbed his hair before he answered. "It's supposed to be the *Slaughter of the Innocents*. But try as I will, I can't get the feeling I want. See there? That hand ought to awake sympathy and pity when you see it, but all it looks like is one of those studies Leonardo's done of the hands of the dead. And the face there, that one?"—he pointed to a portion of the paper where a young woman with wide eyes and open mouth shrieked silently—"it's lifeless. There's no terror, though there ought to be." He took the paper from Ragoczy and set it aside. "It's not just this one. Recently all my work is like that. I pray and I pray but the gift isn't there. It isn't easy anymore. It isn't a pleasure." He dropped into one of the rough chairs by the wall.

Ragoczy saw at once what Sandro said was true. He felt a pang of grief as he realized that Sandro knew as well as he did that his work was not what it had been.

"It's not important. That wasn't what brought you here." Sandro pushed himself out of his chair and forced a conviviality into his voice that he did not feel. "I hope you don't mean to tell me that Francesco is dead. It's more than I could endure today."

In that moment Ragoczy knew he could trust Sandro to keep his secret. "No. I'm not going to tell you that."

Sandro nodded. "Good. I've lost too many of my friends. I don't want to hear that another one is gone. Francesco was a remarkable man. I never felt quite easy about his leaving. I warned him, did you know? I urged him to leave Fiorenza. But now I don't know. I wish he had stayed. I wish someone had stayed who might have stopped what's happened. It's happened to Fiorenza. It's happened to me." He put his hands to his face, then forced them to his sides again. "I didn't want to believe. I still don't want to. But there isn't any choice now. And so I accept, and I Confess with the others and I paint what's safe. They leave me alone if I do that.

I never knew what it could be like. I didn't know Fiorenza would change so much."

Ragoczy stood still, listening to Sandro's hurt-filled words. He clenched his hands to keep from offering the artist comfort.

"Well," Sandro said, mastering himself. "I trust you won't repeat me. My position here is precarious enough without that." He gave Ragoczy a puzzled look. "I don't know why I said that to you. It must be your face." He turned away, adding with a miserable attempt at casual conversation. "Your uncle was a great mystery, but he was kind. I was always very fond of him."

Gently Ragoczy said, "And I of you, Sandro." This was spoken in his own beautifully modulated voice, in excellent Italian, without a trace of the contemptuous manner he had shown to Simone.

Sandro was still for a moment; then he spun around, his golden eyes intent. "Francesco?"

"Yes." He waited, not knowing what Botticelli's reaction might be. He saw Sandro's face tighten and doubt pricked at him. Sandro could still give him away. It would be an easy matter to go to i Lanzi and tell them that the satanic criminal had returned.

Finally Sandro spoke. His words were soft. "You're a fool, Francesco."

Ragoczy shrugged.

Then Sandro came back around the table and embraced him heartily, touching cheeks with him and very nearly laughing. "You're the greatest fool in the world. Gran' Dio, do you know what they'd do to you, those good pious men, if they caught you?"

"I have some idea," Ragoczy said dryly as he stepped

back from Sandro. He did not add that he'd seen it many times before.

"Then why did you come back?"

"Because," he answered with calm deliberation, "Demetrice Volandrai is in prison. And I must get her out."

The enormity of this announcement stunned Sandro. When he could speak, he said, "But you can't, Francesco. You'd be sent to the stake with her."

"Are they sending her to the stake?" Even Ragoczy was surprised at how easily he asked the question, as if it were nothing more than a matter of upholstery or a topic for a debate.

"Not yet, but they will." Once again he sank into the chair. "How did you find out?" He didn't give Ragoczy a chance to answer. "You think I should have told you? If there had been any way, I would have. But I couldn't. Truly I couldn't." He broke off and slammed his clenched fist against the table leg. "That's a lie. I might have found a way. I ought to have found a way. But I'm too frightened, Francesco. I'm frightened for myself." Self-loathing thickened his voice. "I didn't know I was a coward until now."

"Sandro. Amico." Ragoczy spoke compassionately. "You needn't do this to yourself." He came across the room and put his hand on Sandro's shoulder. "I'm not angry."

"I am." Sandro shifted his shoulder so that Ragoczy could no longer touch it. "I hate what I've become."

Ragoczy sighed and moved away from Botticelli. He knew he was close to defeat and he searched his mind for something to say, something that would heal the rift that gaped between them like an open wound.

It was Sandro who broke the silence. "I can't promise anything, because I may not keep it. But I will try to help you. Don't rely on me. Don't ask things of me except silence. Oh"—he nodded—"I know I can do that much. You're Ragoczy's nephew. What's your name again?"

"Germain."

"Germain Ragoczy. An arrogant foreigner full of pride. I'll do that much. And it's little enough." He stared out the window, a deep fatigue in his face now. "What do you want of me, Francesco? What must I do?"

"Why, nothing. Keep my secret." He slung one leg over the edge of the table and balanced there. "I have to find Demetrice, if she's still alive."

"She is. For a little while. The Domenicani want to be sure there is someone to burn at their auto-da-fé." He shook his head. "An auto-da-fé in Fiorenza. Who would have believed it, even five years ago?"

Ragoczy's face was suddenly very serious. "When will it stop? Do you realize that in less than four years Fiorenza had gone backward more than a century?" Idly he toyed with a brush Sandro had put out to mend. "Do you know where Demetrice is?"

"No. She's not inside the city walls. None of them are." He rose slowly this time. "I don't know if I can find out. Estasia might know something, and she might not. And Heaven only knows if she'll tell me."

"Estasia?" Ragoczy put the brush aside. "What has she to do with this?"

"Ah." Sandro made a gesture of utter disgust. "Since she's taken vows, she's the idol of Savonarola's followers. They flock to hear her prophesy, to tell her visions. She sings hymns and they become as popular as Laurenzo's ditties were eight years ago."

"Then Donna Estasia is the nun they're all talking about?" He slammed his fist onto the table. "I should have realized that. Suor Estasia del Mistero degli Angeli. How like her. How entirely like her." He gave Sandro a rueful smile. "You're right, amico. I am a fool. I saw the name, I have heard about her. But I didn't think that Estasia would take the veil. But what else is left for her? She cannot be satisfied by men any longer, and what else is there but God and the Devil?"

"She tried the Devil first," Sandro reminded him. "But of course, she was bound to. And perhaps she'll tire of God." He picked up one of his sketches and crumpled it savagely.

Ragoczy waited until Sandro's violence had passed; then he took Botticelli's hand. "If you can find out where Demetrice is, I would be grateful. But don't take needless risks."

"No," Sandro said bitterly. "I wouldn't do that."

"Stop castigating yourself," Ragoczy said impatiently. "It won't help any of us now." His eyes moved over the room, seeing neglect, noticing the many partially completed works. "How long have you had trouble painting?"

There was a flash of indignation that died as quickly as it appeared. "About half a year. Since I've given in to them, I'd guess." He opened his hands in resignation. "There isn't much left in me. I'm over fifty, did you know? I haven't the strength I used to have." Turning away, he stared out the window into the pale glare of the sky.

"If I found you a patron somewhere else, would you leave?"

Sandro did not turn to ask, "By patron do you mean yourself?"

"Perhaps. There are others who would be pleased to employ you."

The tilt of his head showed that Sandro was considering this. "If I could paint still, yes. But what I'm doing now isn't worthy of patronage. Only the priests like it, and those who want to barter for heavenly favor." He snorted with disgust and did not see the sadness of Ragoczy's expression. It was a while before he spoke again. "Do you still have the *Orpheus* I did for Laurenzo?"

"Yes. Why?"

"Would you let me have it again?" He asked this awkwardly and refused to face Ragoczy when he spoke.

"Why do you want it?"

Sandro clung to his elbows and said miserably, "There is to be a Bonfire of Vanities on the fourth day of March. You knew that? And I have sworn to burn my pagan and fleshly works, or those that I can put my hands on."

"That's a stupid joke," Ragoczy snapped.

Sandro's golden eyes met his dark ones. "It's not a joke. I have sworn to burn those works that are deemed vain."

"No." Fury and devastating sorrow warred in him. "Why? What possessed you? You can't do it." He turned on Botticelli. "Answer me. Why?"

As his big shoulders sagged, Sandro leaned back against the wall. "Because then they'll leave me alone. If I burn the paintings, they'll forget me." He spoke in a calm, flat tone. "You haven't been here, Francesco. There are times I think I'd sell my soul for peace."

"That's what you have done." Ragoczy took an angry step forward. "It isn't worth it, Sandro. Peace is too small a gain." Suddenly there was hurt in his eyes and his next words were a plea. "Sandro. Listen to me. You haven't the right to do this. They haven't the right to ask it of you. It's worse than killing children, because children at least can defend themselves. But art, art goes into the world unarmed, vulnerable to every quirk of fate, and it must survive only by its power to move men not to destroy it. You wonder why you can't paint the *Slaughter of the Innocents*? Think of what you're doing now. It's the same thing. But this is more evil, for even Herod didn't insist that the families put their children to the sword. Look. Sandro. There is so little in this world that is beautiful and so much that is hurtful. But the most fragile beauty can be infinitely stronger than everything that has been done with blood and fire and sword, and neglect." His chest felt tight and he paused to swallow against it. "No one—*no one*—has the right to destroy what another has done. And to make you destroy your own work . . ." Again he stopped, and his voice was coldly level when he said, "I believe in neither Heaven nor Hell. Yet I wish there were Hell, and that its greatest tortures were reserved for men like Savonarola. Forswear your oath. Abjure it. If not for yourself, Sandro, then for the sake of your work."

Through this Sandro had stood silent, his eyes not quite looking at Ragoczy. He crossed his arms, waiting for Ragoczy to stop, and when at last he did, Sandro said, "Perhaps you'd better leave now."

"Sandro . . ."

"No. I've made my bargain. I'll keep it and be damned." He took quick, jerky steps to the door and held it open, calling for his brother. Before Simone appeared, he turned to Ragoczy and said in a soft, fierce whisper, "Never say anything to me about my work again. Ever. For the sake of Demetrice, I'll keep your secret, but ask nothing more of me. Now go." He waited until Ragoczy had come to the door.

"Sandro," Ragoczy said. "I beg you."

"Good-bye, stragnero," Sandro said, and went back into his studio, closing the door behind him.

TEXT OF A letter to Francesco Ragoczy da San Germano
from Olivia, written in the colloquial Latin of imperial Rome:

*To Ragoczy Sanct' Germain Franciscus, Olivia sends
loving, exasperated greetings.*

*What in the name of all the gods is the matter with
you? You got out of Fiorenza by fortunate chance
with the threat of burning over you. And now you
have gone back. Have you forgotten that if you burn,
you die the True Death, as surely as if your head were
severed from your body, or your spine crushed? And
if you have not forgotten, why have you returned
there?*

*Yes, yes, I know. You are in disguise. You've taken
precautions. But how do you know they'll be successful? Don't remind me that I worry too much. One of us
had better worry, and you seem to be incapable of it.*

*Here is the information you wanted. Your letter
reached me in good time. The ship from Venezia to
Napoli had good winds and surprisingly calm seas,
and your associate Gian-Carlo brought it to me with
all speed. What a beautiful man he is, Sanct' Germain.
It would be a pleasure to make him one of our blood.
But since you haven't, I restrained myself as well. I
gather he doesn't know about you. He called you an
alchemist and a shipowner, but nothing else.*

*Alessandro VI very much wants to enforce the ex-
communication of Savonarola. Apparently he tried to
bargain with the Domenicano first, offering
Savonarola a Cardinal's hat, provided that all
preaching stop and that Savonarola leave Fiorenza
and come to Roma where he can be more truly*

watched. I understand that Savonarola's reply was that he preferred a martyr's crown to a Cardinal's hat. You may be sure that as soon as it is possible, Alessandro will arrange it. Certainly Savonarola's rule in Fiorenza cannot last much longer, not with the Pope against him. For say what you will about the Borgia carnality and corruption, he is still the Pope and has the full authority of the Church behind him. Girolamo Savonarola is a madman, if he thinks he can defy the Pope, even so unholy a Pope as Alessandro VI.

There is a movement afoot now, promoted by His Holiness and by young Cardinal Giovanni de' Medici, to bring a charge of heresy against Savonarola. It would be simple to demonstrate it: resistance to Papal Edict is heretical, and it is very well known that Savonarola has continued to preach, to serve Mass, to use the Church as the base of his authority. You may be certain that by summer Rodrigo Borgia or Pope Alessandro, as he prefers to be called, will have his revenge.

I don't know how the Fiorenzeni stand on this matter, but I warn you, my dear friend, that the Pope will not hesitate to use all the force at his command to bring down Savonarola. He may send troops if Fiorenza will not give up their Prior di San Marco. There has been too much flouting of the power of Roma and the Pope. This Borgia Pope is willing to go to war, if that is necessary, to put an end to the rule of Savonarola.

Are you demented, that you insist on this mad course? Believe me, Savonarola is desperate. He has very little time to finish his work, and if that includes,

*as you say it does, the trial and burning of his own set
of heretics, there will be no one safe from accusation.
If by some fluke you actually manage to convince
Fiorenza that you are your own nephew, you will still
be suspect, being an even more uncertain figure than
your "uncle" was.*

*I've spoken to His Holiness, and he has promised
to send orders to Fiorenza specifically forbidding the
trial and burning of heretics until the state of
Savonarola's faith is determined. He has also assured
me that he will require the immediate release of all
those held in prison. It should be no later than March
17 when the documents arrive. Because of the seri-
ousness of the situation in Fiorenza, the Pope has
scheduled the issuing of those orders for seventeen
days from today. The only thing he has ever done more
quickly was arrange his daughter's marriage. In less
than two months, Demetrice will be free.*

*If you were nothing to me, your danger and foolish
loyalty would mean little. But you are precious to me.
And one of the reasons you are precious, I admit it, is
that you are willing to risk everything for those you
love. So pay no attention to my railing at you. Do as
you must. As you did for me, so long ago.*

*My dearest, dearest friend, guard yourself well. I
wish you good fortune. I wish you success. I wish you
victory.*

                                                      Olivia

*In Roma,
the 26th day of January, 1498*

CHAPTER 4

THERE WERE PATCHES of snow at the side of the road and Ragoczy's breath came in steamy puffs as he urged the white mare up the hill. The sky overhead was slate-colored and fading quickly as the afternoon waned.

"This is the last one, Gelata. If there's nothing here, we'll go back to Fiorenza." He gave the mare a reassuring pat and then once again turned his attention to the old, narrow road.

He had been riding into the hills for the last four days, ever since he had had a short note from Sandro telling him that all accused heretics were being kept in one of the old castles in the hills. He had not learned which one, but he gathered it could not be more than about three hours' ride from Fiorenza, for monks were able to go there and return on the same day.

Today he had ridden eastward, and had found a number of villas, a few outpost forts, one of which was almost certainly now being used as a base by one of the gangs of brigands that had become the plague of travelers.

As he rounded the next bend, he caught a glimpse of stone fortifications, of the sort built in the eleventh and twelfth centuries. He pulled Gelata to a halt as he looked ahead, searching for signs of life. Then, cautiously, he dismounted and led Gelata away from the road. He was glad now that she was white, for in the forest, against the patches of snow, she was harder to see. When he was sure she would be safe, he tied her reins to a tree and began to make his way toward the battlements he'd seen.

As he moved through the trees he reminded himself that this might be just another dead end. He had been hopeful the first few times he'd investigated old castles, but his hope had proven groundless and now he had resigned himself to a long search. His first inclination had been to follow the Domenicani Brothers from San Marco, but he had heard they often used devious routes to avoid being followed, and for that reason he knew they would be easily alerted if they saw him. So he had chosen this way, a tiresome search, and only on days when the Domenicani Brothers did not leave Fiorenza.

The stone walls rose up near him now, great solid blocks of stone with short, squat arches marking the windows and door. Smoke belched from three of the chimneys and Ragoczy was mildly encouraged. At least the castle was occupied. He wondered if it could be another brigand stronghold, and rejected the idea at once. A castle was too obvious. And there had been no sentries, no guards to give the alarm at his approach.

A sound stopped him, the sound of chanting. He stood still, hardly breathing. The chanting grew louder, and Ragoczy moved nearer the shadow of the wall. From this vantage point he had a glimpse of the inner courtyard beyond the open sally port a few steps beyond him. As he watched, a procession of more than a dozen Domenicani crossed the courtyard and entered what Ragoczy assumed to be the castle chapel on the far side of the courtyard.

When the monks were all out of the courtyard, Ragoczy moved quickly, beginning a swift search of the outside of the castle. For part of the way he had to cling to the walls of the castle, a rocky drop behind him. He was more than halfway over the cliff front of the castle when he heard a sound. Again he froze, glad that his greenish-brown cloak blended so well with the rocks.

The noise was repeated, a sound barely human. Somewhere not far from Ragoczy's precarious hold on the stone of the castle, a man was coughing.

Ragoczy looked up. About two arm-lengths above he saw a narrow, barred window. A little farther along the wall there was another, and another beyond that. Patiently he began to climb higher, his small feet finding purchase on the stones where a weaker man would not have the strength or the ability to move. His progress was slow, but before the sunlight had wholly been swallowed by the clouds and dusk, he had come even with the first window. He took hold of the bars that covered the window, and pulled himself across the opening, looking into the narrow, dark cell beyond.

The man in the cell coughed again and the fetters which secured him to the wall chinked softly. As far away as he was from the prisoner, Ragoczy knew the man was ill and was likely to die. He considered breaking into the cell and carrying the man to safety: but he knew from the sound of his coughing that there was little chance the man would live, even if he were put into a warm bed immediately and given every available medicine. Ragoczy's face darkened, and reluctantly he moved on.

The next cell held two men, brothers, by the look of them. They stared at each other in sullen silence, fear and hatred almost palpable in the clammy stone room.

After that there was a woman, an old woman in tattered rags. She knelt on the uneven stones that were her floor and prayed, her ancient rosary moving swiftly through her fingers.

Ragoczy had come to the farthest point of the castle, at the steepest part of the cliff. A little farther beyond, level ground waited. There were two more windows, but the forces of wind and rain had smoothed the stone so that moving over it, no matter how carefully, was far more dangero than the rest of the wall had been. He waited while he steadied himself, gathering force for the climb. Then he started to inch his way toward the next window.

The cell was rather smaller than the others were, narrower, with higher walls, and less light. Instead of a cot there was only a straw pallet, and on it a figure in a torn camisa huddled, the shreds of a silk gonella pulled around her shoulders in a vain attempt to stay warm. Though the light was almost gone, Ragoczy saw that the silk was, or had been, green brocade, the same material as the gown he had given Demetrice when she had come to be his housekeeper. The figure moved and two rosy-blond braids fell across the soiled silk.

"Demetrice," he breathed. Carefully he climbed higher, until he could hook one arm over the stone frame of the window. Then he began the exhausting job of pulling the bars away from the window. He worked silently, afraid to call to her for fear he might also get the attention of the monks at the castle. There might well be guards on the ramparts above him, and only so long as he made little noise would it be possible for him to get into Demetrice's cell. As he tugged the second bar away, he remembered ironically how many tales of vampires he had heard in which the vampires were shape-changers. At that moment he devoutly wished it were true.

The last bar came away. He gathered up the other two and flung the three together as far as he could out over the cliff, hoping that they would fall far enough from the castle to be unheard. He hung on, listening, and when he was satisfied that no one had noticed the soft, distant clang, no louder than bells put on cattle, he pulled himself up into the window.

At that moment, he had not thought about how to approach Demetrice. He realized she was lost in a fitful half-sleep, and could not be easily awakened. Catlike, he dropped silently to the floor of her cell, and stealthily he went to her straw pallet.

In one swift movement he had fallen to his knees, one hand over her face to stop her possible scream, the other reaching for the iron fetters.

Demetrice thrashed violently in his grasp, then sank her teeth into his hand.

He had broken the first fetter and was reaching for the other when he could not endure the pain of her bite. He turned her to him, forcing her head against his chest while he broke the second fetter.

She was twisting against him, struggling to get a hand free to hit him, to scratch him, to drive him away. She wondered which of her jailers had broken into her cell at last, for though the monks assured her there would be no abuse from her guards, she had seen the calculating expression in their harsh faces, and while the monks were at prayers, there was no one to protect her.

Ragoczy seized her wrists, but instead of pinioning her hands behind her, he held them between his own, against his chest. "Demetrice," he said, his voice warm and low. "No, Demetrice. No, cara. Hush, Demetrice, hush."

The force of her lunge almost sent her sprawling, but by then she was fully awake and had realized that this was no jailer, no renegade monk. A thousand memories stirred in her, memories of dark, compelling eyes, of endless discovery and learning, of black and silver and rubies and the sign of the eclipse with wings erect. She caught herself and looked up at the man who had risen to stand beside her, one small hand outstretched to pull her to her feet.

"Come, Demetrice," he said, and this time she knew him.

"San Germano?" There was as much disbelief as welcome in her voice and she hesitated to touch him, suddenly fearing that she had gone mad and he was the dream of her madness.

"Softly," he said, just above a whisper.

"San Germano?" she repeated, fearfully putting her hand in his. She felt the fingers tighten and she almost sobbed with relief. He was real. Awkwardly she got to her feet, cold and exhaustion making her body leaden. She started to speak, but a wave of dizziness swept over her and her first step toward him faltered.

Then he reached out, drawing her into his arms, his smooth-shaven jaw against her cheek, his quiet words in her ear. "Amante mia."

"It *is* you," she murmured. "You came."

"Yes." He drew back, but only to be able to kiss her mouth. His lips lingered on hers, not demanding, but wonderfully insistent.

She ascended into his kiss like a diver at last reaching air, like a crocus breaking through snow to the first warmth of spring. She had buried desire with Laurenzo, thinking it dead, and contented to have it so. But now it rose again, and she welcomed it with gladness, as she welcomed the tentative, beginning explorations of Ragoczy's small hands.

In the dim, fading square of light from the window, his shadow lay over hers, one presence merging with another. And then he took her high on her arms and held her back from him. "Demetrice, how much you tempt me."

Although there was some amusement in his voice, she read in his touch, in his voice, in his glowing eyes how much she had shaken him. She trembled as she looked at him, and the words stopped in her throat.

"You're cold," he said softly, and pulled his fur-lined

cloak from his shoulders and in one swift motion wrapped her in it.

Gratefully she hugged the cloak around her, eager for the warmth his body had given it. She sighed deeply, almost lazily as the stiffness which so many days in the narrow, dank cell had given her began to loosen and fade.

A wry smile pulled at Ragoczy's mouth. "I should have done that first." He did not trust himself to touch her again so soon, and he stood back from her, watching as she sank onto the straw, still straight, though on her knees. "I've missed you, Demetrice."

She nodded slowly, but she was thinking of something else. Her eyes stung at his words.

"When there was no letter, I was worried, but I didn't learn of this until the Feast of the Circumcision. If I had known, I would have come sooner." He leaned against the wall, letting his calm, low voice dampen the longing that had flared between them. "It will be difficult, but I will see that you are freed, amica."

In the three years he had been gone, she had forgotten his compelling force, or perhaps, she told herself, she had not seen it because before now she had looked at Ragoczy with the ghost of Laurenzo between them. Now she felt him as a lodestone feels the way north. With an abrupt motion of her hand she silenced him. It was an effort of will not to turn to him and be drowned in his eyes, but she held herself rigid and asked a question that had been born in her years before. "Is it very terrible, what you do?"

Ragoczy closed his eyes in fleeting anguish but his answer was steady. "No, not terrible. Unless you make it so."

"But . . ." She stopped, her mouth suddenly dry. "Does it make me like you?"

He wondered if she knew what she had said, and his face

softened. "Not at first. Eventually, if we come together too often, you will become what I am. Or if you take from me what I take from you."

She was so intent on the turbulence of her mind that she did not hear him when he moved. But she felt him behind her, not touching her, as if a great wind was blowing.

"Well, Demetrice?" He was still, very still, waiting. All the world hung suspended in the silence between them, as if time had learned to move slowly. The small dark cell of rough stone was as vast as space, spreading out around them like the sky. No words passed between them in that immense intimacy, when, hardly seeming to move at all, Ragoczy began to undo her braids, freeing her palely blushed hair from its confining ribbons.

She held her breath as he spread her hair across her back like a veil, draping the strands over her shoulders. Then his hands came to rest against her neck, lying tranquilly on the high, gentle rise of her breasts. A tremor ran through her and his hands withdrew swiftly, cleanly, without taunting, lingering or playfully toying.

"No." She spoke quickly, her breath coming faster as a new urgency was awakened in her.

He hesitated. Slowly he knelt behind her, and not knowing she had done it, she leaned back so that her head rested on his shoulder. Though she would not look at him she took solace in his nearness, in the comfort his body gave her. The rhythm of his breathing sustained her and the curve of his chest against her back supported her without restraint. Gradually his closeness became familiar, his touch as friendly as hot wine on a cold day. Demetrice closed her eyes and turned toward him, into his arms.

His fur-lined cloak still enveloped her, and from it she took a certain measure of privacy, a sanctuary in which her loneliness was preserved, as if his devastating gentleness could be held at bay, if necessary, with fur. Yet the cloak opened. She felt his hands on her body, cherishing her, learning and teaching all the ways of her exquisite elation. The cloak, the ruined gonella, her camisa, were nothing against the warmth of his lips. He cradled her close to him as they lay back on her straw pallet. The caressing words he murmured she barely heard for the thunder that was in her soul. Blinded by a rapture that satisfied a longing she had not known she had, Demetrice surrendered herself to the celebration of her passion.

When the thing she had dreaded for so long occurred, she met his need not with disgust but with rejoicing, in triumph. Her arms tightened around him as her bliss resounded to the limits of her senses. His ardent tenderness evoked a fulfillment more complete than anything she had known before, and phoenixlike, the whole strength of her love rose from the ashes of her grief so that she was reborn.

Late in the night she slept, but wakened to find him watching her, his dark eyes alight. He drew her tight against him, sensing her need. Under his hands her flesh blossomed, yearning toward him with the unending longing that roses feel for the sun.

His joy was as great as her own. He reached to explore the splendor of her, to know every nuance of her pleasure, the very texture of her desire, the entire complexity of her love.

Some little while before dawn he left her, waiting as long as he dared before climbing to her high, narrow window, and making his way down the precarious walls of the castle. A cold, filmy mist wound between the trees and curled against the battlements of the castle, hiding his progress from any sleepy guards.

Demetrice dozed on the straw pallet, warmed by Ragoczy's cloak and the memory of his nearness.

TEXT OF A letter from Ruggiero to Francesco Ragoczy da San Germano:

To my master:

This comes to you by the good offices of a Bolognese merchant who is traveling to Fiorenza, and should be in your hands before the middle of February.

I followed your instructions and left Venezia four days after you did, bringing, as you requested, a small train of baggage on five mules. The journey was fairly fast, all things considered. But it was our misfortune to be set upon by brigands the day we left Bologna. It was a fairly large force, perhaps as many as thirty, though I didn't see more than eighteen. Though we fought against them, by numbers alone they prevailed. I am sad to tell you that Teodoro was killed by them, and that two of the laden mules were taken by the brigands. I've sustained a few injuries and for that reason I am at a monastery near Monghidoro. The care here is excellent, and it should not be more than a week before I am capable of resuming the journey.

The good Fra Sereno is writing this letter for me, as I am not able to do so yet.

It is with the help of these good monks and the Grace of God that I am able to communicate with you at all, for after the brigands attacked us, they left those of us in your employ behind. Tito, though suffering from a serious blow on his leg, yet walked to this monastery and brought back help. If he had not done so, we would have been at the mercy of the brigands and the winter.

Be sure I will be with you again shortly.

Fra Sereno, for the servant Ruggiero il monastero della Carità del Nostro Signor' Brothers of San Ambrogio

Near Monghidoro, February 1, 1498

CHAPTER 5

ALL THE BENCHES for the congregation were filled, though it was only a Tuesday and a market day at that. Near the altar a number of Domenicani Brothers made their final reverent preparations for the Mass their prior was to celebrate that morning. There was a small group of Trinitariani Brothers near the door, one of them carrying a breviary from which he was reading aloud.

Just before the hour of the Mass struck, there was a stir at the back of San Marco. The foreigner Germain Ragoczy stood in the door, resplendent in a roundel of rusty-gold silk. His stiff velvet cap was lavishly sewn with seed pearls and he carried a small golden dagger tucked into his tooled leather belt. The heels of his boots were loud in the hush that greeted his arrival, and every eye followed him as he walked down the aisle. Pausing to genuflect and cross himself most devoutly, he glanced over the assembled Fiorenzeni, and realized with some dismay that even hard-bargaining merchants were in the church, ready to hear Mass and Savonarola's sermon.

A somewhat wheezy chord on the organ gave the signal that the celebration of the Mass was about to begin. Because it was the season of Lent, the monks who entered the church were singing the *Dies Irae*, their awe-inspiring words intoned with a tinge of smug satisfaction.

There was a formal attention paid to the Mass, but when the spiky figure of Girolamo Savonarola mounted the Oratory of San Marco, a new excitement ran through the congregation. Ragoczy could sense the hold Savonarola had over Fiorenza in the taut, almost somnambulistic faces around him. There were women with fists clenched under their chins, their eyes filled with terrified adoration. Ragoczy felt a strange sickness in his mind. He had seen such expressions before, long ago, when Babylonian mothers had watched their infants being thrown into the burning maw of their god, Baal.

"It is the time of year," Savonarola said, "when the sacrifice of Our Lord is remembered. The joyous time of His Birth is past and now is the time when we must contemplate the utter love of His Agony, the death on the Cross." His glance raked over the congregation, accusing every person there of consenting in the death of Jesus Christ. He waited while his faithful squirmed, and then, when he was certain that they were eager for his chastisement, he nodded. "Think of the nails that pierce the beauty of His sacred flesh. Think of the pain He suffered so that you might have glory in Paradise. Think of His Passion, as he hung from His bleeding wounds." Again he paused. "And not one of you is worthy of this. Not one of you is worth the dust in His shadow."

Two older men in the congregation had dropped to their

knees now, and their convulsive sobs echoed through San Marco.

"Yet here you are, accepting the Eucharist as if Grace were available to anyone willing to bend a knee and take a piece of bread into his mouth. How do you live with your hypocrisy, Fiorenzeni? You, who claim to worship that holy being, are not willing to give up your ornaments, your vanities, your profane teachings, or your merchants' pride." He regarded them all with scorn. "So little is asked of you, compared with what He willingly gave, and you refuse Him."

There were more people weeping, and Ragoczy felt his jaw tighten in anger. He pressed his hands together and lowered his head so that no one could see the rage in his eyes.

"I have called for a sacrifice, and you deny it. You hide your trinkets from the Militia Christi so that you may take your little pleasures. But those pleasures damn you to Hell, where the fires will consume you eternally. Then those petty delights will not mitigate your suffering. Then, when it is too late, you will bitterly regret your worldliness."

The sermon was to last only ten minutes, but it was more than an hour later that those of the congregation who were taking Communion filed slowly up to the rail. Many were startled to see the elegant foreigner Germain Ragoczy join them, his hands piously clasped, his eyes bent downward in humility.

Today Savonarola himself served Communion, and he gave Ragoczy a look that in one less holy would have been jealous derision. When he came to the foreigner, he held the Host over the Chalice to make the sign of the Cross. But instead of placing the wafer between Ragoczy's lips, he asked, "Have you fasted?"

Ragoczy answered him honestly. "For three days, good Prior."

But Savonarola was not satisfied with this response. "Your uncle did not take Communion, and he attended Mass rarely."

"My uncle," Ragoczy said in awkward Italian, "was not one of your Church. He was not allowed to take Communion with you. It would have been a great sin if he had."

Savonarola tapped the Chalice, frowning. "He belonged to the Eastern Church? We were united with them, and in agreement, until they disavowed our unity. Those who worship in the Eastern Churches are in error. They should Confess their sins and be received into the True Church and be given Grace. For they do not have the excuse of the heathen, who have not heard the True Church in her might proclaim the promise of God."

"That may be." Then, with a dryness that was lost on Savonarola Ragoczy added, "My uncle was born some years before the brief unification of the Roman and Eastern churches. He would not have profaned your sacraments knowingly."

"But you do accept the sacraments."

"Yes."

"You kneel before me, you know that it is a grievous sin to take Communion if you have any sin upon your soul. You ask for the consecrated Host to be given you."

Ragoczy had an impulse to challenge Savonarola, to remind the Domenican that it was he, not Ragoczy, who was under the pain of excommunication, and that as a result he had no right to serve Mass, let alone question the state of the souls of those seeking Communion, which would not be valid in any case, being, as it was, Savonarola, the excommunicant, who had performed the consecration. "I ask for the Host, yes."

"You are dressed in unchristian finery, Ragoczy," the prior said, apparently enjoying the discomfort he was causing.

"It is appropriate to my rank." Ragóczy was secretly relieved that Fiorenzan sumptuary law still provided that men of title not demean their dignity with common dress. He waited for Savonarola's response.

The congregation had become silent once again, relishing this new confrontation. The veneration they had for Savonarola made them see him as a stern judge protecting them from blasphemy and wrong. But the splendid stranger attracted their notice as well, for his answers were respectful, dutiful and modest. In a few, Ragoczy stirred memories of the Medici days, of the civic pride and the fun of palios, of masques, of processions and tournaments.

"Are you bound by them?" Savonarola scoffed. "If you are indeed born noble, our laws, though superior to yours no doubt, must still be beneath you."

Ragoczy hesitated long enough to bite back a scathing reply. Instead he gazed reverently up into Savonarola's ungainly face. "Good Prior, I don't know why you question me in this way. I have had much hardship in my life. My land is in the hands of Turks and my people are slaughtered. I have fought my enemies for the glory of Christ, and I have done all that I might to protect my subjects. All I desire while I am in Fiorenza is to live in an honorable way, within the laws of la Repubblica and God."

They had arrived at an impasse. Savonarola's voice grew more harsh. "It is an easy thing for a foreigner to claim rank, particularly in a country where war has made so much confusion."

At that Ragoczy let a little of his temper show, and he spoke with asperity. "My lineage is ancient. There have been those of my blood in my native mountains since before the time of Christ. Our line is unbroken to this day, and distinguished."

"And you yourself? What is your degree of nobility?"

"I was born a Prince." It was, he thought with a sardonic light in his eyes, quite true. But that had been considerably more than three thousand years ago, and the people who had given him that rank had long since scattered abroad and were lost in other populations.

"You wear no coronet," Savonarola pointed out.

"You have stated that Fiorenza is a Repubblica, and as such is not receptive to coronets. Italia is not my country. Unless I am called to a royal court, such as the court in Napoli, or to the great court of the Pope, it would be the most profound disrespect for me to wear it."

By now the congregation was wearying of the sport and there was a soft muttering as some of the people jostled one another and began to glance out the high windows at the blustery sky.

Reluctantly Savonarola took a bit of the bread and made the sign of the Cross over the Chalice. Without another word, he placed it in Ragoczy's open mouth.

Holding the bread under his tongue, Ragoczy crossed himself and bowed his head with real devotion. He found the feel of the bread distracting, and tried to remember what it had been like to eat food. That had been so long ago and his recollection was remote, distorted, like a reflection in troubled water. Slowly he rose and returned to his place on the bench, anxious for the Mass to end.

When at last it was over, Ragoczy made his way through the departing Fiorenzeni to the clerk of la Signoria.

Gradazo Ondante had aged much in the last three years. Where before he wore his importance with officious fussiness, he now was bowed under the weight of his responsibilities, and his body was like badly joined sticks under his drab lucco. He gave Ragoczy a curious glance and said, "You have a certain resemblance to your uncle. He was an older man than you, of course, and I think somewhat taller. But there is a similarity."

"Did you know my uncle well?" Ragoczy asked politely, wondering how many others in Fiorenza shared Ondante's opinion.

"I had to deal with him occasionally. He was an imposing man, quite stern and severe." He folded his hands and there was a certain apprehension in his words when he asked, "Why did you wish to speak to me?"

Ragoczy decided to broach the simpler matter first. "I am anxious to regularize my claim to my uncle's lands and goods. No one has yet been willing to tell me what documents and proofs I must present to i Priori in order to do this."

Somewhat dryly Ondante observed, "Your uncle had a better command of our language, too." His eyes focused on the middle distance. "I will have to ask i Priori themselves what they will require of you. Will there be any problem if there is a certain delay? Until the end of Lent it will be difficult to conduct the proper investigation into your claim."

Inwardly Ragoczy cursed. He smiled condescendingly. "If that's what must be done, then how can I object?" In another voice he asked, "And my petition to the law courts, that my uncle's housekeeper and agent be freed, or at least remanded to my custody?"

"Oh. Yes. That." Ondante was plainly uncomfortable. "I have not yet had the opportunity to show your petition to the

Console. It is a difficult matter. Very difficult. You see, the matter of her heresy—"

"Possible heresy," Ragoczy corrected him gently.

"Possible heresy. Yes. It hasn't been settled. And it isn't . . . it isn't desirable that she be given her liberty until it is shown that she is faithful and redeemed to Holy Church."

"But I have offered to vouch for her, and to be responsible for her." This was said so reasonably that Ondante flinched.

"Yes. But your situation is so irregular . . . It's very difficult," he said again, as much to himself as to Ragoczy. "But I will try. It's not fitting that a young woman should . . . The prison is severe, I understand. I'll see if there's anything . . ." His voice dwindled to silence.

"I would appreciate it." Ragoczy realized that he was once again attracting attention, and decided to use it to his advantage. "I feel," he said with sincerity ringing in every word, "that as my uncle's heir, I must do all that he would want for those whom he employed. It is most unbecoming of a man of position to forget the ones who have done him a service, and I know that my uncle was most grateful to his housekeeper. It would be disgraceful to my honor and the honor of my family if I were to neglect my duty to that good woman."

Those members of the congregation who had pressed nearer to listen nodded their approval. Though it was suspicious that Ragoczy was so obviously foreign his sentiments were worthy of any Fiorenzan.

Ondante squinted miserably. "Yes. I understand. Of course." He almost dived into the knot of people around him, painfully glad to escape from the courteous stranger.

As Ragoczy turned to leave San Marco, he saw out of the corner of his eye that from a doorway near the Oratory, Savonarola was watching him.

Text of a letter from Francesco Ragoczy to the Francescan prior to Santa Croce, Orlando Ricci:

> To the most reverend prior of Santa Croce, Germain
> Ragoczy, heir to il stragnero il Conte Francesco
> Ragoczy da San Germano, sends his greeting and be-
> seeches the assistance of the good Francescano.
>
> My heart is much wrung by the many difficulties I
> have encountered of late and it is with a sense of des-
> peration that I, a foreigner and one without friends in
> la Repubblica Fiorenzena, turn to you, good Prior, for
> your guidance and help.
>
> I know not how to think. Here is my uncle's house-
> keeper and pupil, a woman of learning and merit, con-
> fined to prison on the heinous charge of heresy by a
> monk who is in flagrant violation of all the power,
> might and glory of the Catholic Church. Girolamo
> Savonarola was excommunicated by Pope Alessan-
> dro. Yet he preaches at Santa Maria del Fiore and San
> Marco, he gives laws to the state and he is respected
> by all. And his accusations against Fiorenzan citizens
> are heeded and accepted, though he himself stands ac-
> cused by higher authority of great wrongs.
>
> The Vallombrosiani Brothers and the Camaldole-
> siani Brothers stand unalterably opposed to this
> Savonarola, but there is no move to free those unfor-
> tunates who languish in prison as a result of his laws
> and his pronouncements.
>
> Where may I go for help? I must do all that I can to
> save this woman who discharged her duties to my
> uncle with such capable skill. Surely there is some way.

As you know, I am new to Fiorenza and there is no one I know well enough to ask for this help. If you feel that it would not be wrong, your guidance and prayers will be much valued by me.

The power of this Savonarola frightens me, for not only do his political decisions strike at the very foundations of the state, his religious doctrines and contempt for papal authority are a blow at the heart of the Catholic Church. No one can think himself safe, for the state is rendered useless and the Church impotent by his proud rebellion. And just as the few angels who fell from heaven for their misguided loyalty to Lucifer, so the people of Fiorenza stand in like danger from their affection and respect for this Savonarola.

Your words on this are most eagerly awaited. I put my trust in your wisdom and the goodness of your Order. And with humility and gratitude, I await your response.

Germain Ragoczy

In Fiorenza at Palazzo San Germano, the 8th day of February, 1498

CHAPTER 6

THE WHITEWASHED WALLS of Sacro Infante glittered against the dark earth, the new wing still looking painfully raw. A high wind plucked the bare trees with long, lunatic fingers, making them moan. Though the sky was scrubbed bright, a promise of storms came at the back of the wind.

In the chapel, Suor Estasia del Mistero degli Angeli knelt on the cold stones, her hands clasped around her upraised rosary. Her face was dreadfully thin and of a translucent fineness that was quite otherworldly.

She was not alone. Nearby a little man in a Domenican habit watched her, his somewhat protuberant green eyes shining as he studied Suor Estasia. He had been waiting for rather more than an hour but Suor Estasia had shown no sign of coming out of her trancelike state. Savonarola was growing impatient. His sandaled feet ached with cold and he wanted desperately to hear of Suor Estasia's latest visions.

"What do you see?" he demanded in a whisper as he rose from the narrow bench that stood near the altar, generally reserved for the use of those who were too old or too disabled to stand in chapel. His strides were rapid, predatory, as he paced around the whitewashed room. He resisted an urge to seize Suor Estasia by the shoulders and shake her.

But something of his irritation must have penetrated the cloud of her meditation, and at last she lowered her rosary and stared around her, as someone waking from an unpleasant dream in an unfamiliar room might. She put one swathed hand to her forehead, a gesture that for all its restraint was strangely theatrical.

"Suor Estasia?" Savonarola said, coming near her. He bent so that she could see his face.

Suor Estasia blinked, then cried out as she threw herself at Savonarola's feet, tears suddenly flooding her eyes. "Oh, my adored prior, my light of salvation, my Heavenly brother." She grasped his foot and drew it toward her lips. Eagerly she prostrated herself before Savonarola, her face pressed tightly against the leather straps of his sandals.

Urgent as his need was, Savonarola savored that moment, permitting himself a faint smile in appreciation of Suor Estasia's abasement. Then he bent and touched her shoulder. "My child, tell me what you saw."

Her hazel eyes, made huge by the gauntness of her face, shone up at him and her face was radiant. "Oh, holy prior, I see the glory that you have revealed to me."

"But what was your vision? God sends different fragments of Himself to all those who worship Him and are blessed. What you have seen is not necessarily known to me through my visions." He motioned for her to rise, as always feeling uncomfortable beside this woman who was almost half a head taller than he.

Again Suor Estasia pressed her hands together, and tipping her head back, she began to murmur psalms in rapid, rhythmic Latin.

This time Savonarola could not contain himself. He grabbed her shoulders and shook her. "You must tell me. God has given you these visions to aid me in this salvation. You are to tell me at once what you saw."

The psalms stopped and Suor Estasia lowered her head, her face strangely composed, almost vacant. "I saw," she said, dreamily studying Savonarola's eyes, "I saw you surrounded in glory, high above la Piazza della Signoria. You were bright, very bright, shining with a light that no one could look upon. Beneath you, the monks of all the Orders of Fiorenza raised their hands and called for a miracle."

Savonarola's eyes brightened. "What more, Suor Estasia?"

She frowned, trying to recapture the tremendous elation. "I remember I was thinking how sweet was the brightness around you, how it opened its arms, reaching to embrace you. Then, amid the brightness you were lost in a cloud and there were sounds, such sounds, as I have never in this world heard, and they filled my ears until it was a delirium. Ah, I wanted to follow you, to be consumed as you were in that brightness." She stretched out her arms, lifting them as if to welcome a lover.

"A glory on earth? Before all the world?" He was unaware of the greed he felt. Slowly he knelt on the uneven stone floor and said softly, "Suor Estasia, let us pray that this is a true vision, the revelation of God to the world. To be lifted up before all of Fiorenza and taken into radiance." He crossed himself quickly and ducked his head toward his hands.

Suor Estasia dropped to her knees with the slow, languid movement of a swimmer under water. Of their own volition her hands sought her rosary and she held the crucifix between her fingers, lifting the little silver Corpus to her lips as she joined Savonarola in prayer.

When Savonarola left Sacro Infante, he was satisfied at last that Suor Estasia's vision was genuine. He had seen the feverish light in her eyes and had heard her call aloud to God as she lay supine on the chapel floor, her arms stretched out in imitation of the body of Christ above her.

Suor Merzede had stopped him before he left and had expressed concern for Suor Estasia, insisting that what the other nun had seen was not a true vision from God, but a kind of madness. For her envy and folly, Savonarola told Suor Merzede to beg her bread until Good Friday and to use her flail more when she prayed in her cell.

In less than an hour he was within the walls of Fiorenza and crossing the city toward the Francescani stronghold of Santa Croce near the eastern limits of the walls, not far from il Ponte alle Grazie.

Pausing in la Piazza della Signoria, he stared at the bulk of il Palazzo della Signoria, that formidable building, of darker stone than the rest of the city. He thought about what

Suor Estasia had told him, and wondered how long it would be before he looked down on the people of Fiorenza, exalted, hidden in brightness. What would the corrupt Pope's condemnation mean then?

His thoughts were interrupted by a group of youths in the stark dress of the Militia Christi. Each in turn came to him for blessing and Savonarola turned his mind from visions to the reality that confronted him. "My good young soldiers," he told the band gathered around him, "you must be particularly vigilant. You must be guided by the stern teachings of Our Lord and the voice of the Holy Spirit. You must not let pity lure you away from your responsibilities, for it is a false pity that encourages men to remain obstinate in the ways of error."

One of the young men grinned unpleasantly. "We understand, good prior. And we will remember what you tell us."

"Excellent. It is proper that you should be obedient to the instructions of those who are your superiors, and you must always examine your superiors to be certain that they are obedient to the will of God, for as it becomes you to respect and obey your elders as the superior persons they are, so it becomes all men, of every degree, to submit to the will of God, accepting His judgments and welcoming His chastisements, which are meant for His glory and the salvation of our souls."

The oldest of the young men turned his head away, a sly twist to his lips. Unlike a few of the others, he enjoyed his position and the chance to go anywhere in the city unmolested. For him, "superior" meant "stronger," and he knew that his troop of fifteen young men was stronger than almost anyone in Fiorenza. When he turned back again, there was only the greatest modesty and dedication in his reverent expression. "Thank you, holy prior. We'll do what we can to be worthy of the task you set for us."

"It is not I who gives you this task," Savonarola admonished him, but gently. "It is God Who speaks through me. Accept what He deigns to send you, and do Him worship and honor."

The young men nodded, a few exchanging conspiratorial looks, but one, a newcomer to the group, said, "But what am I to do when my father will not accept the word of God? He's said that you are a proud, vain man strutting in the cloak of false religion. He's forbidden me to hear you preach, and to associate with the Militia Christi. He says you are a hypocrite, and are striving for a worldly power, not the redemption of the world." The young man hesitated. "I have tried to reason with him, but he calls that defiance." His face darkened, "He beat me a few days ago, because I went to hear Mass at San Marco."

The enormity of this outrage stunned Savonarola, who regarded the young man in silence. Then his green eyes grew very bright and he stammered as he spoke, so great was his emotion. "I am no hypocrite! I have said nothing in this world that I do not believe is truly inspired by God. If it is otherwise, I pray that God will strike me down with the full force of His wrath." As he said this he recalled Suor Estasia's vision, and the vindication it promised him was calming. "Your father, my son, is in grave error. If he has not confessed his doubts, then he stands in sin. Should he die today, it would be with that stain upon his soul." He studied the young man. "You're Betro Giusto, aren't you? Your father is a mercer, I believe. He depends on the members of the Arte della Lana to sell him goods, otherwise he will have no cloth to sell to his customers and his business will fail. But the Brothers of the Arte are wise. They would not do business with an irreligious man. Particularly if the man is a known heretic."

Betro Giusto had turned rather pale. "My father is in error, good prior, but he is not a heretic. He prays to the Saints and is devout. He goes to Santa Trinita to worship with the Vallombrosiani Brothers. His quarrel is with conduct, not with faith."

"It is good that you defend him. It is fitting that a son defend his father," Savonarola said in his most friendly tone. "But if you would truly help him, you must convince him of the evil of his ways, and urge him to Confess and make a perfect Act of Contrition. It's necessary, believe me. Or you yourself will be contaminated with his heresy, and will yourself need to Confess."

The young man looked horrified. "But he will beat me."

"The martyrs accepted their pain with gladness because it brought them nearer the glory of God. So must you, if you are a true Christian, accept the ignominy that is heaped upon you, because for every insult, every blow, every injustice, there are rewards in heaven that far surpass the trials of earth." He looked at the young men. "Pray for guidance and strength and it will be given to you. Don't wait for justice in this world, because there is none. Men are imperfect and their capacity for wrong monumental. Hope for Heaven, and the Mercy of God."

The young men murmured, then knelt for Savonarola's blessing, their devotion showing in the sincerity of their conduct. As they rose around him, once again dwarfing him, he nodded to them. "Be vigilant. Do not let rank or finery or friendship deter you. Scrutinize everyone in Fiorenza, citizen and stragnero alike. Don't believe appearances, for the fairest face can mask the rottenest sin."

"And my father?" Betro Giusto asked, not willing to depart with the question unanswered.

"He must examine his heart. And you must examine yours. When I was young, like you, living with my father in Ferrara, God had not yet touched me, and I believed my father's words more than those of the Domenicani. He desired that I wed, but I yearned for a woman, the daughter of Fiorenzeni, and told my father that it was this woman I must have. He told me that Fiorenzeni were proud, independent people, who in their vanity despised other cities. But I pleaded, and at last he offered for the woman. Not only did her family refuse, but the woman thought my suit laughable. So far was I from the Grace of God that I railed against that woman and her Fiorenzan family for many days. And then I sought God, and God spoke to me. I left my father's house one afternoon, and entered the Domenican monastery, and did not see my family for seven years while I trained at San Domenico at Bologna. Thus did God show me that my first duty was to Him, and at the same time He revealed to me the sins of worldly vanity and the snare that is laid for men in the sweet flesh of women." He smiled almost benevolently on the young men. "Fiorenza scorned me, and I have repaid her with salvation."

Only Betro Giusto looked askance at this statement. The other young men nodded sagely and waited until Savonarola was halfway across la Piazza della Signoria before they laughed out loud.

The old, austere beauty of Santa Croce did not impress Savonarola as he entered the lean-windowed Gothic stronghold of the Francescani Brothers.

The first Brother he saw, Savonarola asked to inform the prior that Savonarola wanted a word with him. Then he paced the length of the church, noting the front was almost finished, as it had been for many years.

Orlando Ricci was well over forty. His body, which had once been large and hale, was now limp and formless under his habit. He walked slowly, as if his feet hurt, and when he saw that it was indeed Savonarola who waited for him, an expression of ill-concealed irritation touched his face. He schooled himself to a respectful manner and came toward the Domenican prior. "God give you a good day, Fra Girolamo. What a surprise to find you in church."

The conversational dart found its mark. "My excommunication is not valid. The Pope is an incestuous libertine and therefore has forfeited his right to make judgments on godly men."

The prior of Santa Croce had little admiration for Rodrigo Borgia, who occupied the Chair of San Pietro as Pope Alessandro VI. But he said, "The ways of God are not for men to understand. If He has elevated Borgia to his honor, it may be so that his salvation may be the greater, and by his reformation of error, show the world the extent of His Grace." He motioned to one of the chapels at the side of the church. "Would you prefer to speak privately? There are few people here just now, but it might change . . ."

"No." Savonarola glared at Orlando Ricci. "You won't be rid of me that easily, Fra Orlando. I have heard that you have written once again to His Holiness, accusing me of impiety. I warn you now that I will not tolerate such lies being spoken about me. You are to write to the Pope and tell him that you have searched your conscience and changed your mind."

Fra Orlando's smile was almost beatific. "I can't do that, Fra Girolamo. I am as opposed to you as ever."

"What would it take to convince you?" He folded his arms and glared up at the white-haired Francescano.

"A visitation from, God, Fra Girolamo. Nothing less." There was a strangely implacable note in the old prior's voice and something of the strength he had had as a young man came back into his stance.

Savonarola leaped at that. "Yes. Very well. If God were to elevate me, so that I hung over la Piazza della Signoria, surrounded in radiance, borne aloft on a cloud, would you then be convinced?" The brightness of his eyes stilled the derision in the prior of Santa Croce's throat. "Would that be enough?"

"Yes," Orlando Ricci said slowly. "That would be enough."

"Then on that day you will tell the Pope that you believe with me, and recognize that my inspiration is divine?" Savonarola was very excited now, and he leaned toward the older man.

The Francescano studied the Domenicano. At last he said in a slow, measured voice that echoed through all of Santa Croce, "If the day should come when you are elevated above la Piazza della Signoria and you then perform a miracle before all the citizens of Fiorenza, then, if the work you do is godly, I will recant all that I have said in opposition to you."

Savonarola's thick lips widened to a smile. "I was at Sacro Infante today. Suor Estasia has had a vision that would fulfill your conditions for me." He knew that Ricci was not one of those who put their faith in Suor Estasia's gifts, but he thought it would be a victory indeed if this obstinate old man could be made to endorse both himself and the Celestiane nun.

"Then we should know in time if her vision is true." He shrugged easily. "I am old enough that I may be in my grave when your miracle finally happens." From the tone of his voice, he expected this to be the case. He watched Savonarola. "Was that all, reverend Prior of San Marco, or have you more to say to me?"

"There are two other matters," Savonarola snapped, his temper flaring anew. "You realize that this Bonfire of Vanities must have general civic support if it is to be of any use to the souls of Fiorenza."

Rather apologetically, Prior Ricci interrupted him. "Well, no, I don't realize that. I don't realize the need to burn the things you describe as vanities. Much of what has been destroyed already was to the glory of God and Fiorenza. You are making this city a wasteland, and I refuse to lend my help to such an endeavor."

Savonarola raised his voice. "It is the will of God. Our Lord sought out the solitude of the wilderness for His meditation."

"A city is not a wilderness!" Prior Orlando Ricci was angry now. "Our city has been the greatest adornment in all of Italia, and that includes Roma. Three more years of your programs, and the meanest hamlet in Sicilia will be preferable to Fiorenza. No, I will not assist you. I will not tell my congregations to heed your warnings. I will resist your madness with my last breath, and I pray that God will let me live long enough to see you cast into the burning pits of Hell." His face was white and his body shook with rage. He lowered his voice. "I can't ask your forgiveness, good prior, because I repent nothing I have said. And before I bring more sin upon myself, I will say farewell."

In spite of his outward satisfaction, Savonarola had been disturbed by Ricci's outburst. "I will pray for you," he said stiffly.

"And I will pray for you." The Prior of Santa Croce

turned away from the Prior of San Marco, and in a moment he was gone into the shadows of the venerable Francescan church, leaving Savonarola alone in the echoing nave.

TEXT OF A letter to i Priori di Fiorenza from Lodovico da Roncale:

> To the respected leaders of la Repubblica Fiorenza, I, Lodovico da Roncale, Brother in the Arte of builders, wish to reveal a potential danger in the midst of our beloved country.
>
> In four days all Fiorenza will atone for our sins, and each will be called upon to Confess all our guilty secrets. In accordance with the admonition of the great Prior of San Marco, I come forward now with a matter that should have been brought to your attention when I returned to Fiorenza, more than three years ago. At the time it didn't seem important because the culprit had fled before I could accuse him. But now that the nephew has returned, the need is born anew and I take the liberty of addressing you.
>
> As your records will reveal, I was one of the builders first hired to work on il Palazzo San Germano for il stragnero Francesco Ragoczy. There were four of us who were selected from that number to do secret work on the building, and we were sworn to secrecy by a heathenish oath which we were made to sign in blood. This Francesco Ragoczy practiced alchemy, which was no secret. But where he practiced it, and to what end, has never been discovered. That is

*because his hidden rooms have always remained that,
and no one knows what ungodly things were done behind those hidden doors. Even my old Arte Brother
Gasparo Tucchio was uneasy in his mind about the
building. And we have only Ragoczy's word that Gasparo ever left his palazzo that night he disappeared.*

*You should make a thorough search of the place,
including the secret rooms. The Militia Christi are empowered to enter buildings and search through them,
so it is fitting that they go there. Behind the carved
wood at the landing of the grand staircase there is a
door. It is concealed in the carving. But to gain entrance, there is part of the carving that moves, and it
is this that releases the latch of the door. Try there.*

*The reward that the Arte offered for the discovery
of Gasparo Tucchio, dead or alive, will be welcome to
me, for I am in great need. And it would help me clear
my conscience if the mystery were at last solved.*

*I have taken the liberty of speaking to the nephew,
suggesting that he should assist me, as I was an em-
ployee of his uncle, and entitled to a certain sum for
all that I did. He is a very haughty man, and accused
me of trying to blackmail him. A fine thing when a
man can't offer his loyalty to an employer. The nephew
says he knows nothing of such matters, and it appears
to be true that he and his uncle were not close.*

*This is being written for me by Fra Giorgio at San
Felice, and it is he who will see it is delivered. I swear
to him and to you that this is the truth, and that I want
my heart free of deception when the day of contrition
arrives.*

I hope that you will pursue the matter I have disclosed to you. And I thank you for your willingness to hear me.

> the mark of Lodovico da Roncale
> member of the builders' Arte
> by the hand of Fra Giorgio, San Felice

In Fiorenza, February 5, 1498

CHAPTER 7

UNDER HIS TONGUE the Host was bitter. Ragoczy listened to the last prayers and benedictions with scant attention as he wondered what next to do: for the wafer that had been given to him at the Communion rail was poisoned.

The Atonement service had been very long, taking most of the morning and all of the afternoon. And now that it was over and the Mass had been celebrated, most of Fiorenza was sunk into a kind of lethargy. Idly Ragoczy tried to identify the poison, and how swiftly it was supposed to act. He decided that he would not be expected to collapse during the Mass. It was not in the spirit of the occasion, he thought with disgust. No, this day had been for the humiliation of Fiorenza, for bringing shame on everything that had made it beautiful. Death was for later. He would have a little time, then. He returned his attention to the end of the Mass.

When the service was over, Ragoczy lingered only long enough to exchange a few words with Sandro Filipepi. Their manner together was that of polite strangers, but Ragoczy said, "My petition to the Console for Donna Demetrice's release has not been acted upon yet. This worries me, Botti-celli. Have you any suggestions?"

Sandro's golden eyes were troubled. "The whole accusa-tion is ridiculous. All they would have to do is ask for a few questions and they will know she is no heretic."

"Do you know how Domenicani ask questions?" Ragoczy asked gently. "First they take you into a dark room where you are stripped and put into a penitent's robe. Then the torturer shows you his instruments and tells you what they do. And then the Domenicani tell you that if you give them the answers they want, you will not be tortured or put to the Question. Demetrice is a woman of integrity and courage. It would take more than threats to make her say what the Domenicani want to hear. So they would rack her perhaps, since the rack is not torture because it doesn't break the skin. And if she resisted that and did not die, they would resort to torture, probably the boot or hot pincers. And even-tually, so that the agony would stop, she would say anything they wanted to hear. Anything. And so would you, Sandro."

Sandro's face had paled as Ragoczy spoke, but he said, "That may be in Spain, but this is Fiorenza."

"You say this, who are willing to burn your paintings for a little peace?" The incredulity in Ragoczy's voice was rough with hurt.

Unable to meet Ragoczy's compelling eyes, Sandro turned away, a definite hurt in his face. "I don't think . . . Not her."

"Not her?" Ragoczy's question mirrored his disbelief. "And why not her? She was part of the Medici household, which is bad. She loved Laurenzo, which is worse. And she studied at Palazzo San Germano, which is utterly damning. Between those factors and her well-educated mind, she is condemned already."

"But until the petition is heard, there's supposed to be only imprisonment."

"Savonarola can't afford that. Eventually Pope Alessandro will act against him. It must happen soon, because no Pope can afford to tolerate such monumental defiance. If Savonarola is to maintain his position, he must act quickly. The Console is in his power already. If he told them the hearing of the petition must be waived, it would be. Or do you doubt that, Sandro?"

Botticelli shook his head heavily. "No. You're right. God pardon us all, you're right." With a strange, mournful gesture he turned away from Ragoczy and moved quickly away from him through the thinning crowd.

From Santa Maria del Fiore the walk to Palazzo San Germano usually took about ten minutes. Today Ragoczy deliberately took longer. He forced himself to move slowly, uncertainly, as if he were feeling ill. This care was rewarded, as various citizens stopped him to ask if he needed help, which he always politely declined in such a way as to confirm his illness.

It was almost half an hour later that he entered Palazzo San Germano, to be greeted by Ugo and Natale, two stewards he had hired the week before. Natale was well into middle age and felt a determined loyalty to the Medici family, who had employed him three years before. He had been proud to serve Ragoczy because his supposed uncle had been such a noted Palleschi, expressing support of the Medici long after their popularity had waned. Ugo was another matter, being younger, very earnest, and, Ragoczy suspected, working under orders from the Console or Savonarola. That was foolish, Ragoczy thought, but as long as they worked well, Ugo's fanaticism mattered little.

"Are you well, master?" Natale asked with real concern when the great door closed behind Ragoczy.

"I don't know. I don't feel myself." Quite deliberately Ragoczy faltered on the second step as he attempted to climb the grand staircase. "I . . . I'm dizzy."

Natale was the first to respond. He rushed to Ragoczy's side and gave him his arm for support. "There, master. Lean on me."

Ragoczy let some of his weight sag onto Natale's shoulder and spoke weakly. "I'm feeling hot and cold at once." He muttered another complaint in Hungarian, and turned to Natale. "I'm ill. I must get to my bed." With a skillful imitation of the dogged tenacity of the sick, he tried once again to climb the stairs.

"No, master," Natale said, restraining him. "Ugo will go ahead of you and prepare your chamber. You must wait here. Don't hurt yourself more."

Ragoczy accepted this. "I'll wait." He turned quickly to Ugo and saw the smile the young man wore before he could assume an expression of concern. "But work quickly, Ugo."

Ugo raced up the stairs. When he had turned along the gallery, Ragoczy looked at Natale. "Will you get me a warming pan? I don't think I can endure a cold bed just now."

"You must not try to climb the stairs alone," Natale warned.

"I may try again, but if I'm too weak, I will wait for you." He lifted a languid hand. "I don't think I can go far."

Although Natale wore an expression of doubt, he accepted this assurance. "I'll be as fast as possible, master. And I will bring a brazier to burn in your room. There are healing herbs that will make healthful smoke for you . . ."

Ragoczy stopped him. "I know you will do as you think best, and that I will be grateful for it."

Natale gave him a quick smile. "You're kind, master."

He made sure Ragoczy was supported by the banister, then hurried away toward the stairs to the cellars.

Now that he was alone, Ragoczy at last took the poisoned wafer from under his tongue. He looked at it, sniffed it, and wished he had a chance to use his laboratory, so tantalizingly near, to test the bread and find out what Savonarola had given him. He put the little wafer in his long silken sleeve and resolved to rise in the middle of the night and test the bread.

By the time prandium was being served in those few houses that were not honoring the fast day, Ragoczy lay between linen sheets in what he thought of as his public bed. It, too, rested on a layer of earth, and he lay back, doing his best to feign increasing illness.

At first Natale declared his intention of watching his master through the night, but Ragoczy said in a raspy tone, "No. I have a bell by me to summon you, and I will if it's necessary. But I will need you to be alert tomorrow, if I am worse." He touched the elaborate jeweled crucifix that hung around his neck. "I want to pray alone."

Natale accepted this, for prayer was still the surest medicine known in Fiorenza. He fussed around Ragoczy's bed one last time and then bid him good night.

Ragoczy lay back and waited, certain that Ugo would come to see how ill he was.

Ugo did not disappoint him. A few hours later, when night had settled over the city like some gigantic cold bird, the door opened a few inches and Ugo's face peered into the darkened room.

"Who's there?" Ragoczy called in the merest thread of a voice. He rose onto his elbows as if it were the greatest effort, and he clutched the crucifix in his right hand.

"It's Ugo," he said, coming into the room. He was

dressed in a dark, drab houseman's gown, but Ragoczy could see that there was a badge on his sleeve, not the eclipse of his own household, but the fiery sword above the city, the badge of the Militia Christi.

"I've been praying," Ragoczy said as he lay back, seemingly overcome by exhaustion. "But I'm still not well."

Ugo tried not to smile and almost succeeded.

Weakly Ragoczy motioned to Ugo to come nearer. "I don't know what's wrong. Is there a physician in the city who could help me?"

"You should think of your soul, not your body," Ugo sneered, and came to stand by the side of the bed.

"I have thought of my soul," Ragoczy said, raising the crucifix so that Ugo would be sure to see it. "But my prayers are not strong enough. Or I am too ill." He lapsed back into Hungarian as he turned away from Ugo.

There was an undertone of excitement in Ugo's next question. "What's wrong, master? What sickness is this?"

"I don't know," Ragoczy managed to sound both angry and frightened. "I have done nothing. But shortly after Mass I felt faint and now I am filled with pain, as if a fire burned in my vitals." He looked back at Ugo. "Pray with me. I want you to pray with me."

"Of course." Ugo dropped to his knees beside the bed and pulled his crucifix from under his robe. The chain around his neck was very fine and the crucifix of silver. "Dear Lord God, Who looks into every heart and knows all things," he said almost automatically, "though I am wholly unworthy to address You, yet I ask you to hear me for the sake of Your Son Jesus and this stranger who suffers."

Ragoczy echoed the words, smiling with gentle cynicism at the peculiar arrogance in Ugo's tone of voice, as if his assumption of humility automatically granted him superiority over those who did not abase themselves. "That is good, Ugo," he murmured, putting one small hand over Ugo's, which was joined in prayer.

Ugo continued to pray, but Ragoczy appeared to be weakening still. Some little time after midnight, Ragoczy stopped Ugo, claiming to be even worse. "I thank you, Ugo," he whispered. "But I fear I need a priest."

This announcement hardly disturbed Ugo. He crossed himself and rose. "What for, master? Surely you are not in need of Last Rites?"

"I may be." Ragoczy nodded. "Prayer hasn't helped . . ."

"Let me send for Savonarola. He has great strength and God has inspired him to do great things." For the first time Ugo was speaking with genuine enthusiasm. "He will come. I know he will. And his prayers will make you well."

This was exactly what Ragoczy had hoped for, but he said, "Savonarola is a busy man, with many responsibilities. It would be wrong to disturb him on this matter." He left off, panting, one hand clenched on his chest.

"He will come," Ugo promised him. "I will tell him that you are very ill and likely to die without his help." He crossed the room quickly, and added from the door, "I'll wake Natale and he will pray with you while I am gone."

So Ragoczy would have to continue the sham. "I am grateful," he said weakly, and as soon as Ugo had left the room, stretched and rubbed himself to work the tightness out of his muscles.

Natale said little, but he brought candles into the bed-chamber and stood them around the bed. He felt Ragoczy's icy forehead and his face grew grave. When he had put the room in order, he drew a chair near to Ragoczy's bed and said, "Do you want me to read the Scriptures to you? I have them in my chamber."

"Yes. I need to hear holy words." He was lying still, hardly breathing, when Natale returned a few minutes later. "Good. You are back," he breathed as Natale once again took his place in the chair by the bed.

It was more than an hour later when Ugo at last returned. He burst into Palazzo San Germano and raced up the grand staircase, the sound of his shoes announcing him as much as his eager shout. "He's coming," he cried joyfully. "He's really coming!" With this shout he burst into Ragoczy's bedchamber, to be met by the cold fury in Natale's face.

"Recall, if you please, that our master is ill unto death. And comport yourself with the respect you owe him."

Ugo tried to assume the proper demeanor, and almost managed it. His face was somber, but his eyes danced. "It's only that I am happy for our master that Savonarola will come to pray for his recovery," he said defensively.

Natale had a very poor opinion of Savonarola's power, it seemed, for he folded his arms over his chest and said at his most withering, "If there is healing at all, God is the physician. To praise the priest who prays is like praising the rain in time of drought. Each has done only what God gives it to do."

"That's not so," Ugo objected, knotting his hands belligerently. "Savonarola is inspired by God, and God hears him when he prays. He has visions. He knew when Medici was going to die, and he did. He knew that the French would enter Fiorenza."

"Of course he did," Natale scoffed. "He might as well have invited them." Abruptly he stopped the argument. "Our master lies ill and in fear of his life. I won't discuss this now. You may wait at the door for this Savonarola, and when he is come, secure it once again, in case desperate persons try to enter here."

It was difficult for Ugo to admit that Natale's dignity impressed him, but he responded with unaccustomed promptness. He was in the hall when he remembered to ask how Ragoczy fared.

To answer the question, Natale went to the door and spoke in a low voice, hoping that Ragoczy would not hear him. "He's failing. I don't know if he will last until dawn, let alone sunset. He's cold as the grave already, and there's not a drop of sweat on him. When he can speak he says that his bowels are full of devils. He will take no nourishment. See what your Savonarola can do against that." He did not stay to hear Ugo's shocked words, but went back to the chair at Ragoczy's bedside.

As Ugo went down the stairs once more, his mind was troubled. If Ragoczy were indeed hovering near death, then it might be senseless to waste Savonarola's powers on him. He dared not admit, even to himself, that Savonarola would perhaps be inadequate to the task of healing his master through prayer. He stopped in the loggia, thinking that Palazzo San Germano was a lonely place. There should be more to the household than one Hungarian noble and two servants. He recalled that the other Ragoczy had entertained lavishly on occasion, and that he had had more servants. It was a pity that the nephew was not so generous except in matters of vanity. The clothes he wore were grand enough to be worth a year of Masses. And see, he thought smugly to himself, what has become of him. For all his gorgeous clothes and his great station, he lies abed and burning in his guts, and calls for humble monks to help him.

He was still occupied with similar edifying reflections when there was a sharp rap on the door, which jarred him out of his reverie.

As the door opened, Girolamo Savonarola stepped across

the threshold, a pyx in one hand, the Scriptures in the other. His Domenican habit was somewhat disarranged, a silent testament to the haste in which he had prepared. He paused just inside the loggia and glared at the magnificence of the room. "What vanity is here," he remarked. "And this is the man you would have me pray for? A man who wallows in luxury?"

Ugo stared down at his feet saying petulantly, "It is not this man who built the palazzo, it was his uncle. You said you would pray for him."

"Yes. I will pray." He looked back at Ugo. "You have done well, my son. You have told us much of this man that could not be learned otherwise without breaking the seal of Confession. And his Confessor is Francescano." This last was said with sudden rancor, but he went on calmly enough. "You have carried out your responsibilities here quite well. In preferring the welfare of holy Church to the momentary advantage of your employer, you earn yourself a place in Heaven." He gave Ugo a rather preoccupied blessing, then asked, "Where does he lie, this stranger?"

"In his bedchamber, I will show you if you follow me." Ugo had barred the door, and was trying to maintain his composure in the presence of his hero. "Will you follow me, good prior? My master is waiting for you."

"I will come," Savonarola said, motioning to Ugo to precede him up the stair.

The scent of burning herbs assailed them as they entered Ragoczy's bedchamber. Natale was still at the task of putting more of the herbs into one of the braziers that stood near the carved and painted bed in which Ragoczy lay. Natale moved quickly as Ugo came into the room, and in a moment he had brought the prayer stool to the side of the bed. As he passed Ugo, he muttered, "I still think this is foolish."

Ugo made no retort, but the satisfaction in his face was easily read. Savonarola pushed past the two servants and approached the bed with the intensity of a hunter stalking bear. At last he put out his hands to Ragoczy's face and felt how gelid he was. "You are in mortal danger," he informed Ragoczy.

Ragoczy nodded, a motion that was so slight it barely pressed the pillow. "I fear so," he agreed. He tried to lift his crucifix but the effort was too great. He closed his eyes, knowing that if Savonarola looked too deeply, he would know that he was in no danger whatever. "Pray for me, good prior. You are my last hope."

The Domenican prior hesitated, oddly pleased with the stranger's helplessness. He looked at the face, so tormented and so peaceful, and reluctantly admired the bravery of the man, who endured his suffering with patience. "Are you resigned to accept whatever God wills?" he asked.

"I am." The words were so soft that Savonarola had to strain to hear them. The foreigner tried to cross himself, but the gesture was feeble, ineffective, and his hand dropped back to his side.

An unfamiliar frustration gnawed at the monk as he fell to his knees. He went through the first of the ritual with the barest modicum of attention while he tried to fathom what it was about the stranger that bothered him. "Holy Father God, Son and Holy Spirit, Sacred Trinity, I beg that You will hear me and grant my prayer. For I have served You all my life, given You my devotion and faith. In Your name I have scourged vice and sin from the land, and in Your name are the mighty and the worldly cast down. Therefore, I ask that You look upon this unworthy mortal who lies before You, and examine his heart. If he is worthy of Your great gifts, if he be not eaten up with venality, if he is capable of understanding Your mercy, then heal him of this great ill that threatens to take his life."

Ugo watched, rapt and attentive, while Natale stood apart, his face a mask, showing no emotion of any kind.

Savonarola lifted his hands, and his harsh voice filled the room. "I ask that You hear me, I ask that You come into this suffering creature, and for Your glory, heal him. I ask that You chastise him with this sickness, so that he will ever turn away from perdition. And if he is corrupt and vain, then I ask that You strike him, so that his sins will no longer contaminate the earth, so that he will be banished from the company of men to dwell with demons in the eternal fires of Hell, where all who are vicious must go. Judge this man, I ask of You. If his life is one of merit, save him, now and forever. But if he aspires to be redeemed and is bloated with evil, destroy him as You have destroyed all those who have mocked You."

On the bed, Ragoczy moved a little, and made a sound in his throat. His fingers moved restlessly over the covers.

"See this man. See what a creature he is. If his illness is a judgment on him for his impiety, cast him forth and let him howl in Hell through all time. Save him only if he is virtuous, and if You find him worthy of life, and if You are willing to let me be the means of his discovery." Savonarola's voice had risen to a kind of shriek and he rose high on his knees. He stayed that way for some little time while the herb-scented smoke grew denser. Then slowly he sank back onto his heels. "I can do no more. Now it is God Who will decide whether I am to have the glory of saving this man's life." He got to his feet somewhat unsteadily, the pyx still dangling from the chain in his hand.

Natale coughed, and the sound was perilously near a snort. Ugo turned on him, glaring, then turned back to Savonarola. "You have done more than anyone could have asked. If he dies, it is as you say, the will and judgment of God. And if he lives, then it is your prayers that have saved him, for his own did not prove effective." He knelt before the little prior. "You are a man of miracles, blessed Savonarola. No one can deny that." There was a certain defiance in the last words, and he waited for Natale to take up the argument.

But there was none. On the bed, Ragoczy moved again, and with a tremendous effort sat up. His bedshift was disarrayed, and he moved with difficulty. He looked squarely at Savonarola. "Good Prior," he said in a weak, clear voice, "I thank you for your prayers. God has heard you."

It was difficult to know who was the most startled. Ugo gave a kind of scream, and Natale's eyes filled with tears. Savonarola turned white and there was an unpleasant light in his green eyes.

From the bed, Ragoczy went on, letting his voice grow stronger as he spoke. "The fire that burned in my guts is dying. My hands are growing warm. Good, holy prior, you have done this. It was your work alone that affected me. I feel as though I had been filled up with loathsome poison and have been purged of it." He determined to be less grim. "I owe you much, prior. Here." With trembling hands he reached to the table beside his bed and took one of the rings he had worn earlier that day. It was a large polished emerald, one that had come from Burma. He felt a momentary pang at the thought of giving it up, but it was a small price to pay to have beaten Savonarola at his own game. "Here. Take this. It is the best that I have. Be certain that in later days I will see you are paid as you deserve."

Woodenly Savonarola approached the bed, and with no expression whatever he held out his hand for the ring. "This is a great vanity," he said automatically, hardly looking at the jewel.

"Then sell it and use the money for the glory of the Church." Perhaps, he thought, that would save it from the Bonfire of Vanities.

"I will consider it." He took the ring, and without another word he strode from the room.

"See him out, Ugo," Natale said, and as soon as the younger servant was gone, he approached the bed. "Did he do it, master? Was it his prayers?"

Ragoczy wondered briefly how far he could trust Natale. He looked at the servant. "I don't know, Natale. But I do know that I had little chance for survival without his help." If he had not died, he would have been accused of diabolism or other heretical arts, for Savonarola was waiting for him to die. And if he had not asked for help, his death was required.

"Ugo will have it all over Fiorenza that this was a miracle and that Savonarola saved you." There was a measure of reproach in that statement.

"Let him. Let Savonarola have full credit, so long as he will also take full responsibility." He did not know how flinty his dark eyes had become as he stared at the door.

Natale flinched at the sight of his master, but wisely decided to say nothing. A man brought back from the brink of death was entitled to his anger.

Later that night, when the promise of dawn waited in the eastern sky, Ragoczy left his bed and went at last to his laboratory, the poisoned wafer in his hand. He thought momentarily about the desperation that had driven Savonarola to so rash an act, and though he disliked to admit it, he began to have doubts that he would prevail. As he set to work on the wafer, he banished those worries from his mind, resolved to accept defeat only when he died the true death.

By sunup he was back in his bed, ready to receive the

long line of visitors, who, through the day, came to congratulate him on his fortunate healing.

TEXT OF A letter from Alessandro di Mariano Filipepi to Francesco Ragoczy da San Germano:

> To the nephew of his old friend Francesco Ragoczy, Botticelli sends his greetings and rejoices with him that he was spared from death by the intervention of Prior Savonarola.
>
> I heard of your deliverance only a few hours after it happened, but I have been busy with a commission and therefore have not had time enough to send you this note until now. First, let me tell you how pleased I am that you escaped death. If you were the most despised man in Fiorenza, yet no one would wish you to die alone, unprotected and friendless in a foreign country. But my pleasure extends to more than your rescue. A few days ago you warned me of what might befall those who are in the keeping of the Domenicani, and you described to me some of the wrongs done in Spain, intimating that such might occur here. Now that Savonarola has miraculously restored you to health, how can you think that such a man as he would ever allow any man or woman in his care to be harmed in the way you described? Think of the prayers that Savonarola said for you, and then consider Donna Demetrice's plight. Be certain that she stands in no danger from one selfless as Savonarola.
>
> Rather than suspect this excellent Domenicano, be sure that you are sincere and prompt in the expression of

your thanks. You owe him too much, Ragoczy, to accuse him capriciously of crimes he would never commit.

I have had your note saying that you will not return the painting I have requested. I can't come and take it away from you, of course, but I warn you now that the Militia Christi might enter your palazzo and if they should find it, they are very likely to confiscate it and it will be burned, in any case. I ask you, if you do have it, return it to me. I cannot pay you what you paid me for it, but that should not be a consideration between us, because this is to the mutual benefits of our souls.

Francesco, Francesco, you were my friend, why do you refuse me this? I didn't paint it for you, you merely took over Laurenzo's commission. I know it is not a question of money, because you are too rich to care about the price of the work. But does not my peace mean something to you? Are you unwilling to help me gain the calm I have missed for so long? I ask you again, send me the painting.

Again, I am glad you didn't die. I will pray for you.

> Sandro
> via Nuova, Fiorenza
the 23rd day of February, 1498

CHAPTER 8

PRIOR ORLANDO RICCI opened his hands, a gesture of despair. "I have done all that I can, Signor Ragoczy. I have had no response from His Holiness, and my authority is neither greater nor lesser than Savonarola's. But he has usurped the force of the state as well as the leadership of his Order. In the face of that power, I am impotent."

Ragoczy nodded slowly. "I see. And there's nothing else either of us can do?" He looked up at the ornate beams that crowded the ceiling, almost blocking the view of the vault. "Can we delay him, even a week?"

"What good would that do?" the Francescano asked. "The week would give him more opportunity to create a climate of approval for his auto-da-fé. And you, if you were strong in your opposition, might make yourself suspect. If he once convinces Fiorenza that heresy is rife in the city and that only the stake will abolish it, then the city will indeed be laid waste with the fire of God's Wrath, just as he predicted." He turned to look toward the altar, framed by tall, thin windows that in the morning were alive with light; but now, with the sun low in the west, a bright smear behind clouds, the whole church seemed drab, forlorn and lifeless.

Although it was dangerous to do so, Ragoczy decided to trust the prior of Santa Croce. "I have heard from . . . an associate of mine, living in Roma, that Pope Alessandro intends to issue a formal charge of heresy against Savonarola. My information is not official," he added as a caution to Orlando Ricci. "I don't know if the Pope will make the charge, not wholly. But I have found that my . . . associate is very reliable."

"Heresy?" If the old Francescano was surprised by the word, it did not reveal itself in his words or his bearing. "Heresy. At last."

Ragoczy was silent. "Do you think we could force a delay? Knowing this?"

The prior of Santa Croce regarded the foreigner in the elegant dark red damask silk. "Why should it matter to you?"

"If I'm to be human, I must care about humanity. And I have an obligation to my uncle's servant."

Orlando Ricci winced, "I beg you not to dissemble with me. The fabrication of a nephew will do well enough for most of Fiorenza, but I pray you will be honest with me. I have known you to be Francesco Ragoczy from the day after you returned."

Ragoczy's face was guarded, but a tension was winding in him. "How?"

"Your voice, when you sing. I heard you once or twice when you and Laurenzo would stroll about the streets singing. When you've heard as many monks singing flat as I have, you value a voice that's true. And there is a quality to your voice when you sing, a texture that I've never heard before or since." He laughed once, very sadly. "The other day I heard you join in a hymn, and I knew."

"I hope, good Prior, that others are not so acute." After a moment of silence he said, "What will you do? I am under pain of arrest still. The accusation of diabolism still stands—"

"My dear Ragoczy, you've stood in this church for the last hour, and I have not seen you shrink from me, from the altar, or any holy thing here. We've passed powerful shrines and relics and you have not cried out in pain, nor have burns or welts appeared on your skin. You regard all these things with becoming respect and you do not stink of brimstone. Because of this and because of the source of the accusations against you, I'm reserving my judgment. And I honor you for your courage, whatever you are." He turned and said in another voice, "It's nearly time for Vespers, I must leave you. But come again, as soon as you have confirmation on

the Pope's action. You have my word that I'll give you what
help I can, but it may not be much. There is too much fear
and support for Savonarola in Fiorenza and any aid I give
must be in secret. On the day Savonarola is cast out as the
Devil in monk's robes that he is, I will acknowledge in public all you have done for Fiorenza." With that he sketched a
blessing in Ragoczy's general direction before hurrying
away through the church.

Ragoczy did not linger at Santa Croce. Night was already
gathering in the sky, and he had a great deal to do before the
next morning, when he would again try to address the Console on Demetrice's behalf. He was grateful that Ruggiero
had arrived at Palazzo San Germano at last for there were
tasks that only Ruggiero could perform for him. His manservant had recovered from the worst of his wounds though he
still limped when he walked. Between that limp and the dark
stain on his skin which had been colored with oil of walnuts,
he was quite effectively disguised, and at the moment answered to the name of Ferrugio.

While Ragoczy paused in la Via della Primavera to speak
with a spice merchant, the supposed Ferrugio was vainly attempting to keep a large troop of Militia Christi from ransacking Palazzo San Germano. He shouted to the youths as
they pulled a huge, elaborately framed painting of the *Triumph of Paris* off the wall. The heavy frame cracked as it hit
the marble floor, and two of the young men set to work with
short knives, slicing through the handsome face of Paris and
the opulent curve of Helen's shoulder.

From the landing of the grand staircase four of the Militia Christi searched the elaborate carving for the release of
the lock of the hidden chambers rumored to be at the back
of the landing. As he watched, Ruggiero was secretly

pleased that he had taken the time to be sure that entrance had been locked from the inside.

Two more of the young men were racing up the stairs to the gallery on the second floor when Natale appeared, holding a steward's staff. "Not one step farther, ragazzi." He moved the staff so that it effectively blocked the top of the stairs.

The leader of the group glared. "You must move. It's our duty to seize vanities."

"Not while I'm here to stop you." Natale looked as if there were nothing he would like better than to smash a few of the arrogant young men with his thick staff. Smiling, the Militia Christi took the challenge.

Even before he reached the main door of Palazzo San Germano, Ragoczy knew something was seriously wrong. Though nearly half a block away he began to run, his long cloak of tooled red leather flying out behind him like wings.

The sound was hideous, a combination of nails pulled from their beds and crockery breaking. Ragoczy paused on the threshold, his face set into grim lines as he saw Ugo conferring with a leader of this troop of publicly sanctioned vandals. Near the top of the stair Natale lay in a heap, a large reddened lump on his forehead. Two of the young men held Ruggiero, mocking his attempt to break away from them.

In the middle of the loggia, scattered and broken on the marble floor in addition to the ruined painting were several brass scales and gauges from his measuring room, a small spinettino, a large viol, two T'ang Dynasty jade lions, a bolt of Turkish silk, a few carved rosewood chairs, a number of enameled bowls, and a tied bundle of illuminated music manuscripts. As Ragoczy watched, four more of the young men ran in dragging a large screen of intricately carved wood inlaid with ivory. They tossed this onto the heap, cheering as the delicate wood broke.

"Stop! At once!" Ragoczy's command filled the loggia like the tolling of a great bell.

It was as if the air had been sliced with an ax. All the young men stopped abruptly, and turned toward the elegant figure in the door. The clatter of broken wood falling on marble seemed horridly loud, and as ominous as the sound of cannon.

Ragoczy walked into the silence, cold rage in his penetrating eyes. His jaw tightened as he looked down at the wreckage before him. Then he lifted his gaze to the troop of Militia Christi.

Afterward none of them could say why they had been so frightened. Ragoczy was unarmed, a man of no more than medium height, elegant to the point of foppishness. And yet as his dark, luminous eyes met each of theirs in turn, a kind of dread touched them, a sense that Ragoczy's foreignness was more than a matter of language and geography.

The leader of the troop raised his chin. "We are empowered to eliminate all Vanities—"

"Be silent. " The words were soft, almost a whisper, and they stung like a lash.

The leader glared defiantly. "I am Ezechiele Aureliano. Savonarola himself entrusted me—"

"I said be silent." He spoke conversationally and his menace was all the greater. He regarded the two young men holding Ruggiero. "Release my houseman. *Now*."

Shamefaced, confused, the two young men frowned, exchanged bewildered looks, and let go of Ruggiero.

"Ferrugio," Ragoczy told him, "see to Natale."

Ruggiero nodded and without a word shouldered his way

through the young men and climbed the stairs to where Natale lay.

No one spoke as Ragoczy walked around the pile in the middle of his floor. He bent and touched one of the spinettino's keys and the string jangled tunelessly. There was a kind of blind pain in his face at the sound. Next he picked up one of the jade lions. The front right paw was broken off and the right side of the head was smashed, turning the lovely jade cloudy, as if it were a plant touched by frost. Ragoczy stood, holding the jade lion in the crook of his arm. His glance never wavered from the little statue.

"Get out of my house. All of you." His words were distant, quiet, terrifying.

Most of the young men were glad to obey, sensing that they were escaping a danger far greater than they knew. They went stiffly, a residual fear making them clumsy.

But Ezechiele Aureliano stood his ground. "You have no right to do this. The Militia Chris—"

Ragoczy spun around on him. "I have no right? *I?*" The wrath in his voice, in his eyes was so fierce that Ezechiele Aureliano backed away from it and stumbled as his foot caught against some debris on the stairs. "You say that, you who caused this . . . this *obscenity?*"

Ezechiele scrambled to get away from Ragoczy. He missed his footing once again, but then fled, shouting as he went, "You'll regret this, stragnero!"

When the door had crashed shut, Ragoczy stood very still, his hands lovingly, mournfully assessing the damage to the jade lion. At last he put it down on the stair and turned his attention to Ugo, who waited, sullen and defiant, on the landing.

"They're good Christians," Ugo began, ready to defend the Militia Christi and the destruction they had brought to Palazzo San Germano.

"They are pernicious savages." His brows flicked together. "And you are one of them."

"I believe with the holy prior of San Marco . . ."

Ragoczy ignored this entirely. He asked of Ruggiero, who leaned over Natale, "How is he, Ferrugio?"

"I don't think his skull was cracked, but the blow has left a serious bruise." Ruggiero stood. "He'll have to lie down for a while, and he may need a physician later."

"I'll carry him to his chamber." Ragoczy pushed past Ugo, moving fastidiously, as if unwilling that any part of his garment should touch his servant.

"But what about me?" Ugo demanded as Ragoczy reached Natale.

Ragoczy barely glanced back at him. "You not only permitted, you invited the destruction of my valuables. What would you do, in my position?"

"I would be grateful that my servants wish to save me from Hell." This was shouted. The sound was strident and it was obvious that Ugo knew he had gone beyond what could be tolerated.

"Would you? Then you may be grateful that I will not allow you to remain here where there is so much sin and vice. You have until sunrise tomorrow to leave this place. If you are not gone by then, I will send for i Lanzi. Believe this." Ragoczy looked away from Ugo, and his icy contempt vanished. "I'm ashamed. He was harmed in my service."

Ruggiero seemed not to hear this. "His chamber is waiting, master. I'd carry him, but I'm not strong enough yet." He was embarrassed to admit this, and under the dark dye his skin flushed.

"Never mind," Ragoczy bent, then lifted Natale into his arms, carrying him as easily as he would a child. On the stair below, Ugo stifled a gasp, realizing what strength Ragoczy must possess to carry a man larger than himself without noticeable effort.

Undecided, Ugo took one hesitant step up the stairs, then changed his mind, fearing what Ragoczy might do to him. He knew now that he had been treated with great forbearance, and that he could not count on Ragoczy's continued restraint. Until he had seen Ragoczy overwhelm the Militia Christi, he thought he had never seen anyone more compelling and more dangerous than Savonarola. Those traits had attracted him to the little Domenicano, because force fascinated him. Now he had seen someone stronger, much stronger, someone who used that strength, with formidable, alien discipline. By comparison, Savonarola's railing at sin was only childish histrionics. Ugo walked down the stairs, dejected, and could not bring himself to look at the beautiful broken things piled up before him. He hurried away to the cellars, feeling cheated, feeling lost.

When Natale was safe in bed, Ragoczy and Ruggiero returned to the loggia. They both were reluctant to sort out what was piled there, but at last Ragoczy dropped to one knee. "Make a list, Ruggiero. I want a record of what was done."

"As you wish, master." He studied Ragoczy compassionately, knowing how much Ragoczy loved beautiful things.

Ragoczy had retrieved a miniature of a Byzantine prince which looked more like an icon than a portrait. He stared at it, rubbing the archaic face with his thumb. "Well, at least the *Orpheus* is safe. I should have put more of this in the hidden rooms."

"Don't chide yourself," Ruggiero admonished him.

"Who better? You'd think by now I would have learned . . ." He broke off. "Make the list, old friend, I'm going to find a physician." He turned away so that Ruggiero could not see and would not pity his grief.

TEXT OF A letter from Germain Ragoczy to i Priori and la Signoria:

> *To you excellent governors of Fiorenza, I, Germain Ragoczy, nephew and heir to the holdings and estate of Francesco Ragoczy da San Germano, am driven by circumstance to address a complaint.*
>
> *The day before yesterday, in the evening, members of the Militia Christi came to Palazzo San Germano and engaged in acts of vandalism to a considerable extent. Attached to this letter is a list of the items they destroyed. Though I am in sympathy with the cause of religion, the callous invasion of private homes cannot be tolerated, no matter what your current laws permit.*
>
> *Some of the items which the young men saw fit to seize and damage or destroy are neither my property nor the property of my uncle, and as they are my responsibility, I am now bound by the law and my conscience to make good on those pieces of art, those musical instruments and those goods that were, in fact, the property of others, most of whom are not, in fact, Fiorenzeni.*
>
> *If you have provisions for restitution of damages, I would appreciate a meeting to decide the amount at your earliest convenience.*
>
> *At this time, I would like to remind you that you have yet to hear my petition for the release of Donna Demetrice Volandrai, who is currently being held at an unknown place on a charge of heresy. Perhaps when you allow me to present my claim for settlement, you would be willing to hear my petition on her behalf.*

I ask you good Priori to consider my position. I have many obligations to my uncle, not only as his heir, but as benefits the honor of our ancient house. You are anxious to discharge the law equitably; no less am I anxious to see that I accomplish my tasks. Certainly it is to our mutual benefits to settle all these matters as quickly as possible.

Be certain that I await your response most eagerly and will place myself entirely at your disposal.

Germain Ragoczy

At Palazzo San Germano,
March 2, 1498

CHAPTER 9

A MIZZLY, DRIVING rain had made the stones slippery, and the hazard of crossing them was great. Thin shards like fingers plucked at him from their beds of loose mortar as he made his way over the castle walls. Ragoczy was forced to cling desperately as his feet and hands struggled to maintain their hold on the slick wall. Once a narrow ledge crumbled under his left foot and he had to clasp the wet stones in a fervent embrace while he searched for secure footing on another perilous outcrop.

After what seemed hours, but in fact was little more than thirty minutes, Ragoczy lifted himself onto the stone frame of the high window of Demetrice's cell. He paused there, in part to listen to the sounds within and in part to steady himself. The castle was quiet, the stillness of a frightened animal in hiding. The air around it seemed to quiver with un-namable dismay. His fine brows twitched together. What could have happened here, that fright permeated the very stones? Still frowning, he dropped silently to the floor of the cell, landing in a crouch, prepared to fight.

When he was not attacked, he straightened up and made his way, with more caution than seemed necessary, to the darkest corner of the cell, where Demetrice's straw pallet covered the floor. "Demetrice?" he said softly, and the walls murmured her name after him, eerily.

The cell was empty. He touched the fetters hanging open over the pallet, the cold iron telling him nothing, except that she had been gone from the cell for some time. His fear for her increased as he patted the chilly, sodden straw. He felt for his cloak which she had hidden there, and discovered it was gone.

He went to the heavy door, worry making him awkward. Very carefully he tugged at the brace, and to his surprise the door swung inward on recently oiled hinges. Very carefully, every sense acute, he stepped out into the narrow, torchlit hall, his eyes moving restlessly over the time-darkened stones. To the left and the right the hall was the same. There was no indication of which way she might have gone, or of where she could have been taken. He lingered, undecided, at the door of her cell.

A metallic scrape and clang echoed along the hall, the re-verberation making it impossible to tell where the sound had originated. At the sound a shriek of despair came from the adjoining cell, and other wordless voices joined the heartrending lament.

Ragoczy ducked back into the cell, and dropped himself into the far corner, under the window. He pulled his old black guarnacca around him, so that he became part of the deepest shadows. Now he was grateful that he had risked wearing black, for in any of the gaudy colors he wore as disguise he would have been as bright as a tilting target. He pressed himself to the uneven stone floor and waited.

There were steps in the hall, heavy sounds from two, and light, faltering steps from the third. As last they paused and in a moment the cell door creaked open. Wavering torchlight licked the walls with brightness as the two jailers pushed Demetrice nearer her pallet.

"Hold your arms up," one of them ordered.

"I can't." Her voice was quite calm, but more tired than Ragoczy had ever heard it. There were scuffing steps and a soft gasp, and the unmistakable chink of metal closing on metal and the crinkle of chain. Then the heavy steps retreated and the door was pulled to. Then there was the solid impact of a bolt driven home and a lock turning.

Only when these sounds had died away and there were no more footfalls in the hall did Demetrice allow herself to sob.

Ragoczy got to his feet slowly, unmindful of the dank walls and the cold now. He looked through the gloom of the cell, and with all his heart in his voice he said, "Demetrice. Demetrice mia."

She stifled her tears and her eyes widened as she peered into the dark. "San Germano?"

"Yes." He came nearer, stopped less than an arm's length from her.

As his eyes searched her face, he whispered, "Are you well? Were you hurt?"

She nodded affirmation but said, "No." Her voice was unsteady but she stubbornly refused to weep. "But I was frightened. So frightened." In supplication she extended her manacled arms to him. "Please. San Germano. Please." Her voice broke.

Tenderly he took her in his arms. Softly he kissed her forehead, her eyelids, the curve of her cheeks and at last her mouth, her lips parting under his. They stood so for some time, until her breath quickened and color came back into her face. Ragoczy stepped back and was secretly pleased that Demetrice leaned toward him as he did. "Gioia mia, wait, wait." He reached for the iron that bound her wrists. "First this."

But she pulled away. "No. Last time they saw the locks were broken and they said it was Devil's work, like the broken bars on the window, though I told them that I had thrown a loose stone at a bird perched there, and the bars . . ." She bit her lower lip as tears filled her eyes. "No. No."

Ragoczy wiped her face. "About the chains. What did they tell you?"

"These are new. See? They were blessed by the monks, so that I could not escape again. They said if I did, they would know for sure. They said they would cast the devils from me." She stopped abruptly and horror filled her eyes.

"Ah, Demetrice." There was so much sorrow, so much regret in the way he spoke her name. "If you are frightened, then in the morning before I leave you, I will secure you once again so that they will never know. Give me your hands."

It was an effort for her to lift them. "I can't. No."

A terrible thought lanced through him. "Torture? Have they tortured you?"

She shook her head numbly. "Not yet. Today they tied me by the hands and lifted them high in the air with a rope over a beam. I had to stand on tiptoe or my shoulders would ache. After a while I ached no matter what I did. They gave me no water, and the torturers searched my body for Devil's marks.

At least," she added contemptuously as she fought revulsion, "that's what they said they did. But I think they did it for their pleasure."

Ragoczy had seen other men who derived their satisfaction from humiliation and pain, as he once, long ago, had derived it from terror. He said nothing, letting Demetrice speak so that she could rid herself of the shame she had endured so that it would not fester in her, poisoning her life.

"They asked me questions. The same questions over and over. It made no sense. And then they made me watch while they examined another woman, an older woman. She had refused to answer their questions at all, and so they were doing hideous things to her, with heated irons. Her skin. The smell." Suddenly she gagged and leaned against the wall. "When she fainted, they told me that if I would not admit my heresy, they would brand me. And worse." Her legs grew weak and she dropped onto the straw of her pallet, shivering uncontrollably.

He sank down beside her. "Gioia mia." Carefully, kindly he drew her into his embrace. "You have much courage, Demetrice, and I honor you for it. And I promise you with my blood that I will not let them kill you. Not now or ever." This time his kiss was more urgent, evoking a response from her.

A gust of wind filled her cell and the cold drove her more tightly against him. "Don't leave me, San Germano," she whispered into his shoulder.

"I won't." He smoothed her hair back from her face and asked, "Shall I lie beside you to keep you warm, be your companion for tonight? Or do you want . . . more?"

"Can you just lie beside me?" she wondered aloud.

"Of course. I would prefer to love you, but that, amica mia, is up to you. Either way, I will not leave you unless you tell me to go." His voice was low, persuasive, musical. With an effort he refrained from touching her.

She stared down at the manacles binding her wrists and the chains attached to the bracket sunk deep into the wall. Her arms ached abominably and her head felt like ice. "I hate this," she said with loathing in her voice. She hesitated, then thrust both hands toward Ragoczy. "Unfasten them. But only if you can lock them before you go."

"Certainly," he said, and took great pains as he pulled the fetters apart. "You see? I need only put this pin back, so, and they will lock as well as ever." As he spoke he kissed her arms where the metal had chafed her. "Now, cara Demetrice," he said with more ease than he felt, "what do you want me to do?"

He had removed his short mantle and reached to put it over her shoulders, but she drew back as it touched her. "It's wet!"

"Yes. It is raining tonight," he said, a sad amusement lurking in his eyes. "Does it displease you?"

"Oh, no. No. But if your clothes are wet, you might become ill, or take chill . . . ." She stopped, looking confused.

"That," he said ironically, "is impossible, amica mia."

"Is it? But if you stay that way, in damp clothing . . ." Then she gave a soft cry and flung herself into his arms. "I don't care if you're soaking. I don't care if water poured from the ceiling. Hold me. Dio infinito, hold me." All her strength was in her arms then, and she ignored the pain of it and pressed close to Ragoczy, feeling the thick woolen guarnacca and his chest and thighs beneath. His moist clothes did not bother her at all.

He returned her kisses ardently, lingeringly. His hands sought out the opening of her penitent's robe, and then, be-

fore he roused her more, he breathed deeply and held back
from her. "Demetrice, gioia mia, listen to me. Listen."

She tugged at his clothes, now needing more from him.
"San Germano, I don't mind the damp, truly I don't. The
mantle will dry soon enough." Then she saw his face and
knew it was not the wet clothes that concerned him. At once
she was serious. "What is it?" she asked, touching him, apprehension in every line of her body.

"You know what I am, Demetrice. And you are still disgusted by it occasionally." He saw her objection and hurried
on. "I know you weren't disgusted before. It isn't myself
that disturbs you, it's the idea of what I am."

"But I was wrong. You're not like that at all." She had
flushed, knowing how accurate he was. She was not comfortable with his vampirism, even though he had given her
transcendent pleasure.

"I *am* like that, Demetrice. It's my nature. And if I love
you too often, if you welcome me too much, you will be . . .
tainted by me. If I taste of you tonight, so soon again, there
is some very little danger. Not much, for usually it takes
several . . . encounters before transference is possible. But
when there is such intensity, so much love . . ."

"Are you saying that I might become a vampire?" There
was no accusation in her question. The horrors she had
known in the last two days had banished her more trivial disgust of what he was.

"If we continue this way. Five times, perhaps six at the
most, and the thing is certain." He held her face in his hands,
yearning in his eyes. "There are no words for how I want
you. Even the most profound are paltry beside the feeling
that wells in me now as I see you, touch you, feel the sweet
weight of your body against mine. Demetrice, if you could
endure to share blood with me, I would rejoice to have you

among my kind. But you shy away at that thought. Even now, when you've already spent one night in my arms, you think distastefully of what was done. Oh, you don't forget the pleasure, but the method bothers you." He dropped his hands to his sides. "If you cannot endure my love, then deny me. For your sake, deny me."

"Deny you?" She was incredulous. "With the threat of the rack waiting for me? With the stake to look forward to?" Her laughter became a sob. "I loved one man with all my being and I lost him. And I thought that no one would ever reach me so completely again. You, you are what I thought never to find. My memories of Lauro are as sweet and as bitter as they ever were. But you have given me another love, as rich as wine. Not only with your body, though that is much more than I guessed it might be, but with your care. I know how much you risk for me."

"Do you?" His hands covered hers.

"San Germano, if my life is to end soon, then let me die consumed with love. I can think of nothing better to know in this world than your love. I want nothing more."

"And if you live, what then?" He tilted her face upward.

"Then I still want you." As she said it, she knew it was the truth. She moved back from him, pulling away, but only far enough to open her penitent's robe.

The cell was cold, and gooseflesh rose on her pale skin. Ragoczy saw this, and reached for his mantle, and then changed his mind, casting the sodden garment aside. With skillful, loving hands he warmed her and his lips made a litany of her flesh. There were many hours ahead on this blustery March night and he took the time this afforded him to discover all the wonder of her, and to praise her until what passed between them was an anthem that in its beauty banished fear.

When at last she dozed, replete, in the circle of his arms, she murmured, "Remember the manacles."

He kissed the curve of her breast again. "I'll remember," he promised, and gathered her close against him.

TEXT OF A letter to Francesco Ragoczy da San Germano from Gian-Carlo Casimir di Alerico Circando.

> _To his reverend teacher and beloved friend, Gian-Carlo in Venezia sends hasty greetings to Fiorenza._
>
> _I have your orders and I will carry them out as you have instructed me. I leave this evening for Mestre, will go from there to Padova, then I will travel south to Bologna, where I will wait for you. I will send a messenger to Fiorenza if you have not arrived in Bologna by the tenth day of April. Should I discover that you have been taken by Savonarola's Domenicani, I will make every attempt to free you, and to that end, I carry a letter from Il Doge Barbarigo. Should that prove to be useless, I have also the letter from your Roman associate, Olivia. If I discover that you have died or been killed, I have your burial instructions and only if your spine is broken or your body wholly crushed or burned am I to see it laid in holy ground. Otherwise, I am to bear your remains back to Venezia in the chest you have already provided._
>
> _If you have other instructions, or there is a change in what I must do, I will be at la Locanda dei Sassi Verdi. The innkeeper is named Isidoro da Rivifalcone, and he is paid to be discreet. Any message you send_

*will be delivered promptly and your confidence re-
spected.*

    *Until I see you again, I will faithfully carry out
your instructions and pray for your safe return.*

                             Gian-Carlo

*In Venezia,
the 4th day of March, 1498*

CHAPTER 10

NEAR LA LOGGIA della Signoria the faggots were being
stacked, ready for the Bonfire of Vanities that would begin
soon after Mass was over at Santa Maria del Fiore. Two
large troops of Militia Christi supervised the placing of the
wood, while others established barriers in la Piazza della
Signoria to keep the expected crowd at bay. The afternoon
was wonderfully bright, preternaturally clear though the air
was cold.

On the north side of la Piazza della Signoria a small
group of artists stood with Sandro Filipepi. One of them, an
ugly young man whose powerful arms and chest declared
him to be a sculptor, kept looking at the paintings that were
leaned up against the nearest building. Occasionally he
shook his head.

With the artists was the white-haired Marsilio Ficino, his
old eyes fading now both in color and sight. "Botticelli," he
said in an undervoice as he plucked at the artist's sleeve,
"don't do it."

Sandro shrugged Ficino's hand away. "I have sworn I would. I have no choice."

The old philosopher shook his head. "You always have a choice. It's immoral to ask this of you. You aren't bound by your oath, not to an excommunicant monk." He looked once toward the stacked paintings. "At least spare the *Solomon and Sheba*. It's biblical, Sandro. It's a religious painting."

"Is it?" Sandro asked vacantly. "With Solomon reclining with Sheba, his hand on her hip and her breasts thrust forward? It's lascivious. Think of the lust it incites." He spoke as if by rote, the words curiously flat.

"But Solomon loved Sheba. Aren't the Prophets and Kings in the Testaments allowed to love anymore?" Ficino saw that Sandro was no longer listening. He turned away, furious at his own helplessness.

In a little while the Vacca began its slow, mooing toll, calling the citizens to la Piazza della Signoria. The youths of the Militia Christi gathered together near their carefully stacked wood and waited for the procession that had just left the cathedral.

The sound of chanting blended with the droning peal of the bell, casting a gloomy pall across the bright day. The chanting grew louder, the monks being now under the spell of the occasion. A few of them danced as the procession neared la Piazza della Signoria, their bodies moving in strange, almost spastic gyrations, as if enthralled.

By this time la piazza was quite full and the Militia Christi were once again enforcing the boundaries they had established earlier. Many people strained to get nearer, to watch more closely the destruction of the precious Vanities that were waiting for the flames.

When at last the procession entered la Piazza della Signora the gathered crowd was greedily silent. This was what they had come to see. The monks chanted faster, more loudly, and those devout who watched fell to their knees and began to pray aloud. The sound of prayer became an antiphony to the chanting and the sound of the bell. The monks in their black habits over white cassocks moved around the entire piazza, their chanting becoming a shout. In response the crowd began a rhythmic clapping. This, too, became faster until the continuous noise rolled like thunder over the red roofs of the city.

Then, abruptly, all fell silent as Savonarola mounted the steps of la Loggia della Signoria to address them. They waited while the prior of San Marco glared at them, while he motioned significantly to the faggots. At last he spoke, "Today God has given you an opportunity!" He held his hands up to indicate that they were not to interrupt him. "God has granted you a reprieve that you may repent at last your great and terrible sins!"

A sigh like the distant sea rushed through the huge crowd. Almost all of Fiorenza's forty thousand people shared in that sigh, and pressed forward in anticipation.

"Here! Today! At last you will have an opportunity to show your devotion to the will of God. Here you will cast away those worldly baubles that bind you to your sins!" He motioned to the Militia Christi. "These young soldiers of God will prepare. You will see their piety shining in their eyes as they light the fires that burn for your salvation!"

The gentle sound grew louder, and more of the monks began to dance. A few people in the crowd near the front of the barricades began to sway in sympathy with the dancing monks.

Two bonfires were laid as the monks danced. The Militia Christi worked fast, the young men eager for the approval of Savonarola and the praise of the citizens of Fiorenza. The first bonfire was quite large and stood on the south side of la piazza. But the other was somewhat smaller, on the northeast side of la piazza, and it was here, on this smaller bonfire, that attention was focused, for this was where Sandro Filipepi, known as Botticelli, was to burn his works. Ezechiele Aureliano had been given the responsibility of laying the fire, and he worked with zeal. He had five young men to help him and he supervised them with a fine air of authority.

"Sandro, let me take one or two of these away." The voice was soft, gently modulated, with only a trace of a foreign accent.

Botticelli turned swiftly and saw Ragoczy at his side. "Francesco!"

"Germain," he corrected with a smile. "Let me take two of the paintings. Spare those. There will still be more than twenty to burn. Surely no one will miss these."

Sandro's eyes grew hard. "I can't do that."

"Why not? Let me take the *Persephone*. That legend has always appealed to me. The painting is not offensive. Only the Domenicano's madness would see it so." He had not spoken loudly, but Sandro had the impression that he was shouting.

"I cannot. I took an oath."

"Break it. For your work. For those beautiful, fragile creatures whose flesh is cloth and paint." Suddenly he took Botticelli by the shoulders and looked searchingly into the artist's golden eyes. "Sandro, do you know what you're doing? Truly know?"

Across la Piazza della Signoria Savonarola was shouting to the Militia Christi, praising them more fulsomely than before, reciting the names of the dedicated young men who were soldiers for God, for redemption. The young men, as they heard their names called in turn, glowed with embarrassed pride.

Botticelli tried to break away from Ragoczy's hold, and was somewhat startled to find he could not. The foreigner's hands were much stronger than he had realized, and the compact, muscular body would resist anything but outright assault. "Leave me alone, Francesco."

One last, desperate time Ragoczy pleaded with Botticelli. He saw out of the corner of his eye that the Militia Christi was coming to gather up the paintings, and that their arrogant leader, Ezechiele Aureliano, was smiling in malevolent anticipation. "This is wasted, Sandro. Because next to them"—he nodded toward the paintings—"neither you nor I nor that maniac Domenicano mean anything. There is more humanity, more reality in those figures than in half of the people gathered here to watch. Sandro. Please."

"You'd better leave, Ragoczy." His voice was flat, and without waiting for Ragoczy to respond, he turned to the nearest of the Militia Christi. "I'm ready. Help me carry the paintings."

The smile on Aureliano's face widened in spite of his efforts to appear solemn. "You must do it, Filipepi. Otherwise it isn't real sacrifice."

For just a moment there was a kind of sickness in Sandro's face, a loathing. Then it was gone and he shrugged. "Very well. Show me what I must do." He shouldered his way past Ragoczy, refusing to meet the reproach in his face.

"The small ones first," Aureliano instructed. "Save the large ones for last. The most indecent is the *Diana and Actaeon*. It's large enough to save for the last. This *Jupiter and Io* or the *Semele* will do for Savonarola's lesson."

"Lesson?" Sandro asked, the word almost strangled him as he spoke it.

Aureliano's face was wonderfully bland as he regarded the painter. "Yes, of course, Savonarola will use your work, that you yourself so justly condemn, to inspire others to destroy their Vanities. He will show the error of the work, and tell how it damns us all."

Botticelli put his hands to his mouth as if he feared he might vomit. He forced himself to be calm, and when he could, he lowered his hands and said, "That isn't necessary."

"But it is." Aureliano was grinning unashamedly. "If you are not sincere in your repentance, then how can we expect sincerity of others? The corruption inherent in the art will be revealed, and where lust has been engendered there will now be only disgust." He rocked back on his heels.

Sandro glanced wildly around him, looking for help. There were only the mocking faces of the young men and a few Domenicani Brothers separating the paintings into stacks. He took one step forward, but his way was blocked by the Militia Christi. Beyond, the monks continued their work. Botticelli wondered fleetingly what would happen if he cast himself instead of his work into the flames. He started toward the nearest monk, who bent over the *Persephone* and *Semele*, and it was only then that he saw the monk wore heeled boots of blue leather. He almost laughed at that, amazed at Ragoczy's audacity. He felt a moment of elation, which he quickly stifled. He looked at Ezechiele Aureliano and his heart tightened like a fist in his chest.

"We will begin soon," the Militia Christi leader said. "Whenever you're ready."

Sandro gave one last, quick glance at his *Semele* and *Persephone*, then said, "Very well. Bring the *Jupiter and Io*. More people know that story."

"You must carry it," Aureliano stood very straight and the twist of his mouth was faintly contemptuous.

"Why not?" Sandro said to the air, and went to the stack of paintings. He picked up the *Jupiter and Io*, studying it critically, as if it were someone else's work, someone he did not know. Io reclined, gloriously blonde, languid, abandoned, surrounded and supported by a cloud that was aglow with all the colors of dawn and sunset, a cloud that was like a man, perhaps, with a handsome face dimly perceptible in the cloud. The line of Io's neck was particularly effective, he thought, and the movement in the cloud that might be hands. He was startled to realize the work was good, better than he had ever thought his painting to be.

"Filipepi." Aureliano spoke sharply, cutting through Sandro's thoughts.

"I'm coming," Sandro said, and reluctantly took the gilded frame in his hands. The Militia Christi made a path for him through the crowd and as Sandro entered the empty center of la Piazza della Signoria he heard the rustle of the people made suddenly silent.

Botticelli followed Aureliano through la piazza toward the Loggia della Signoria, where Savonarola waited for him. He studied the little Domenican prior, aware now of how ugly Girolamo Savonarola was, how angular, how shrunken. He experienced a moment of terrible revulsion, and then it was over.

"Fiorenza," Savonarola cried out as Botticelli brought the painting to him. "Here is one who has grown great in his fame and in his error, for he has been driven to paint such things as Christian men must be shamed to look upon. Here." He reached for the painting and motioned for two of the Militia Christi youths to lift the painting into the air. "See the fruit of his talent, which might have shown the world the glories of God! Here is the aggrandizement of lust, the representation of pagan pleasures. See the wantonness of the woman, how she displays her body without shame, how she is made lewd by the voluptuousness of her thighs which welcome the monstrous intrusion of Jupiter, who is no better than the Devil!"

The crowd was pressing forward, eager to see the painting and be disgusted. Sandro heard the strange sound the people made, and he wanted to cry out to them that Savonarola was mistaken, that this was painted to show pleasure, and the delight of the body. This was not lust, but beauty. Behind him there was a sound of flint striking steel, and almost immediately the rush of flames as lighted straw was tossed onto the smaller bonfire, kindling the wood laid there.

"But Sandro Filipepi has repented his sin," Savonarola announced to Fiorenza. "See, with his own hands he takes his iniquitous work"—he motioned to Sandro to do so—"and with his own hands, in pious acceptance of the strictures of God, he consigns the perfidious thing to the flames!"

Sandro moved as if asleep. He took the painting and clasped it to his chest as he carried it to the flames. Hotter than the waiting fire, self-hatred raged in him as he lifted the picture and cast it onto the fire.

The crowd and the flames roared together and Sandro looked through the flames to see the exultant figure of his brother, Simone, as he raised his hands to heaven, and beyond him, framed by a black Domenican hood, the stricken face of Francesco Ragoczy.

As the stink of burning paint and cloth filled la Piazza della Signoria, Ragoczy pressed the *Semele* and the *Persephone* close against him under the Domenican habit. When he could bear to look no longer, he made his way through the crowd, murmuring that he had to return to San Marco.

He was halfway there when another groan from the crowd told him that a second painting had been consigned to the flames.

Transcription of a vision of Suor Estasia del Mistero degli Angeli:

> In the name of the Father and of the Son and of the Holy Spirit, Amen. In reverence to the Blessed Virgin and all the company of Saints, Angels and Martyrs who are the Hosts of Heaven, let it be set down here what the Power of God has shown to me.
>
> When I was languishing in the world, a prey to all the follies of the flesh and the cravings of the body, before my soul conquered my sin-ridden thoughts, I shared the abode of my cousin Sandro di Mariano Filipepi, who is known also as Botticelli. It was there that I saw so many of those shameless paintings which yesterday were given to the cleansing flames. Thinking on that glorious moment, I turned my thoughts to God and His Splendor, of His Radiance that shines so brightly that the Archangels are all but blinded by it. Before Him all the kings of the earth fell in awe, and there was nothing so beautiful as His beauty. The most sacred painting was a humble, insulting reflection of His Glorious Beauty. The most sublime hymn was screeching compared to the sweetness of His Voice.
>
> My soul soared aloft, rapt in the sight of Him, and there I saw how the fires of Fiorenza reached to Heaven. The stench of burning paintings and finery were to God as the most fragrant incense. The vile ashes of clothes, furniture, wigs, lace, brazen statues that littered la Piazza della Signoria were changed and formed a flowering wreath that crowned His brow and shone with the Light of His Face.

The leap of the flames was a dance to Him, and the prayers that rose to Him sounded with the loveliness of lutes and trumpets. As the tokens of Vanity and Envy were consumed, God was glorified. For there is nothing so beautiful as God. Nothing better merits our souls than the thought of God. Nothing better adorns us than virtue and worship, for piety weaves a robe that not even the master of l'Arte di Calimala can duplicate.

In the vision I saw God embrace Fiorenza in acceptance of this sacrifice, and the fiery sword that burned in His Right Hand was turned from us and raised toward the hellish sink that is Roma. But He was watchful, for not all shared in our offering. There were some who would not give up their worldly goods for the greater rewards and treasures of Heaven. Those unchristian souls who took away two of the paintings that were to be burned will share with the pagan works all the fires of hell. God will not be cheated, and even now He waits to destroy those who mocked the sincerity of our purged sins.

My voice is hoarse from singing His praises. My eyes are heavy from the joy of beholding His Glory. My poor weak body is sunk in fatigue from the vigils of prayer and fasting that have brought me close to the Throne of God.

God has given me to know that His great plan for the Salvation of Fiorenza is soon to be accomplished. Savonarola will be raised up, and unworthy though I am, unbearable, all-consuming glory, bright as flowers in the sun, will be my lot through the goodness and the Mercy of God.

O Fiorenza, be fervent in your prayers. Be rigorous in your faith. Do not now desert the triumph that

*is so near at hand. As we cast out the unrighteous
and the heretical ones who have brought us this terrible depravity, be sure that there will be joy in Paradise and that we will be redeemed through the acts
we perform in these days. Set an example in holiness
that all the world will seek to emulate. Free yourself
from the hideous bonds of the flesh and learn to
praise the might of God with your chastity and your
devotion. Reflect on the Mercy of God, that will receive the greatest sinner in Heaven if he repent.*

*The Love of God pierces all armor and defeats all
opposition. The armies of Angels and Saints and Martyrs are in heaven for our salvation and the elevation
of our souls. I have seen how much joy is felt in
heaven when one sinner casts sin away and embraces
virtue. I have seen the compassion of the Angels for
those who are tempted, and the tears that are shed by
those holy beings would rend the heart of the most
corrupted and venal of men.*

*What is love among men when compared to the ce-
lestial fraternity? What is success in the world when
death strikes down even the mightiest and the greatest
treasures turn to dust? Only the Glory of God remains. And if we turn from God, we turn from the
Eternal Source of life and the Eternal Goodness that
is the light of the world.*

> *by the pen of Fra Milo*
> *from the lips of*
> *Suor Estasia del Mistero degli Angeli*

*At Sacro Infante, near Fiorenza,
the 5th day of March, 1498*

Chapter 11

WHAT IS THE meaning of this outrage?" Ragoczy demanded as he was ushered into the Madonna chapel of Santa Maria Novella. He pulled his arms free of the grasp of the two lancers who had brought him to the old Domenican church and glared into the darkness. Next to the mercenary soldiers his bearing was disturbingly aristocratic, and his indignation was as genuine and legitimate as the medieval frescoes on the far wall. Ragoczy straightened his heavily embroidered sleeveless cote that was worn over a sleeved tunic of stiff green satin. His heeled boots were tooled blue leather and the hat on his short-cropped loose curls was thickly sewn with pearls.

Two of the old Domenicani Brothers seated behind the long table set up in the Madonna chapel exchanged worried glances, but the third, a man of little more than twenty, regarded Ragoczy sternly. "You will be seated. It is for us to ask questions."

"I'll stand," Ragoczy said shortly, and looked again at the young Domenicano. Something stirred in his memory. The night of the celebration . . . what was it? Twelfth Night! The monk before him had been the leader of the followers of Savonarola who had broken into his palazzo and caused such havoc. His face did not change expression, but he realized that he was much more vulnerable than he had thought at first.

"You are Germain Ragoczy, are you not? Heir to the perfidious Francesco Ragoczy da San Germano?"

Ragoczy gave him a haughty stare. "I would not have put it that way. But Francesco Ragoczy was my uncle and I am

his heir. If I am ever allowed to settle his estate." This
pointed remark was not wasted. The two older Domenicani
exchanged looks and one very slightly shook his head.

"When certain matters have been answered to our satisfaction, then the estate will be settled, one way or the other."
The younger monk rapped out the words.

"And have you already decided what those acceptable
answers are? Tell me at once, so I may be prepared to lie to
your order." Ragoczy folded his arms and waited.

The young Domenican Brother said, "I am Fra Mario
Spinnati." He studied Ragoczy closely, studying his reaction
to this announcement.

Ragoczy raised his brows and asked, "You are willing to
tell me who you are? You must be very certain of yourself."

This was not what Fra Mario had hoped for. He rose to
his feet, his breath coming quicker. "You are wearing blue
boots. Boots of tooled leather. With heels."

Obligingly Ragoczy raised one foot and inspected the
boot as if he had never seen it before. "So I am."

Fra Mario's control slipped badly. "*And you were wearing them at the Bonfire of Vanities!*" The sudden shout rang
through the old church.

"Very likely," Ragoczy agreed, standing on both feet
once more.

"You were wearing them then. I know because you were
seen."

Ragoczy shrugged. "I wasn't trying to hide myself."

"But why were you there?" Fra Mario demanded.

"I suppose for the same reason many others were there—
to see Botticelli's paintings for the last time." He knew this
answer was a dangerous one, but he hoped it might lessen
the impact of the accusation he knew was coming.

"The citizens of Fiorenza were there to see an end to Vanity," Fra Mario insisted.

"Were they? Then why did so many weep when the paintings burned?" His eyes met Fra Mario's with controlled intensity.

"They wept," Fra Mario said unsteadily, "because they were filled with joy. They were free." Too late he realized that the foreigner had succeeded once again in putting him on the defensive. He tightened his hands. "Is that why you stole the paintings?"

"What paintings?" Ragoczy asked.

"The *Semele* and the *Persephone*." The monk's question was a challenge, and he was clearly waiting for the chance to take up the battle in earnest.

"Are they missing?" Ragoczy asked.

"You know they are!"

"You've told me." Ragoczy saw the slight confusion on the two older monks' faces and felt relief. The matter was still between Fra Mario and him. "I'm glad," he added thoughtfully, "that someone had the courage to take them."

This had all the effect he had hoped it would. Fra Mario took a few hasty steps around the end of the table, his jaw set pugnaciously. "You say that, foreign dog!"

"Yes," Ragoczy agreed calmly. "I say it. Because I believe it. And whoever it was, in time the world will be grateful to him."

"And would you have taken the paintings?"

Ragoczy knew from this question that Fra Mario was less convinced than he had been. He studied the monk evenly. "Yes," he said at last. "If I had had the opportunity, I would have made the attempt. But I would have tried to take the *Jupiter and Io* instead of the *Semele*." His eyes never wavered from Fra Mario's face, and his candor perplexed the Domenicano.

One of the older monks interrupted at this point, "Signor' Ragoczy," he said in a surprisingly strong voice, "I am Fra Stanislao. I would like to ask you a few questions."

"Of course," Ragoczy said, recognizing a far more dangerous opponent in the old monk than Fra Mario had been. "I will do my best to speak truthfully."

Fra Stanislao nodded noncommittally. "You say you are the heir of Francesco Ragoczy?"

"I am."

"Do you have proof of that?"

"I have a patent of arms which should be familiar to you: the eclipse, winged erect on a silver field. I have also letters from my uncle, and a document from two Hieronomiani Brothers, reporting the death of my uncle and giving his last Will." There were few of the Hieronomiani Brothers in Italia, for their strength was greatest in Spain. The assumption would be that Francesco Ragoczy had gone into Spain or perhaps Portugal. "I believe he was in the company of an alchemist of his acquaintance, a Magister Branco."

Fra Stanislao nodded again. "Are you willing to produce these documents?"

Ragoczy sighed as one much put upon. "I have been trying to show someone at la Signoria my documents since first I arrived in Fiorenza. If your examination of them would hurry the conclusion of the settlement of my claim, let me send word to my houseman Ferrugio and he will bring the documents to you."

If this assertion impressed Fra Stanislao, nothing in his manner or expression revealed it. "That may be for later." He glanced at a parchment in front of him. "Now, this matter about Donna Demetrice Volandrai. You have been seeking to secure her release."

"I have been," Ragoczy agreed, his senses suddenly very alert. "My uncle specifically bade me see that Donna Demetrice was given housing and a pension of her own in return for her service to him. He charged me with the task of seeing that she was protected and provided for."

"But she stands accused of heresy," Fra Stanislao pointed out mildly.

"It is a crime to which she has not, as I understand it, yet Confessed. Accusations mean little. And it may be that her tuition from my uncle in the science of alchemy has contributed to her accusation. Until she is condemned, I would dishonor the memory of my uncle to abandon Donna Demetrice." He stood somewhat straighter and let his accent become stronger and harsher. "I do not know how it is in Fiorenza, but in my Transylvanian mountains, when the honor of your name and your family is in your hands, you are doubly damned if you betray either."

At last there was a reaction from Fra Stanislao, the merest touch of anger in his voice and the abrupt way in which he put down the parchment. "Honor is part of Christian life. And I hear that you are a Christian. A Catholic, in fact."

Ragoczy nodded slightly. "I am. I attend Mass regularly, as I am certain you know." He decided to take a certain risk. "Is it only Fra Mario who thinks I have stolen Botticelli's paintings, or do you agree with him?"

Fra Stanislao frowned. The foreigner had anticipated his question and he was thrown off stride. "I have reserved judgment so far."

"If you wish, search Palazzo San Germano. The Militia Christi have already, but it may be that they overlooked something in their eagerness to destroy my uncle's treasures." His voice was louder and his brow darkened. "But I ask that if you desire another search, that someone be sent who will supervise those young men, so that more will not be damaged."

"You sound angry, Signor Ragoczy," Fra Mario said smugly.

"I *am* angry. So would you be if you had seen the wanton destruction that was brought to my house." Ragoczy stepped nearer the table where the Domenicani waited. "Do you want to search the house?"

Fra Stanislao made a gesture of dismissal. "If you are so willing to have us there, the pictures must be elsewhere."

"What?" Ragoczy demanded, and looked at the monks with a kind of arrogance. "I see. If I will not allow you to search Palazzo San Germano, it is because I have the paintings there. If I do allow you to search, it is because I have the paintings somewhere else. That condemns me no matter what I say and makes it unnecessary for you to ask such questions of a Fiorenzan. Foreigners are better suspects, are we not?" He half-turned from the table, indignant.

"It's not foreignness," Fra Mario insisted, ignoring the warning gesture from Fra Stanislao. "We know you're mixed up in this somehow. You were seen near the paintings. You were talking with Botticelli."

"I haven't denied it," Ragoczy said, relieved. "He had asked me to return to him a painting my uncle had bought from him a few years ago. I made a search for it and could not find it. I told him so. I also told him I was glad that it wouldn't have to burn." He decided to take another chance. "I tried to look at the pictures before they were consumed, but the Militia Christi had a tight guard on them. Only Domenicani were allowed to handle the works. So I watched from as close as I was permitted to stand." He knew that several of the Militia Christi members would testify to that if they were ever asked. And luckily no one had seen him in his hiding place when he pulled the Domenican habit over his own clothes.

Reluctantly Fra Stanislao nodded. "So we understand. But one of the young men claimed to have seen a monk wearing blue tooled leather-heeled boots."

Ragoczy's laughter was startling, and Fra Stanislao crossed himself to protect himself from the impiety of it. "I beg your forgiveness, good Domenicani," Ragoczy said when he could speak. "But the thought of a monk in my shoes . . ." He let his mirth possess him again. "It's ridiculous. I admit that I stood very near one or two of the monks who searched through the paintings, and it is possible that someone looking quickly might have seen my boots near the feet of one of the Brothers. But to think anything else . . ." He mastered his laughter this time.

Fra Stanislao regarded him coldly. "It is possible that the young man was mistaken." He fingered the parchment, his face revealing nothing. "The auto-da-fé is to take place on the tenth. Today is the sixth. Tomorrow or the day after, Donna Demetrice will be examined by members of our Order, to determine if there has been heresy committed. She has maintained that there was none in her initial examination, but the examination was not rigorous."

Ragoczy turned cold. "What do you mean, not rigorous?"

"I mean," Fra Stanislao informed him in his most deliberate manner, "that so far she has been threatened only. She has refused to answer us. So it will be necessary to submit her to the Question."

The Question, as Ragoczy knew well, meant some form of torture. He did not betray his dread as he lifted his brows again. "I should think her oath would be enough."

This time Fra Stanislao shook his head regretfully. "You don't understand. The Devil is cunning and his ways are devious. You have never met this woman, you don't know what she might be capable of doing. For the salvation of her soul, her body must suffer. For the glory of God, she must accept chastisement and Confess the truth."

This cool recitation brought a smile to Fra Mario's lips and he turned to Ragoczy. "When the Question is finished, if she has proven innocent, she will be released to your care."

"How does she prove herself innocent?" Ragoczy asked, knowing the answer.

"She dies, foreigner. She dies."

But this was too much for Fra Stanislao. "It is enough that she demonstrate her innocence under Question. If she dies, it is proof of her redemption. But if she lives and convinces us, then it will be a simple matter to see that she is restored to you. If, of course, she is found to be guilty, she will burn on the tenth, with the other heretics."

Ragoczy gazed down at the Domenicani Brothers. "Tell me, of those you have in prison who are accused of heresy, how many have demonstrated their innocence and lived?"

Fra Mario answered the question, with relish. "None. But there are eleven of the accused yet to be examined."

"I see. How convenient." Ragoczy stepped back. "Well, good Domenicani, what now? Are you proposing to accuse me of heresy, to be sure of my compliance with your plans? Are you going to insist that I stole Botticelli's paintings? Or are you going to send for my documents, and find out whether or not I am who I say I am?"

Fra Stanislao's mouth was a tight line, and he spoke as if the words were painful. "Time enough for your proof after the auto-da-fé. But you must understand our position, and our concern for our city and the state of your soul. We are assigning a guard to you, who will stay with you until we decide what is to be done. If you make any attempt to escape or to trick your guard, we will know that you are not what you claim, and we will order you arrested and imprisoned."

Ragoczy's eyes glittered unpleasantly. "I see. Just as you condemn me if I don't allow you to search my house and condemn me if I do, you guard me, and if I accept the guard I must betray my house and name and oath, but if I refuse the guard, I convict myself of heresy and am dishonored. Very neat, good Brothers." He looked around the empty church, staring out of the elaborate screen of the Madonna chapel.

Not one of the monks seemed to hear the sarcasm in his words. Fra Stanislao was unperturbed as he said, "The whole matter will be resolved in a few days, Signor Ragoczy. You might as well accept things as they are with a good grace. Fra Sansone"—he signaled for the Domenicano to approach—"will be your guard."

Fra Sansone deserved his name. He was tall, broad-shouldered and muscular in a way that not even the Domenican habit could disguise. He acknowledged Fra Stanislao and turned a passively hostile gaze on Ragoczy.

"Fra Sansone," Ragoczy said politely. "I will do my humble best to make you comfortable. If that is not also a sin?" he added, addressing his remark to Fra Stanislao.

The old monk had little humor left in him. "You will do yourself and Donna Demetrice a great service if you treat this man with as much circumspection as possible. Fra Sansone was once part of the secular arm of the Church. He still has great capacity for such tasks." By which Fra Stanislao meant that Fra Sansone had been a torturer. "I trust you understand me, Ragoczy."

"I understand," Ragoczy answered grimly.

"In that case, you may leave. We will speak again on the eleventh." Fra Stanislao motioned to his companions.

"And in the meantime? How will I know what has become of Donna Demetrice? How will I know how I must defend myself, if there are accusations laid against me?" His indignation was no longer feigned.

"On the eleventh, Ragoczy," Fra Mario said, enjoying his power over the foreigner. "I fought your uncle once. He wasn't as big a man as you are, but he fought well. It would be a pleasure to compare your abilities."

Ragoczy did not answer this provocation. Instead he looked at Fra Stanislao. "And I suppose I cannot Confess or attend Mass until the eleventh?"

"That is correct," the old Domenicano said, no longer interested in Ragoczy.

"And if I object?" He leaned against the table, putting his weight onto his hands. "Answer me, good Brothers. What if I should object?"

Fra Stanislao met his eye levelly. "Then you will accuse yourself of heresy. And your fate will be the same as that of all heretics. You will die at the stake and your ashes will be scattered to the four winds. Until the eleventh, Signor Ragoczy."

TEXT OF A letter from Pope Alessandro VI to Girolamo Savonarola:

To the irreligious and disobedient excommunicant Girolamo Savonarola in Fiorenza, His Holiness Alessandro VI issues final warnings.

We are distressed to learn that you, in your pride and all-devouring vanity, have chosen to defy the See of San Pietro and Holy Church. Though you are excommunicant, you persist in celebrating Mass and administering the Sacraments, which not only damns you the more, but condemns those who in misguided trust receive these sacred things from your blasphemer's hands.

Therefore, we have begun a Process against you, which will demonstrate that in your continued and unrepentant rebellion against us, you are guilty of the most pernicious heresy, and for that you will suffer the ultimate penalty, both in this world and in the world that is to come.

But God is merciful and is more delighted with the return of the strayed sheep than in the faithful flock. Were it not for this, the Process would be served without warning and without opportunity for you to recant and abjure your impious ways. We would betray the trust of San Pietro if we allowed such a course to be followed. Therefore, you will have one week to repent in public for your disobedience and continued defiance of our Bull and our Interdict. Your repentance must be sincere, your Confession complete and you must publish it abroad for all the world to read. Then you must surrender yourself to the Superior Generale of the Domenicani, and from him learn in which monastery you will serve as immured anchorite.

On this, the feast day of San Tommaso Aquino, you would do well to think of his example and to accept the judgment of the Church. By this act you would spare your congregation much suffering and much

terrible doubt. You will keep them from greater sin,
and for that, much will be forgiven you.

We will learn of your compliance with rejoicing. Or
we will strike you down with the full weight of the
Church Militant and the Will of God.

> *Alessandro VI*
> *Pontifex Maximus*

See of San Pietro
Roma, the feast day of San Tommaso Aquino,
the 8th day of March, 1498

CHAPTER 12

GELATA TOSSED HER head, eager for a gallop. Ragoczy tightened the reins and leaned forward in the saddle. The gloom of the stable was relieved by one candle only and its light revealed Ruggiero's dark-dyed face near the door.

"How long will Fra Sansone sleep?" Ruggiero asked as he prepared to draw back the bolt on the door.

"He should be awake by midmorning, and I will be back long before then. If he gets restless in the night, burn some of those dried leaves I gave you in a little brazier in his chamber. That should be enough to keep him out." He drew his dark cloak more tightly around his shoulders. "I'll leave by la Porta Corsa del Prato. That gate is open all night for the privy workers. I'll come back by another gate." He checked his boot and found the knife there. "I'm ready. Draw back the bolt."

Ruggiero hesitated. "What do I say if you are asked for? One of the Domenicani may call."

"Tell them I am at prayers and cannot be disturbed. And make certain that none of them see that there are cases packed. They'll know we're leaving if they see that."

"Depend on me," Ruggiero said, as he had so many times before.

"With my life, old friend." He moved forward in the saddle as the door swung open and was away into the night before Ruggiero had bolted the stable door again.

Fiorenza was ghostly under the cold stars. Ragoczy rode through the empty streets, listening to the rattle of his mare's hooves as she trotted toward la Porta Corsa del Prato on the west side of the city near the Arno. Once he pulled her to a walk as they passed near Santa Maria Novella, for a few of the monks' cells showed the glow of candles and echoed with the murmur of prayers. The delay was a minor one, and in a few minutes he had passed through la Porta Corsa del Prato, past the privy workers who took the night soil from the city, and was away into the darkness.

It was treacherous to ride at a gallop through the night. Too many dangers attended on it, so Ragoczy held Gelata to a strict trot, while he studied the road for hazards. Once the mare shied at the howl of a dog, and once he thought he heard pursuers and urged her into a gallop. But then they were far into the hills and the old castle was around the next bend. Ragoczy let the mare drop to a walk and he looked about, seeking out a new hiding place for her. At last he dismounted and pulled her into the shelter of a boulder. The distance to the castle was greater than before, but he feared that as the day of the auto-da-fé neared, the vigilance of the Domenicani would increase. He tied Gelata to a thick tree root that was deeply embedded in rock, and then he made his way, secret as a shadow, toward the bulk of the castle.

This time the stones were dry and his desperation gave him speed. In less than a quarter of an hour he was pulling himself over the stone frame of her cell's high window. He dropped swiftly to the floor, calling to Demetrice as he moved toward her. His voice was hardly more than a whisper and he was not entirely surprised that she did not hear him.

She was huddled on her pallet against the wall. Ragoczy dropped to one knee beside her and leaned toward her, touching her shoulder gently to waken her.

With a painful gasp she opened her eyes, eyes that were bruised and puffy, the lids abraded, beneath a badly cut forehead where the blood had only recently dried. "No . . ." she whispered.

Ragoczy's eyes narrowed as fury burned in him. His hands were deliberate in their care, ministering to her terrible bruises and wounds as efficiently as possible. He longed for a candle or a lantern but knew that he courted disaster if there should be light seen in Demetrice's cell. Rage and anguish warred in him every time Demetrice moaned, every time he found a new swelling or cut or burn.

When at last he had done all that he could, he tried again to wake her. The backs of her hands were raw, and so he placed his kisses on her palms, whispering her name again.

This time her lids fluttered and opened as far as the swelling would allow. Her eyes were agonized and bright and she brought up one hand to protect her face. "No more. No more. I said what you wanted. I said it. I said it." Her voice was rising and her body twisted. She smothered a shriek as she cringed away from him.

"Demetrice, no. It's San Germano. Demetrice. Demetrice." He moved nearer, and pain keen as steel stabbed him as she shrank away, horror in her beaten face.

"I'll say it again. I will. Anything. But no more. No more." She started to cry, thin, wailing sobs that were the worse for being quiet. "No more. No more."

"Demetrice," Ragoczy said again, sinking back away from her so that she need not be afraid. "It's San Germano. It's Francesco, amica mia. I've come back, as I said I would."

He hadn't truly expected her to hear him, but she blinked suddenly and then began to weep as a child does, with a kind of determination, and it was a moment before Ragoczy realized it was for relief.

"San German'," she said when her sobs had stopped. Cautiously she extended her hand toward him, saying as sadness thickened her words, "I told them I was a heretic. I said that I had profaned the Cross and mixed the Host with excrement." She shook her head slowly in disbelief. "I had to tell them. They wouldn't have stopped if I hadn't."

He took her hand, being careful not to touch where the skin had been torn away. "It's not important," he said in as reassuring a tone as he could manage. He knew that was true. Her Confession was expected. The auto-da-fé was now less than two days away and Savonarola was eager for victims, for his last gesture of defiance against the authority of Roma and the Pope. He longed to take her in his arms, to cradle her there, protecting her from the hideous sentence that had been passed upon her.

"But I'll burn," she said calmly. "They told me that. I will burn in this world and the next." Her eyes closed in a momentary spasm of distress, but this was quickly mastered and she went on resignedly. "Your petition didn't work. But nothing would have, would it, San Germano?"

"Probably not," he allowed, remembering his interview

at Santa Maria Novella two days before. In the dark he could not see the full effect of the bruises on her face, but he knew they were ghastly from the large areas of darkness on her fair skin.

Her eyes were melancholy. "Well, we've shared love." She was silent a moment, then added, "You know how much it distressed me at first, but I'm sorry now there were so few chances . . ."

Ragoczy's eyes brightened. "There is one last chance."

"Yes. I'm glad of that." She tried to lean back but the stones hurt her and she was forced to sit upright again. "I'm afraid of the flames, San Germano. I wish I had resisted them longer, and died today." Ordinarily such an admission would have revolted her, but after her ordeal all the terror had gone out of suicide. "I'm not a martyr, Francesco," she said, using his name for the first time.

"What?" he said absently as he turned away from his racing thoughts. For a moment he was uncertain as to whether he should tell her what had filled his mind. Then he put such concerns behind him. He moved a little nearer to Demetrice so that she could see his face in the wan square of light from the window. "Demetrice, listen to me. I can't save you from death, not entirely. But there is something I can do. I can give you a kind of . . . deliverance."

She stared at him, bewildered. "Deliverance? How?"

Again he took her hands, and this time she let them lie in his. "Do you remember my warning? That if there was too much love between us you might in time become like me? Do you remember that there is another way to change? If you share blood with me, then your change is assured. Now. Tonight."

"But there is still the stake," she said softly, not daring to hope that he might save her.

"Not if you're already dead. Then they'll take you to be buried away from sacred ground, and the first nightfall after that, you will wake again. Into my life." He was talking quickly now, the words almost running together.

"But how would I die? If they torture me again in the morning, it might happen . . ." There was a sickness in her face that told more than the anguish in her voice how much she dreaded what might happen.

"No. Not that way." He felt the knife in his boot. "I will show you how. Two little cuts, Demetrice mia. Two little cuts and the Domenicani cannot touch you again." He caressed her face with gentle fingers. "Share blood with me, Demetrice. Accept life. Save yourself. Please."

She heard the sincerity in his soft words and though she tried to build disgust in her heart for the thing he suggested, she found it was impossible. Every movement hurt her and tomorrow it would be worse. They had promised her the rack tomorrow, and she had seen for herself what it would do. Suddenly she shuddered and pressed her hands to her face.

"No, Demetrice," Ragoczy pleaded, fearing he had lost her. He was reluctant to reach out to her and possibly give her more pain. There was little more he could say if she refused him. He wished he had told her more gently so that she would not be frightened.

In a low voice she asked, "What do I have to do?"

He breathed deeply, gratefully. "Let me love you as I have before, Demetrice. But this time, you will do as I do. I will make a small cut. You need taste very little. And when that is done, I'll show you how the other . . ." He caught her in his arms and felt his embrace returned. "I must be hurting you," he murmured to her hair.

"It doesn't matter," she told him before she kissed his

mouth. If her wounds were not forgotten, at least they seemed less important. She tore her penitent's robe from neck to hem and pressed his head against her breasts.

His hands were kind and sure, and where they went, his kisses followed, tracing out the loveliness of her, salving her bruises with tenderness, warming her, succoring her. The intensity of his desire was revealed only in the slight tremor of his hands. He spoke softly as he sought out her joy and his beautiful voice was as sweet as the deep strings of a lute. "There was a woman like a star who burned white-hot in the vastness of the sky. Like Venus hung in the sunset she was radiant with splendor that was all her own. When she walked the trees shook for love of her and the humble earth caressed her feet. To lie beside her was to fill your temples with the pulse of the tides which are ever drawn to worship the moon. To savor her lips was to taste eternity and be nourished by it. Who can say all the extent of her glory?"

The wildness of her response surprised Demetrice, for previously she had been accepting, almost passive, waiting for Ragoczy to waken the passion that slumbered in her. But now with his words tolling through her, she reached anxiously for him, yearning for his unendurable sweetness. Her mouth sought his to stop the hymn, then lingered where he had opened his riding mantle.

He made the nick high on his chest, then slipped the knife back into his boot. With urgent open lips he kissed her again, then leaned back. "Come to me, Demetrice. Come to my life."

Before his compelling words her reluctance faded. As her mouth touched the wound he breathed sharply, pleasurably. He drew her nearer and at last she lay atop him, pressing his body with her own, desiring to blend her flesh with his until they became wholly united in rapture.

When at last he moved she accommodated him, exulting as his sharp kisses loosened the last bar against her joy. Nurtured by his love, glorified by his lips, she surrendered the inmost part of herself and was filled with triumph.

She was still trembling with the force of her victory when he spoke to her again. "Demetrice, are you ready?" She heard the question as she sometimes heard thought, in a majestic awesome sound. Without speaking she held out her hands.

"The great women of Roma, when the Caesars ruled there, would have their musicians play to them as they died this way. We have no musicians here, and no perfumed bath. But I will hold you, amica mia, and if you like, I will sing to you." He tried to read her face in the gloom, but could not.

The little knife was cold so he held it to warm it. The cuts were quickly made, two neat incisions slid in under the wrist tendons. After making sure that the arteries were indeed severed, Ragoczy braced himself against the wall and pulled her into his arms, holding her close to him. "You must keep your hands down, amante mia. Press your palms to the floor so that the cuts stay open." His arms tightened and there was a distant look in his eyes. Somewhat later he began very softly to sing, not the melancholy laments of lost love or the soaring lyrics of passion, but Laurenzo's time-haunted praise of fleet, brief youth.

Quant'e bella giovenezza
Che si fugge tuttavia
Chi vuol esser lieto, sia;
Di doman non c'é certezza.

Dreamily Demetrice recognized Laurenzo's words, and she felt a tug at her soul as she remembered the happily sleepless nights in his arms. For a moment the memories were so real that Laurenzo's presence was almost tangible. And then she felt Ragoczy's small hand smooth back her hair, and she wondered at his generosity that gave her not only his love to comfort her, but Laurenzo's as well. She tried to smile, but it was too much effort. Instead, she snuggled closer to his chest and with a contented sigh closed her eyes.

TEXT OF A letter from Febo Janario Anastasio di Benedetto Volandrai to Marsilio Ficino, written December 19, 1497, and delivered on April 19, 1498:

> To his most deeply revered master and teacher, Febo Volandrai sends his respectful greetings from Paris.
>
> This will come to you through the good offices of Rene Benoit Richesse, a fellow student of mine who is journeying to Mantova and Roma to continue his studies. He has agreed to deliver this in exchange for an afternoon in your company, learning from you. I trust that for my honor you will agree.
>
> I have heard only recently of my sister's arrest, and I find myself quite helpless. How did she come to be so accused? I thought that all was well with her and that she was still under the protection of the foreigner. I can only assume that she is still studying alchemy, which I warned her was unwise. Of course, the whole matter is foolish and I am certain that a few questions will have settled the problem long before this reaches you.

But that brings me to the reason for this letter. I need your advice, dear master. I have been uneasy in my mind for some time about my sister's situation there as the housekeeper for the foreigner. She assures me that there is no fleshly dealing in their association, and with the foreigner gone so many years now, I believe that if there was earlier, the passion by now must be over. Yet she continues in his care. It is not good for her to be thus beholden to him. Foreigners are often unaware of the difficulty they impose on others in cases like these, and it is in general preferable that the matter be solved.

My studies are such that I cannot interrupt them just now, but if you think it wise, I will send for my sister and find some appropriate employment for her here in Paris. With the stigma of heretical accusations attached to her reputation, life in Fiorenza may be quite difficult for her. In another six months I will have a break in my studies and then I may journey again to Fiorenza to find Demetrice and bring her away with me.

Of course, if you think it would be possible, it would be more convenient for me if she remained there in Fiorenza, but not, of course, if there is any real danger to her. I trust to you to tell me in what danger she stands and to suggest what solutions will be the best for all concerned.

You realize, I'm certain, that I feel very much in Demetrice's debt. It was she who provided the funds for my continued studies here, and I'm very grateful. But she would be the first to tell you that such hard-won education should not be treated lightly. Remember this when you write to me of her. Most certainly

I'm aware of my obligations to her, but I know she would be greatly disappointed if I despised the sacrifices she has made for me only to rush to Fiorenza to find all this has been a minor disruption or a foolish mistake, long since explained and resolved.

Should her benefactor return to Fiorenza, I urge you to speak to him as my deputy and suggest that he cut his association with her, since it is largely from that association that this current difficulty springs. I am sure you will know how best to say it so that he will understand what is expected of him. It's unfortunate that he had to take her in, for it was inevitable that there would be some trouble arising from that. But vision in retrospect is always so much clearer. Had I realized how very much compromised she was by her situation, I would have insisted that she join me in Wien. But no one told me and I have had little opportunity to consider her particular situation until recently.

I pray you will write to me as soon as is practical for you. Unless there is genuine danger, don't interrupt your work unnecessarily. Demetrice is most competent for a woman and no doubt would resent interference from you or me if she was able to deal with it herself.

With the hope that you are well, my dear master, and that your fears for Fiorenza have proved groundless, I commend myself to you and express in advance my gratitude for your good counsel, and your kindness to my sister.

Febo J. A. di B. Volandrai

In Paris, at the Université
December 10, 1497

CHAPTER 13

IT WAS LATE afternoon before Fra Sansone brought news of
Donna Demetrice's death to Palazzo San Germano. The
large monk was still suspicious about his unnatural sleep the
night before, and he regarded Ragoczy with an unfriendly
eye. "Word has been sent," he said in querulous tones.

"Of what?" Ragoczy asked in a bored voice, though he
hoped it was about Demetrice.

"The heretic woman has revealed herself." Fra Sansone
was satisfied with the news. "She has committed the ultimate
sin and taken her own life, confirming her Confession."

Ragoczy turned away from his table where he was measuring out spices into the balance of one of his brass scales,
a look of mild irritation clouding his features. "What do you
mean?"

Fra Sansone was delighted at the question. "I mean, foreigner, that the woman you were so determined to save has
shown herself to be a heretic and rather than face the puri-
fying flames has taken her own life in the night."

Though it was difficult, Ragoczy forced himself to react
slowly. "That's impossible," he said, irritated. "My uncle assured me she is . . . was someone who lived by Christian
principles. You Domenicani might have killed her through
torture, but it's ridiculous to say that she committed suicide." He finished measuring the spices and tipped the fragrant powder into a small box, turning his attention to the
next container. "Who told you this?"

Irritation was getting the better of Fra Sansone, and because of it he revealed more than he had intended. "I had it
from Fra Stanislao himself, not an hour ago. The woman

was to have recounted her heretical acts today, but when the guards came to her cell less than an hour after sunrise, she was already cold. Her wrists had been cut and there were mysterious marks all over her body."

Ragoczy remembered the marks, and knew there was nothing mysterious about them. "Indeed?" he said.

"Yes. She and three others died last night, but she was the only one to abandon Christ and take her own life. The others proved their innocence in succumbing to the Question. They will be given Christian burial after the auto-da-fé. But she is another matter." Fra Sansone lifted his hands and folded them piously. "She will be thrown into a pauper's grave at the crossroads."

"Perhaps the good Domenicani will allow me to see to her burial," Ragoczy suggested with just enough uncertainty to satisfy Fra Sansone. "My uncle enjoined me to see that she is cared for. I cannot let her be so wholly abandoned."

"She was a heretic," Fra Sansone reminded him, glaring.

"She was also my uncle's housekeeper," Ragoczy said firmly and at last turned away from weighing spices. "Where is she?"

This was not precisely what Fra Sansone had hoped for, but he grudgingly answered the question. "She will be brought to San Marco after sunset. If you go there, you may be able to arrange to see to her burial." His face set into unattractive lines. "But it may not be possible. They may insist that she be buried as the heretic she was. Ask anything you want, however." His expression was most unpleasant now. He glanced around the weighing room, at the shelves filled with various instruments of measurement. "Vanities," he proclaimed.

"How can you say that?" Ragoczy asked, determined to maintain his pose. "These are all used often, and it is not a sin that besides being functional, they are beautiful." He put his hand on the spice chest, a piece of heavily carved furniture with fifty little drawers in its front. "Any stout wooden box will hold spices and any well-made chest may be fitted for drawers, but would you not prefer this to mere pieces of wood made into a box, with no thought to the grain and the color?"

Fra Sansone scoffed as his hands at his sides twisted at the remembered pleasure of breaking things. "If your soul is worth two pieces of fitted wood, what is it to me?"

"The Cross, I believe, was made with two pieces of fitted wood. Certainly an excellent example." His tone was absent, for he once again busied himself with measuring spices. Though he could hear Fra Sansone's anger in his breathing, he paid no attention as he carefully drew open the little drawer filled with cinnamon. Before he began to spoon out the powdered spice, he said, "If you have anything more to say, please say it now. If not, leave me, and be sure that you close the door tightly. Otherwise, the wind may scatter the powder. And spices, you know, are almost as costly as gold."

"I will leave you," Fra Sansone said between his teeth.

"Thank you. Oh, and if you see Ferrugio, send him to me, will you?" The angle of his head and the slight condescension in his voice were masterpieces of arrogance, and they produced the expected results: Fra Sansone muttered a response and rushed out of the room, slamming the door forcefully behind him.

When Ruggiero came to the measuring room somewhat later, his worried face told Ragoczy that he already knew of Demetrice's death. "You were too late?" he asked softly.

"No. The Domenicani were." He half-sat on the edge of the table, one leg dangling negligently, his high red boot catching the light as his foot swung. "They're bringing her here, to San Marco. I'll go there after sunset and claim the body. We can lay her in her native earth—and I trust you have it?—tonight and she will be ready to leave with us in the morning. If we go before the auto-da-fé, we'll have many leagues between us before anyone knows we've left."

Ruggiero nodded. "I have the earth. Not very much, but I ordered the alchemist in Rimini to send more to Venezia, and I've dispatched instructions to Gian-Carlo."

They spoke in that strange tongue that was Ragoczy's native language. "Is this precaution necessary?" Ragoczy asked, amused.

Ruggiero shrugged. "I saw Fra Sansone in the gallery as I came up the stairs."

"It's wisest, then." He chuckled, picturing the frustration of the listening monk. "Where have you put the earth? And how much is there?"

"At the moment there are two sacks of it in the stable." He paused and went on somewhat awkwardly. "Are you certain that she will make the change? You've only been with her three times. It might not be enough." Ruggiero's passive face was at variance with the worry in his voice. "I admire her. I wouldn't like to lose her."

"It is enough," Ragoczy said shortly. "We shared blood."

This sufficiently startled Ruggiero that he raised his brows and let out a low whistle. "You told me you doubted she'd be willing."

"And I was. But they tortured her yesterday—pardon, that's incorrect. They only Questioned her, because her skin was not deliberately broken. They were going to do more today. By comparison, vampirism was welcome." An old, old bitterness hardened his voice. "After we shared blood, she let me cut her wrists and the thing was assured."

Ruggiero nodded, and said with a little difficulty, "Do you think she'll mind?"

He had voiced a fear that had been haunting Ragoczy since the night before. "I don't know. I wish there were a way to have her released, alive. If I could have had her case delayed long enough to stop Savonarola, it would have been another matter. She would have had a choice then. As it is, she's not used to the idea. She accepted me because the alternative was death by torture. Not a very flattering thought, is it?" He shook off his mood. "Well, we won't know until late tonight. If she is truly angry, I'll have to arrange for her to go elsewhere until she understands."

"I will talk to her," Ruggiero said as he went to the door. "I'll wait for you at the courtyard gate when you bring her. That way, Fra Sansone won't have to be distressed by her." Suddenly he pulled the door open and Fra Sansone stepped back guiltily.

"I have instructions," he said, and glared into the measuring room.

"So you have," Ruggiero agreed. "By all means tell your superiors every word that passed between Ferrugio and me." He smiled sweetly and strode across the room. "It's growing late. I'll leave for San Marco shortly." For the benefit of Fra Sansone he added, "I trust you'll have everything in readiness to receive the body."

Ruggiero bowed slightly, his houseman's gown whispering as it brushed the floor.

San Marco shone in the dusk, every window alight, and the brightness spilling out onto the street and the buildings around it, filling Piazza San Marco with a square of brilliance that spilled from the open door of the church.

Ragoczy entered by that door, his silken sleeved tunic throwing back the scintillating lights from hundreds of tiny, polished diamonds worked into the neck and shoulder of the fine white brocade that was further decorated with black piping at the high neck, down the front closing, and at the hem and wrists. White boots reached almost to his knees and the black heels were studded with polished gems. A short white cape hung over one shoulder and was held across the chest with braided cords of black silk. His white cap made his dark hair even darker and set off his dark eyes.

One of the Domenicani who bustled through the church, preparing for the great event that was to come in the morning, saw him and stopped his errand to ask, "You are the foreigner, aren't you?"

"I am. I wonder if you will be kind enough to direct me to whoever is empowered to release bodies?" He spoke respectfully and with a becoming deference to the monk.

"What body?" Belatedly he rolled up two of the parchments he held and tucked them under his arm.

"I understood from Fra Sansone that the bodies of the condemned heretics were to be brought here. Since one was the servant of my uncle, I feel it my duty to give her proper burial, even though she may not lie in hallowed ground." He leaned toward the monk and added, "I know the request is irregular. But I have obligations."

"Of course, of course," the monk said nervously and fingered the parchments under his arm. "That would be Fra Cataline. He's on the south side of the church. There's a little room there, near the side door . . ." He glanced nervously around. "That's Fra Cataline."

"Thank you, good Brother," Ragoczy said, wishing he had had a chance to see what was written on the parchments. He turned and crossed the church, pausing only long enough to genuflect before the altar.

A number of monks waited outside the little room near the south door of the church. Ragoczy moved up to them and asked if there was some problem. No one answered him.

He decided to get attention. "Where is Fra Cataline? I must see him. It's urgent." His voice was loud enough to be heard throughout the church. He had a thick accent so that his very foreignness would force response from those around him.

Almost at once a man of late middle age in a Domenican habit burst out of the little room. His expression was harassed as he glared at the monks. "I've told you that you can take no one until I finish the certificates!"

"A thousand pardons, good Brother. But it was I who called you." Ragoczy shouldered his way through the monks and regarded Fra Cataline evenly.

Fra Cataline regarded the glittering stranger with curiosity. "And who are you?"

"Germain Ragoczy," he replied, bending the full force of his compelling eyes on Fra Cataline. "I have come to claim the body of Demetrice Volandrai. She died last night, while in your care."

"Claim her?" Fra Cataline said with an exasperated gesture. "You must do that after the burning."

"What?" Ragoczy resisted the impulse to grab the monk and shake him. "Why not now? Surely there's no purpose in keeping her here longer."

Fra Cataline gave an exaggerated sigh. "Of course not. The bodies aren't here, any of them. They were earlier."

"Then where are they?" His voice was low and his manner respectful, but Fra Cataline quailed before him. The other monks, seeing their fellow's barely concealed terror, stepped back and crossed themselves, taking covert glances at the foreigner in white.

"At . . . at la Piazza della Signoria," Fra Cataline stammered, then turned away from Ragoczy's eyes. "The prior, the blessed Savonarola, has given orders . . . that all who have died unrepentant be burned with the other heretics."

Ragoczy's eyes closed. Anger, pain and despair coursed through him and for an instant he felt a fierce desire to rend and maim every Domenicano monk in all of Fiorenza.

This passed and was replaced by determination that was fed by his sense of impending loss.

"Signor stragnero . . ." Fra Cataline said uncertainly, "you may have the ashes. Our prior won't forbid that."

Abruptly Ragoczy swung around on his heel and as the monks parted before him, his swift strides took him from the church. His thoughts raced before him, and by the time he arrived back at Palazzo San Germano he had his instructions ready for Ruggiero.

"But what if it isn't possible?" his manservant asked when he had heard the new instructions.

Ragoczy shook his head, and his dark eyes were sad. "Then, my friend, leave Fiorenza instantly. Make sure the Botticellis are carried on my mare. She's fast and her gaits are even."

"And you?" He knew the answer, but fear drove him to ask.

"It will be too late for me, Ruggiero. If I fail to save Demetrice, I'll be dead. Truly dead."

T EXT OF A letter from Suor Merzede, Superiora of the Celestiana convent, Sacro Infante, to Girolamo Savonarola, prior of San Marco:

With a humble heart, the Superiora of Sacro Infante sends her greetings to the blessed Girolamo Savonarola, prior of San Marco, in Fiorenza.

Though I have no wish to distress you, or bring difficulties upon you, good Prior, I must write to you before the matter is out of hand. You have proclaimed that tomorrow there is to be a great auto-da-fé wherein many heretics will be burned to the glory of God and the salvation of Fiorenza. You have further ordered that Suor Estasia del Mistero degli Angeli be there to tell of her visions and to sing her hymns.

Good prior, most earnestly I beg you to reconsider. I realize you think that I am jealous of Suor Estasia, and certainly her particular abilities have brought her a great deal of attention, and have much influenced the life of all of us at Sacro Infante. But I did not become a nun to receive praise, but so my life might be of service to God. I am grateful that our convent has become well-known, for it is in this way we are granted the opportunity to do good in the world.

Good prior Savonarola, I must warn you that Suor Estasia is not well. She has been fasting most rigorously for the last month and it has made her weak. But more than that, she is filled with strange apprehensions. She herself has said that never has she experienced such sensations, and though they are for her most rewarding, as they increase in severity they make her behave strangely. Last night she opened her habit and scourged herself unmercifully and in a way that I cannot in modesty describe. She said that such chastisement purged all the devils of the flesh, but there was a fever in her eyes as she said that.

I greatly fear that if you bring her to Fiorenza now and expose her to all the heady excitement that must attend such an occasion, Suor Estasia will be cast into such a state that she may do herself or others some hurt. Being inspired by the Holy Spirit, she does not always remember the limitations of her human body and therefore is vulnerable to many things.

You may recall some of the excesses she committed before she was redeemed to God through her Confession to you, and subsequent absolution. Her soul is still volatile and for that reason the light of piety burns in her more brightly than in many of us. Pray for her, but do not, I ask you, expose her to such an experience. Only last week her cousin Sandro Filipepi visited her, and he himself expressed concern for her. You know that someone as devout in the exercise of his faith as is Filipepi would not worry capriciously.

Surely the heretics will burn equally well whether Suor Estasia is there or not. And surely Fiorenza will derive as much benefit from the auto-da-fé with Suor Estasia here, in prayer, as it would if Suor Estasia addressed them herself from those wooden platforms that have been constructed for the burning.

It is not too late. I will await an answer to this tonight. I will keep the vigil with Suor Estasia. Already she lies in the chapel, her face pressed against the stones, her arms out to the side in imitation of Our Dear Lord. She has hardly moved for more than an hour but she has declared that her devotion must be perfect, and she must be wholly consumed in the radiance of God. She has her scourge with her, the one you presented to her, the one with metal hooks on the seven lashes.

*Good prior, I fear for her. I fear what she might do.
Let her remain here where she may be protected and
looked after by her Sisters, who love and revere her.
Her faith is strong but flesh is fragile. Do not test her beyond her endurance. God cannot want that of her, and if
you ask it, you do her a terrible disservice. Her reverence for you is such that if she were a woman living in
the world, I would say that you had become the God
of her idolatry and that her devotion bordered on the
blasphemous.*

*Consider well, good prior, and do not endanger
one who is as selfless in her zeal as Suor Estasia. I
will await your answer while I keep the night vigil
with Suor Estasia. If at dawn you have sent no answer,
I will most reluctantly send her to you, as you have
commanded me to do.*

*In all things, I am most obedient to you after my
obedience to God and my Order.*

> *Suor Merzede*
> *Superiora of Sacro Infante-*
> *Celestiane Sisters*

Sacro Infante, near Fiorenza,
9th day of March,1498

CHAPTER 14

THE FIRST LIGHT of dawn lay like a stain along the hills east
of Fiorenza. The streets were still dark but the red roofs had
taken on a subtle glow, as if they smoldered. Above the river

a low, wraithlike mist hung, waiting to creep away at the touch of the morning. Birdcalls had just begun, anticipating the church bells.

But this morning Fiorenza was already awake. Around la Piazza della Signoria the people were gathering as they had gathered to watch the burning of Vanities. Today it was another burning, this time of heretics, and though some of the citizens shook their heads sadly, thinking it a scandalous day, that Fiorenza was as dangerous as Spain, more of the citizens reprimanded them for the weakness of their faith and assured their faltering fellows that there was as much good in burning heretics as there was in burning Vanities.

The Militia Christi was busy in la piazza, building up the faggots around the stakes which were set up on wooden platforms; as the fires took hold, the floors of the platforms would collapse and would, in effect, bury the wretched heretics in flame. There were nine such platforms, and a tenth structure along the front of il Palazzo della Signoria waited for Savonarola to harangue the condemned one last time before the fires were kindled. Builders inspected the platforms, searching for flaws and imperfections.

As the morning bells began to ring over Fiorenza, a group of monks approached la piazza. Most of the monks carried one end or the other of a hurdle on which were tied those destined for the stake. Seven of the heretics gazed unbelievingly at the city around them. Their eyes were red and blurred with suffering. Under their penitent's robes their abused bodies were matted with blood and filth. The remaining two heretics were naked, one man and one woman. The man had succumbed to the torture of the boot, and the legs which dangled on either side of the hurdle were nothing more than distorted sacks of crushed bone in swollen flesh. The other was Demetrice, her flesh eerily pale so that even the hideous bruises were dimmed by her loss of blood. One concession had been made: she was tied facedown on the hurdle so that she would not be wholly exposed to the inquisitive eyes of the crowd.

A murmur of interest filled the waiting people. They were not too great a number yet, not more than two or three thousand. These were the fascinated, the angry, the eager. They pressed forward to watch as the heretics were moved from their hurdle to the platforms and secured there in chains. It was a slow process, and by the time the task was complete, the sun was just lifting over the eastern horizon, sending long streamers of golden light down the mountains and into Fiorenza. The mist over the river was beginning to dissipate.

From the western quarter of town, the Domenicani of Santa Maria Novella came in procession, and with full deliberation they stopped before each of the nine platforms while Fra Stanislao pronounced anathema on the heretics.

The crowd was more restless now, and rapidly growing in numbers. The Militia Christi left the platforms and set to work policing the limits of the crowd, making sure that the citizens would be far enough away from the fires to keep from being singed by the terrible heat. The citizens grumbled at this treatment, but complied.

At last Savonarola arrived, and after a few words with Fra Stanislao and Ezechiele Aureliano, he mounted the long platform by il palazzo and looked over the crowd. He felt a surge of satisfaction at the sight. In spite of everything, he had at last humbled Fiorenza and saved her. Neither the power of the Medicis nor the power of the Pope had been sufficient to stay his crusade against sins. Glowing with an emotion which he did not know was pride, he stepped forward, raising his skinny arms to heaven.

The crowd slowly fell silent, and some of their number

dropped to their knees to pray. The rising sun touched la Piazza della Signoria at last, shedding impartial splendor on heretic and citizen alike.

"Fiorenzeni!" Savonarola shouted out suddenly. "Behold your triumph! This day, at last, the ungodly are cast out!" His voice was harsh and it echoed down the narrow streets and over the waiting people. He waited while the susurrus of voices faded before going on, savoring the moment. "See here? See what becomes of those who will not put their trust in God!" He pointed at the figures chained to stakes, surrounded by waiting faggots.

Ragoczy moved through the crowd, his magnificent white clothes and foreign grandeur making him a path. He stayed away from the front ranks of people, not willing to expose himself until the last possible instant. Demetrice was badly placed, being on one of the inner platforms. That would mean carrying her body through the exiguous gap between two other pyres, which by then would be burning. His eyes narrowed as he calculated the best route. There was only one way that would be safe, and it would mean crossing Savonarola's platform and going east, toward the familiar bulk of Santa Croce.

There was another disruption as the ox cart from Sacro Infante forced its way through the crowd and stopped near Savonarola's platform. Five of the white-habited nuns got out, one of them wearing a deep frown. The crowd hissed and rustled in anticipation, for one of the nuns was Suor Estasia del Mistero degli Angeli.

Suor Merzede pulled at Suor Estasia's arm as they neared the platform. "You don't have to do this, my Sister. If you are too distressed, I will take you home."

Suor Estasia turned dreamy hazel eyes on her Superiora. "I am fine, Suor Merzede. Truly I am. I feel my soul yearning for glory. God will enter me today, He will inspire me, giving me fulfillment I have never experienced." Fasting had made her painfully thin and her smile was a skull's grimace. She lifted her rosary and kissed the crucifix. "It will be glorious today, Suor Merzede."

Savonarola had seen the arrival of the party from Sacro Infante and smiled sourly. He motioned to Suor Estasia del Mistero degli Angeli to mount the platform with him. Then he turned back to the crowd. "Today, good Fiorenzeni, we celebrate the Feast of the Forty Martyrs. Today our thoughts must be on those valiant Roman soldiers, who, for their faith and the Love of God, died on the ice while their heathen leaders tempted them to recant with fires. Think of those men, bound together, naked, the lake around them, the night blowing with snow and their comrades in arms watching with fear. Think of them standing in that freezing night, on the ice-covered lake. Think of how their flesh was hurt, and then was numb as God released them and welcomed them to His triumph."

Suor Estasia knelt beside him and bent to kiss his feet. "I am come, dear master. You have called me and I am here." She looked up into his eyes and crossed herself, her face as rapt as if she saw God Himself.

For a moment Savonarola turned his attention away from the crowd and looked down at Suor Estasia. He made the sign of the Cross over her, then shot an angry glance at Suor Merzede, who stood at the other end of the platform. Their eyes locked; then Savonarola turned back to the crowd.

"Think, now, of these loathsome heretics!" He held his arms up to the pitiful figures chained to stakes. "Think of their atrocious sins! Think of how they are like the fires that tempted the Forty Martyrs, and how their temptations will shortly consume them."

Ragoczy was closer to Savonarola's platform now, but still far enough away not to attract the monk's attention. He touched one man on the shoulder and moved nearer the front of the gathered crowd.

One of the heretics, a man with dislocated shoulders, turned his pain-crazed eyes toward Savonarola and in a cracked voice shouted, "You're the temptation! You're the heretic! You're excommunicated! You have no authority to do this!" He stopped, coughed up blood and slumped in his chains.

A young man in the drab guarnacca of the Militia Christi climbed onto that heretic's platform and gave him a blow in the face with a short cudgel. This was greeted with cheers and he jumped down grinning.

At the far end of la piazza, where the sunlight gave a golden glow in the walls, Ezechiele Aureliano stood with two other members of the Militia Christi. Beside them were short torches, the heads covered with rags stiff with pitch. Next to them stood a brazier in which a charcoal fire burned. Aureliano reached for one of the torches and thrust it into the brazier. In a moment it flared to life and he held it up, wishing that it would shine more brightly against the sunlight.

On the platform Suor Estasia began to sway rhythmically, making a strange, low moaning in her throat as she moved. Her eyes were rolled back in her head and the lids only half-closed over them. The crowd began to take up her swaying, all of them intent on her. She stood up suddenly, nearly falling over with the violence of her motion. Her arms extended, her bandaged hands giving her the look of a large white bird about to fly. When her breath came through her teeth in sharp gasps she lifted her arms higher, crying out incoherently. Then she shouted, "O God! O God! Why won't You speak to me?"

Savonarola and Suor Merzede exchanged glances, his worried, hers significant. He started toward Suor Estasia, but by then the visionary nun was speaking again.

"Is it that so much sin is here, that You remain hidden from me? You are like light beyond a cloud. Shine forth! Shine that we may be guided by Your light to the Mercy Seat!"

The crowd groaned in sympathy with Suor Estasia. There were strangled sobs now from some who watched, and the murmur of prayers was stronger, a countermelody to the words from the platform.

"Do not desert us! See, we offer You these creatures, heretics all, and purge ourselves at the same time we give them to You in sacrifice for the expiation of our sins!" Suor Estasia dropped to her knees once more, sobbing hysterically.

Savonarola knew the moment. He shouted out to Ezechiele Aureliano, "It is time!"

Aureliano grinned broadly and handed the lighted torch to the nearest member of the Militia Christi. "The wind is from the south. Start in the north. Otherwise you'll work in smoke."

The outbreak of shoutings, of wailings and prayers, was unbelievable. The cacophony drowned out the rush of flames as the torches were thrust in among the faggots at the foot of each stake.

Ragoczy moved quickly. Taking advantage of the confusion, he pushed through the crowd and broke out into la piazza. The light of the fires caught the diamonds on his white silk tunic and for a moment they blazed red as rubies. He glanced quickly around him, and then rushed toward the stakes in the center of the platforms.

There was a cry from one of the Militia Christi, but the noise of the crowd was too great. Only one man heard the shout, one of the builders who had made the stakes and platforms and stood as near as he dared, watching the pyres flare into life. He saw where the young man had pointed, and he ran toward the white-clad stranger.

Ragoczy was almost between the first stakes when the builder's hand closed on his shoulder. At another time caution would have stopped Ragoczy before he used his remarkable strength while so many could see, but seconds were too precious for this circumspection. He reached back for the hand that held him, and with a sudden jerk flung the man into the air and over him. The builder crashed to the ground and shouted as his hands touched burning wood. He rolled away, then reached for the leg of the stranger. The black-heeled boot came down full force on his hand and the builder screamed. He was still screaming when two small hands fastened on his arms and lifted him to his feet. Dark, penetrating eyes glared into his, and in that moment before he was thrust back into the flames greedily consuming the nearest heap of faggots, Lodovico recognized the foreigner. "You're *Francesco* Ragoczy," he said in wonder before the searing pain claimed him.

Although the fight with Lodovico had taken little more than a minute, it was enough time for two youths in the guarnacca of the Militia Christi to run into the center of the stakes, six of which were now burning. One held a short sword and the other a torch, and both were determined to drive him into the flames.

Ragoczy stepped back, but only to get more room. When he had distance enough he came out of his crouch, kicking upward at the young man holding the torch. His foot caught the other's jaw, snapping his head back and tossing him half his body length, to land against one of the unlighted pyres.

The other young man took a wild swing with the short sword, but instead of moving aside, Ragoczy let the sword pass him, then stepped squarely up to the young man and forced his arm back even farther than his slice could carry it. Slowly, inexorably his arm was borne back until there was a terrible grating snap and the arm hung down, the bone splintered at the shoulder.

Now all the pyres were blazing and Ragoczy could feel the heat pull at him, insinuating itself around him, anxious to feed on his clothes and his body.

A great cloud of dark, greasy smoke rolled skyward, and the brightness of the dawn was dimmed by it. The rush and cackle of the fires masked the screams of those they consumed.

Ragoczy ran the few steps that separated him from Demetrice's stake, and then leaped upward to land on the platform beside her. He saw that the ends of her hair were beginning to burn and he pulled a knife from his boot, gathered her hair at the nape of the neck and swiftly cut it away. Her chains were terribly hot, but he took them and pulled at them until they broke.

In the crowd there were shouts now as the wind blew the smoke away. People pointed, shrieked, screamed as the foreigner lifted the naked body of Demetrice Volandrai free of the chains and the stake.

On his platform Savonarola heard the new, strange commotion, and fear stabbed at him. He could not see through the smoke to the various pyres, but he knew something was going wrong. Quickly he ran to the end of the platform where Suor Merzede stood in furious silence. He glared at her, as if accusing her of this disruption. "What is happening?" he demanded.

"I cannot see, good prior. I don't know." The nun's face, framed by her white coif and gorget, seemed unreal but her hostility burned as hot as the flames at the stakes.

With an impatient oath, Savonarola moved away from her and tried again, futilely, to see through the smoke. This was impossible, and so he motioned for one of the Militia Christi, but the smoke hid them as well, and shouts were useless over the deafening noise of the crowd, the fires, the dying heretics.

It was no easy thing to balance Demetrice over his shoulder, but Ragoczy managed it. He could smell burning flesh and the sweaty stench of the crowd. His feet were getting hot, and he knew if he were to keep his protective earth in his boots, he must get away from the flames immediately. One last adjustment of Demetrice's weight and he jumped from the pyre onto the flagging of la Piazza della Signoria.

Landing between the fiercely burning pyres was hellish, and Ragoczy forced himself not to look at the holocaust around him. There was one break in the flames, and one break only. It led to Savonarola's platform, where Suor Estasia stood, her hands extended toward the flames as if in benediction.

Savonarola was still at the other end of the platform when a hideous apparition appeared out of the roiling smoke in front of Suor Estasia. It took him a moment to realize that what he thought was a visitation of demons was in reality a man in blemished white carrying a body across his shoulder. He started toward them, and froze as Suor Estasia screamed, a long, shuddering sound that cut through the rush of the fires and the sound of the crowd.

Ragoczy had just gained the platform as he saw Suor Estasia. He saw the recognition in her eyes and for a moment could not move. He held Demetrice's body more firmly and met Estasia's tormented hazel eyes. "Estasia," he said as gently as he could.

"Francesco." She reached out her covered hands to him, seeing him as she saw her visions. "Is it me you carry? Where do you take me?"

Ragoczy swallowed once, and searched for an escape. With his free hand, he touched Estasia's half-open lips. "Don't betray me, diletto mio. Don't. Prego."

She stared at him, at the whiteness of his clothes, not seeing the soot that clung to them, watching the fire flash in the diamonds on his chest. "No," she whispered as she touched her lips where his fingers had been.

He nodded, and turned, moving toward the end of the platform away from Savonarola.

Estasia watched him, the same somnambulistic glaze to her eyes that she sometimes wore in trances. "No," she repeated to herself. "I won't betray you." Slowly, methodically she began to tear at her habit, first pulling off the coif so that her close-clipped chestnut hair came into view. "Won't betray you," she repeated as she ripped the wrappings off her hands with her teeth.

At the far end of the platform, Savonarola watched with horror as Suor Estasia pulled away her garments. Behind him Suor Merzede began a steady, anguished weeping.

Many in the crowd saw Suor Estasia as she gradually shed her garments, and they watched in fascination as the nun stepped along the platform, her hands moving over her emaciated body. Her face was transfixed as she prayed. "O God, Who sent me this messenger to show me Your love, forgive me. I was blind to Your caresses." She lifted her shrunken breasts and massaged the nipples. "See how my flesh warms to You. O God, possess me! I am Your hand-maiden, I long for Your embraces, I offer my body to Your pleasure, to Your delight."

Savonarola started toward her, and she reached for him, drawing him against her side, which was still welted with angry red from the use of her scourge. Languidly she kissed his mouth as her hand pressed at his habit, seeking his gen-itals. The Domenican prior of San Marco yelled and struck out blindly with both hands, then ran back toward Suor Merzede, his face filled with revulsion.

The fires were burning fiercely and Suor Estasia smiled at the raging pyres. Slowly, deliberately she climbed down from the platform as Francesco Ragoczy had shortly before. She looked at the furnace that the stakes had become and she looked at the crowd that watched her with awe-stricken eyes. She began to sing.

Ragoczy was almost through the crowd when three Domenicani Brothers started in pursuit of him. The press of people made it hard for them to reach him, but they slowed his escape as well. Carefully he moved Demetrice so that she was better-balanced, then he began to look for a weapon other than the knife in his boot.

The first Domenicano to reach him was easily dealt with. The monk was older and unhealthily stout. Ragoczy's arm delivered at full force across his belly sent him to his knees at once. The second and third were another matter. Ragoczy forced himself through the crowd as the Domenicani got nearer.

The fire boomed with fury as Suor Estasia stood before it, her face alight with love. "Behold me, God, how I long for you." She pressed her hands between her thighs, throw-ing her head back as her first spasm shook her. "Your love, God, Your all-consuming love." She stretched her hands forward into the fire, laughing delight as the skin blistered and blackened. "Let me be part of You!" she cried. "O God, my lover, my spouse, my savior and redeemer! Nothing but You! Ravish me! Destroy me!"

There was a horrified silence in the crowd now, and everyone who could see strained to watch as Suor Estasia del Mistero degli Angeli walked, burning, into the fire.

TEXT OF TESTIMONY written by the prior of Santa Croce, Orlando Ricci, presented as part of the Process against the excommunicant Domenicano Giroloma Savonarola:

> To His Holiness Pope Alessandro VI, Pontifex Maximus, Fra Orlando Ricci of Santa Croce in Fiorenza commends himself and in dutiful compliance to His Holiness's instructions, gives account of that terrible day, March 10 of this year, wherein the perfidious heretic Girolamo Savonarola caused to be burned eight men and women of Fiorenza on the false charges of heresy, which said burning resulted incidentally in five additional deaths: those of Suor Estasia del Mistero degli Angeli, a builder called Lodovico da Roncale, two young men of the Militia Christi (which unjust and tyrannous organization of Fiorenzeni youths the said Savonarola employed to carry out his illegal schemes) and a young woman who in her effort to save her father who was one of the martyred souls, rushed into the fire and died.
>
> Many of those who stood by were burned. Some had great blisters, some had hair and eyebrows singed

away. There was much catastrophic confusion and it seemed for a time that the whole city must burn, for there were none to bring water, though the Arno is only a few steps away from la Piazza della Signoria.

Before these terrible fires were lit, the said Savonarola exhorted the people to approve the acts, declared that they were pleasing to God and that as such would redeem the city from sin. Now, this is proof of Pride, of infamous Vanity, of the most gross blasphemy, for an excommunicant is without the access to God, and being denied the sacraments is in a state of mortal sin.

The activities of this said Savonarola have been disastrous to Fiorenza for other reasons as well. Good men have been driven away from us because of his accusations and activities. Many of the scholars who were wont to live and teach in Fiorenza have fled in fear for their lives. Artists of great repute who with their work have adorned all Roma as well as Fiorenza are no longer willing to paint here, since their work is judged by the severe and unreasonable standards of the San Marco Domenicani. Musicians cannot work, for music is forbidden most days. Mercers, seamers, and other merchants have not been able to sell their wares, for they have been forbidden to make or purchase such textiles as are deemed vain by Savonarola. As most of Fiorenza lives by the loom, such edicts condemn the people to hunger and poverty. Foreigners, who previously flocked here to learn of us, now are afraid to come within our walls because they might be accused of heresy on the weight of being foreign alone.

Good, Holy Father, the evil of the said Savonarola is an offense to God and the Church. The stench of him reaches even to Heaven, where Angels vomit from it. For the sake of our religion, for the sake of peace, for the sake of Fiorenza, condemn this mad excommunicant priest as he condemned so many others. He is a rabid dog, infecting all he bites.

This I swear is true, and by my vows as a Francescano, I pray God that I be cast out and damned for eternity if I have said anything that was not accurate and honest. I cannot say that I am without malice, for I hold much against the creature who has caused Fiorenza so much suffering. I pray God that He will lift this burden from my heart so that I may forgive this heinous enemy of mankind as Our Lord forgave those who brought Him to shameful death.

Orlando Ricci
Prior of Santa Croce
Francescano

In Fiorenza, March 12, 1498

Chapter 15

RUGGIERO HELD THE bay gelding's head as Ragoczy tied the large bundle to the saddle. "Are you sure she's secure? It might be dangerous once we start to move."

"It will hold," Ragoczy said, giving the straps an experimental tug. "Where do we change horses?"

"There is a place on the road to Bologna. They raise race-horses there. I have purchased four for our use."

"Good." Ragoczy looked back over his shoulder to the thick black cloud hanging over la Piazza della Signoria. "We must leave soon. The worst of it is almost over, and one of those Domenicani I fought with is sure to be coming around." He brushed the soot and cinders off his white silk. "What about Fra Sansone?"

Ruggiero almost smiled. "He had the misfortune to lock himself into one of the cellars. An odd mistake, but he was not aware of the danger."

Ragoczy's fine brows raised. "You must tell me some-time how you managed that." He went to the packhorse and pulled at the straps. "The paintings?"

"They're there. Under the sacks."

"Excellent." He reached for Gelata's bridle but paused one more time to touch the shapeless bundle that held De-metrice. "I hope there's enough earth. She must wake tonight if we're to get to Bologna in the appointed time." This required no comment and got none. "It can't be helped," Ragoczy said quietly. A moment later he had vaulted into the saddle and was pulling Gelata's head around. He took a last look at the courtyard of Palazzo San Germano. "I will miss this house. I will miss Fiorenza." Then, without another word, he dug his jeweled heels into Gelata's side and rode out of the iron gates. Ruggiero fol-lowed immediately, leading the two other horses. The gate to Palazzo San Germano was left open, for it was empty but for crates that would soon be gone as well.

Passage through the streets was easy. No one had left the auto-da-fé yet and there were few strangers entering Fiorenza these days. Ragoczy made for la Porta Santa Croce, glancing occasionally toward the stern tower of il

Palazzo della Signoria, where an iron lion clung to the pole that topped it.

The two lancers on guard at the gate were more interested in the chaos around la Piazza della Signoria, and aside from an inquisitive look at the two packhorses, made no attempt to stop Ragoczy and Ruggiero as they rode out of Fiorenza. But neither of them took comfort from this. They had at the most an hour before they were pursued. Savonarola had been cheated, and he would not be satisfied until punishment had been meted out.

The road into the hills was filled with the awakening splendor of early spring. Freshets ran beside the track and new flowers rose from the earth. The scent was almost clean enough to take away the ghastly odor of roasting flesh that still filled Ragoczy with disgust.

At the top of the second rise, Ragoczy called a halt and looked back toward Fiorenza. Most of the smoke over la Piazza della Signoria was drifting away. The fires at last were dying. At this distance the city seemed unreal, a kind of toy, and the Arno a strip of silver laid through it to give it worth. The pale walls of the houses and their red roofs reminded him of pictures he had seen long ago in Greece. As he watched, he saw a line of tiny horsemen leave the Santa Croce gate in double file. The sun winked on their metal breastplates.

"Lanzi," Ragoczy said, pointing.

"How far behind us?" Ruggiero was nervous.

"Not quite an hour. If we didn't have the other horses and the burdens they carry, it would be time enough. But as it is, I don't know."

"Shall we look for a place to hide?" Ruggiero suggested, not very hopefully.

"And be trapped?" Ragoczy frowned. "I wish there was

another road through the mountains. It's too dangerous to strike out on our own." He turned in the saddle. "There's nothing for it. We'll have to outrun them. How long until we get to the first change of horses?"

Ruggiero looked even more uncomfortable. "More than an hour. The farm is in a little hollow higher in the hills."

"It will require skill, old friend." There was no blame in his words, just a kind of fatigue. "No faster than a trot, or the horses will drop out from under us."

The sun was almost overhead when they came to the farm. No one rushed out to see them and no smoke curled from the chimney. Ragoczy gave Ruggiero an inquisitive look. "They're gone, I thought it best. They were paid in advance, and told go to market or to church."

"Are you sure the horses will be here?" Ragoczy asked sharply. "I don't want to be trapped here. Gelata can't take another hour of this."

"They're here. I had their oaths."

Ragoczy knew how capriciously oaths could be kept, but he said nothing. He swung out of the saddle and looped Gelata's reins over the gate to the paddock. The stables were beyond the paddock, a low building with wide doors and a roof badly in need of repair. As he walked across the paddock he felt eyes on him, and bent over to draw his knife from his boot. He reached the stable, still convinced he was being watched. He opened the door carefully and peered into the dark. Four horses were tethered inside. He closed the door, and as silently as possible he went around the building, his knife ready, to the far door.

This, too, proved to be safe, and deciding that the lancers who pursued them accounted for the sensation, he went into the stable and inspected the horses. He ran his hands over the legs of each horse, searching for trouble and finding none. He checked their hooves and found them sound, though one of them was unshod. He would put Demetrice on the unshod horse, since she was the lightest burden. Satisfied, he went to the door and signaled to Ruggiero.

They changed mounts quickly, working silently most of the time. Ragoczy still had the nagging sensation that they were under observation, but nothing supported the feeling. In a quarter of an hour they were ready to be on their way again, but it was with a slight pang that Ragoczy turned Gelata loose in the paddock. She was a fine mare, full of stamina and with little temperament to mar her responsiveness.

The road grew steeper and as high clouds gathered in the west, the sunlight began to fade. Ruggiero said nothing but he knew as well as Ragoczy that the distance between them and the lancers was narrowing. It was well past noon when the dun gelding carrying the chests began to labor, his breath coming in great gulps and sweat darkening his mouse-colored coat.

"What ails the beast?" Ragoczy snapped, glancing back at the dun. The horse's eyes were rolling and his tongue protruded. Hating to do so, Ragoczy pulled in and dismounted, catching the dun's lead rope and going to his head. Heaving flanks and foam told their tale. Ragoczy patted the dun's neck, then checked him out with determined hands. At the end of it he gave Ruggiero a bleak look. "I couldn't swear to it, but I'll wager he was given salt last night and all the water he could drink this morning. With all that in his gut, it's amazing he got this far."

Ruggiero blinked in alarm. "But why?"

"Who knows. But it wasn't for any good." He began to unstrap the chests from the packsaddle. "We'll have to carry these on our mounts." He nodded at Ruggiero's dismay. "Yes, I know. The lancers may very likely catch us. But what else can we do? We haven't any cannon, or even a sword between us. We can't ambush them, and we can't leave the trail, not now. There's a storm building up in the west, and we can't afford to be lost in it." By now he had undone the first of the chests. "Here. Strap it to your saddle."

Ruggiero obeyed automatically, saying as he finished attaching the chest straps, "What about brigands?"

"That had crossed my mind," Ragoczy admitted. He had the other chest off the dun now, and was securing it to the saddle of the roan he rode. "I hope we're wrong. But I wouldn't depend on it."

With an uneasy glance at the unwieldy bundle that held Demetrice, Ruggiero asked, "Will it work, do you think?"

Ragoczy shrugged. "I hope so. But I don't know." He finished lashing down the chest and climbed back into the saddle. "We must not force the horses now. We may need them later for a sprint."

Ruggiero acknowledged this with a sound between a groan and a sigh as he gave his mount a sharp kick in the ribs. He could tell from the way the animal moved that he was not used to carrying so much weight.

Clouds had blown across the sky and there was a stiff wind blowing by the time they stopped again. Ragoczy motioned for a rest and turned in the saddle. "They're no more than a quarter-hour behind us now," he said without rancor. "We'd better start looking for a hiding place, or some boulders we can roll down the hill on them."

Ruggiero nodded but said nothing. It was late afternoon and he ached from the long and difficult ride. The next change of horses was still almost an hour away, and he knew with icy certainty that long before then the lancers would be upon them. He glanced at the lump that was Donna Demetrice. "What do you think we should do about her?"

"Well"—Ragoczy sighed——"if it comes to a fight, we must make sure she's out of the way. There may be trees we can hide her under, or a barn somewhere." He knew as well as Ruggiero that it was highly unlikely. "We'll put one of the chests with her, and hope that one of us can explain what she must know." Wearily he set his horse in motion once again.

It was much darker when at last they heard the sound of hooves behind them, and knew they could not escape any longer. Ragoczy felt a certain pleasure in coming out of the saddle to fight at last. They were at the crest of a little rise, and that gave them a mild advantage in sight, but as they had nothing to use, neither cannon nor gun nor cross-bow, the matter was unimportant. Ruggiero took the horses and led them off the road, to a little stream that gushed merrily down the hillside. Ragoczy called after him, "Make sure you stay on this side of the water. If Demetrice wakes, without earth in her shoes she won't be able to cross it."

"How long until sundown?" Ruggiero asked as he tethered the horses near the stream.

"I'm not sure. The clouds are so heavy it's hard to tell. I doubt if it's much more than an hour away, if that." He pushed at a large boulder that stood beside the road, but even his preternatural strength could not move it. "It will give us some cover, that's something," he said. He remembered the horn and wood bow that he had carefully packed in the chests that were to follow him. At the time it had seemed advisable to travel with as little burden as possible, and he had long felt that weapons invited trouble. Now he missed the bow. And his swords, one of Toledo and one of Damascus steel. There was a third sword, a very special one, that he had won in combat with a Japanese warrior very far from home, but that, too, was packed away.

He walked to where Ruggiero had tethered the horses. "I want some rope," he said.

Ruggiero thought a moment. "How long?"

"Somewhat wider than the road." His eyes met Ruggiero's and there was renewed hope in them. Ruggiero nodded and began to search through the small packs both of them carried on the front of their saddles. At last he produced a thin rope measuring about four times the height of a man.

After that they worked quickly, securing the rope at one end and hiding themselves at the other. "Remember," Ragoczy said as they tested it once more, "don't lift it until the first horses are almost on it."

"I won't," he said.

"As soon as the first lancers are down, grab whatever weapons you can get your hands on. If you can't reach the lancer go for the horse's legs. It will cripple the horse, but it can't be helped. It's a waste." He glanced up as the first few drops of rain spattered down. He narrowed his eyes. "Mud may help."

Ruggiero tried to smile and failed. "My master . . ."

"What is it, old friend?"

Ruggiero thought over the words and at last said, "It was worth it." Then he turned away and put his mind to trapping horses.

The waiting was difficult, but it did not last long. In a short while the clop and jingle of the lancers grew nearer, blending oddly with the gentle purr of the rain.

"Ready?" Ragoczy whispered as the lancers were almost upon them. Ruggiero made a gesture. Ragoczy nodded and set his legs.

"Now!"

The rope snapped up, tightening across the lead horses'

knees. The horses reared, stumbled and plunged as the pair of horses behind them pushed into them. One of the two lead horses slid and fell on its side and in a moment there was chaos.

Waiting only until they were certain that the lancers were too much disordered to present a united defense, Ruggiero and Ragoczy raced from behind the boulder that had hidden them, moving precariously near flying hooves and twisting bodies.

Ragoczy reached the column first, and with care he snatched a double-handed broadsword from one of the lancers. As soon as he had a firm hold of the scabbard he stepped back, holding his prize to him until he could toss the scabbard away and bring the blade into play.

The lancers toward the rear were not caught in the trap and they were forming themselves for attack, ready to take on Ragoczy and Ruggiero.

Ruggiero had grabbed a lance, and though the weapon was unwieldy on the ground, he set it where he could use it while braced against the boulder.

The rain was pelting down quite heavily now and the road was becoming slick with mud. Ragoczy almost had his feet go out from under him as he avoided the thrust of a short sword from one of the lancers. He moved away from the road, knowing that his white garments made him a better target than Ruggiero, who wore rust-colored clothing.

Near the end of the column orders were barked out, and six mounted men left the road, fanning out as they did, their lances held low.

Ragoczy moved back toward the trees, going carefully so that he would not slip on the wet ground. The sword he carried was worse than useless, for as long as the lancers held their weapons, he could not get close enough to fight them.

Ruggiero shouted to him, but the words were lost in the howl of the wind. He dared not look around now, for the lancers were much too close, and a lance in the back would be the True Death as surely as the flames would be.

There was another shout, and louder, and the sound of more horses. Even the lancers pursing Ragoczy heard it, and for a moment they hesitated, looking around for the source of the noise.

He had barely time to raise his head before Ragoczy saw perhaps twenty mounted men come hurtling around the bend of the road. At the sight of the lancers, the brigands—for they most certainly were brigands, as their long swords and old-fashioned armor showed—checked their plunge, but only long enough to draw their weapons and plunge furiously into battle.

Ragoczy did not wait to see more. He signaled Ruggiero and raced for the trees. He was soaked now, and his finery hung on him in clinging layers. He paused under the trees and waited for Ruggiero to catch up with him.

"How long will that go on?" Ruggiero asked, cocking his head back toward the road.

"I don't know. Not long, I'd think." He looked up through the leaves into the rainy sky. The clouds were bloated with water and there was almost no color left in them. "Sunset," Ragoczy said tersely, and started off through the woods.

The horses were still tethered, waiting where they had been left. Nearby, under an inadequate and clumsy shelter of cut branches, lying on the sack she had been carried in all day, was Demetrice. Her face, now wet, was no longer deathly pale. A faint blush colored her cheeks, and though she was still, it was the stillness of sleep, not of death.

Ragoczy went onto his knee beside her. The old gonella

of rust-red velvet she wore was heavy with water and he shook his head at the feel of it.

The noise of the fight was much louder; then there were shouts and horses were heard fleeing.

"The lancers are winning, I think," Ragoczy murmured. "We can't stay here much longer."

"Will she waken?" Ruggiero wondered aloud. "Or should we carry her?"

Gently Ragoczy touched her face and noticed that her mouth softened into a smile. "We wake her, Ruggiero." He took her hand in his, ignoring the rain and the renewed scuffle of horses on the road behind them. "Demetrice," he said softly. "Demetrice."

Her eyelids tightened, and then very slowly they opened. She looked around, bewildered, seeing the forest, the rain, the dark, and the face of Ragoczy, glistening with rain, leaning above her. "Fran . . . cesco?" she said and put one hand to her head. "Don't leave yet."

"I'm afraid we have to," he said, tightening his grip on her hand.

"How did it get so wet? Is it another torture? Did the jailers do it?" The questions came quickly, with no time for answers. She rolled onto her side and held herself on her elbow. "But this isn't my cell!"

"No," Ragoczy said, and waited.

"Where are we?" This was almost a cry and her amber eyes were wild. "What place is this?"

"We're on the road to Bologna. Well, not quite on the road." He was silent while she tried to understand. Suddenly she snatched her hand away from him and pulled her wrist close to her face. The two neat cuts were still there, but seamed and white, like the scars on ancient wounds. Her eyes flew to his again. "You *did* do it."

"Yes." He longed to take her into his arms again, but he knew her shock was too great to allow that. Instead he put his hand to her cheek. "Demetrice, this morning, though you were dead, you were chained to a stake in la Piazza della Signoria and the wood around you was lighted. If you had been alive, the same thing would have happened."

"No." Demetrice tried unsteadily to rise. "But what are we doing here?"

Ragoczy's smile was almost apologetic. "We're trying not to be caught either by brigands or by lancers. And we must leave quickly." She let him pull her to her feet and she held his hand tightly as he led her to the horses. As she got into the saddle, she saw the chests tied to Ragoczy's and Ruggiero's saddles, and said, "I hope you have dry clothes in there."

"Well, no," Ragoczy said as he mounted once more.

"What do you have in there, then?"

There was a noticeable pause before he answered. "There is earth from Rimini in the chests. Your native earth."

She frowned, and for the first time she felt the icy prickle of belief touch her spine. "My native earth?" she asked slowly.

"You'll find you need it, Demetrice. All of our kind do." Then, before she could say anything more, he kicked his horse to a trot and in a little time they were once more on the road to Bologna.

TEXT OF A letter from Marsilio Ficino in Fiorenza to the poet Cassandra Fedele in Venezia:

To my very dear colleague and valued friend Cassandra Fedele, Marsilio Ficino sends greetings from Fiorenza on this Feast Day of San Germano di Parigi.

I thank you from the depths of my heart for the delightful poems you sent me last month. They came at a good time, for April was filled with excitement and your poems complemented that excitement for me.

By now you must have heard that Savonarola has been condemned as a heretic, but perhaps you did not know that the sentence, hanging and burning, was carried out just five days ago, in la Piazza della Signoria, the same place that he committed his atrocious auto-da-fé little more than two months ago. It was an eerie feeling, watching him as he hung high over the heads of the few people who gathered to watch him. Some monks, in an excess of zeal, cried to him to perform a miracle now, if indeed God inspired him and protected him. I don't know whether he heard or not, because the flames were very bright and he was quickly hidden in the smoke.

I have not much admired Alessandro VI, but in this he has done well. His judgment was ruthless, but nothing less than ruthlessness would have prevailed against one as wholly demented as Savonarola had become. It may be true that even a Borja y Lara is useful to the Papacy.

Fiorenza has not recovered from the excesses of Savonarola's reign. Many of i Priori and the Console are his creatures and only time and calm judgment will remove their influence from our government. But yesterday I saw a young woman wearing a lace wreath in her hair, and it was heartening. The fast days are not so strictly enforced now, and since the

Militia Christi has been disbanded many of our citizens are bringing their beautiful things out of hiding once again. I will not live to see Fiorenza restored, I know, but I am grateful to God for letting me live long enough to know that the city is not lost, and that all the things that Cosimo and Piero and Laurenzo cherished have not died.

I understand that Ragoczy is in Venezia. When next you see him, remember me to him, will you, my friend? He did a very courageous thing coming back to Fiorenza as he did. It probably would not be wise for him to visit us again, but his bravery will be long remembered here.

Sandro has taken his cousin's death very badly. She is the one who immolated herself during the auto-da-fé. I think she must have been mad, but Sandro is much tormented in his soul. He paints very little now, but talks of doing a vast allegory in praise of Suor Estasia.

It may be that in doing such a painting he will at last resign himself to the Will of God and learn to forgive himself for what was, after all, none of his doing.

I have come upon some excellent translations of Aristotle, which I am taking the liberty of sending to you with this letter. My messenger is one of the servants of Cardinal Giovanni, for though he is not allowed back in Fiorenza, his servants are. As he is carrying other messages on to Venezia, he was kind enough to offer to bring you this.

Be certain that this bears my love and my blessing to you. You will never know how much your kindness meant to me in my time of greatest despondency. But I know, and God knows, and it will shine from you like the purest light when the Judgment comes to us all. In this world and in the next I treasure you, Donna Cassandra.

Marsilio Ficino

In Fiorenza
the 28th day of May, 1498

EPILOGUE

TEXT OF A letter to Francesco Ragoczy in Venezia from Olivia in Roma:

To Sanct' Germain in Venezia, Olivia of the Eternal City sends loving greetings of the same sort.

So Demetrice is going to leave you after all? You may not believe this, but for your sake I am truly sorry. It is unfortunate that she had to make the change before she was prepared. If there had been more time, undoubtedly she would not feel as she does. She is an intelligent and sensitive woman, you tell me, and in time the wounds will heal and she will not be distressed by what you are and what she has become.

Yet I know this is painful to you. For so long you have wanted someone who knows you for what you are, understands it and loves you for it. I'm not sure such a woman exists, but if she does, if she ever does, I hope with all my heart that you will find her and love her until the end of time.

From what you have told me about the other, Estasia, it may be just as well that she burned. If she had made the change when she died, she would have been the sort of vampire who gives our kind the hideous reputation we have gained. You have seen that happen before. We are like elephants, my dearest friend. Most elephants live happily with people, enjoying them, and help them. But it is not by these that elephants are known, but for the rare one that turns rogue, that rampages through towns, killing all in its path. One with the hunger of Estasia would have been a rogue among us. Because of her death, we are all spared danger and pain.

Another one of the cardinals has died and of course the blame is laid at Alessandro's door. Why he should bother to poison a feeble old man of eighty-six I can't imagine. But the Borgias have a certain reputation and it haunts them as surely as ours haunts us.

When you leave Venezia, come to Roma for a time. I have missed you and with all this fear of poisons and plots, my life is severely circumscribed for the time being. Perhaps we might go to one of the old villas at Ostia, or visit Sicilia. I have a small boat of my own, with provisions for carrying earth, so you need not fear to be sick.

I thank you for the painting. As you know, Semele is one of my favorite allegories, though after all this time I am flattered you remember. I will do as you request and not hang the painting where it can be seen. But how can anyone have believed that something that beautiful was evil? Never mind. Even if you could explain, I would never understand.

You must excuse me. A very beautiful young man has just arrived and I am most interested in learning more of him. I will write again later, perhaps. Oh, Sanct' Germain, I wish that you will find what your soul is seeking. And if my love will help or lend you courage, you know that you have it, as you always have.

Olivia

In Roma, on the Feast of the Blessed Virgin, a horridly hot August 25, 1498

ABOUT THE AUTHOR

Chelsea Quinn Yarbro is the author of dozens of fantasy, horror, and young adult novels, including the 15 books of the Saint-Germain series. A frequent speaker at library, literary, and SF/fantasy conventions, she has been nominated for the Edgar Award, the World Fantasy Award, and the Bram Stoker Award.

THE NEWEST IN THE SAINT-GERMAIN SERIES

By Chelsea Quinn Yarbro

"[A] character who is alays worth watching."
—*Locus*

NIGHT BLOOMING (0-446-52981-8)

In the court of king Karl-lo-Magne (Charlemagne), Santus Germainius meets an albino woman, Gynethe, who exhibits stigmata. When accusations of witchcraft fly, Gynethe must make a desparate choice in order to survive.

AND COMING SOON!

MIDNIGHT HARVEST (0-446-53240-1)

Fleeing Spain at the beginning of their Civil War, Saint-Germain leaves behind his numerous business concerns for the States, unaware that a ruthless assassin is pursuing him.

"A veritable Prince Charming of the darker arts."

—*Publishers Weekly*

AVAILABLE FROM WARNER ASPECT

BACK IN PRINT!

Return to Saint-Germain's beginning's with
the first two novels in Chelsea Quinn Yarbro's
acclaimed series.

✦   ✦   ✦

HOTEL TRANSYLVANIA

A Novel of Forbidden Love

(ISBN: 0-446-61100-X)

The classic that first introduces the tormented hero
who has walked the earth throughout time,
battling for honor…and love.

✦   ✦   ✦

THE PALACE

(ISBN: 0-446-61009-2)

Set in Pre-Revolutionary France, Saint-Germain
finds danger threatening the city and his
lover, and must face a terror that only he can over-
throw.

✦   ✦   ✦

AVAILABLE IN MASS MARKET

FROM WARNER ASPECT